LORD
OF THE
FORSAKEN

NORA NIGHTINGALE

Copyright © 2026 by Nora Nightingale

All rights reserved.

No part of this book may be reproduced in any form or by any electronic or mechanical means, including information storage and retrieval systems, without written permission from the author, except for the use of brief quotations in a book review.

Cover art by Anna Stone.

A NOTE BEFORE YOU BEGIN

This is a love story wrapped in shadows. Within these pages you'll find violence, blood, political scheming, and characters who don't always make kind choices. There are explicit love scenes, themes of grief and loss, betrayal by people who should have been trustworthy, and a death realm that earns its name.

...Oh, you turned the page?
You like it dark, don't you?
Don't worry. So does he.

*For those who built walls to protect themselves.
May someone climb them anyway.*

I.
BRYNN

Brynn pressed her ear against cold metal, blocking out her own breathing and the creak of the manor settling into the night. She listened for the pins shifting inside, each click telling her what to do next.

Fifth pin catching. Seventh needed pressure from below. The third had been filed down. Sloppy work from whoever had serviced it last.

Listen to the lock, Brynn. Every lock has a voice. Learn to hear it, and no door in the kingdom can keep you out.

Two years since they'd strung Gareth up in the square, and his voice still lived in her head. Kept her fed. Kept her one step ahead of the noose.

Barely.

She adjusted her grip on the tension wrench and slid her rake deeper into the lock. Her picks were works of art, each one shaped and filed to specifications that had taken months to perfect. In the darkness of this cellar, they were extensions of her fingertips.

Sixth pin. Stubborn little bastard.

The kingdom's laws were clear about thieves: the first offense cost you a hand, the second cost you your head. Those who survived the first punishment had two choices: starve in the streets or take the king's coin to die on some foreign battlefield.

She'd seen too many of Gareth's students take that coin. The lucky ones came back with more missing limbs. The unlucky ones didn't come back at all.

Better to be very, very good at not getting caught.

The seventh pin surrendered with a satisfying click. Too easy.

She froze, tension wrench halfway through its final turn.

In ten years of this work, easy meant trapped.

Behind her, the corridor was silent. No footsteps, no hushed conversations, no jingle of weapons announcing guards. Just the manor settling and her own pulse hammering in her ears.

But she was already inside the mechanism, and backing out empty-handed meant another week of watered-down stew that tasted like dishwater and regret. The merchant who'd hired her had been specific: Roderick's private vault, third level down, behind the wine cellar. Take the small strongbox, leave everything else, and then disappear.

Twenty silver pieces. A month of real food and a bed that didn't smell like horses.

Worth it.

She finished the turn. The lock clicked open. She eased the door back on well-oiled hinges, and the silence sent ice flooding her veins.

She pushed the door open slowly, every instinct screaming that she should be running in the opposite direction.

The vault should have reeked of metal and coin. Instead, this place smelled like stone and age. Her breath misted in the darkness, which made no sense three levels underground in late spring.

She fumbled for the oil lamp at her belt, hands steady despite the growing certainty that she was somewhere she absolutely should not be.

The flame caught, casting shadows across the walls of black stone. Carvings covered every surface. Skulls with empty eye sockets. Ribs like ladder rungs. Bones arranged in patterns she didn't recognize.

Get out. The voice in her head sounded like Gareth. *Get out now.*

She took a step backward toward the door.

It slammed shut.

She spun, grabbed the handle, and pulled.

Locked. From the outside.

She cursed the merchant who'd hired her. The suspiciously detailed intelligence about Roderick's vault. The conveniently easy locks that led her down to this exact spot.

She'd walked right into it because the pay was good, and she'd thought she was clever.

Gareth would've smacked the back of her head for missing the signs. "There's no such thing as an easy score, girl. Just traps you haven't spotted yet."

Her lamp revealed a circular chamber stretching upward into darkness, the domed ceiling lost beyond the light's reach. The floor beneath her boots was so smooth she almost slipped.

And there, in the exact center of the room, sat a chest.

Even from across the chamber, she could tell it didn't belong to this place. Where the stonework spoke of ages long dead and buried, the chest looked maintained. Cared for. Fresh footprints in the dust around it. Recent visitors, multiple sets, all leading to and from that single point.

Whatever was in that chest, someone valued it enough to keep returning.

Why?

Voices echoed down the stairwell outside. Multiple people. Moving fast, not bothering with stealth now that the door was sealed.

She crossed to the chest. If she was trapped, if this was all a setup, she needed to know what she'd been set up for.

The chest was dark wood, bound with silver, its surface covered in symbols that matched the walls. Five keyholes were arranged around a central mechanism. The most sophisticated lock she'd ever seen.

And it was already open. Lid raised just enough to show darkness within.

Her jaw clenched. Of course it was open.

The voices grew louder outside, words becoming clearer.

"—been down here long enough. Move faster, you idiots."

No time to think, no time to plan. She lifted the lid.

Twelve tools lay nestled in black silk. Dark metal that seemed to drink her lamplight, edges that shifted when she tried to focus on them. Each one was engraved with words:

Ward-singer. Soul-binder. Death-reader.

Names that meant nothing and everything.

She reached for what looked like a delicate pick, fingers closing around cold metal.

The world shifted.

Heat flooded up her arm, shocking in its intensity. The tool recognized her. She could feel it responding to her touch, humming with a frequency that resonated in her bones.

She gasped and nearly dropped it, but the tool wouldn't let her. It had warmed to match her skin, fitting her grip like it had been made for her hand.

Whispers filled the chamber. The echo of voices speaking in a language that felt familiar, even though she couldn't understand it. They came from the tools themselves, and they sounded... welcoming?

What are you?

The shadows around her lamp deepened, stretching toward her fingers like they were curious. Like they recognized something in her they'd been waiting for.

She grabbed a second tool, shaped like a key but with edges that refused to stay still. That same warmth spread through her hand.

Boots thundered on the stairs outside.

She couldn't make sense of it. Couldn't understand what was happening. She shoved both tools into the hidden pockets of her vest, the warmth pressing against her ribs like a second heartbeat.

Whatever these things were, she wasn't leaving them for whoever had set this trap. If someone wanted them badly enough to lure a thief down here, they were valuable. And if they were valuable, she could use them. Figure out what they were, sell them if possible, or at least bargain for her life with them.

Assuming they didn't kill her first.

The iron door crashed open, and the first guard rounded the corner, sword drawn and torch held high. Behind him came three more in House Greymont colors, and finally Lord Edmund Greymont himself, younger son of a duke who was hungry for recognition and willing to do questionable things to get it.

His dark eyes swept the chamber, landing on her standing beside the open chest. His smile widened into something that made her skin crawl.

"Well, well. The infamous lockbreaker, finally caught in the act." He stepped closer, studying her face. "Though I must say, your reputation for choosing targets doesn't quite match your performance tonight."

She kept her face blank. "I was hired to steal from Roderick's vault. Wrong room. Just bad intelligence."

"Oh, I don't think there's anything wrong about tonight at all." His eyes gleamed. "In fact, I think it's going exactly as planned."

One of the guards moved toward the open chest, reaching for the remaining tools.

"Don't—"

The guard's scream cut off Edmund's warning as the tool seared his palm. He stumbled backward, clutching his hand, and the smell of burned flesh filled the chamber.

"Death magic," another guard whispered, making a warding sign that wouldn't do him a damn bit of good. "She's cursed."

"I'm not cursed!" The words came out sharper than she intended, defensive in a way that made her sound guilty. "I don't even know what's happening!"

But even as she said it, she felt the lie. The tools weren't hurting her. They felt protective. Like they recognized something in her touch that made her safe from whatever had just burned a man's hand to the bone.

Which meant she was special. Lucky her.

Lord Edmund stepped closer.

"Fascinating," he said softly. "Very fascinating indeed."

He gestured to his guards. "Take her upstairs."

The guards moved in, spreading out to cut off any escape routes.

Brynn moved.

She faked left toward the widest gap between guards, then pivoted right at the last second. The first guard lunged to grab her arm. She twisted and drove her fist into his throat. He staggered back, gagging.

"Don't hurt her!" Edmund's voice cracked through the chamber.

The hesitation was all she needed. She ducked under another guard's outstretched arms and made for the door.

Almost there. Almost—

Something slammed into her from behind. The guard she'd hit tackled her to the stone floor, driving the air from her lungs. She bucked and thrashed, got an elbow into someone's face, and heard a satisfying crunch of cartilage.

"Damn it, hold her still!"

Hands grabbed her arms, her legs, her hair. She kicked hard and connected with something soft—a grunt of pain. But there were too many of them, and they were too strong.

They hauled her upright, pinning her arms behind her back with enough force that her shoulders screamed in protest.

She was breathing hard, heart hammering. One guard had a bloody nose from her elbow. Another was clutching his ribs from her kick. The one who'd tackled her was still wheezing, and he looked furious.

She fought down a smile.

"Spirited," Edmund observed, brushing dust from his fine coat. "Good. You'll need that."

He nodded to the guards. "Bind her hands. And don't try to take those tools from her. They've clearly chosen their keeper."

The guards wrapped rough rope around her wrists, tight enough to bite. One of them patted her vest pockets, felt the tools inside, but didn't try to remove them.

Edmund turned toward the door, already losing interest. "Bring her."

The guards dragged her toward the stairs. She fought every step, but it was useless now. They had her, and they knew it.

The tools pressed warm against her ribs, humming softly, almost like they were trying to comfort her.

Or maybe claiming her, piece by piece, as she was dragged toward whatever fate Edmund had planned.

II.
BRYNN

Lord Edmund's private study was crowded. His guard captain waited near the desk, the castle's priest hovered by the window, and two minor nobles lingered, clutching wine glasses from their interrupted meal.

Brynn stood in chains worth more than everything she'd ever stolen, still wearing her dark leather work clothes, feeling every inch the criminal she was supposed to be.

"The law is clear," the priest said, consulting a leather-bound tome. "Theft from a noble house: lose your hand. But theft involving death magic..." He glanced at her unmarked hands. "You burn for that."

"Standard protocol," the guard captain added, hand resting on his sword hilt. "Take her hand first, per theft laws. Then the burning."

Brynn's stomach dropped. They meant now. Not tomorrow, not after a trial. *Now.*

Her eyes went to her hands, still bound in front of her. Ten fingers that had picked a thousand locks, that had fed her for a decade, that had touched those tools and survived. In the next few minutes, she'd lose one. Then they'd burn what was left.

"How brutal," she managed, keeping her voice level through the cold dread settling in her gut. "At least you're consistent."

"Bring the block," the guard captain ordered one of his men.

The guard moved toward the door. She could already hear it in her mind. The thunk of wood hitting stone, the scrape as they positioned it. The smell of old blood that never quite washed out.

This is happening. This is actually—

"Wait."

Every head turned toward Lord Edmund. Even the guard, his hand on the door, froze.

He had remained silent until now, watching her with those dark, beady eyes. He stepped closer, studying her face with sudden interest.

"The tribute selection is in one month," he said slowly, thoughtfully. "The Death Lords require five mortal tributes each decade to maintain the barriers between their realm and ours."

The priest frowned. "My lord, the tribute selection follows old protocols. We typically send—"

"We typically send criminals, the condemned, those who have nothing left to lose," Edmund finished smoothly. His gaze never left Brynn's face. "I think our thief here qualifies. And her unique abilities might serve a purpose there." He gestured toward her unmarked hands. "She touched death magic and survived."

Ah. Not mercy. Just a different kind of execution.

"You want to send me to die slowly instead of quickly," she said. "So generous."

"I want to send you to die usefully," he corrected. "One month in my dungeons, then the tribute ritual. Or we can proceed with the burning right now." He tilted his head slightly. "Your choice."

The guard captain shifted his weight. "My lord, if she's dangerous enough for death magic charges—"

"Then she's dangerous enough to be useful to the Death Lords," Edmund cut him off. "We need to send tributes anyway. Why waste the opportunity to gain favor?"

They were all staring at her now, waiting for her response. As if she had a real choice between burning in the next hour or buying herself a month.

One month. Four weeks to find a way out of this nightmare.

She'd probably fail. The dungeons under Greymont Castle were legendary. No one escaped them. And even if she did, where would she go? Every lord in the kingdom would be looking for the thief who'd touched death magic and lived.

But one month was better than burning today.

She straightened her shoulders and met Edmund's gaze without flinching.

"One month it is."

His smile suggested he knew exactly what she was thinking and found it amusing. "Wise choice. Though I should mention: escape attempts will result in immediate execution. No second chances."

The urge to roll her eyes was almost overwhelming. "Got it."

His eyebrow rose.

"Take her to the cells," he told the guard captain. "Maximum security. No visitors, no exceptions. We can't risk losing such a valuable tribute."

As the guards hauled her toward the door, Edmund's voice followed her out.

"You're the Death Lords' problem now."

His tone suggested he thought that would be the end of the problem. That she'd walk into death's realm and disappear like every other tribute before her.

He had no idea who he was dealing with.

III.
DANTE

The Throne of the Forsaken rose from the dais like a monument to death itself. Massive ribs arched overhead like cathedral vaults, curving inward to form a canopy of bone that seemed to breathe in the flickering light. A towering spine formed the back, each vertebra the size of a man's head, while armrests were hewn from femurs so large they could only have belonged to giants or things that had never been human at all. The entire structure gleamed in the twilight, fifteen feet of polished bone that commanded the hall.

But it was the base that drew the eye. Thousands of smaller bones woven together in patterns suggesting supplication. Hands stretching upward, frozen mid-grasp, as if the dead had clawed their way toward the throne and been trapped reaching.

The throne room stretched beyond the reach of torchlight, bone beams arching overhead and disappearing into shadows that moved with their own purpose. The walls were lined with skulls—hundreds of them, perhaps thousands, arranged in neat rows from floor to ceiling. Cold blue flames burned in their eye sockets, casting the hall in ghostly light that made the shadows dance. Some of the skulls had too many eye sockets. Some had jaws that hung slightly open, as if frozen mid-scream.

Columns of black marble rose between the skull-lined walls, carved with names of the forsaken dead in scripts that predated human memory. The floor was a mosaic of teeth. Yellowed ivory and bone-white fitted together in spiraling patterns that pulled the eye toward the distant throne. They crunched softly underfoot, no matter how lightly one walked.

Dante sat within this monument to death, black-gloved hands resting on bone armrests while his shadows pooled around the throne's base. Dark extensions of his will that seemed to merge with the reaching hands carved below.

No one approached closer than twelve feet. His courtiers, bound souls in court dress that had long since ceased to follow mortal fashions, formed their usual semicircle. Translucent but solid, they served without hesitation and never, ever tried to get closer to their lord.

They'd learned. Eventually, they all learned.

"The soul of Isabel Graves seeks judgment," his chamberlain announced from the great doors.

A young woman stepped forward, her dress once fine but now stained with soot and blood. She knelt exactly at the boundary, but her shoulders didn't shake like most. When she lifted her head, her eyes held the hollow darkness he recognized: the look of someone who had stared into the abyss until it stared back.

"Speak."

Silence fell across the hall. Every soul present held whatever breath they still possessed, and frost began forming on the nearest torches.

"My lord, I thought I was clever." Her voice didn't shake. "My family owed debts we couldn't pay. The moneylender said he'd forgive everything if I spent one night in the old Moore manor. Just one night. Prove it wasn't haunted."

The shadows around Dante's throne writhed.

"I lasted six hours." Her voice cracked. "The things that lived there... they didn't kill me quickly. They fed on me first. Made me watch them take pieces of my soul while I screamed for help that never came. I died begging for it to end."

Terror. Despair. Cursed death. She belonged here.

Dante had seen it a thousand times. The cruelty that turned ordinary deaths into forsaken ones. Someone always profited from manufacturing despair.

"The moneylender knew," she whispered. "He'd sent eight others before me. The manor needed feeding, and desperate people cost nothing."

Dante leaned forward. Every soul in the hall pressed backward.

"You want revenge."

"I want him to know what I felt. I want him to die the way I died—"

"No."

The word echoed across the hall. Isabel's face crumpled.

Dante waited until she looked up at him again. Until those desperate eyes met his.

"Your wants are irrelevant." His voice was flat, empty of anything that might be mistaken for compassion. "You died screaming and forsaken. That terror is the only thing about you with value, and I will use it. The moneylender will live out his natural life and die peacefully in his bed, wealthy and content. Your suffering will power the ward-barriers that protect the realms. That is your purpose. That is all you are worth."

His hand tightened on the armrest. Bone creaking under his grip. Mercy only prolonged suffering. He'd watched it happen too many times to count. Better to break them quickly than let hope fester.

He let that sink in. Watched hope die in her eyes all over again.

His fingers relaxed on the armrest. The mask he'd perfected centuries ago remained firmly in place.

"You will serve in the Tower of Screaming Winds for one thousand years, where every soul who enters will experience your final moments on an eternal loop. Be grateful your death serves a function. Most don't."

The Tower was the cruelest assignment in his domain. A place where the dying moments of the terrorized played endlessly, maintaining the ward-barriers through concentrated fear. Those sent there didn't fade, didn't find peace, didn't even have the mercy of forgetting.

They relived their worst moments forever, their agony powering the realm.

It was necessary. The barriers required a specific frequency of terror to maintain stability. Without souls like Isabel feeding power to the system, the boundaries between life and death would collapse. Thousands would die.

One soul's eternal torment weighed against the extinction of the realms.

The balance was simple. His feelings about it were irrelevant.

Isabel's mouth opened in silent horror. No sound came out. The weight of eternity had crushed whatever protests she might have offered.

"Remove her," he said. "Before her despair becomes tedious."

Two shadow-guards materialized and lifted Isabel from the floor. She didn't resist. Couldn't. The certainty of her fate had broken her all over again.

The court watched in silence as she was led away. No one offered comfort. In the Court of the Forsaken, hope was a lie, and everyone learned that eventually.

Dante settled back into his throne, shadows coiling tighter around the base. Another soul broken. Another thousand years of screaming. Another piece of his realm's terrible function fulfilled.

He'd stopped counting how many he'd sent to the Tower long ago.

"Next."

The chamberlain consulted his scrolls. "A territorial dispute between the houses of Grimwald and Thorne. Both claim salvage rights to the battlefield at Raven's Cross."

Ridiculous. They were always fighting over salvage rights, boundary lines, and perceived slights that had festered for ages, as if any of it mattered. As if death made their petty squabbles anything but pathetic.

"Grimwald claims the field by right of higher death count among their house soldiers," one representative began. "We lost—"

"Both houses will share the field," Dante interrupted. "Alternating salvage rights by lunar month. Disputes will be settled by single combat to the death." He paused, letting his shadows pulse outward.

"If you waste my time with this again, I'll assign the territory to neither house and let it rot."

The representatives bowed quickly and withdrew, their relief at escaping his presence written across their faces.

Good. Fear was efficient. It saved time.

"Next."

A minor noble approached, stopped at the invisible line, and bowed low. "My lord, I seek permission to—"

"Denied."

The noble's head snapped up. "But my lord, you haven't heard—"

"I don't need to." Dante's shadows coiled tighter. Whatever the request, the answer would be the same. It always was. "Whatever you want, the answer is no. Dismissed."

"My lord, please, if I could just explain—"

The temperature in the hall dropped ten degrees. Frost spread across the floor toward the pleading noble, who stumbled backward with a strangled sound.

"You're still here," Dante observed. "I was certain I'd dismissed you."

The noble fled.

Dante watched him go, his expression unchanged. His shadows flickered with irritation. The fool had been making petitions for seventy years, always wanting something, always believing persistence would be rewarded. It wouldn't. But he would return next month with some new plea, and the answer would be no then too.

Persistence wasn't a virtue. It was just another form of stupidity.

Three more petitions followed. Resources. Mercy for some old punishment. Expansion into the outer territories. He dismissed each with a gesture, no longer bothering to listen to the details. Nothing they wanted mattered. Nothing they offered changed the fundamental truth: they were dead, he was their lord, and the hierarchy would remain intact until the end of existence.

By the time Dante dismissed the court for the day, his courtiers couldn't get away fast enough. They bowed, scraped, and backed away with movements refined by countless years of service.

None of them ever turned their backs on him. That would require trust, and the Forsaken court had no use for trust.

As the great doors closed behind the last retreating soul, Nathaniel approached and stopped at the boundary. Dante's advisor had served the court longer than most could remember.

"My lord," Nathaniel said, his translucent form more solid than most bound souls, "urgent word from the mortal realm."

"Proceed."

"The tribute selection has been completed. The ceremony is scheduled for one month from now. Your presence is requested along with the other Death Lords."

The tribute ceremony. Another decade, another mortal sacrifice, another inevitable corpse.

"All five courts are expected to attend?"

"Yes, my lord. The formal summons arrived this morning."

Dante narrowed his eyes. He hadn't bothered attending the last two. The mortals died within weeks regardless of which court claimed them, and watching the other Death Lords fight over doomed humans had lost its entertainment value an eternity ago.

"You think I should go."

It wasn't a question. Nathaniel wouldn't have brought it up otherwise.

"I think, my lord, that the other courts have noted your absence from the last two ceremonies."

Politics. Even in the realm of death, appearances mattered to those who still cared about such things.

Dante didn't. But the other Death Lords did, and ignoring them completely would create complications he didn't need.

"The tribute will die within weeks. My presence or absence changes nothing."

"Yes, my lord. But the ceremony serves other purposes. Information is shared. Alliances are maintained. And given the recent disturbances in the ward-locks..."

Nathaniel let the sentence hang unfinished. His voice had softened on that last phrase. The careful suggestion of someone who'd learned exactly how far he could push. The old advisor had perfected the art of planting thoughts without overstepping.

Dante's fingers drummed once against the armrest. It was the only reason Nathaniel had survived this long.

"Prepare for travel," Dante said finally. "I'll attend."

"Yes, my lord." Relief flickered across Nathaniel's translucent features. "Shall I send word of your participation?"

"No. Let them wonder."

Nathaniel bowed and withdrew, leaving Dante alone in the throne room.

His jaw tightened. Countless tributes over countless centuries. All of them corpses.

The first had been some noble's daughter. Pretty thing, he supposed. She'd arrived in silk and trailing perfume, spent her days weeping in the chambers he'd assigned her. She lasted two weeks before fading away, becoming translucent like his bound servants until one morning she was no longer there.

The second had tried seduction. She'd worn revealing gowns, positioned herself in his path, spoken in honeyed tones about service and pleasure. He'd explained why distance was the only option. She'd ignored the warning. When she'd finally worked up the courage to touch him, death claimed her before her fingers met his skin.

After that, the details blurred. Poison attempts. Hiding in towers. Suicide jumps. Madness from the twilight.

His hand flexed against the armrest. He'd given them safe quarters, servants, everything except proximity to himself. It hadn't mattered. The realm killed them, or he did when they got too close.

He'd stopped going to check on them after the tenth one died. If they lasted long enough to require his attention, someone would inform him. Usually, they didn't.

This new tribute would be no different. The only question was whether they'd last six weeks or sixteen before death found them.

But first, he had more pressing concerns than another doomed mortal.

Dante rose from his throne, shadows swirling around him as he strode toward the northwestern wing. The ward-keeper had reports waiting, and those failures were actually worth his attention.

The journey through his palace took him past corridors where the architecture shifted from grandeur to something older, stranger. Here, the walls weren't lined with skulls but made of them. A tunnel of interlocked bone, jaws hinged open to form the passage.

Skeletal hand sconces emerged from the walls at intervals, cupping cold flames. Some beckoned. Some pointed deeper into the darkness. One, near a junction he rarely used, was frozen in a gesture of warning.

The hands twitched sometimes. He'd stopped noticing.

The ward-keeper's chambers occupied the highest tower in the northwestern wing, where the barriers between realms were thinnest and most easily monitored. The staircase spiraled upward, carved from ancient bone. The walls were studded with remnants that gleamed in the perpetual twilight. The dusk seemed deeper here, tinged with aurora-like streaks of green and silver that danced across the sky visible through tall windows.

The air hummed with residual magic from the barriers and tasted faintly of dust and old graves.

Dante climbed the spiral stairs, shadows streaming behind him. He found Keeper Theron hunched over a table covered in maps, charts, and fragments of ward-stone that glowed with unstable light.

"My lord." Theron straightened, his elderly frame marked by decades of exposure to raw death magic. Unlike the bound souls that served in the main court, the ward-keeper was still technically alive, though the distinction had blurred considerably over his forty years of service.

"Show me."

Theron gestured to the largest map spread across the table. Red marks dotted the eastern territories. "Seventeen locks showing signs of failure in the past six months, my lord. The pattern is concerning."

Dante studied the markings. The failures formed a rough circle around the central ward-core, the massive nexus point that anchored all barriers in his domain.

Seventeen failures in six months. After an eternity of stability.

"Define failure."

"Energy fluctuations at first. Minor degradation in the binding matrices. Then, a complete shutdown." Theron picked up a piece of ward-stone, its surface cracked and lifeless. "This is from the Thornwick crossing. It stopped working two weeks ago."

Dante took the stone fragment, his gloved fingers tracing the dead runes carved into its surface. The locks were supposed to last millennia. They were built by the original architects, using magic that predated the current realm's structure, to maintain the barriers between life and death until the end of existence.

They did not just stop working.

"How long from first fluctuation to complete failure?"

"Varies, my lord. Some took months to degrade completely. Others failed within days of showing the first signs."

"External cause?"

"None that we can find, my lord. No damage, no interference, no sign of tampering. The seals appear to be degrading from within." Theron's frustration was evident. "But there's nothing that explains how or why the damage is occurring."

Dante set the dead stone back on the table. After millennia of stable operation, the barriers didn't spontaneously decay.

His shadows curled tighter around his feet.

"You've attempted repairs?"

"Of course, my lord. But..." Theron gestured helplessly at the lifeless fragments scattered across his workspace. "We maintain the system, yes, but we don't truly understand it. Not the way the original architects did. The deepest knowledge was lost centuries ago. We're..." He hesitated, then continued with apparent frustration. "We're caretakers, my lord. Not builders. I can't fix what I don't fully comprehend."

"Useless, then."

Theron flinched but didn't argue. Because it was true. His wardkeepers could maintain functioning systems, replace damaged components, and follow the instructions left by their predecessors. But the fundamental understanding of how the locks actually worked? That knowledge had died with the original architects.

Inconvenient.

And potentially fatal, if this pattern continued.

"Have you contacted the other domains?"

"I sent inquiries yesterday, my lord. Lord Caelum's ward-keeper reports minor fluctuations but no complete failures. The other courts claim no significant issues."

Dante's shadows writhed, agitated.

"Double the patrols," he commanded. "Post shadow-guards at every seal showing signs of instability. And send word to the Archive. I want the original construction records for the ward-stone network."

"My lord, those records are sealed. The Archive-keepers require a formal petition—"

"They require nothing." Dante's voice dropped to the tone that had silenced entire courts. The temperature in the room plummeted. "They will provide the records, or I will retrieve them personally. The distinction is theirs to make."

Theron bowed quickly, understanding the threat for what it was. "Yes, my lord. I'll send word immediately."

"Good. Dismissed."

The ward-keeper fled in relief.

Dante stood alone in the tower chamber, studying the map. Seventeen locks forming a circle around the central core. No explanation for the failures.

His realm was failing. Possibly all the realms, if the other Death Lords were hiding their own problems.

His shadows writhed around him, restless.

And now, a ceremonial obligation that would waste time watching frightened mortals be claimed by courts that would let them die anyway.

IV.
BRYNN

One Month Later

Brynn shifted against the rough wooden bench of the prison wagon, her wrists chafing where the iron manacles had worn the skin raw. Two days of travel had numbed her to most discomforts, but the sobbing from the girl beside her was beginning to grate on nerves already stretched thin.

"Please," the girl whispered for the hundredth time, tears streaming down cheeks that had probably never known real hunger before today. "Please, there has to be another way. My father has gold, he could pay—"

"Your father sold you to pay his debts," Brynn said quietly. "Crying won't change that."

Though at least your father was alive to make that choice. Brynn's parents were dead. Had been for ten years now. She shoved the thought down.

Morgan, the girl who'd given her name between sobs, flinched as if she had been struck. Across the wagon, three other tributes sat in their own private misery. A middle-aged woman who hadn't spoken since they'd loaded her into the wagon stared at nothing with empty eyes. A young man barely past boyhood, his lips moving in constant prayer to gods who'd already abandoned him. An older man in merchant's practical clothing sat rigid, jaw clenched, trying to maintain some shred of dignity in the face of inevitable death.

All of them marked for death. All of them too broken by fear to see the opportunities that still remained.

Brynn had spent her month of imprisonment more productively.

The strange tools Lord Edmund's men had confiscated were long gone, locked away in some vault where scholars could decipher their construction. But the two pieces she'd palmed during her capture, a delicate probe and a tension wrench that warmed when she held it just right, remained hidden in the specially sewn pocket of her vest.

One month of imprisonment had given her time to prepare in other ways. She'd convinced her guards that a condemned woman deserved final comforts, playing the role of a frightened girl seeking solace in stories. They'd brought her books. Old tales about the Death Lords and their realms, the kind of folklore meant to frighten children into obedience.

The guards had thought her a fool, seeking escape in fairy tales while awaiting her doom. But she'd read every word, learning what she could. The five Death Lords and their domains. The Courts of Violence, Consumption, Lingering, Mourning, and Forsaken. Not enough to save her, but enough to know what she might face.

The landscape beyond the wagon's barred window had been changing for hours. Gone were the rolling farmlands and tidy villages of the inner kingdoms. Here, the trees grew gnarled and leafless even though it was spring, their branches reaching toward the sky like skeletal fingers. The grass had turned from green to a dull brown, brittle and dead. Even the air tasted different, thinner, with a metallic undertone that made her mouth water unpleasantly.

"We're getting close," she murmured, more to herself than the others.

Morgan's sobbing intensified. The praying boy's voice cracked on whatever plea he was making.

Through the bars, Brynn caught her first glimpse of their destination rising from the horizon. The ritual grounds sat atop a massive hill that looked unreal, its slopes bare except for standing stones arranged in concentric circles around the summit. Even from miles away, the place radiated menace. The kind that settles in your bones and makes you understand why people cross to the other side of the road to avoid walking too close to certain ruins.

But danger could be studied. Could be understood. Could be used.

"Look," she told the others, her voice cutting through Morgan's sobs. "Up ahead."

They looked. The praying stopped mid-word. The empty-eyed woman's head turned for the first time in two days. The older merchant's gaze surveyed the hill with the same practicality Brynn recognized in herself. Even Morgan's crying hiccupped to a halt.

The ritual grounds weren't just old; they were older than the kingdoms themselves, older than the roads leading to them, maybe older than the human settlements that had sprung up around them. The stones crowning the hill weren't carved from any quarry Brynn knew. They were black as night, so dark they seemed to have no surface at all. Runes covered every visible surface, symbols that seemed to pulse with their own slow heartbeat.

"Gods preserve us," the young man whispered.

"The gods aren't invited to this party." Brynn kept her gaze on the ritual grounds ahead, refusing to let her voice waver. "That's rather the point."

Their wagon crested a slight rise, revealing the full extent of the ritual grounds. The hill was surrounded by what once had been a town, but the remaining buildings felt off in the same unsettling way as the place itself. Houses with too many angles, doorways that didn't quite connect to roads, windows that seemed to look inward instead of outward. People still lived here. Smoke rose from chimneys, laundry hung from lines. But Brynn suspected the residents weren't entirely human anymore. Places like this changed those who lingered too long in their influence.

"How do you know so much about this place?" the empty-eyed

woman asked suddenly. Her voice was raspy from disuse, barely above a whisper.

"I don't," Brynn admitted. "I just pay attention. One month isolated in a cell gives you plenty of time to think, and thinking beats crying any day of the week."

She didn't mention the dreams that began after her encounter with the strange tools. Dreams of stone circles and death magic, of voices speaking in languages she'd never learned but somehow understood. Dreams where she stood in places like this and felt welcomed rather than threatened. Reading about the Death Lords and the barriers between realms only made the dreams more vivid and specific, until she could no longer tell what was from the books and what came from something deeper.

The wagon wheels changed rhythm as they began climbing the hill. The road here was paved with stones that looked too much like bone for comfort, fitted together without gaps or mortar. The standing stones grew larger as they climbed, until each one towered above the roadway.

"I can't do this," Morgan whispered. "I can't. I'll die of fear before we even reach the top."

"Then you'll die," Brynn said. "But dying of fear here is still better than dying of fear after you've been chosen by something that feeds on terror. So pull yourself together and save the panic for when it might actually help you."

Harsh, maybe. But she'd learned in the last ten years that kindness was a luxury none of them could afford. The guards escorting their wagon weren't the ones who would decide their fate. That honor belonged to creatures who measured mortal lives in moments and found most of them wanting. The Death Lords wouldn't be impressed by tears or moved by pleas.

They might, however, be intrigued by defiance.

The wagon finally reached the summit and came to a stop before gates that looked like they belonged in nightmares—two massive archways flanked by pillars of bone-white stone, each carved with faces. Hundreds of them, twisted in expressions of terror and despair, their mouths open in silent screams. The gates themselves were forged from metal so dark it seemed to swallow light, and they weren't just closed. They were sealed with what looked like dried blood, dark stains coating the metal in patterns that suggested desperate hands clawing at the surface from the inside. Guards waited beyond the threshold. They wore human faces, but their eyes held no white, only solid black. When they breathed, their chests rose and fell in perfect unison, like puppets pulled by the same strings.

"End of the line," called the wagon driver, a grizzled man who'd spent the entire journey refusing to meet any of their eyes. "Everyone out."

The manacles were removed from their wrists, only to be immediately replaced by ceremonial chains. Lighter in weight but far more ornate, each link carved with symbols matching the standing stones. Brynn realized the chains would mark them as tributes, property of the ritual, claimed by old laws that outweighed any kingdom's authority.

As they were led through the gates and into the ritual grounds, Brynn caught sight of the amphitheater where their fates would be decided. Stone benches arranged around a central platform, every surface carved with more of those writhing runes. The air here was so charged with otherworldly energy that it made her teeth ache, and the hidden tools pressed against her ribs felt warm, as if responding to this place.

Above them, the sky was starting to darken even though it was still early. This wasn't the natural evening gloom, but rather a darkness that indicated the boundary between worlds was growing thin, allowing things from the other side to push through.

Brynn was guided down the worn steps with the other tributes, their ceremonial chains jingling with each step. The sound echoed oddly in the vast space, creating strange harmonies. She counted the levels as they went down—thirteen terraces, each marked with different symbols.

"Sweet gods," the empty-eyed woman breathed, her voice barely above a whisper. "What is this place?"

No one answered her. Even the guards seemed reluctant to speak within these walls.

The central platform was raised just high enough that everyone in the amphitheater would have a clear view of whatever happened there. It was perfectly circular, perhaps thirty feet across, made from stone the color of old bone, weathered grey and smooth. Five smaller circles were carved into its surface, each inlaid with a different metal: silver, gold, copper, iron, and something that looked like shadow.

Those circles were where they would stand, where they would be examined like livestock at market.

Around the platform's edge ran a channel carved deep into the stone. It was stained dark, and she didn't want to think about what had filled it during past ceremonies. The whole structure looked as if it had been designed for sacrifice, though she supposed that was exactly what this was—just a sacrifice with prettier words and formal protocols.

Officials in ceremonial robes were settling onto the higher benches, their faces hidden beneath hoods that cast shadows darker than nature should allow. These weren't the same people who sentenced them or brought them here. These were the witnesses, the record-keepers, the ones who would document which Death Lord claimed which tribute for whatever grim purpose lay ahead.

"The old ways," one of them intoned, his voice carrying impossibly well in the vast space. "The ancient pacts. The bargains that keep the realms in balance."

Morgan started sobbing again, a broken sound that seemed to be absorbed by the stones themselves. The young man was praying under his breath in a language Brynn didn't recognize. Possibly one that predated the common tongue, pulled from some half-remembered religious tradition his family had preserved.

But Brynn found herself studying the platform with interest. The metal inlays in the smaller circles hummed with residual energy, making the hidden tools pressed against her ribs grow warmer in response.

This place seemed to know her, just like the tools had. Just like her dreams had suggested it would.

The air above the platform was starting to shimmer, reality warping like heat waves.

"Look," she murmured to the others, nodding toward the sky above the amphitheater.

The darkness she'd noticed from the wagon was deepening, but it wasn't spreading evenly. It was gathering in specific patterns, forming what looked like doorways in the air. Five doorways, each one edged with a different color of light: green, silver, red, gold, and something so deep and dark it was less a color than an absence of light.

The Death Lords were preparing to manifest.

Around them, the officials fell silent. The only sounds were Morgan's muffled sobs and the steady clinking of their chains as the tributes shifted nervously on their feet.

Brynn straightened her shoulders and lifted her chin. She'd survived one month in Edmund's dungeon, two days in a prison wagon, and thirty years of a world that had tried repeatedly to kill her. Whatever came through those doorways would see her standing tall.

V.
BRYNN

The first to manifest was Lord Caelum of The Mourned.

He stepped through the green-edged doorway like a concerned father arriving to comfort grieving children, his presence immediately easing the oppressive weight that had been building in the amphitheater. Where the other doorways crackled with volatile energy, his portal closed behind him quietly.

Caelum appeared younger than Brynn had expected. He looked about forty, with kind eyes and graying hair that spoke of wisdom rather than age. His robes were pristine white, cut in simple lines that managed to look both humble and regal. When he surveyed the amphitheater, his gaze lingered on each tribute with genuine sympathy.

"Peace," he said, and his voice carried to every corner of the amphitheater without being raised. "You are all far from home, but you need not fear. Death comes to all mortals, but it need not come with suffering."

Even Morgan's sobbing quieted at his words.

Pretty words from a pretty package. But underneath all that compassion, he was still one of them. Still a Death Lord. Still something that fed on mortal souls.

The crash of steel on stone shattered the moment.

Lady Seraphina of The Violent burst through her red-edged portal, landing in a warrior's crouch. Rising to her full six feet, she revealed razor-wire bindings in her blood-red hair and armor that left her scarred arms bare. Each scar marking a life she'd taken.

When the Lady of the Violent smiled, her teeth were filed to points.

"Brother Caelum," she said. "Still trying to calm them before the choosing? You know it changes nothing."

"Compassion changes everything," Caelum replied mildly. "But I don't expect you to understand that."

Seraphina's laugh was like shattering glass.

Now there was honesty. At least this one didn't pretend to be anything other than what she was. Violence personified, brutal, beautiful, and completely unapologetic about it.

The third Death Lord slid through his gold-edged portal like he owned the world. Lord Vex of The Consumed stepped onto the platform, and immediately the air grew thick with the scent of wine that had turned to vinegar.

He had the kind of beauty that made bad deals look tempting. Sharp cheekbones, full lips curved in a perpetual half-smile, gold eyes that promised everything and delivered nothing. Dark hair that looked like he'd just rolled out of someone's bed and couldn't be bothered to fix it. His skin had a faint blue undertone, something cold-blooded beneath the charm. His clothes were rich velvet and silk that had seen better days, elegant but worn at the edges like a nobleman who'd gambled away his fortune but refused to admit it.

When he moved, there was something hungry in the way his gaze swept over the assembled crowd, a desperate craving of someone who could never have enough of anything.

"Caelum. Seraphina." His voice dripped with false sweetness. "How delightful to see you again. Though I must say, this year's offerings look rather ordinary."

Another charmer. The kind who'd smile while picking your pocket and make you thank him for the privilege.

The fourth arrival brought with it the scent of flowers past their prime.

Lady Thessa of The Lingering emerged from her portal like morning mist, taking shape. Her gown flowed around her like fog, shifting with each movement, and when she turned her distant gaze across the tributes, Brynn felt seen and forgotten at once.

Spirits followed in her wake. Translucent figures that might once have been human, their forms shimmering. They arranged themselves around her with the devotion of courtiers, though their eyes held the hollow emptiness of souls that had forgotten why they refused to cross over.

"Brothers," she said, and her voice seemed to echo from far away. "Sister. How lovely to see you all again. It's been far too long since we gathered like this."

"Only ten years," Seraphina pointed out. "Hardly an eternity."

"Time moves differently for those of us who linger," Thessa replied with a smile that was both sad and knowing.

Four Death Lords stood in the amphitheater now, each one representing a different aspect of humanity's final moments. But the most feared portal remained sealed. The one edged with darkness that devoured light.

The officials on the higher benches had gone perfectly silent. Even the wind had stopped moving through the stone passages. The entire amphitheater held its breath, waiting for the arrival of the one Death Lord whose very name was spoken in whispers.

The darkness around the fifth portal began to deepen.

Brynn's pulse quickened, her body reacting before her mind could stop it. Whatever was coming through that doorway made every survival instinct she had scream *run*.

Shadows poured from the doorway before he did. They spilled across the amphitheater floor like black water, reaching toward the assembled crowd with grasping tendrils before withdrawing at some unspoken command.

The temperature dropped so fast that a shiver ran through her.

Then he stepped through.

The Reaper. Lord of The Forsaken.

And hells damn her traitorous body, but the first coherent thought that formed in her head was: *Oh. Oh no.*

She'd expected a monster. Something grotesque, something that matched the nightmare stories whispered in taverns about the Lord of Despair and Forsaken Deaths.

She got devastation wrapped in a deceptively civilized package.

He towered over most, easily exceeding six feet tall, with a lean, muscular build that suggested danger. His black hair fell to his shoulders, framing a face with sharp cheekbones and a straight nose. His mouth was set in a hard line, as if smiling was something he rarely did.

But it was his eyes that made her breath catch and her pulse spike traitorously.

Black irises, set against whites that made the darkness starker. Not dark brown or deep gray, but true black. Lightless voids that made her think of falling into deep water with no bottom in sight. They didn't catch the torchlight like normal eyes. They swallowed it.

Her survival instincts screamed. *Run. Hide. Survive.*

Her body had other opinions, though. Significantly less clothed opinions that would get her killed.

Down, girl. Death incarnate. But what a way to go.

Black gloves covered his hands entirely. No skin visible anywhere. His armor was fitted with black plate over dark leather, each piece edged in silver that caught no light. A high collar framed his jaw. Even standing still, he looked ready for war.

When his gaze swept across the amphitheater, Brynn felt the temperature drop another few degrees. Frost began forming on the stone benches. The shadows that had preceded him made the carved symbols in the stone glow with cold light.

He surveyed the space, boredom flattening his expression. The officials, the other Death Lords, and finally, the five tributes who stood chained on the platform below.

His expression held nothing but complete indifference to the mortal lives being bartered like commodities.

That should have been reassuring. Instead, it was somehow more terrifying than if he'd looked at them with hunger or malice.

"Well," Lord Caelum said into the silence. "Now that we're all here, shall we begin?"

The guards, those wrong-moving things that looked almost human, prodded the first tribute forward. The young man was barely past sixteen, his noble clothes now wrinkled and stained from the journey. He walked to the center of the platform on shaking legs, stopping in the middle of the largest circle.

The moment his feet touched the inlaid metal, the symbols around the platform's edge began to glow with cold blue light, making the shadows dance strangely across the carved stone. The boy whimpered as energy crackled through the air around him, his hair lifting as if touched by invisible winds.

Four of the Death Lords leaned forward, studying him.

Lady Seraphina spoke first, her voice cutting through the charged air. "Too soft. He'll break before I can use him properly." She leaned back dismissively, scarred arms crossed.

"Fear has its own value," Lord Vex murmured, his dark eyes fixed on the trembling boy. "But this one's terror is pedestrian. Ordinary. I require more sophisticated forms of despair."

Lady Thessa tilted her head, studying the tribute like she was watching a memory fade in real time. "He has no unfinished business, no burning regrets. Nothing to anchor him should he pass into my domain. He would fade within days."

Lord Caelum stepped forward, extending one gentle hand toward the boy. "Come, child. You've suffered enough. Let me offer you peace."

Relief flooded the boy's face. Whatever horrors he'd imagined, being claimed by The Mourned was the best fate possible. He stumbled toward Caelum on unsteady legs, tears streaming down his face.

"Thank you," he whispered. "Thank you, my lord."

Caelum's smile was genuinely kind as he placed a gentle hand on the boy's shoulder. "Rest now. Your suffering has ended."

The Reaper hadn't moved. Hadn't spoken. Hadn't even looked at the boy being claimed. His black eyes remained fixed on some point off in the distance, his expression suggesting he found this entire proceeding beneath him.

Like he had far more important things to do than waste time selecting terrified mortals.

The second tribute was the middle-aged woman. She walked to the center circle like a ghost moving through familiar motions, her empty eyes reflecting the cold light of the platform symbols.

This time, Lady Seraphina straightened with interest. "This one knows loss. Real loss. The kind that turns sorrow to rage and rage to strength."

"She's already broken," Lord Vex observed. "Where's the satisfaction in claiming something that's already been consumed by grief?"

"Broken things can be reforged," Seraphina replied. "Made into weapons sharper than they were before."

Lady Thessa shook her head. "Her spirit has already begun to linger. She's caught between what was and what might have been. She belongs with me."

"She belongs where she can serve best," Seraphina snapped. "I claim her."

"As do I," Thessa said calmly.

The two Death Lords stared at each other across the platform. The temperature began to rise as Seraphina's power flared, while spirits materialized around Thessa like a gathering storm. The woman in the center circle swayed on her feet, caught between two competing claims, each pulling from a different direction.

Lord Caelum raised his hand for peace. "Ladies, please. The girl clearly bears the weight of unfinished sorrow. That speaks to both your domains. Perhaps we should let her choose."

"Choose?" Seraphina's voice was sharp with surprise.

"A rare honor," Caelum said gently. "But not unprecedented. When claims conflict, the tribute may select their own fate."

The woman looked between the two Death Lords with eyes that held no hope, only indifference. Finally, she spoke.

"I can't let go," she said. "I can't stop thinking about what I've lost."

Lady Thessa smiled, an expression both sad and triumphant. "Then come to me, child. We'll ensure you never forget a single moment of what you've lost."

As translucent spirits led the woman away, Brynn felt her stomach clench. She had just seen someone choose eternal haunting over the chance of being turned into a weapon. That said, everything about what awaited them in these domains.

The Reaper still hadn't moved, still hadn't shown the slightest interest in any of the proceedings. His shadows shifted restlessly around his feet, but his expression remained one of boredom.

The third tribute was the older merchant. He approached the center circle without faltering, his jaw set in grim determination. When he stood in the circle, and the symbols flared to life around him, he didn't flinch.

"I know what I am," he said before any Death Lord could speak. "A merchant who cheated his customers, who lied and stole and built his fortune on the backs of those who trusted him." His voice was flat, resigned. "I deserve whatever comes."

Lord Vex leaned forward with sudden interest. "Guilt. Self-awareness. The knowledge of one's own corruption. How delicious. You'll spend eternity dwelling on every choice that brought you here."

"Better that than pretending I was anything other than what I am," the merchant replied.

"Indeed." Vex stood and approached, his smile promising unpleasant things. "You'll do nicely in my domain. We appreciate honesty about one's vices."

As Vex led the merchant away, Brynn revised her read of the man. He'd known exactly what he was doing when he confessed. Choosing the devil he understood over the ones he didn't.

The fourth tribute was Morgan, and Brynn's chest tightened as the sobbing girl was pushed toward the center platform. Morgan's legs gave out halfway there, and she collapsed to her knees in the circle, shaking so hard the chains around her wrists rattled like wind chimes.

"Please," she whispered, the word barely audible. "Please, I just want to go home."

The Reaper spoke for the first time since arriving, his voice carrying easily, low but clear.

"Pathetic."

One word. Delivered with such cold dismissal that even Morgan's sobbing stuttered to a halt. His black eyes hadn't even entirely focused on the girl. She wasn't worth his complete attention.

"Fear without strength. Despair without defiance. She offers nothing of value."

Hells, he really was a piece of work, wasn't he? Brynn had met cruel men before, plenty of them in her ten years of thieving, but this was something else. This was cruelty that didn't even care enough to be deliberately vicious—just complete indifference, as if Morgan's terror was beneath his notice.

"Someone take her before her weeping becomes insufferable."

Lady Seraphina stood with a sharp smile. "I'll forge something useful from this raw material. Fear can be turned to rage with the right pressure."

As armored spirits stepped forward to lift Morgan from the platform, the girl was still sobbing. But there was something different in her tears now—a spark of something that might have been anger beginning to burn through the despair.

Four tributes claimed. One Death Lord yet to choose. One tribute remaining.

Brynn walked to the center circle without waiting to be pushed.

The moment her feet touched the inlaid metal, the symbols around the platform's edge began to glow with the same cold light as before. Energy crackled through the air around her, but she kept her spine straight and her chin high.

Even if her heart was hammering and every instinct screamed that she was standing in the direct line of sight of something that could erase her from existence with a thought.

"Another peasant," Lady Seraphina said with a dismissive wave. "Probably die of fright before anyone can make use of her."

"Unremarkable," Lord Vex agreed, already losing interest. "No particular obsessions, no consuming desires. Hardly worth the effort."

Lady Thessa nodded absently. "Nothing draws me to this one. No unfinished business, no desperate attachments."

Lord Caelum offered Brynn a gentle smile. "You seem calmer than the others, child. That's wise. Peace makes any transition easier."

But the Reaper had gone perfectly still.

While the other Death Lords dismissively discussed her like she wasn't standing right there, he studied her with such intensity that the frost around his feet spread even further across the stone. The shadows surrounding him stirred, reaching toward her before pulling back like they'd been burned.

"You're not afraid."

An observation delivered with something that might have been surprise if Death incarnate were capable of such emotions.

Brynn met those lightless black eyes directly. "Should I be?"

"Everyone else is."

Fair point. Morgan had been sobbing. The merchant had confessed his sins. The empty-eyed woman had chosen eternal haunting. Even the noble boy had looked at these Death Lords like they were his executioners.

But Brynn had learned a long time ago that showing fear to predators was the fastest way to become prey.

"Fear seems like a waste of energy," she said. "Besides, you're all going to choose someone anyway. Cowering won't change that."

The other Death Lords had gone quiet, watching this exchange with sudden attention. Lord Caelum looked concerned. Lady Seraphina's eyes had narrowed with interest. Even Lord Vex had stopped examining his nails to pay attention.

But the Reaper's expression didn't shift—just that same cold, unblinking stare from something that had never been human.

Then he descended from his position, shadows flowing around him. The other Death Lords shifted, surprise clear on their faces. Even the officials in the higher seats leaned forward. Whatever was happening, it clearly wasn't standard procedure.

When The Reaper reached the edge of the circle where she stood, the symbols blazing beneath her feet suddenly shifted to something darker. Black fire edged with the faintest hint of silver light. The air between them crackled with energy that made everyone else in the amphitheater take an involuntary step backward.

He stopped just outside the circle's boundary. Close enough that she could see her breath misting in the cold radiating from him, that his shadows reached toward her like they wanted to touch before jerking back.

Brynn's muscles locked. Every nerve ending fired the same message: *run*. Put distance between herself and the apex predator studying her like she'd done something unexpected. Cold sweat slid down her spine. Her hands had gone numb at her sides.

She didn't move.

Couldn't afford to. Not with every Death Lord watching. Not with her life balanced on whatever judgment he was making right now.

So she forced her spine straight. Braced her knees before they could betray her with trembling. And met those lightless eyes, even though looking directly at him felt like staring into an abyss that stared back with hungry interest.

His head tilted fractionally. Shadows wrapped around his form, moving with the patience of something that had eternity to decide whether she was worth the hunt.

Up close, he was even more devastating than from a distance. Those black eyes, the sharp planes of his face, the controlled power in every line of him. Everything that had caught her attention across the amphitheater hit twice as hard at this range.

No. Absolutely not.

But her pulse hammered anyway, and she couldn't tell anymore if it was pure fear or something far more dangerous.

His jaw clenched once. Just a flicker of tension in that perfect, terrible face. Then his eyes darkened, and she knew. Whatever he'd just decided, he wasn't happy about it.

The silence stretched. The amphitheater held its breath. She counted her own heartbeats—one, two, three, each one too fast, too loud—and willed herself not to break eye contact first.

Then his shadows surged forward.

They wrapped around her ankles first, then her wrists, where the chains hung. Testing. The cold sank through her skin, deeper than it should. His power pressed against her, sliding along her spine, her ribs, searching for weakness. For the moment she'd break and give him reason to walk away.

Her skin came alive where the shadows touched. Every defense stripped away, every secret exposed, like being examined down to her soul.

Her breath came shallow. Each inhale was a conscious effort. Her hands trembled now, beyond her control. But she didn't look down, didn't flinch, didn't do anything except hold his stare and pray he couldn't see how badly part of her wanted to run.

And how another part, smaller and infinitely more foolish, was caught by the way he looked at her. Something that widened his eyes for a heartbeat before his expression went cold and flat.

The shadows retreated slowly. They circled her wrists once more before finally releasing her.

He straightened slightly, pulling back. The movement should have brought relief.

It didn't.

Those black eyes remained locked on hers with an intensity that made her skin prickle.

Her heart pounded. Fear she could handle. Fear kept you alive. But this awareness of him as something more than just a threat? This was the kind of distraction that got people killed.

His hand flexed at his side. Once. The only visible crack in that perfect control.

When he finally spoke, his voice was low. Rough. Her pulse jumped before her mind could process the words, something tightening low in her stomach.

"You're mine, thief."

The other Death Lords looked shocked. The officials whispered frantically. Even Lord Caelum had straightened with what looked like concern on his face.

"Brother," Caelum said slowly, his gentle voice strained. "Are you certain? She could find peace in gentler hands."

"She could find strength in mine," Lady Seraphina added, though her tone suggested she wasn't particularly invested in the argument. "The girl has a spine. I could work with that."

The Reaper ignored both of them. He kept studying Brynn's face.

"The choice is made," he said.

His voice held no room for argument. Just made it clear he'd kill anyone who tried to challenge his claim.

Well. That was either the best or worst thing that had ever happened to her.

Guards approached to lead her away. Different guards than the ones who'd brought them here, wearing armor marked with symbols that matched the darkness of his shadows.

Brynn caught fragments of whispered conversation from the officials in the higher seats.

"The Reaper has never claimed anyone before."

"He didn't even attend the last two ceremonies."

"Why would he start now?"

None of it sounded encouraging.

"Move," one of the guards commanded.

Brynn was led to where the five Death Lords stood waiting beside portals that had begun opening in the air. Each doorway showed a glimpse of the realm beyond. Caelum's portal revealed gardens where white flowers bloomed in eternal golden hour, while Seraphina's showed training grounds where warriors practiced under a blood-red sky.

The Reaper's portal was a rectangle of darkness. No glimpse of what lay beyond, no hint of the domain that awaited her. Just black that seemed to pull at the edges of her vision.

Perfect. Walk through the door marked "certain death" and hope for the best. Her life choices had always been questionable, but this might be a new low.

"Any last words?" Lord Caelum asked gently.

Brynn looked around the amphitheater one last time. At the officials who'd documented her fate, at the other Death Lords who'd found her unremarkable, at the guards who served laws older than memory.

Then she looked at The Reaper, who waited beside his portal. His black eyes met hers, and for just a second, she could have sworn she saw something shift in that lightless gaze.

Interest, maybe. Or curiosity about this mortal who'd looked Death in the eye and refused to blink.

"I'm harder to kill than I look," Brynn said.

Several of the officials exchanged glances at her boldness. Even Lord Vex looked mildly impressed.

But the Reaper's expression didn't change at all.

"We shall see," he said, and gestured toward the portal.

The crossing felt like being pulled through ice water while someone played discordant music inside her skull. Reality twisted around her, up and down, losing all meaning as she was dragged from one realm into another. The ceremonial chains around her wrists grew so cold they burned her skin, and the air she tried to breathe tasted of copper and endings.

Then her feet hit solid ground, and she stumbled forward onto flagstones that crunched softly beneath her. Smooth bone tiles, she realized with a lurch of her stomach. Fitted together like cobblestones.

She was no longer in the mortal realm.

Behind her, the portal snapped closed with a sound like breaking bones, cutting off the last connection to the world she'd known.

Ahead stretched corridors where massive ribs arched overhead, meeting at spines that ran along the ceilings. Bone sconces lined the walls, skeletal hands cupping cold blue flames that cast flickering shadows.

Welcome to the Court of the Forsaken.

VI.

DANTE

He didn't look back. Looking back would acknowledge the problem.

But he could feel her behind him. Scanning corridors, studying the bone sconces, mapping exits.

Her chains clinked with a steady rhythm.

Hundreds of tributes had passed through his domain, and not one had ever walked in like they were already planning their escape.

The ritual had proceeded exactly as expected until she'd stepped into that circle. When the thief had walked to the center platform without being pushed and met his gaze directly, the ward symbols had changed from cold blue to bright white flame.

The wards had never blazed white before. His shadows had reached for her before he could stop them, instinct overriding his control.

Even now, the shadows around his feet stretched toward her. He wanted to snap them back, force them under his control. But doing so would reveal how much her presence unsettled him. He hadn't spent centuries perfecting that mask just to let it slip now.

Her defiance should have irritated him. Instead, satisfaction flickered through his chest before he buried it.

He'd grown weary of sobbing tributes. At least this one was different.

Ahead, the doors to his throne room stood open. Massive doors framed by crossed femurs, their handles shaped like curled skeletal hands.

His court was in their assigned positions. Close enough to attend, far enough to survive.

Everything just as it had been for ages.

Except his shadows kept reaching for the woman he'd claimed barely an hour ago.

"My lord." One of his servants materialized ahead. "The court awaits you."

Dante's chin dipped once. His court always awaited him, bound by magic older than their memories, compelled to serve whether they wished it or not. But tonight felt different.

Tonight, they were curious.

The tribute stepped through the doorway behind him.

And stopped.

Dante waited for the collapse. The begging. The desperate tears.

Instead, her head lifted. She swept her gaze across his court, tracked the walls, the chandeliers overhead, the floor beneath her feet.

Her attention settled on his throne, studying it like she was calculating its weight, its value, its weaknesses.

"Interesting decor."

Servants made sounds of shock. One spirit flickered so violently it nearly lost its form. Even his bound warriors shifted uneasily.

Dante's jaw clenched. "You find my throne room interesting?"

"The sight lines are excellent." She gestured from the throne to the doorways, chains clinking. "You can see every entrance from that seat, and anyone approaching has to cross significant ground to reach you. Good defensive positioning." Her gaze swept the twelve-foot boundary around his throne. "Though I notice everyone stays well back from the center. Is that by choice, or by design?"

No one had spoken to him like this in centuries. As if his throne room were a fortress to solve rather than a monument to everything he represented.

His shadows wound tighter, fighting his control. He forced them still through sheer will, refusing to let them betray his reaction.

Dante walked toward the throne. Power rolled off him in waves, dropping the temperature. Frost spread across the floor.

She straightened her shoulders and walked deeper inside.

Such a waste. She'd get herself killed within the hour.

He reached his throne and turned to face her. The boundary stretched between them. From this distance, he could study her without the complications of proximity.

Smaller than she'd seemed at the ritual. Average height, maybe, but the ceremonial chains looked heavy against her lean frame. She carried them without apparent discomfort. Chestnut hair caught the blue flames, turning auburn where light touched it. Those sharp eyes continued their sweep. Green, he noted. Looking at the architecture, the carved names, the way shadows pooled in corners.

Callused hands, visible even from this distance. Working hands.

A strand of hair had come loose, falling against her throat. It moved slightly with her breathing.

He looked away.

"Well?" He settled into his throne. "Are you going to stand there all evening, or do you have something to say?"

She met his gaze directly.

One shoulder lifted in a shrug that sent chains clinking. "Nice place. Bit excessive on the death imagery, but I suppose that's the point."

A spirit lost its form entirely, dissipating before frantically reforming. A warrior's sword rattled in its sheath.

Dante leaned forward. The temperature plummeted. Frost spread across the armrests beneath his gloved hands.

"Excessive."

The word came out flat—a warning most mortals would have recognized.

She didn't even blink.

"Well, yes." She gestured at the walls, the throne, the floor. "It's very 'look upon my works and despair.' Effective, but it does rather announce itself, doesn't it?"

She was critiquing his interior design. Standing in his throne room, surrounded by the bound souls of those who'd displeased him, and offering decorating advice.

His remaining servants pressed against the walls.

Dante straightened in his throne. Ice spread rapidly outward. Several servants fled, abandoning their posts rather than witnessing what came next.

Her foot moved forward. One step closer to the boundary no one else dared cross, chains clinking.

She was walking toward him while ice formed in the air and shadows writhed across the floor.

Careful, thief. That curiosity of hers would get her killed faster than fear ever could.

His shadows surged toward her, wrapping around her shoulders, her arms, touching her with an eagerness that had nothing to do with his will. They'd never done that before, never reached for anyone without his explicit command.

Yet they curled around her like greeting an old friend.

Then they found the chains. A sharp snap of metal. The ceremonial cuffs split apart and clattered to the floor, the sound ringing through the silent chamber.

He dragged them back by force of will, fighting their resistance. His jaw clenched with the effort.

"You're still not afraid." The words came out flat, stripped of inflection.

She looked at him. Really looked at him. Her chin lifted slightly.

"No." Her voice remained steady. "You don't scare me, Reaper."

The title fell from her lips casually, without the reverence or terror others showed when speaking it.

Her pulse jumped in her throat when she said it. Just once. Visible proof that some part of her recognized the danger, even if her voice didn't waver.

She should be afraid, even if she were too stubborn to show it.

Shadows surged forward again, testing that boundary. The temperature dropped so rapidly that their breath misted.

"I am the Lord of the Forsaken." His voice dropped to that whisper that had made armies surrender. "I rule over humanity's darkest final moments. The sight of me has driven mortals mad. My presence has ended bloodlines."

She waited a beat. "Yes. I've heard all of that." A pause. "Very impressive."

His hands clenched on the throne's arms. Ice formed under his gloved fingers, spreading across the bone. The crack echoed through the silent chamber.

Shadows pressed toward her again, aggressive and seeking.

She didn't step back. Didn't flinch. Her eyes narrowed slightly. A soft exhale escaped her, visible in the freezing air.

"You should run." The words came out rougher than intended. His throat tightened around them, voice dropping to something raw. "You should be terrified. You should be begging for mercy I will never grant."

Her head tilted. A moment passed. Then she shook her head slowly. "I don't think so."

His fingers dug deeper into the bone. Another crack. Louder this time.

This would end badly. *For both of them.*

But he couldn't quite make himself care about the consequences. Not when she stood there seeing things no one else had seen, asking questions no one else had dared to ask.

He should send her to Caelum. The Lord of the Mourned would take her gladly. Natural deaths were kinder, gentler. She'd fade peacefully in white marble halls under eternal golden light instead of learning to navigate shadows and ice.

She'd be safer there.

The thought made his shadows coil tighter.

"You're staying."

She blinked. The first sign of surprise she'd shown. "I'm what?"

"You're staying. In my court." He leaned back against his throne, forcing casualness into his posture. "Until I decide what to do with you."

Her eyebrows rose slightly. "And how long might that take?"

"Weeks. Months. Years." One shoulder lifted in a dismissive shrug. "Time moves differently here. I have nothing but patience."

The frost around his throne began to recede slightly.

"There are rules." His voice dropped to that tone that ended all discussion. "Break them, and I will kill you. Slowly. Painfully. In ways that will make you beg for the mercy of simple execution."

She straightened slightly.

"What rules?"

"First: Don't touch anything that doesn't belong to you. My domain is filled with objects that will kill mortals in ways I won't bother to heal."

"Second: Don't touch anyone without permission. My servants are bound by magic older than your civilization. Disrupting those bindings could free them. Or destroy them entirely."

He paused, letting both rules settle.

"And if you damage my property through ignorance or carelessness, I will ensure you regret it."

"And the third rule?" she asked when he didn't immediately continue.

Dante studied her. The unwavering gaze, the complete lack of deference, the way she stood in his throne room like she belonged there.

The way his shadows kept reaching for her despite his restraint.

"Don't touch me." His voice dropped, losing its theatrical edge and becoming something more honest. "Ever. For any reason. No matter what circumstances arise."

The words carried weight different from his previous threats.

She studied him for another long moment.

Then her chin dipped once in acknowledgment, like a soldier receiving orders rather than a prisoner accepting terms of captivity.

"Understood."

His servants shifted uneasily, waiting for him to punish such casual address.

He didn't.

Dante gestured to one of his bound spirits.

"Escort her to the west wing. Third floor. The purple rooms."

The spirit bowed before turning to the tribute.

"If you would follow me, my lady."

She turned to leave, boots echoing softly on the floor.

Dante watched her go. The straight line of her shoulders. The pace suggested she was still mapping exits.

A muscle ticked in his jaw.

When the doors closed, his court remained silent.

Finally, Nathaniel cleared his throat.

"My lord. The West Wing. The purple rooms. Those are..."

"I know what they are." Warning edged every word.

Nathaniel took a step back.

"Shall I inform the household staff of any special requirements?"

Dante considered the question, thinking of the woman who had just walked out of his throne room. Who had looked at him and seen the person beneath the power.

"Tell them to treat her as they would any other member of my inner court." He let the words carry weight. "And tell them that anyone who fails to show appropriate respect will answer to me personally."

Nathaniel bowed and hurried to carry out his orders, leaving Dante alone on his throne surrounded by melting frost and cracked bone.

She had disrupted the order he'd maintained for so long.

He should have killed her when she first spoke out of turn.

The reaching hands at his throne's base seemed to curl more tightly, as if they too were unsettled by the change she represented. Somewhere in the skull-lined walls, a jaw clicked softly. The sound might have been settling. Might have been agreement.

VII.

BRYNN

The door closed behind her with a sound like a tomb sealing shut.

Brynn stood frozen for a couple of full heartbeats. Then she let out a breath she didn't realize she'd been holding, her hands shaking as she pressed them against her thighs.

Holy shit. Holy shit.

She'd just told The Reaper, the actual fucking Reaper, the Death Lord everyone in the kingdom whispered about in terror, that he didn't scare her. She'd walked right up to his throne when his entire court kept twelve feet back. She'd met those dark eyes and refused to flinch.

And now she was alone, and her knees felt like water.

She moved to the nearest chair, its frame carved from pale bone, the armrests ending in curled skeletal fingers. She sank into it before her legs could give out completely. Her hands were still trembling. She pressed them flat against her knees, trying to stop the shaking through sheer willpower.

Get it together, Brynn.

She forced herself to look around the room properly. The walls were covered in dark purple silk, so deep it was almost black, but this was no ordinary fabric. Woven into the silk were scenes of death, hauntingly beautiful tableaus that seemed to move and depict the scene. A woman in a field of flowers, her soul rising from her body. A battle frozen mid-slaughter, warriors falling in almost graceful poses. A child sleeping peacefully while a shadowy figure bent over the bed.

The images moved. The woman's soul drifted higher. The warriors fell further. The shadow's hand reached closer to the sleeping child.

She looked away.

The furniture was carved from wood so dark it was almost black, but bone accents decorated every piece. Drawer pulls shaped like finger bones, a mirror framed in polished bone. The bed was massive, its headboard formed from curved bones that arched overhead like protective arms. Or a cage. The posts were wrapped in carved bone vines bearing flowers that, on closer inspection, were tiny skulls with petals.

Someone here really loves their bone collection. Either that, or there's a truly impressive graveyard somewhere nearby.

The absurd thought steadied her slightly. Made this feel less like a nightmare and more like a very strange place with very strange decorating choices.

Guest quarters. Not a cell. Not servant's lodgings.

What the hell did that make her?

She moved to the windows. Always check your exits, even when you know there aren't any. The heavy curtains, made of that purple silk, were pulled back to reveal something that made her stomach drop all over again.

The sky hung in eternal twilight, deep purple bleeding into midnight blue, never brightening to day or darkening to full night. In the distance, palace spires of black stone and pale bone rose against that unchanging sky, their Gothic architecture stark and severe. She could see ribcage archways connecting towers, windows framed in what might have been jawbones. Figures in dark robes walked between the spires, their movements unnaturally smooth, too fluid to be entirely human.

She let the curtain fall and backed away from the window, her hands shaking again.

She just told him she wasn't scared. She looked him in the eye and said he didn't scare her.

The worst part? She'd meant it in the moment. Standing there with his entire court watching, with those dark eyes fixed on her like she was something he couldn't quite figure out, she'd felt more alive than she had in months. More herself than she'd been since the moment guards dragged her out of that underground chamber.

But now, alone in this too-fancy room with death scenes shifting on the walls, the fear caught up.

She kept moving. Better to map her cage than stand still and let the panic settle in.

The bathing room was carved from black marble veined with white, looking unsettlingly like exposed bone. A chandelier of tiny interlocked finger bones hung overhead, holding candles that burned with that same cold blue flame. When her fingertips accidentally brushed the edge of the tub, warmth pulsed under her palm.

She jerked her hand back so fast she nearly lost her balance.

"Don't touch anything. Don't touch anyone. Don't touch me."

His voice echoed in her memory, all rough command and danger. She'd spent years learning to read people: merchants, marks, city guards who could smell desperation streets away. But the Reaper was a locked vault. All sharp edges and shadows that moved on their own.

Like those black gloves he never removed, even sitting on his own throne of reaching bone hands. Like how his entire court kept twelve feet of distance as if their lives depended on it. Like how they'd looked ready to faint when she'd walked right up to where they wouldn't dare go.

Like how he'd gone still when she'd gotten close, then practically snarled at her to stay back.

What kind of Death Lord needs that much distance from everyone?

She should investigate more. Map the room properly, test the door, and look for weaknesses. But exhaustion slammed into her hard enough to make her stumble. The journey through the death realm, the terror of the selection, the month in a cell before that. It all crashed down on her at once.

Her legs gave out. She barely made it to the bed before collapsing onto silk sheets that felt too smooth against her skin. The bone-frame headboard arched over her. On the wall beside her, the death tapestry showed a young woman drowning, her expression peaceful as bubbles escaped her lips.

Don't look at it. Don't think about it.

Sleep dragged her under before she could fight it.

DREAMS CAME IN FRAGMENTS. Black eyes watching her like she was a threat. Shadows reaching for her with desperate hunger before snapping back. The Reaper's voice, low and rough. The death scenes on her walls coming alive, figures stepping out of the silk to circle her bed.

Three sharp knocks jolted her awake, heart already racing.

Twilight glow filtered through the curtains. Slightly lighter than before. Morning, she assumed. She'd slept through the entire night.

"Miss Brynn?" A woman's voice called through the door. "I've brought breakfast."

Brynn sat up, trying to shake off the lingering nightmares. The drowning woman on the wall had drifted lower, her peaceful face now turned toward the bed.

"Come in."

The door opened. A woman stepped inside carrying a silver tray, and Brynn had to blink twice to convince herself she was seeing correctly. She looked solid enough. Dark hair pulled back in a practical knot, sharp cheekbones, clothes that seemed real. But something about the way light passed through her was off, like looking at someone standing behind frosted glass.

"You need to eat," she said, setting the tray down on the small table near the window. The clink of metal on wood sounded real enough.

"Thanks." Brynn studied her, the no-nonsense set of her mouth, the way she moved like someone who'd stopped being impressed by much of anything a long time ago. "I'm Brynn."

"Naia." She moved to leave.

"Wait." Brynn gestured to the tray. "Is there anything I should know? About all this?"

Naia paused, one translucent hand still on the door handle. She turned back to study Brynn with new interest. "Most tributes are too busy falling apart to ask questions."

"I'm not most tributes."

Approval flickered across her features. "No, you're not. You're still standing, for one thing."

The way she said it made Brynn's chest tighten. "Should I not be?"

Naia was quiet for a long moment, as if weighing her words. "The girl before you spent her first three days curled up in her bed, crying." A pause. "The one before her tried to climb out a window on the second night." She glanced toward the curtains. "Thirty-foot drop into thorns that bite back."

"What happened to them?"

"What happens to all of you, eventually." Her voice went neutral. "The death realm isn't meant for mortal hearts. It pulls at you, bit by bit."

"How long do I have?"

"Depends on how smart you are. How cautious." She crossed her arms, and Brynn noticed her fingers looked more solid when she was thinking hard. "Some manage weeks. The longest lasted almost two months. Smart girl, kept her head down, learned the court politics."

"What happened to her?"

"The realm got her in the end. It always does." Naia's voice went flat. "Woke up one morning and she was just... done."

Dread crawled up Brynn's spine. On the wall, the death tapestry seemed darker than before. The drowning woman's hand had risen, reaching toward the surface that would never come. "And the others?"

"Most fade bit by bit. But some..." She moved toward the door, then stopped. "There was one girl who thought she was different. Thought she could change the rules."

"What did she do?"

Naia's back was still turned, but Brynn could hear the tension in her voice. "Tried to seduce him. Thought if she got close enough, pretty enough, he'd let her past all that distance he keeps."

"What happened?"

When Naia looked back at her, her expression was haunted. "She learned why everyone calls him The Reaper. And why the distance isn't cruelty. It's the only thing keeping you alive."

Brynn's mouth went dry. "What does that mean?"

"It means his control isn't perfect." She met Brynn's eyes, and for a moment she looked completely solid. Afraid. "The distance is mercy. Remember that." She moved to the door. "I'll return in an hour to help you dress for court."

The door closed behind her, leaving Brynn alone with the sound of her own heartbeat and the death scenes shifting silently on the walls.

She forced herself to eat. Bread, fruit, tea. Though she barely tasted any of it, her mind was elsewhere. Girls who got too close and learned hard lessons. The way The Reaper's jaw had clenched when she'd stepped into his space. The way his shadows had seemed to reach for her before he'd jerked them back.

She checked her vest draped over the chair. Her fingers found the hidden pockets along the inner seams. The two small tools were still there. The delicate probe and the tension wrench that warmed in her palm. Good.

She moved to the wardrobe and stared at its contents for longer than she cared to admit.

Three gowns hung inside, each more elaborate than anything she'd ever worn. Deep purple velvet with silver threading that caught the light like spider silk. Black silk with bone buttons carved into tiny skulls. Dark blue with sleeves that would trail past her fingertips.

All of them screamed Death Court nobility. All of them would mark her as either trying too hard or entirely out of place.

She picked the blue. If she was going to stand out in a room full of purple shadows and death imagery, she might as well commit to it. Let them see she wasn't trying to blend in.

The fabric felt strange against her skin—too smooth, too expensive, nothing like the rough cotton she was used to. The neckline was lower than she preferred, but higher than the others. The sleeves were fitted to her wrists, leaving her hands exposed. She wondered if that was intentional, if everyone would be able to tell she wasn't wearing gloves like he did.

She was struggling with the back lacing when a knock at the door interrupted her frustration.

"Come in," she called, grateful for the help.

Naia entered and moved behind her without being asked, her translucent fingers surprisingly quick with the intricate lacings. "Blue was a good choice," she said. "Shows you're not trying to disappear into the shadows."

"Should I be?"

"No." She pulled the laces snug. "Hiding never works here. Better to stand out for the right reasons than the wrong ones." She finished with the laces and stepped back. "The Reaper has summoned you to attend morning court."

"Of course he has." Brynn took a breath.

On the wall behind her, the drowning woman had finally stopped sinking. Her eyes were open now, staring directly at Brynn with an expression that might have been a warning.

Or welcome.

VIII.
BRYNN

The throne room was even more overwhelming the second time. She'd thought she'd prepared herself, but walking back through those femur-framed doors, stepping onto the floor of teeth that crunched softly beneath her feet, seeing the thousands of skulls watching from every wall with blue flames burning in their sockets—it hit differently in the silence of morning court.

The vaulted ceiling disappeared into shadows where bone chandeliers hung like the ribcages of giants. Death-woven tapestries she'd barely noticed last night now drew her eye. Battles, massacres, figures being dragged into darkness by hands emerging from the ground. Images designed to remind everyone precisely where they were and who ruled here.

And on the throne of reaching hands sat the Reaper, looking every inch the Lord of the Forsaken.

Darkness pooled around the base of his throne, curling between those frozen bone fingers that strained upward from the dais, stirred by whatever simmered beneath his stillness.

He wore fitted black, emphasizing his lean strength. Dark pants tailored for movement, chest armor crafted from black metal, catching the blue firelight from countless sconces—long sleeves despite the comfortable temperature. Black leather gloves disappearing under those sleeves, never removed.

Rule three. Don't touch him. Ever.

She wondered what those gloves were protecting—him, or everyone else.

His dark gaze found hers the moment she entered, tracking her movement across the room. His expression shifted, too quick to read, before settling back into cold indifference.

Her stomach tightened. She'd faced worse. Noble houses full of guards who wanted her dead. This was just another room where she didn't belong. She could survive it if she acted like she did.

"You may observe from there," he said, gesturing to a spot along the wall. His voice carried easily in the vast space, that low roughness making her breath catch. "Close enough to see and hear everything. Far enough to stay out of the way."

She took her position, her back against bone, empty sockets flanking her on both sides. They seemed to watch the proceedings with the same attention she did.

The morning's business was a parade of nightmares dressed up as paperwork.

A dispute between two minor lords over territory in the Screaming Marshes. She filed that away as a place to absolutely never visit. A request to relocate several hundred tormented souls from one wing to another, discussed with the same casual tone someone might use for moving furniture. Then reports on ward-locks throughout the realm. None of it made sense to her, but it concerned him. His shadows wound tighter with each update, wrapping around the throne's base.

He was good at this. Decisive without being hasty, listening to full arguments before making judgments. His voice carried authority, but he didn't seem to enjoy the power; it was more as if he were managing necessary business that required ultimate decision-making.

What struck her most was the distance.

Every petitioner stopped at that invisible twelve-foot barrier; none of them dared cross. No closer. When he gestured them forward, they took the smallest step possible, their feet barely lifting from the floor. When he leaned forward slightly, they retreated as if pushed by force.

It wasn't just respect. It was dread so deep it had become reflex.

But dread of what? He hadn't threatened anyone all morning, hadn't raised his voice above that low, commanding tone. If anything, his judgments seemed fair, even merciful by Death Lord standards. He'd reduced a soul's torment sentence. He'd granted better working conditions in the palace kitchens.

Her gaze drifted to those gloves again. To the distance he maintained. The way darkness reached toward people but never quite touched them, as if leashed by invisible chains.

His touch killed. That had to be it. Why else would he keep everyone at arm's length, warn her so specifically, wrap himself in gloves like armor?

The atmosphere shifted when a representative from the Court of the Mourned arrived.

She swept into the room, her white robes a stark contrast against the bone-and-shadow architecture. Pale hair caught the blue firelight like spun silver, the fabric glowing with its own inner light—the kind of ethereal beauty that made you think of angels, until you noticed the coldness in her eyes.

Everything was designed for maximum impact. Even her movements were meant to make you forget she was deadly.

Her approach was confident, stopping at that boundary as if she had done this many times before.

"Lord Reaper," she said, offering a formal bow, managing to convey respect without submission. "I bring greetings from Lord Caelum and a request for an emergency council of all five Death Lords."

"I will consider it." His response was neutral, but Brynn caught the slight tightening around his eyes. The subtle way his shadows drew closer to him, wrapping around the bone armrests like protective serpents.

He didn't like this. Whatever this messenger was asking for, he didn't trust it.

"Lord Caelum believes immediate discussion is warranted." The representative's smile revealed nothing. "There are matters requiring urgent consultation among all five courts. The barriers between realms have been experiencing unusual fluctuations."

That got his attention.

He leaned forward slightly, and Brynn noticed how the representative's hand moved instinctively to her throat, fighting the urge to retreat. Like getting closer to him, even by a few inches, triggered every survival instinct she possessed.

"What kind of fluctuations?" His voice had dropped to that quiet tone, making her spine straighten.

"Ward-locks going dark without explanation. Souls are crossing over in the wrong locations. Minor issues, but concerning." The representative paused, turning toward Brynn. "Perhaps a tribute with special talents might have insights into such magical anomalies?"

Every head in the court followed.

Heat flooded her neck as dozens of eyes appraised her with new interest. Spirits, bound servants, warriors. All of them were suddenly very aware of her presence.

She kept her expression neutral, her posture relaxed.

"Perhaps." His voice went flat.

Power flickered at the edges of the dais like flames responding to wind that wasn't there. The throne's base seemed to strain higher. Just his power reacting to whatever he was feeling.

"Though I find it curious," he continued, weighing each word, "that these fluctuations are just now being reported. Ward-locks don't fail silently. Someone should have noticed this earlier."

The representative's smile never wavered, but her posture shifted subtly. A fractional tensing, suggesting she'd expected this challenge.

"Lord Caelum wanted to gather all perspectives before raising an alarm," she said smoothly. "He looks forward to your counsel on the matter. Your expertise with the ward system is, after all, unmatched."

Flattery. Appealing to his pride.

But the Reaper didn't look flattered. He looked suspicious.

"Tell Lord Caelum I will attend his council," he said finally. "And that I expect a full accounting of these 'minor issues' before I arrive."

The representative bowed again, deeper this time. "Of course, my lord. He will be pleased by your cooperation."

The representative couldn't leave fast enough, her quick pace through the bone-framed doors not quite masking her relief. After that, the remaining court business felt different.

More whispered conversations among the courtiers—speculative glances in Brynn's direction. More tension radiated from the dais where the Reaper sat in thoughtful silence, his shadows writhing around him like agitated snakes, curling around the throne's base.

The courtiers wondered what she was, and why a tribute would have talents related to ward-locks.

She wondered that herself. What had she done to those tools in the vault? Why had they glowed when she touched them? And why did he watch her the way he did? Like she was an anomaly he hadn't accounted for?

When the final petitioner was dismissed, and the room began to empty, Brynn started to slip toward the exit along with the others.

"Thief."

The Reaper's voice carried across the space, stopping her mid-step. The remaining courtiers paused, watching.

"You will dine with me tonight. Eight bells. Don't be late."

No *would you* or *if you please.* Just commands delivered in that rough voice, sending unwanted heat down her spine.

He rose without waiting for her answer. Shadows flowed around him as he strode from the room, the throne seeming to grasp after him as he left.

Leaving Brynn standing there on a floor of teeth, every gaze in the room fixed on her.

IX.
BRYNN

When the eighth bell chimed somewhere in the depths of the palace, a sound like bones striking bones, a servant appeared at her door.

"My lady." The translucent figure bowed. "The Lord Reaper requests your presence at dinner."

Brynn followed through corridors that twisted in ways that made no sense—left, right, down a staircase carved from what might have been a single massive horn—until she was thoroughly lost.

Probably the point.

The grand hall could have comfortably seated fifty people. Instead, it seated two. One at each end of a table so long she could barely make out the Reaper's expression in the candlelight. The distance between them felt absurd, like they were shouting across a canyon to have a conversation.

Or like he was making a point about the space he needed to keep between himself and everyone else.

The room seemed built for isolation. The high ceiling disappeared into shadows where chandeliers of fused vertebrae hung like inverted spines, their cold blue flames casting everything in ghostly light. The walls were lined with more death-woven tapestries. Scenes rendered in thread so fine the figures seemed to breathe. A king dying on his throne while his court celebrated, unaware. A ship sinking beneath waves made of grasping hands. Lovers embracing as darkness crept up behind them.

The table was carved from wood so dark it was almost black, polished to a gleam. Candelabras lined its length—spinal columns rising from the surface with candles nestled in the topmost vertebrae, their flames flickering silver instead of gold. The chairs had armrests that ended in skeletal hands, fingers curled as if waiting to grip whoever sat in them.

Shadows gathered in the corners and along the walls, deeper than they should have been. They moved when nothing else did, shifting and coiling.

His power. Restless even during dinner.

Servants appeared and disappeared like ghosts, placing plates and filling glasses before melting back into dim corners. The food was elaborate—roasted fowl with rosemary, root vegetables glazed in honey, and brown bread. The wine was rich and smooth, with an aftertaste that lingered like smoke.

Everything was perfect. And completely awkward.

He sat at the far end, framed by those skeletal armrests. His posture was flawless, his attention focused on his meal.

Probably never had a day of back pain in his immortal life.

She caught herself slouching and straightened.

He'd removed the ceremonial armor but kept the long sleeves and gloves. Still maintaining that barrier even while dining.

She watched him cut his meat with exact movements, managing knife and fork with ease. Everything about him was controlled, like he'd spent a lifetime perfecting the art of never making an unnecessary movement.

She lasted approximately five minutes before the silence became unbearable.

"So," she said, raising her voice. "Interesting day at court."

He continued to cut his meat without looking up. "Was it?"

His voice carried easily across twenty feet of table, doing inconvenient things to her pulse that she firmly ignored.

"The representative from the Mourned Court seemed friendly," she tried.

He looked up at her, silverware paused midway to his mouth. "Friendly."

Flat. Skeptical. Like she'd just suggested the sky was yellow.

"Well, not friendly exactly." She was already regretting this attempt at conversation. "But diplomatic? Polite?" She gestured vaguely with her fork, avoiding the spinal candelabra near her plate. "She seemed very interested in the ward-lock problems."

"Indeed."

One word. He'd given her one word and gone back to his meal like the conversation was finished.

This was going to be a long dinner.

She took a sip of wine and tried again. "Have you known the other Death Lords long?"

"Centuries."

"That's a long time to work with the same people." She was determined to extract more than single-word responses if it killed her. Which, given where she was, remained a distinct possibility. "Do you get along well?"

His knife and fork clinked against the plate. "We coexist."

"Right. Coexist." She attacked her vegetables with more force than necessary, honey glaze making them shine. "And the emergency council meeting...is that a regular thing, or...?"

"No."

She waited for him to elaborate. He didn't. Just kept eating, as if this were an everyday dinner conversation.

Maybe for him it was. Maybe he'd forgotten how to talk to people after so long of everyone being too terrified to speak to him.

She tried a different approach. "The palace is beautiful. All those tapestries in my room, the craftsmanship is incredible." She glanced at the death-woven scenes surrounding them now, the sinking ship's passengers frozen mid-scream. "Do you know who made them?"

"Artisans."

Her jaw clenched. She gripped her glass tighter to keep from throwing it at him. "Right. Artisans. Living artisans or...?"

"Dead."

"Of course they are." She took another, larger sip. The alcohol was starting to warm her blood, loosening the control she usually kept on her tongue. Reckless, but at this point, she'd take reckless over this excruciating silence. "This is delicious, by the way. The wine. Do you make it here, or do you import it from somewhere else?"

He set down his utensils slowly. Those dark eyes fixed on her across the length of the table, seeing too much. The armrests curled tighter, though surely that was just the flickering light.

Her breath caught.

"Are you always this talkative?" he asked.

The words held an edge—irritation, or possibly amusement. With him, it was impossible to tell.

"Are you always this charming?" she shot back before she could stop herself.

The crash of a dropped plate echoed from somewhere near the wall. One of the servants had fumbled their tray in the quiet hall. A bone-handled serving knife clattered across the floor.

Shadows wrapped tighter around his chair. Responding to his mood. The same way it had in the throne room when he'd been suspicious of the Mourned Court's representative.

He gave her a measuring look down the table's length, and she could have sworn she saw his lips twitch. "Yes."

The admission was so unexpected, so bluntly honest, that she let out a slightly shaky laugh. "Well, at least you're consistent."

He picked up his glass and took a sip, studying her. The candlelight caught in the crystal, refracting through the wine. Behind him, the tapestry showed the dying king's crown rolling from his head, though she was certain it had been firmly in place a moment ago.

"You're nervous."

Not a question, but she lifted her chin anyway. "I'm not used to dining with Death royalty."

"I'm not royalty."

"What are you then?"

"A Death Lord." He set his glass down. "Nothing more."

Nothing more. As if that wasn't impressive enough. As if being one of five beings who ruled over all of death was somehow mundane.

"Right," she said, hearing the skepticism in her own voice. She took another sip, warmth spreading through her chest. Feeling just bold enough to push. "The representative mentioned my 'special talents.' What talents is she talking about?"

He was quiet for a long moment, his fingers tapping silently against his glass. His shadows shifted with each tap, keeping time. In one of the bone-framed mirrors, she caught the tapestry behind her—the lovers had turned to look toward the approaching shadow. They hadn't been looking before.

"The tools you stole reacted to you," he said finally. "Word travels between the courts."

Her pulse jumped. "What do you mean they reacted to me?"

"They responded to your touch. Grew warm, glowed." His dark eyes met hers from the far end of the table, pinning her in place. "Death artifacts don't typically do that for mortal thieves."

The way he said it made it clear that was exactly what he thought she was. Nothing special. Nothing important. Just someone who'd stumbled into something she didn't understand.

"So what does that make me?" She kept her voice level even as frustration built in her chest.

"Useful."

She set her fork down with more force than necessary, the clatter echoing in the vaulted space. He'd gone back to his meal as if the conversation was over. As if reducing her to a single word—useful—was sufficient.

"That's it?" she pressed, leaning forward slightly. The armrest pressed against her forearm. "Just useful?"

His eyes snapped up, and the temperature in the room dropped several degrees. His shadows pressed closer to his chair, restless and agitated. The flames in the ribcage chandeliers guttered.

"For now," he growled.

A warning wrapped in two syllables.

Her heart skipped. She looked down at her plate, picked up her fork, and suddenly found her vegetables fascinating. Too aware of

The Reaper watching her, of the tapestry figures that had shifted positions, the armrests that felt closer than before.

Right. She'd pushed too far, asked too many questions. Forgotten for a moment that a friendly dinner conversation didn't exist with the Lord of the Forsaken.

They finished the rest of the meal in silence.

But this silence felt different from the beginning. Charged. Like a boundary had shifted between them that neither was willing to acknowledge.

When the last course was cleared away, he stood and left without a word. Shadows flowed after him like a cloak, and the skeletal hands on his abandoned chair slowly uncurled, releasing nothing.

Brynn sat there, alone at a table built for fifty, her heart still racing from a two-word warning.

X.
DANTE

A couple of days later, Dante stared at the reports scattered across his desk, but the words might as well have been written in forgotten tongues for all the attention he was paying them.

Two incidents in the past week. Ward-locks going dark without explanation. Souls crossing boundaries they shouldn't be able to breach, appearing confused in domains where they didn't belong.

The archive-keepers had returned yesterday with troubling news: the original construction records of the ward-lock network had disappeared long ago. Without those records, tracking the current failures back to their root cause would be nearly impossible.

The incidents alone warranted investigation, but not necessarily his attendance at Caelum's emergency council. The other Death Lords could speculate and theorize without his input. They usually did. But the pattern bothered him. Two failures in one week after centuries of stability, and now the convenient absence of historical records, suggested either accelerating decay or something more intentional.

And if it was intentional, he needed to understand who benefited.

The emergency council meant hours away from his territory. Hours he couldn't afford to waste on speculation and theater.

Unless he brought resources.

Caelum's representative had suggested as much. *Perhaps a tribute with special talents might have insights into such magical anomalies.* The words had been directed at the thief, not him. The entire court had turned to appraise her like she was a curiosity on display.

He'd given a flat "perhaps" and steered the conversation elsewhere. But the suggestion lingered.

Since when did the Court of the Mourned take interest in his tribute?

He pushed back from his desk, shadows coiling tighter. The death tools had reacted to the thief in ways that defied ages of magical theory. Her composure in his court, her complete lack of fear when any sane person would have been terrified. Those traits could prove useful.

Or dangerous. Possibly both.

"She comes with me," he said aloud to the study, testing how the decision sounded.

The shadows around him settled as if even they approved. Ridiculous. He didn't need approval from his own power.

Dante left his study and made his way through the castle's corridors toward her chambers. The walk gave him time to consider what he would tell her about the meeting.

When he reached her door, he raised his hand to knock before catching himself. He'd ruled this castle since its founding without announcing his presence to anyone. He entered where he wished, when he wanted.

But he knocked anyway. Sharp. Giving her exactly one second to prepare.

"Come in," came her voice from the other side.

She was seated at the writing desk near her window, wearing the blue silk she seemed to favor. She'd removed the outer layer and rolled up her sleeves, revealing forearms marked with scars from her thief days. Papers were spread before her. Court records she'd requested. She'd been studying protocols and power structures, making notes about hierarchies and precedents.

"Working late?" he asked.

"Working early." She glanced toward the window where eternal twilight cast its usual ambiguous light. "I'm not sure I'll ever get used to the lack of sunrise here."

"Few mortals do." He stopped a distance away, maintaining the space he always kept between himself and others. His shadows curled restlessly at his feet, and he forced them still. "I need you to attend a meeting with me today."

Her eyebrows rose. "What kind of meeting?"

"The emergency council Caelum requested."

She set down her pen and turned to face him fully. The movement drew his attention to the hollow of her throat, where her pulse beat steadily—no fear response. After days in his domain, she still showed no terror.

"And you want me there because...?"

"Because the tools responded to you in ways they shouldn't have," he said, shadows shifting against his will.

"Where's the meeting?"

"The Bone Temple. Neutral ground."

"I see." She was quiet for a moment, her expression thoughtful. "What should I expect from the other Death Lords?"

The question was practical. She was already thinking like someone who belonged in his world rather than someone trapped in it.

"Caelum will appear reasonable and concerned. He usually is." Dante's voice flattened. "His domain values peace and comfort above all else. Don't trust the compassion. It serves his interests first."

She nodded, filing away the warning.

"Seraphina values strength. She'll respect you if you show spine." His shadows darkened. "But she'll eat you alive if she smells weakness."

"And the other two?"

"Vex sees everything through obsession and desire. He'll try to read what you want most and use it against you." Dante's jaw tightened. "Don't let him get close enough to touch you."

His shadows shifted restlessly at the thought.

"Thessa knows things," he continued, forcing his voice level.

"Things that haven't happened yet, things that should be forgotten. Don't trust anything she tells you, but don't dismiss it either."

Her expression sharpened as she absorbed each warning.

"Any particular reason they might see me as a threat?"

"You're mortal in a realm of immortals. You've survived days in my domain when most tributes don't last one." He paused, considering how much to reveal. "And you're under my protection. That alone will make them curious."

"Curious how?"

"The Reaper doesn't protect people." His voice went cold. "The Reaper kills them. My reputation doesn't include mercy."

She studied his face with that unflinching stare that made his shadows restless. "But you do show mercy. I'm still alive."

"You're still alive because you're useful."

The words came out harsher than intended, but he didn't soften them. Better she understand the terms clearly.

She was quiet for a moment, then nodded once. "I understand."

"Be ready in twenty minutes," he said, then turned and left before his shadows could betray anything else.

XI.
DANTE

Dante maintained his grip on the portal's anchor, feeling the familiar disorientation as they passed through spaces between realms—places where neither life nor death held dominion, where existence itself became negotiable.

Most mortals didn't handle travel well. The tribute before her had spent an hour vomiting. The one before that had collapsed entirely.

The thief handled it like she'd been born to it.

Her eyes widened as reality twisted, but she didn't lose her footing when the world reformed. No nausea, no disorientation. Just sharp awareness as she took in their new surroundings.

Adaptable. Dangerously so.

"How often do you do this?" she asked, voice even.

"As little as possible."

They had emerged at the crest of a hill in the neutral realm. The Bone Temple rose before them, its soaring spires carved from ivory that gleamed with light in the night.

This was where the Death Lords met when business affected all five domains. A place built before any of them had claimed their thrones, when the barriers between realms were still being negotiated by powers whose names had been lost to time.

The air here tasted of nothing. Not the metallic tang of his domain or the sweetness of Caelum's realm. Just space waiting to be filled with whatever the assembled Death Lords brought to it.

"It's..." The thief paused, searching for words. "It feels like a cathedral. But one built for darker prayers."

The observation was more accurate than she knew. His shadows shifted with approval—or what would have been approval, if he allowed such things.

Other portals were opening around the temple's perimeter. Caelum's arrival came with silver light and the sound of wind through gardens. Seraphina's portal brought the clash of weapons and the scent of spilled blood. Vex materialized in wine-colored mist, while Thessa faded into view as if she'd been there all along.

Each entrance was designed to announce its maker. A display of power and personality, serving as both a greeting and a warning.

"Stay close," Dante murmured as they began their descent. "But not too close. Six feet, no closer."

She glanced at him with questions in her eyes, but didn't ask them aloud.

Learning when to stay silent. Good.

"Say nothing unless directly addressed," he continued. "When they look at you, look back. Show no fear, but no challenge either."

"Understood."

As they descended the steps, he was acutely aware of her presence six feet behind him. Could hear her breathing. Could sense her attention taking in their surroundings.

The central chamber opened before them—vast, circular, with a vaulted ceiling. At the center, a five-pointed star was inlaid in different metals on the floor. Each point held one of the thrones.

His throne was black marble, naturally. Polished to a mirror finish that reflected twilight. Caelum's was white, veined with silver, warm and somehow comforting even from a distance. Seraphina's chair was weapons forged together with silver wire. Vex's throne looked like crystallized wine, deep purple-red shifting between solid and liquid. Thessa's seat was apparently made of solid moonlight, casting no shadow while absorbing the darkness around it.

The other Death Lords were taking their positions. But Dante noticed how they watched him approach.

No. How they watched her.

Every eye tracked the mortal who walked six feet behind him instead of maintaining the customary twelve-foot boundary.

She walked with her chin up and shoulders straight, projecting confidence without arrogance. To anyone watching, she looked like exactly what she was supposed to be. A useful tool being brought to assist with realm business.

But Dante caught the subtle signs. The way her gaze swept the arena, noting exits. How she positioned herself to keep all the Death Lords in her line of sight while appearing to look straight ahead. The tension in her stance spoke of readiness.

His shadows stirred with pride. Uncomfortable, unwanted pride.

When they reached his throne, Dante settled into the marble seat. The thief took her position six feet to his right. Close enough to be clearly under his protection, far enough to avoid triggering proximity warnings.

In centuries of these meetings, none of them had ever brought a mortal.

"Brother Dante," Caelum called out warmly from his throne, white robes pooling around him. "How good of you to join us. And you brought your tribute. Excellent. Her circumstances could prove invaluable to our discussions."

The way he said "your tribute" carried emphasis, though his tone remained cordial.

His shadows thickened around his throne. "You said it was urgent."

"Indeed." Caelum's expression grew grave. "But let us not ignore our manners. Lady Seraphina, I believe you remember our brother's... advisor?"

From her throne of bound weapons, Seraphina leaned forward with interest. Her crimson hair caught the light, and the razor wire binding it glinted. "The little thief who wasn't afraid of The Reaper. I remember you from the ceremony."

"Lady Seraphina," the thief replied with a nod.

No tremor. No hesitation. Facing down a Death Lord who could tear her apart with bare hands, and she sounded like she was negotiating market prices.

"Still alive after a week in the Forsaken domain," Seraphina observed with something that might have been approval. "That's more than most manage. Tell me, girl. What's your secret?"

Before the thief could answer, Vex interjected with amusement. "Oh, I think we can all see what her secret is." He leaned back in his crystallized wine throne, dark eyes glittering with pleasure. "How fascinating that our Reaper has developed protective instincts. Tell me, little mortal, what hold do you have over the Lord of the Forsaken?"

Dante's shadows flared around his throne. Frost spread across the floor beneath his feet as the temperature dropped ten degrees in an instant.

"Lord Vex," he said, voice carrying warning.

The threat only seemed to delight Vex further. "Come now, brother. Surely there's no harm in curiosity? It's simply so rare to see you take a personal interest in anything." His smile turned sharp. "Or anyone."

"The girl shows promise," Dante said flatly, forcing his voice emotionless. "Nothing more."

"Promise," Vex repeated, tasting the word like wine. "How deliciously ambiguous. Promise for what, I wonder?"

Dante's hands flexed at his sides. His shadows writhed around his throne, frost patterns spreading outward in fractals. He was seconds from doing something he wouldn't be able to take back.

Before the situation could escalate further, Lady Thessa spoke for the first time. "The threads around her are unusual," she said in her whisper, tilting her head as if listening to sounds only she could hear. Her translucent form flickered between solid and ethereal as she studied the thief with intensity.

"Meaning?" Caelum asked gently, though Dante caught the sharp interest beneath his tone.

"Meaning the threads around her shimmer differently than most mortals." Thessa's pale eyes remained fixed on the thief. "Past and future tangled in her presence. Whether that's significant or merely curious remains to be seen."

An uncomfortable silence followed. Dante's shadows shifted, responding to his unease at having the thief scrutinized so closely by beings whose motives he couldn't fully read.

The thief, to her credit, met Thessa's unnerving stare without flinching. "I'm here to assist with whatever emergency brought this council together, my lady. Nothing more."

"Are you?" Thessa's smile was both sad and knowing. "How refreshingly direct. Though I wonder if you understand what forces have drawn you here."

"Enough riddles," Seraphina cut in with bluntness. "If the girl has unusual circumstances, let's understand what they are. If she's here to help, put her to use. Standing around speculating serves no purpose."

"Such a direct approach," Vex murmured appreciatively. "Though I do wonder what useful purpose a mortal tribute might serve in matters concerning immortal realms."

Dante's shadows shifted at the dismissive tone. The frost around his throne spread another foot.

But before he could respond, Caelum intervened smoothly.

"Brothers, sisters," he said, voice cutting through tension. "Perhaps we should address why I called this emergency council." He gestured gracefully toward the center of the star. "We have a crisis that affects all our domains. Shall we discuss what each of us has observed?"

Dante forced his shadows to settle. "Very well. What crisis?"

Caelum leaned forward in his marble throne, expression troubled. "Ward-locks failing across multiple domains. I've experienced... concerning losses in my realm."

"How many?" Seraphina asked sharply.

A pause. Caelum's expression grew more troubled. "More than I'm comfortable admitting. But I'd like to hear what others have experienced before I reveal the full scope."

The temple fell silent. No one rushed to volunteer information.

"I've had failures," Seraphina admitted reluctantly. "Not catastrophic, but unusual."

"Define unusual," Vex drawled.

"Define your losses first," Seraphina shot back.

Vex's smile was sharp. "Ladies first, I insist."

The tension in the temple ratcheted higher. Each Death Lord watching the others, calculating, weighing whether cooperation served their interests or exposed vulnerabilities.

"This is why I called the council," Caelum said with reproach. "If we can't trust each other enough to share information, how can we address a crisis that threatens all our domains?"

More silence. The weight of centuries of rivalry and suspicion hanging in the air.

Finally, Thessa spoke, her voice barely a whisper. "Two stones in my domain have gone dark. Ancient stones that survived the realm wars. Their loss troubles me."

"Two," Caelum repeated thoughtfully. "Thank you for your honesty, sister." He turned to Seraphina. "And you?"

Seraphina's jaw tightened, clearly unhappy about revealing weakness. "Three stones. All border wards."

"Five in mine," Vex admitted after another pause. "Though my operations remain unaffected."

All eyes turned to Dante.

He weighed what to tell them. The others didn't need to know the full extent of the damage in his territory. Not yet. Not until he understood what was happening.

"Two failures in my territory this week," he said. "Both ancient stones that should have lasted another millennium."

"And I've lost six," Caelum said quietly. "Six stones in the past week alone."

The number stunned the assembled Death Lords into silence.

"Six?" Seraphina repeated. "In one week?"

Caelum nodded gravely. "My domain has been hit hardest, though I can't fathom why. Natural deaths should be the most stable transition."

"That's eighteen stones across all five domains," Dante said slowly. "More than we've lost in the past century."

The math was damning. Even for immortal beings accustomed to thinking in epochs, eighteen failures in one week represented a crisis.

"Any common elements among the failed stones?" he asked.

"Age," Caelum replied. "The oldest stones seem most vulnerable, though I can't be certain that's significant."

"Location patterns?"

"None that I can determine," Seraphina said with frustration. "Border stones, internal stones, high-traffic areas, isolated locations. No consistency."

"Which suggests either random decay," Thessa observed softly, "or forces affecting the ward system that we don't yet understand."

His gaze swept the assembled Death Lords. Caelum appeared genuinely concerned that his domain had been hit the hardest. Seraphina radiated frustration at a problem she couldn't solve with violence. Vex seemed more interested in the theater than in the crisis itself. Thessa watched everything with that unnerving stare.

And six feet to his right, the thief stood still, her expression neutral. But he caught the slight tension in her shoulders, the way her gaze moved from speaker to speaker.

She's listening, really listening, and filing away every detail.

"Coordinated investigation seems prudent," Caelum said. "Share information about stone locations, failure patterns, and any unusual phenomena observed."

"You're suggesting we open our domains to inspection," Vex said with amusement. "How trusting."

"I'm suggesting we work together to solve a problem that affects all of us," Caelum replied with patience. "Unless you believe the failures will simply stop on their own?"

Dante considered the proposal. Everything Caelum suggested was logical, practical, and necessary if they were truly facing coordinated failures. Yet something nagged at him.

"I'll consider coordination," he said finally. "But I won't open my domain to unrestricted access."

"Of course not," Caelum said with understanding. "We each have security concerns. Perhaps we could start with shared reports? Information exchange without requiring physical access?"

Silence stretched. No one wanted to commit.

"I'll consider it as well," Seraphina said finally, which meant no.

Vex examined his nails. "Perhaps."

Thessa's form flickered, which could mean anything.

Caelum smiled as if this constituted agreement. "Then we'll coordinate through regular reports when possible. Share patterns as we're comfortable and compare data."

He let that settle for a moment.

"Speaking of working together," Caelum continued, his tone shifting slightly, "there is one other matter that concerns me..."

Caelum's gaze moved to the thief. "Your tribute, brother. Given her circumstances, perhaps she would be more comfortable in a domain better suited to mortal limitations."

The temple fell silent except for the whisper of shadows moving around Dante's throne.

Then even those stopped.

"Explain," Dante said, voice neutral despite the warning prickling down his spine.

"The Forsaken domain is harsh, brother. Beautiful in its way, but..." Caelum gestured delicately. "Despair and terror weigh heavily on mortal hearts. My realm offers gentler transitions, peaceful crossings. She would thrive there."

"She's proven useful in my domain," Dante said evenly.

"And she could be equally useful in mine," Caelum replied smoothly. "Perhaps more so, given that comfort and safety allow for clearer thinking. Fear clouds judgment, brother. You know this."

"The girl has a spine," Seraphina interjected. "But even steel breaks under enough pressure. A week in the Forsaken realm..." She shook her head. "Most mortals don't last."

"Precisely my point," Caelum acknowledged. "Why waste her potential by subjecting her to hardship? In my domain, she could explore whatever connection she has to the old magic without the constant stress of survival."

Each word was reasonable. Each argument logical. And every sentence made Dante's shadows writhe with agitation.

"She stays with me."

The words came out harder than intended, shadows flaring around his throne in a display that made the other Death Lords sit back. Frost spread across the floor in patterns radiating outward from where he sat, the temperature dropping fifteen degrees in seconds.

Caelum's eyebrows rose in surprise. "Brother, I meant no offense. I'm concerned for her welfare—"

"She. Stays. With. Me."

Each word carried the weight of command, echoing off the temple's walls and settling into the silence that followed. The wards hummed in response to power radiating from his position, and the metal star inlaid in the floor began to glow with cold light.

For a long moment, no one moved. No one spoke.

Then Vex began to laugh, a rich sound full of delighted malice. "Oh, this is wonderful. Absolutely wonderful. Our Reaper has found something he doesn't want to lose."

"I protect what serves my interests," Dante replied coldly, fighting to regain control of his display. The frost around his throne stopped spreading, but didn't retreat.

"Of course you do," Vex said with a knowing smile. "How very practical of you."

His tone made it clear he didn't believe a word of it.

Dante's shadows roiled, but Caelum raised a hand for peace. "Brothers, sisters, please. I withdraw my offer." His smile remained warm, understanding. "Clearly, Dante values his tribute's contributions too highly to consider alternatives. I meant only kindness."

"Your kindness is noted," Dante said stiffly.

"Though I hope you'll reconsider if the situation becomes too dangerous for her," Caelum added gently. "My domain will always be open to any mortal seeking refuge from harsher realms."

"Understood," he replied.

But as the conversation moved on to logistics and coordination plans, his shadows remained restless around his throne. The frost at his feet refused to melt.

XII.
BRYNN

Brynn woke to the sound of rain against stone, though she'd learned not to trust her ears in this place. The drops struck the window in patterns too rhythmic to be natural, each impact creating flares of blue light that faded almost too quickly to see.

On the wall beside her bed, the drowning woman in the death-woven tapestry had finally surfaced. Her silk-threaded eyes stared directly at Brynn now, one hand reaching toward the bed frame.

The council meeting kept replaying in her mind. The way the other Death Lords had studied her like a prize to be claimed. The undercurrents she sensed but could not fully decode. And worst of all, the moment when his voice had dropped to that growl.

She stays with me.

The words had echoed through that bone temple with finality. Every immortal present had heard the claim beneath them. Whatever game the Death Lords were playing, she was now a piece on the board, whether she wanted to be or not.

And the way he'd looked at Caelum when the offer was made. Like he was considering murder. She'd seen killers before, had worked with a few, stolen from more than she could count. But she'd never seen someone go from complete control to violence so fast.

Over her. A thief he'd known for barely a week.

What the hell was that about?

She pushed the thought aside and swung her legs out of the bone-framed bed, bare feet hitting stone that should have been cold but somehow held just enough warmth to be comfortable.

Everything in this realm seemed designed to unsettle. Beauty twisted just enough to feel off, comfort offered with an edge that suggested it could be withdrawn at any moment.

The twilight filtering through her windows offered no clue about actual time, but her stomach suggested it was well past dawn by mortal standards. Though what constituted morning in a place where the sky never brightened was anyone's guess.

That's when she noticed the wardrobe.

The doors stood slightly ajar, revealing glimpses of fabric that hadn't been there when she'd gone to sleep. She crossed the room, passing the chair with its skeletal hand armrests, and pulled the wardrobe open, then stopped short.

Where three gowns had hung before, an entire wardrobe now waited. But these weren't just more silk confections meant for formal dinners. Someone had provided options.

Gowns in varying shades of blue hung alongside practical clothing. Midnight blue silk appropriate for court functions. Steel blue velvet that struck a balance between elegant and understated. Deep sapphire that would catch the light.

But interspersed with the formal wear were clothes designed for someone who might need to move. Work. Maybe even fight.

Tunics cut close to the body, with room to move. Riding pants in dark gray that looked like they'd stay in place during activity. A jacket in sapphire blue with reinforced seams and what felt like hidden pockets along the inner lining. The kind of details that showed an understanding of concealed tools.

And boots. Real boots, not delicate slippers. Dark leather with good tread. Footwear you could run, climb, and fight in if necessary.

Everything was in shades of blue.

She ran her fingers along the nearest tunic, noting the quality. These weren't servants' clothes or basic wear. The fabric matched the court gowns in quality, but was cut for utility rather than display.

Someone had noticed her preference for the blue silk and accommodated it.

She'd spent years learning to read people's intentions through their actions. Gifts always came with strings attached. Kindness always had a price. Considerations were usually the prelude to demands.

So what was the angle here?

But even as she questioned it, she appreciated the craftsmanship. The cuts that didn't sacrifice elegance. The hidden pockets were positioned exactly where she would have placed them herself. The boots that looked like they'd been made for her feet.

Whoever had arranged this understood what she needed. And more unsettling, understood what she would want.

She selected the midnight-blue tunic and fitted gray pants, adding the jacket with its hidden pockets. The clothes fit perfectly—either magic or a highly observant eye for measurements. The fabric felt luxurious but practical enough that she could forget she was wearing it.

When she caught her reflection in the bone-framed mirror, she barely recognized herself.

Gone was the desperate thief in stolen noble's clothes. Gone was the overdressed tribute drowning in silk. This version of her looked lethal, as if she belonged in this world of death magic and politics.

Like someone who might survive here.

Weeks ago, she'd been a prisoner waiting for death. Now she stood in a Death Lord's palace wearing clothes chosen for her preferences and needs, surrounded by purple silk walls where death scenes shifted when she wasn't looking.

Three knocks at her door interrupted her thoughts.

"Miss Brynn?" Naia's voice carried through the wood, but tension threaded through her tone. More formal than usual, but also more urgent.

"Come in," Brynn called.

The soul entered carrying a breakfast tray, but her usual manner seemed strained. The translucence that marked her as one of the dead flickered more noticeably than normal, as if whatever animated her was struggling with emotion. She set the tray on the small table near the window.

"Thank you for the clothes," Brynn said, gesturing toward the wardrobe. "They're perfect."

"The Reaper was quite specific in his requirements." Naia's eyebrow arched as she gave Brynn an assessing look. "He also requests your presence in the deep chambers."

Brynn paused in the middle of lacing her boots. The bone fingers of the chair's armrests seemed to press against her forearms, though surely that was her imagination.

So it had been him.

The Death Lord, who barely spoke to her beyond instructions. Who maintained distance at all times. Who looked at her like she was a problem he hadn't figured out how to solve yet.

That same Death Lord had personally selected her wardrobe. Right down to the reinforced pockets and sturdy boots.

After yesterday's display in front of every Death Lord in existence.

"The deep chambers?" she asked, keeping her voice neutral.

"Below the palace proper. Where the oldest foundations lie." Naia's voice flattened in that way that suggested bad news. "Few are brought there."

"And fewer still come back unchanged?" Brynn guessed, echoing the pattern from their first conversation.

A ghost of a smile flickered across Naia's face. "You learn quickly. Yes."

Brynn finished with her boots and stood, testing the fit. They felt reliable. Like someone had considered what she might need them for. "What's down there that requires my presence?"

"Old magic," Naia said. "The kind that remembers things we'd rather it forget."

That wasn't ominous at all.

"Any advice for someone about to descend into ancient magic chambers?"

"Be careful what you touch," Naia said seriously. "The old magic recognizes things about people that they haven't figured out about themselves yet. Sometimes that recognition comes with consequences."

Brynn studied her face, looking for more warnings. Behind Naia, the death-woven tapestry showed the battle scene—warriors falling in almost graceful poses. One of them had turned his head since yesterday. He was looking toward the door now. "What kind of consequences?"

"The kind that changes you. Permanently." Naia moved toward the door, then paused. "But then again, perhaps change is exactly what's needed."

After Naia left, Brynn stood there for a moment, processing.

The Reaper had summoned her to work with old magic after giving her clothes suited for dangerous conditions. Or running. Or fighting her way out.

She retrieved the tools from where she'd hidden them beneath her mattress, slipping them into one of the jacket's inner pockets. The fabric muffled any sound they might make against each other.

She was adjusting the jacket's fit when a different knock sounded at her door. Heavier than Naia's, more authoritative.

"Enter," she called.

The door opened to reveal one of his death knights, the tall figure's armor glowing dully in the twilight. Unlike the servants, this one radiated an aura of contained power that made the air feel thicker.

"Lord Reaper awaits," the knight said, voice carrying the echo of someone who had died in battle and chosen to keep fighting. "I am to escort you to the deep chambers."

Brynn nodded, though her pulse quickened. Whatever was about to happen, there was no turning back now.

The knight stepped aside, waiting for her to precede him into the corridor.

"This way," the knight said, turning toward a section of the palace she'd never been to before.

XIII.
BRYNN

The death knight led her through corridors that shifted as they descended. The ribcage tunnels of the upper levels gave way to something older, more primitive. Here, the walls weren't constructed from bone. They were bone. Massive segments fused directly into the bedrock, as if the palace had been built inside the skeleton of a creature too large to comprehend.

The air grew thicker as they descended, pressing against her skin. Each breath tasted of old magic and damp stone. The sconces here burned a deeper blue, nearly purple.

"How much farther?" she asked, her voice echoing strangely in the stairwell.

"Not far now," the knight replied without turning. His armor clinked softly with each step.

The stairs beneath her feet became less uniform, carved from stone veined with pale striations. Her new boots found purchase on each step. He'd chosen them, knowing she'd be walking down here.

That's when she noticed the runes.

At first, they were just shallow scratches in the wall, easy to miss in the flickering light. But as they went deeper, the markings became more elaborate. More deliberate. Symbols carved into stone, arranged in patterns that seemed to shift when she wasn't looking directly at them.

She found herself tracing one of the patterns with her eyes, following curves that seemed almost familiar. The markings themselves seemed newer somehow. Or perhaps they refused to fade.

Where had she seen this before?

But the memory, if it was a memory, slipped away before she could grasp it.

The knight paused at a heavy door that made her stomach turn. Ribs curved together to form planks, fused at joints that still showed their original structure. Black iron bands wrapped around it like bindings holding something in.

"Beyond this point, I cannot accompany you. The Reaper awaits within."

He pushed the door open, and it swung silently.

The chamber beyond was carved entirely from solid rock. But the rock was riddled with ancient remains. Massive fossilized formations jutted from the walls and ceiling, creatures that had died here long before the palace was built, their skeletons becoming part of the foundation. The ceiling arched high above, supported by structures that reached down from the darkness.

Runes covered every surface. These weren't the faint scratches she'd seen in the stairwell. These blazed with blue light, pulsing steadily.

In the center of the room, standing within a circle of symbols that glowed brighter than the rest, stood The Reaper.

But not the Death Lord she'd grown accustomed to seeing.

This version wore a black shirt, sleeves rolled up to his elbows, exposing forearms corded with muscle. Pants that actually fit his form instead of formal court attire. Worn boots planted firmly in the runic circle. His dark hair was tied back, not left loose as it usually was.

He still wore his gloves.

But seeing him like this—sleeves rolled up, hair tied back, dressed for work instead of intimidation—sent heat crawling up her neck.

Stop that. He's still a Death Lord who could kill you with a thought.

Her eyes caught on the line of his wrists where glove met bare skin, then snapped back to his face before he could notice.

Too late.

His gaze traveled over the clothes he'd selected, and for a moment his mask slipped. Then indifference settled back into place.

"You wanted to see me?" she said, proud that her voice didn't waver.

"The ward-locks are failing faster than expected," he said. "We need to understand why."

The door closed behind her with a sound like joints settling, and Brynn realized this was no casual meeting. Whatever he'd brought her down here to see, it was severe enough to warrant descending to the palace's foundations.

"And what am I supposed to do about failing ward-locks?" she asked.

He stepped out of the runic circle, shadows shifting around him as he moved. The practical clothes made him less intimidating somehow. Or maybe just intimidating in a different way. Less "the embodiment of death" and more "extremely dangerous man who knows exactly what he's doing."

Her lips pressed into a flat line.

Great. So much better.

"Follow me," he said, already moving toward an archway.

He led her through the opening framed by massive formations carved with more of those pulsing runes. Beyond it lay another room, carved from the very heart of the palace's bedrock.

This chamber was smaller, more claustrophobic. The walls pressed close, entirely fossilized remains fused into solid barriers. The air thrummed with energy.

Built directly into the walls were mechanisms of crystal and metal, pulsing with energy. Most radiated a steady glow, their components turning in patterns that seemed almost organic, like the mechanisms had grown here rather than been installed.

But one stood out.

Its light flickered erratically, stuttering between vibrant blue and sickly yellow. Gears twisted and strained against one another, the grinding echoing off the walls with an almost pained quality. Crystal components shimmered with unstable energy, as if caught in a struggle.

Even from across the room, she could sense the chaotic energy. Something was deeply wrong.

"These locks maintain the barriers between realms," he said, his voice quieter than usual. The chamber seemed to absorb sound, making even his low tones feel intimate. "The failing one is a primary stabilizer. If it goes completely dark, souls will be able to cross between life and death without control."

As she studied the chaotic patterns, something strange began to happen. The longer she looked, the more layers revealed themselves. Not just the surface mechanisms, but deeper currents of energy weaving between the components. Patterns that danced and intertwined, resonating in her mind in ways she couldn't quite grasp.

She knew this. Somehow, she knew how this worked.

"You've tried to repair it?" she asked, though she suspected she knew the answer.

"I lack the skills to work with mechanisms this intricate." His jaw tightened slightly. Barely noticeable, but she was learning to read his micro-expressions. "These locks require a skill I don't possess."

He'd just admitted weakness. To her.

He moved to a stone alcove and withdrew a weathered leather pouch from a hidden crevice. From it, he produced several small tools that looked similar to the ones she'd taken from that noble's chest. But these were larger, more complex, each one expertly crafted.

They glimmered faintly in the blue light.

"These will work with the two you have in your jacket," he said.

Brynn's hand moved instinctively to the inner pocket where she'd concealed her tools. "How did you—"

"I can sense their magic." His black eyes met hers, and she felt the weight of that stare. "Those tools carry the resonance of the same power that built these ward-locks." He studied her more intently, and she resisted the urge to step back. "Show me both sets."

Reluctantly, she pulled her tools from her pocket. They were warm to the touch. Warmer than they should have been, just from sitting against her body. When she held them next to the ones he'd given her, they seemed to recognize each other somehow.

The metal hummed faintly.

"These aren't just lockpicks," she said, the realization hitting her.

"No." He moved closer to the failing mechanism, and she followed, hyperaware of his presence beside her in the cramped chamber. "They're designed for something far more complex."

"And you think I can fix this because...?"

"Tell me what you see when you look at that ward-lock." He gestured toward the device.

She focused on the chaotic patterns, and they resolved into something that made perfect sense. Like reading a language she'd somehow always known but never consciously learned.

"It's not broken," she said slowly, confidence building with each word. "Foreign elements are disrupting the core mechanism. Look at how the energy flow is being redirected through those secondary channels. If we remove the interfering components, it should stabilize."

He went very still beside her. That stillness meant his complete attention was focused on something.

On her.

"You can see the energy flows," he said quietly.

She nodded. "Can't you?"

"No."

The single word held weight. Meaning. She looked at him, but his expression was neutral.

He approached the mechanism. "I need your help," he said, the words coming out with reluctance.

The Death Lord who'd claimed her in front of everyone needed something from her.

"We need to stabilize this before the barriers collapse completely." He glanced back at her, his gaze unwavering.

Brynn studied the failing lock, watching the erratic patterns dance across its crystal components. "What do you need me to do?"

"These locks maintain the barriers." He moved to stand beside the device, close enough that she could feel the cold radiating from his shadows. "This one stabilizes the boundary between life and death in this sector. If it fails..."

"Souls cross over without control," she finished.

"Yes." He gestured to the tools in her hands. "You said you could see how the flows are disrupted. I need you to show me what you mean."

She approached the mechanism cautiously, acutely aware of his presence just behind her.

"Here," she said, pointing to where crystal and metal components intersected. "The flow should be moving in a smooth circuit, but it's being forced through these side channels instead. Like..." She paused, searching for the right comparison. "Like water trying to flow through a pipe that's been partially blocked."

He stayed at a distance, but his shadows stretched forward to where she was pointing, tracing the pathways she described. The dark tendrils moved, following her words.

"I can see the components," he said, "but not the energy patterns you're describing."

"Really?" She looked at him in surprise. "But you're so powerful. Surely you can—"

"Power and skill are different things." His hands flexed at his sides. That tell she was learning meant he was uncomfortable. "Continue."

She raised an eyebrow at the dismissal. "Well, lucky for you, I apparently have the skills."

The shadows around his feet shifted restlessly at her tone, but he didn't respond.

Touchy. He hated this.

She turned back to the mechanism, running her eyes along the pathways she could see, but he couldn't. "There are foreign elements blocking the flow. They don't belong here."

"Foreign elements?"

"Little bits of something that aren't part of the original mechanism. They're wedged into points where the energy tries to flow." She traced the pattern with her finger, not quite touching the crystal. "If I can remove them, the pathways should clear."

He was quiet for a long moment. When he spoke again, his voice was flat. "Can you do it safely?"

She studied the obstructions more closely. They resembled shards of something foreign. Darker than the surrounding crystal, angular where everything else was smooth.

"Maybe. But I need to understand how these tools work first."

He moved behind her, close enough that she could feel the weight of his power pressing against her back. In the cramped chamber, his presence was overwhelming. Shadows curling at the edges of her vision, cold radiating from him like winter.

"The tools respond to intent as much as technique," he said, his voice low and rough. "Hold one and focus on what you want to achieve."

She selected one of the needle-thin implements, trying to ignore the way her pulse had quickened. The moment her fingers closed around it, warmth spread up her arm, and the tool seemed to wake up.

The metal hummed faintly, and suddenly she could sense the mechanism's structure more clearly than before.

"Interesting," he said quietly, still standing close behind her.

She barely heard him. The tool was showing her things. Where to apply pressure, which components could be safely manipulated, how the flows wanted to move if given the chance.

It was like having a conversation with the mechanism.

"I think I can fix this," she murmured, already reaching for a second tool.

"You're sure?"

She looked up at him over her shoulder, surprised by the question. His dark eyes were fixed on her with an intensity that made her pulse jump. In the blue light of the ward-lock, he looked less like a court politician and more like something ancient. Something that had been here as long as the foundations themselves.

"Are you doubting my abilities?" she asked, keeping her voice light.

"No." The word came out rougher than usual. "I'm concerned about what might happen if we destabilize it further."

Fair point. But as she studied the mechanism, she felt that same certainty she'd experienced when unlocking the impossible. This was simply a more complex version of the same principle. Finding the pressure points. Understanding how the pieces wanted to move.

"I can do this," she said, straightening her shoulders.

He held her gaze, and whatever flickered in his eyes was gone before she could name it. The chamber seemed to hold its breath around them. Or perhaps that was just her imagination.

Then he stepped back to give her room.

"Tell me what you need."

XIV.
BRYNN

She started with the smallest obstruction, holding the tool steady between her fingers. The element looked like a splinter of glass wedged between two crystal components.

"I need to apply pressure from this angle," she explained, positioning the tool delicately, "but if I push too hard—"

"The crystal will fracture." A tendril of shadow slipped past her shoulder, wrapping gently around the component to brace it. "Try now."

The support was perfect. Firm enough to stabilize the mechanism, gentle enough not to interfere with her work.

She pressed the tool against the obstruction and felt it give.

"More pressure on the left side," she murmured, adjusting her grip.

Another shadow-tendril appeared, providing the counterforce she needed. The obstruction shifted, then came free with a chime of crystal against metal.

"One down." She looked up to find him watching her intently. "That actually worked."

"You sound surprised."

"I am." She selected a broader tool for the next blockage. "I've never worked with anything like this before."

Yet the work came naturally. Lockpicking instincts, probably. Reading mechanisms by touch was the same skill, just on a grander scale.

They moved to the second obstruction, deeper within the mechanism's core. She had to reach into a channel between rotating gears, the tool barely fitting through the gap.

She reached for another tool just as he moved to adjust the shadow support. His hand hovered a breath away from hers.

They froze.

Time stopped. His hand was so close to hers that she could feel the cold from his glove. Could see the way his fingers had gone rigid, like he was forcing himself not to move closer.

Or pull away.

She could feel his attention on her. Could hear the way his breathing had changed. Slower, more restrained. Like he was fighting some battle.

He withdrew first, shadows pulling back with him.

She blew out a breath and turned her attention back to the mechanism, trying to ignore the way her hands had started trembling slightly. "I can't see what I'm doing from this angle."

"Describe what you need."

"Something to hold this gear steady while I work behind it." She paused, then decided to test something. "And can you make the shadows glow? Just a little?"

She felt him go still behind her. "They don't usually—"

"Please. I just need enough light to see where the blockage is attached."

After a moment's hesitation, the shadow wrapped around the gear began to glow faintly. Not bright, but enough to illuminate the space she was working in.

It was beautiful.

"How did you know they could do that?" he asked quietly.

She paused, realizing she had no idea where that knowledge had come from. "I... I'm not sure."

The third obstruction required both of them to work in coordination. She held three tools simultaneously, while his shadows supported five pressure points. It was like having extra hands that responded to her thoughts before she could voice them.

"Lift the crystal housing," she said, and shadows were already moving to comply.

"Hold that gear." A shadow-tendril was already in place.

"I need something to catch this piece when it comes free." A curl of darkness formed a small basket beneath her work area.

They worked in silence, the only sounds the chime of tools against crystal and the hum of energy. Her hands moved, and his shadows were already there. Again and again. Like he knew what she needed before she did.

She'd never worked with anyone like this. Never this smooth, this synchronized. Ten years as a thief, and she'd always worked alone. Had to work alone. But this was different. This was trust she hadn't expected to feel.

"You're getting better at this," he observed as she successfully removed the fourth blockage.

"So are you." She wiped sweat from her forehead with the back of her hand. "Your shadows are practically reading my mind."

His shadows shifted slightly, almost like a shrug, but he didn't respond.

The fifth obstruction was the most challenging yet. A tangle of material wrapped around the mechanism's primary conduit. She had to work from three different angles, using four tools in sequence while he channeled power to keep the system stable.

"Now," she said, and felt power flow through the shadows exactly as she needed.

"Hold," she added, and the energy stabilized instantly.

"More on the left." But the power was already shifting before she finished the sentence.

When the obstruction finally came loose, they both exhaled in relief.

The sound echoed in the chamber, and she became aware of how close he was standing, how they were breathing in sync, how his shadows were still wrapped around the mechanism, around her tools, around the space where she was working.

Almost like they were wrapped around her.

"How many more?" he asked, voice rough.

She studied the mechanism's interior, counting the remaining dark splinters, trying to ignore the way her skin had started tingling where his shadows were closest. "Three. But they're in the core assembly. I'll have to..." She paused, considering the challenge. "I'll need to disassemble the flow chamber partially."

"Is that safe?"

She looked at the mechanism, its crystal components pulsing with energy, and felt that certainty again. "With the right support, yes. But I'll need your shadows to hold twelve different components in alignment while I work."

"Twelve?" The shadows around him stilled completely.

"The core is more complex than the outer layers." She pointed to the arrangement of gears and crystals. "Each piece has to be held at the right tension, or the whole thing could collapse."

He studied her for a moment, and she couldn't read his expression. "Walk me through it."

———

They worked with such intensity that everything else fell away. Twelve shadow-tendrils held components in suspension while she painstakingly disassembled the core, removed the obstructions, and began the reassembly.

She lost track of time. Lost track of everything except the mechanism, the tools, and the way they moved together.

"Tension on the primary gear," she murmured.

His shadows adjusted instantly.

"The third crystal needs to rotate two degrees clockwise."

The component turned smoothly.

"Power flow to the secondary chamber, but keep it at half strength."

Energy flowed as specified.

Her hands moved, and his power followed. Immediate and

unquestioning, a synchronization that shouldn't be possible between two people who barely knew each other.

"Last one," she said, reaching for the final obstruction buried deep in the heart of the assembly.

This piece was larger than the others, more firmly wedged. She had to apply pressure while maintaining balance across all the suspended components.

One wrong move and everything would collapse.

"Steady," he said, his voice tight with concentration.

She could feel the strain in his shadows. Holding twelve components in alignment demanded immense power. Could sense his focus narrowing down to this single task.

She applied pressure to the obstruction, feeling it resist. More pressure. The crystal components around it started to vibrate, resonating with the stress.

"Careful," he murmured, and she felt his shadows tighten their grip.

Almost there. Almost—

The obstruction gave way, coming free with a sound like breaking glass. All the elements were gone, the pathways clear, and the mechanism was ready to function as it was designed to.

"There," she said, sitting back on her heels, breathing hard. "That should do it."

He moved closer, shadows shifting around him as he prepared to channel power into the now-clear pathways. "Ready?"

She nodded, both of them watching as he began feeding energy into the mechanism.

For a moment, everything seemed to work. The erratic lights stabilized. The grinding sounds stopped. The crystal components began turning smoothly, one by one.

Relief flooded through her. They'd done it. They'd actually—

Then, instead of closing and sealing properly, the mechanism burst open like a door thrown wide.

The blue light flashed into blinding white, and alarms blared throughout the castle, a sound that seemed to shake the stones.

Oh no. Oh no no no—

"Get back!" he shouted, but it was already too late.

Souls began pouring through the breach—a flood of spirits from other realms. Ghostly figures swirled around the chamber, some flickering between translucent and solid, others manifesting as nothing more than wisps of cold light. Their cries echoed in chorus, a cacophony of longing and despair.

Brynn stared in horror at what she'd unleashed. "What have I done?"

He moved to shield her as the figures pressed closer, his shadows rising defensively around them both, swirling like a dark cocoon. She could feel his power ramping up, cold and vast and barely restrained.

Amidst the chaos, she could hear the echo of footsteps in the corridors above. Others rushed to investigate the disturbance, each stride growing louder.

More souls poured through the breach, their forms filling the chamber with chaotic light. The ward-lock blazed brighter, the opening widening with each passing second.

XV.
BRYNN

The souls came through in waves. Peaceful figures in flowing white robes who should have passed quietly materialized alongside violent shades still marked by the wounds of their brutal deaths. Desperate souls with hollow, hungry eyes pressed against those consumed by obsession, flickering between solid and translucent with every heartbeat.

This was bad. This was very, very bad.

The chamber was filled with clashing energies that made the air feel heavy and suffocating. Cold spots gathered where the peaceful dead clustered while searing heat radiated from the violent ones. The presence of the obsessed spirits created a nauseating vertigo that made her vision swim.

She'd broken something that had been holding back entire realms' worth of death, and now—

"No, no, no." Brynn lunged toward the ward-lock mechanism. The device blazed with unstable light, its opening growing wider with each spirit that passed through. "Close, damn you!"

She pressed her hands against the crystal housing, trying to force the mechanism shut through sheer will. The tools scattered on the floor around her feet, forgotten in her desperation to undo what she'd done.

Nothing happened. The magical flows she'd been able to see so clearly during their repair work were now a tangle she couldn't begin to unravel. The ward-lock pulsed with malevolent energy, as if feeding on her panic.

Stupid. So stupid. Poking at the pretty magical lock like it was some noble's strongbox. Except nobles didn't keep interdimensional soul-floods in their vaults.

More souls poured through. A child-spirit no older than ten, tears streaming down translucent cheeks as she called for her mother. A warrior still gripping the sword that had failed to save him, eyes burning with the need for one final battle. An old woman clutching a locket, lips moving in endless repetition of someone's name.

They shouldn't all be here together. They belonged in different domains, different realms, guided by Death Lords who understood their particular needs. Instead, they swirled around the chamber in growing confusion and distress.

Her chest tightened. She'd seen that look before, on the faces of orphans in the street, lost and calling for families that would never come. These souls wore the same desperate confusion, and it was her fault.

"I can fix this." Her voice rose with panic as she grabbed for the tools, hands shaking so badly she nearly dropped them. "I can fix this, I just need to—" Her breathing came fast and shallow. "I broke it, I broke everything—"

"Look at me."

She turned toward him. He stood between her and the most dangerous spirits, shadows forming defensive walls, but his dark gaze was focused entirely on her.

"Breathe." He stepped closer. "You didn't break anything."

The certainty in his voice made her racing heart slow slightly. "But I—"

"Focus on my voice, not the chaos." His shadows shifted, creating a small pocket of calm around them while still holding back the displaced souls. "You can see the flows better than anyone who's ever worked these locks. Trust what you know."

The space he'd created felt intimate, even with the chaos mere feet away. She could hear his steady breathing even as his power strained against the supernatural storm. His voice had dropped to that low, commanding tone that seemed to resonate in her chest, making her want to listen, to obey, to—

Before she could process that thought fully, a soul broke through his defensive barrier. One of the obsessed spirits, its form shifting between that of a young man and something far more twisted. It lunged toward her with desperate hunger, reaching for the life force that blazed so temptingly warm in this realm of cold death.

His shadows slammed into the spirit with force, wrapping around it like chains and dragging it back into the containment area he'd created. The violence of the movement was effortless, controlled, and absolutely terrifying.

Right. Death Lord. Not someone who should make her feel safe.

But the effort left him momentarily vulnerable, and three more souls slipped through the gap.

"The mechanism." His voice stayed steady through the strain. "Can you see the flows now?"

As she focused on the ward-lock, one of his shadows brushed against her wrist. Cool and gentle, at odds with the violence she'd just witnessed. It seemed to beckon her hand toward a tool she'd overlooked in her panic, its presence a quiet reassurance in the havoc.

She couldn't afford to think about how that felt. Couldn't let herself wonder why his shadows touched her with such restraint when they'd just crushed that spirit like it was nothing.

With the shadow's guidance, she forced herself to look past the chaos and focus on the ward-lock. The magical patterns were still there, buried beneath layers of unstable energy. Twisted, yes. Unstable, absolutely. But not random.

"The closing sequence has been redirected." The realization made her stomach drop. "The lock isn't broken. It's been modified to do exactly this when anyone tries to repair it."

A trap. This whole thing had been a trap, and she'd walked right into it.

"Can you reverse it?" His power flared as more violent spirits tested his barriers.

She studied the modified pathways, trying to trace them back to their original configuration. It was like trying to untangle a knot while blindfolded, with someone constantly pulling on all the wrong strings.

"Maybe. But not while it's actively drawing souls through." She gestured toward the blazing aperture. "I need you to stop the flow so I can work."

"I can't close what I can't see." Strain roughened his voice with the effort of containing so many displaced souls. "But I can redirect it."

His shadows began moving in new patterns, not trying to hold back the flood but to channel it. Dark tendrils reached toward the ward-lock's opening, weaving themselves into barriers that guided the soul-flow into more manageable streams.

The control was breathtaking. He was conducting a symphony of death magic, each shadow moving with purpose, creating order from chaos. She'd watched street performers juggle fire, seen master craftsmen at work, but this—

This was power choosing discipline over destruction.

"There," he said through gritted teeth. "Work quickly."

Brynn grabbed the specialized tools from where they'd scattered, her hands trembling only slightly as she approached the modified mechanism. The souls still came through, but now in slow pulses rather than an overwhelming flood.

She could do this. She had to do this. Because if she didn't, this disaster would be her fault, and he'd probably decide she was more trouble than she was worth after all.

The first modification was embedded deep in the lock's core. A twist in the magical pathway that turned what should have been a closing command into an opening trigger. It was elegant work, she had to admit. Subtle enough that no one would notice unless they knew exactly what to look for.

"Whoever did this knew these mechanisms better than the people who built them," she muttered, carefully applying pressure with one of the needle-thin tools.

"Later," he said, his shadows straining against the effort of containment. "Fix first. Analyze after."

Fair point.

She pushed aside her growing suspicions and focused on the immediate problem—one modification at a time. One twisted pathway slowly coaxed back into its proper configuration.

A peaceful spirit drifted past her elbow. An elderly man who smiled at her kindly before continuing toward where the peaceful souls were supposed to go. The sight gave her a surge of hope. She was doing something right.

"Flow's reducing," she reported.

"Good. Keep going."

The second modification was harder to reach, buried behind a maze of crystal components that hadn't been displaced in ages. But as she worked, something strange began to happen. The tools seemed to remember the mechanism's original configuration, guiding her hands to the right pressure points and the correct angles of approach.

More souls found their proper paths. The violent shades began drifting toward whatever dark realm they belonged in, their aggressive energy fading as they moved away from the world that had never been meant to hold them. The obsessed spirits flickered and grew translucent, their desperate hunger easing as they accepted the pull toward their destined domain.

"Almost there." Sweat beaded on her forehead despite the otherworldly cold. "One more modification and the flow should normalize."

The final twist was the most complex. A knot of redirected energy that had turned the entire closing sequence inside out. But now that she understood the pattern, she could see how to undo it.

She inserted two tools simultaneously, applying pressure from opposite directions. One of his shadows wrapped around her hands, steadying them with a cool touch.

The modification resisted for a moment, then suddenly gave way with a soft click. She heard his quiet exhale of relief as tension flowed from his shadows.

The ward-lock's blazing light stabilized, the soul-flow shifting to a manageable trickle before stopping entirely. The mechanism settled back into place with a deep, satisfied hum that resonated through her bones.

In the quiet that followed, Brynn could hear her own ragged breathing and his steady breaths. The chamber was still full of displaced spirits, but they were no longer pouring in from other realms.

"Is it closed?" she asked.

"Sealed." His shadows gradually released their defensive positions, one lingering against her wrist for just a moment longer than necessary. "Though not as securely as it should be. This will require ongoing monitoring."

Brynn sank back on her heels, suddenly exhausted. Around them, the displaced souls continued their confused wandering, but the immediate crisis was over.

She'd done it. She'd fixed what she'd broken. And he—

He hadn't yelled, hadn't punished, hadn't even looked particularly angry about the fact that she'd nearly destroyed his realm.

Before she could fully process that, heavy footsteps echoed in the corridor outside. He straightened immediately, his attention shifting to the approaching sounds they'd been hearing throughout the crisis.

Whatever softness might have existed in the last few minutes vanished. His shoulders squared, his expression cooling into that mask of authority she'd seen in the throne room. The transition was so seamless that she almost doubted what had just passed between them.

Almost.

She stared at the now-stable ward-lock. "This was planned," she said. "Every detail of it."

"Yes."

"The modifications were designed to trigger exactly when someone tried to repair the damage. They wanted the ward-lock to fail catastrophically."

He moved closer to examine the scarred mechanism, and she noticed how his shadows still moved with that restraint around her.

"The question is why."

The chamber door swung open to reveal three death knights in bone-white armor, their hollow eye sockets glowing with cold fire.

"Lord Reaper," the lead knight said, his voice carrying the distant echo of the long-dead. "The magical disturbance has been contained?"

"For now." His shadows gathered around him, no longer reaching toward her. "Secure this chamber. No one enters without my direct permission."

"What of the displaced souls?"

"Already redirected to their proper domains. Post guards at all ward-lock sites. If there are other sabotaged mechanisms, we need to be ready."

"Understood, my lord."

As the death knights moved to secure the chamber, the Reaper approached Brynn. She was still crouched on the floor, exhaustion and shock finally catching up with her.

She looked up at him and saw only the Lord of the Forsaken looking back.

"We need to discuss what we've learned," he said quietly, his voice neutral. "But not here."

XVI.
DANTE

As they left the deep chambers behind, Dante noted that the thief moved without the trembling he'd expected. Her breathing stayed even after what she had just endured, though her fingers flexed unconsciously, as if still gripping those ward-tools.

Most would have collapsed after such an experience. She had witnessed catastrophic magic failure and fixed it with his help.

His shadows stirred restlessly as they climbed the steps, drawn toward her in a way that defied his usual control. They wanted to reach for her again, to wrap around her wrists like they had during the repair work. He forced them back with an effort that shouldn't have been necessary.

She was mortal. Fragile. Temporary. The fact that she'd survived one crisis didn't change her fundamental nature.

"Where are we going?" she asked.

"My private study." He kept his voice level.

She nodded, and he noticed the exhaustion creeping into her movements. The slight drag in her step, the way she gripped the banister just a fraction longer than necessary. The adrenaline was fading.

"You handled it better than most," he admitted, surprising himself.

She glanced at him, wariness in her gaze. "Most people don't get the luxury of falling apart when something's trying to kill them."

He found that oddly reassuring. She understood survival in a way his courtiers never would. They'd died once already and had nothing left to fear. She still had everything to lose.

The study was one of the few rooms in his domain that prioritized function over intimidation.

The room was narrower than his other spaces, almost cramped. Tall black-wood shelves lined the walls, filled with books. Every surface was covered with something useful. Stacked volumes, rolled maps, instruments for measuring magical resonance, and a collection of ward-stones in various states of repair.

The room smelled of old paper, leather bindings, and the faint metallic scent of magic. Cold blue flames burned in a small hearth. His shadows moved independently, adjusting documents, ensuring nothing was disturbed without his knowledge.

A large table dominated the center, its surface dark stone set into a frame of polished bone. The only apparent concession to his realm's aesthetic. Maps covered it: translucent sheets displaying the ward network with connections pulsing faintly. More maps were pinned to the walls between shelves, some so old the edges had gone brittle.

This was a working space. No comfortable chairs, no softness. Just a single tall stool by the table where he stood for hours reviewing realm business, and hard wooden benches along the walls.

She paused in the doorway, taking in the space.

"This isn't what I expected," she said finally.

"What did you expect?" He moved to the table, watching her reaction from the corner of his eye.

"More skulls? Torture devices? Another throne made of bones?"

He felt a flicker of amusement. She was exhausted, probably terrified on some level, yet still defiant. "I leave the theatrics for public spaces. Here, I have work to do."

She moved toward the table, her attention drawn to the maps. The ward network seemed to respond to her proximity. Connections brightening slightly, pathways becoming more defined.

Interesting. The magic recognized her, even here, where he'd spent centuries working alone.

Her fingers hovered just above the surface, tracing the energy flows as if she could feel the magic beneath her fingertips. The movements were unconscious, instinctive.

"There are so many," she murmured. "How many ward-locks keep the barriers stable?"

"Hundreds." He had moved closer while she studied the map. Close enough to catch her scent. Warmth. Life. Something that had no business being appealing in his realm of cold and death. "Each realm intersection requires multiple stabilization points. I've spent years learning to read these patterns."

"And if even a fraction are compromised..." She met his gaze, intelligence cutting through the weariness.

"Months," he said grimly. "Maybe less before total collapse."

The weight of that knowledge settled between them. Someone had orchestrated this specifically, targeting the ward system.

And somehow this mortal thief had become essential to stopping it.

"Tell me more about the other Death Lords," she said. "Who has access to ward-locks across all domains?"

Dante studied her for a moment, impressed by her directness. She wasn't asking who might want to create chaos. She was focused on who could actually pull it off.

"Each of us has access within our own domains," he replied. "Cross-domain access requires explicit permission or an in-depth understanding of the underlying structure."

"What about maintenance? There must be technicians."

"Ward-keepers." He gestured to the dimmer pulse points on the map. "We all employ specialists who monitor the locks for irregularities. But they can't manipulate the core magic. That requires abilities most lack."

She traced a path on the map, connecting his domain to another realm. Her finger moved with confidence. "So they can spot problems and fix minor damage, but nothing deep. Nothing structural."

"Exactly." He watched her, noting how her brow furrowed slightly as she processed the information. "Which means either someone with centuries of experience..."

"Or someone who knows the system well enough to bypass normal access." She finished his thought without hesitation.

He nodded, though his shadows flickered with grudging respect. Few could follow his reasoning that quickly, and even fewer would dare interrupt him mid-sentence. She did both without seeming to notice.

"How much documentation exists about the original construction?"

"Very little. Most of the architects' records were lost long ago." He gestured to one of the shelves, where a handful of volumes gathered dust. "What remains is fragmentary."

She turned from the map, her expression sharpening. "The tools I took from that vault. You said they were connected to the ward magic."

"Yes."

"How would a minor noble acquire something that old? That powerful?" She looked genuinely confused. "Those tools seemed significant. Not the kind of thing someone just stumbles across."

His shadows shifted restlessly. He had wondered the same thing. The tools' presence in that vault made no sense—ancient artifacts of immense power, sitting in some nobleman's collection like common curiosities.

"I don't know," he admitted, and the words tasted strange. He was accustomed to having answers, to understanding the patterns of his realm. This blind spot unsettled him more than he cared to examine.

She nodded, her gaze returning to the map. "Too many coincidences."

"Indeed."

Someone had orchestrated these events, leading to this moment. The tools appearing in that vault. Her theft at the exact right time. The tribute system delivering her to the death realm just as the sabotage really began to manifest.

Now he found himself relying on the one person who could identify and repair the damage—a mortal thief who should be dead within weeks.

Instead, she stood in his private study, tracing ward patterns with uncanny understanding, asking questions that cut straight to the heart of his investigation.

His shadows moved restlessly, unsettled by possibilities he wasn't ready to admit. This ran deeper than simple sabotage. Someone had planned this with an intent that disturbed him, manipulating events over the years. Possibly centuries. To achieve this exact setup.

And he had no idea who. Or why.

"I have a proposal," he said at last.

XVII.
DANTE

Dante found himself reluctant to continue. His fingers traced the edge of the table, shadows coiling around his wrists. He didn't ask for help. Ever.

But the alternative was watching everything collapse.

"The ward-locks are failing," he said. "What we witnessed tonight will happen again unless someone can identify and reverse the sabotage."

She stood across from him, hands hovering above the maps. The large table between them felt both necessary and frustrating. Close enough to catch the subtle shift in her breathing, far enough that his shadows had to resist bridging the gap.

"Someone is targeting the entire system," he continued. "They know these mechanisms better than the people who built them. They know exactly how to ensure any repair attempt triggers catastrophic failure."

Her fingers traced a connection between two distant realms. "How many other locks show signs of tampering?"

He gestured to several dim pulse points scattered across the map. "At least a dozen that we've identified. Possibly more."

She looked up at him. "You want my help."

His shoulders tensed. She wasn't asking or offering, just stating a fact, forcing him to admit what they both knew.

"I need your assistance with the ward-locks."

She didn't answer immediately. She was weighing her options, preparing to bargain with a Death Lord in his own domain.

Bold. And deeply inconvenient.

"What happened tonight was mostly luck," she said slowly. "I was just trying things until something worked. How exactly do you expect me to help with an entire network?"

Training a mortal in death magic was dangerous under the best of circumstances. Training one to work with ward-locks deliberately sabotaged to kill anyone who touched them—

"With proper training—"

"Training." She stepped back from the table, crossing her arms. "From you."

"Yes."

"In exchange for what?"

His shadows shifted at the challenge in her tone. Not because he couldn't afford whatever price she named, but because it meant acknowledging she held the upper hand.

That a mortal thief had something he desperately needed.

"What do you want?" he asked.

She was quiet, her gaze moving around his study. Books, maps, shadows moving independently through the space. When she looked back, her expression had shifted to something more guarded, but he caught the way her pulse jumped when their eyes met.

His shadows noticed too. They always caught her reactions.

"Freedom," she said at last. "I'm not your prisoner, and I won't be treated like one. If I'm going to help, it's because I choose to, not because I'm trapped here."

Freedom meant she could refuse, could walk away. It meant treating her as an ally rather than a convenient asset.

But an alliance was what he needed. She'd already proven her value during the crisis.

"Within reason," he said slowly. "The timeline for this crisis doesn't allow for—"

"I understand urgency." She cut him off.

The temperature dropped several degrees.

She either didn't notice or didn't care. "But I won't be kept locked in chambers or dragged around like baggage. I need to be able to move freely in your domain, make decisions about my own safety."

He exhaled through his nose. "Agreed."

"And protection." Her chin lifted. Defiance masking vulnerability. "If I'm going to be working with magic that makes me valuable, I need guarantees that I won't end up dead because someone decides I'm a threat."

His shadows drifted toward her before he could stop them. The thought of someone targeting her triggered an unexpected surge of protective anger.

He reminded himself that she was just a necessary asset.

His shadows disagreed. They wanted to wrap around her, shield her, and ensure nothing could reach her without going through him first.

"You'll have my protection and political backing with the other courts," he said.

"What about practical details?" All business now. "What exactly are you asking me to do? How dangerous is it? What happens if I can't fix whatever's broken?"

She negotiated as if she knew her own worth, holding her ground even when facing him.

He found himself respecting that.

"You'd help me investigate other ward-lock sites," he said. "Identify sabotage, attempt repairs where possible. As for danger..." His shadows rippled. "Considerable. Ward magic at this level can kill if mishandled."

She looked down, teeth catching her lower lip.

"Anything else?" he asked.

"That's it." Her eyes met his directly. "I help because I choose to, I'm protected while I do it, and I know what I'm getting into before it tries to kill me."

Cleaner than he'd expected. She wasn't asking for things he couldn't give. Just respect her choices and acknowledge the risks.

"Agreed," he said.

The acknowledgment seemed to surprise her. Her guarded expression softened, and he caught a glimpse of relief she couldn't quite hide.

"So we have a partnership?" she asked.

"We have an alliance," he corrected. The distinction mattered. "Temporary, until the crisis is resolved."

"An alliance." She tested the word, then nodded. "What happens now?"

"Now," he said, moving toward the shelves, "your education begins."

But as he reached for a text, he reconsidered. She would be useless if she collapsed from exhaustion. The crisis was urgent, but running her into the ground served no one.

"Tomorrow," he corrected himself. "Your education begins tomorrow."

She blinked. "Tomorrow?"

"You're exhausted. Trying to absorb magical theory in your current state would be inefficient." He turned toward the door, then paused. Extending invitations wasn't something he did. Orders came naturally. Asking felt foreign. "When did you last eat?"

She opened her mouth, then closed it, apparently trying to remember.

"I'll take that as confirmation." He moved toward the door. "You need food."

She stared at him. "Are you asking me to dinner?"

"I'm stating that you require sustenance, and we might as well discuss our arrangement while you eat." He opened the door, shadows moving ahead into the corridor. "Unless you prefer to eat alone in your chambers."

"No," she said quickly, following him. "Dining together is practical."

His jaw clenched. His shadows reached for her before he pulled them back.

"Practical," he repeated.

XVIII.
DANTE

The private dining chamber was smaller than the formal hall where court meals were served, intimate in a way that formal spaces never achieved. The table was carved from walnut, its legs ending in elegant clawed feet that might have been decorative. Or might have been actual talons, preserved and repurposed. Candles flickered in sconces shaped like cupped hands, their fingers more delicate than the crude claws in the deep chambers, almost graceful in their stillness.

The walls were paneled in dark wood rather than lined with bone, but death hadn't been banished entirely. Subtle carvings wound through the wooden panels. Vines that, on closer inspection, were actually spine segments linked together, flowers with petals that resembled finger bones arranged in delicate whorls. The kind of details you might not notice unless you looked closely. The type that revealed itself slowly.

His shadows moved through the space, ensuring everything was properly arranged. A habit so automatic he barely noticed it anymore.

She took in the room with the same watchful sweep she had applied to his study, noting the exits, the sight lines, the way the shadows moved independently of any natural light source. Her gaze lingered on the carved panels, recognition flickering across her features as she decoded the bone-vine patterns.

He found her vigilance oddly comforting in its predictability.

"Sit wherever you're comfortable," he said, taking his usual place at the head of the table.

She chose a chair that gave her a clear view of the door but was close enough that they could converse without shouting. The armrests were smooth dark wood, their ends curved into shapes that suggested knuckles, joints. Hands folded in repose rather than grasping.

She was close enough that he could read her expressions, note her reactions.

Close enough that his shadows kept trying to drift toward her, seeking her presence like she was some lodestone they couldn't resist.

He forced them back.

Servants appeared. Translucent figures that glided through the air without disturbing it. They set dishes before them, their forms solid enough to handle physical objects but bearing the faint luminescence that marked them as inhabitants of the death realm. The serving pieces were elegant: a wine decanter with a stopper carved from what might have been a small vertebra, and platters edged in silver filigree that echoed the bone-vine carvings on the walls. Once their tasks were complete, they faded back into the shadows, leaving no sound of footsteps or rustle of clothing.

The meal was familiar fare transformed by its passage through realms where death and life intermingled. Roasted meat that retained its savory richness but carried undertones of the otherworldly—magic woven into every bite. Fresh bread that looked ordinary but felt substantial in a way that suggested it would nourish more than just the body. Wine that tasted of dark berries and earth, but left a lingering coolness on the tongue that spoke of magic woven into its very essence.

She ate quickly, like someone who'd learned not to waste opportunities for good food, but her eyes kept darting to him, clearly unsure of the protocol for dining with a Death Lord.

"I don't poison my dinner guests," he said dryly. "If I wanted you dead, there are more efficient methods than tainted wine."

She paused, a piece of bread halfway to her mouth. "That's oddly reassuring."

"I thought so."

The corner of her mouth quirked upward for an instant as she settled back in her chair. The slight smile transformed her expression entirely, softening the sharp edges.

His shadows rippled around him at the sight, and he found himself wondering when the last time was that someone had smiled in his presence without fear.

"How long have you been a thief?" he asked, partly to redirect his thoughts and partly because he found himself genuinely curious.

She looked up sharply, as if trying to determine whether this was some test. "Ten years."

"What did you do before that?"

The guarded expression returned immediately, her shoulders tensing. "Does it matter?"

"Perhaps not." He cut a piece of meat, giving her space to decide whether to answer. "I'm simply curious about the person I'll be working with."

She was quiet for a moment, absently tracing the rim of her wine glass. He could see her weighing whether to share. The candlelight caught on the glass and on the delicate bone-flower carvings in the panel behind her.

"I never planned to become a thief," she said finally.

"People rarely do," he said. "What changed?"

"My family died." The words were flat, devoid of emotion. "What about you? Were you born to be the Death Lord of despair and terror?"

The deflection was skillfully done, turning his curiosity back on him. He found himself almost admiring the technique.

"In a manner of speaking," he said. "My nature was evident from an early age."

"Your nature?"

He hesitated. There was too much to explain, and most of it she wasn't ready to hear. The whole truth about what he was, what he could do, and the reasons why isolation wasn't merely a preference but a necessity.

"I am what I am," he said instead. "The title 'Reaper' isn't ceremonial."

She studied his face, and he had the uncomfortable sense that she was seeing more than he intended to reveal.

"Is that why you live like this?" she asked quietly. "All the distance, the isolation, the way everyone fears to get too close?"

His voice went flat. "It's safer for everyone."

"Safer for them, maybe. What about for you?"

The question caught him off guard. No one asked about his safety, his well-being. They worried about protecting themselves from him, as they should. The idea that isolation might cost him something beyond loneliness had never factored into anyone's considerations.

Including, until recently, his own.

He turned his wine glass slowly, studying her across the table. She looked curious, not judgmental. As if she wanted to understand rather than condemn.

Reckless. That kind of interest could lead him to places he couldn't allow himself to go.

"Safety is relative," he said finally.

"So is loneliness."

His grip tightened on his wine glass, and his shadows drew tighter around his chair. She had no right to see that clearly, to name things he'd spent a lifetime refusing to acknowledge.

"Is that what you think this is?" he asked, his voice neutral. "Loneliness?"

"I think," she said, taking a sip of wine before continuing, "that you've spent so long protecting everyone from what you are that you've forgotten what it might be like to have someone who doesn't need protecting."

He found himself watching her across the table. She waited for his response with that same patience she'd shown during the crisis, willing to hear whatever he said next without flinching from what he might reveal.

"Tomorrow," he said, shifting back to safer ground, "we'll begin with basic magical theory. You'll need to understand how different types of death magic interact before we attempt any field work."

"Field work?"

"Visiting the other compromised sites. Testing your abilities on ward-locks that aren't conveniently located in my palace." He leaned back in his chair, studying her reaction. "Are you having second thoughts about our alliance?"

"No," she said without hesitation. "I'm just trying to understand what I've gotten myself into."

"Something dangerous," he said honestly. "Something that will likely get more dangerous before it's resolved."

"I figured that part out." She met his gaze. "What I'm still figuring out is you."

"What do you want to know?" he found himself asking, and immediately regretted the invitation. Understanding led to connection, and connection led to vulnerability he couldn't afford.

But apparently, his mouth had other ideas about what was wise.

"More than you'd probably want to share," she said with a faint smile. "But I suppose we have time for that."

"We do," he agreed, though he wasn't entirely sure what he was agreeing to.

She turned her wine glass between her fingers, considering. "How old are you?"

"Old."

"That's not an answer."

"It's the only one I have. After a certain point, counting becomes irrelevant." He watched her file that away. "Time moves differently here. Years blur."

"That sounds sad."

"It sounds like a fact."

"Those aren't mutually exclusive." She took a sip of wine. "What do you do? When you're not maintaining wards or terrifying courtiers?"

The question caught him off guard. No one had ever asked him that. His court feared him. The other Death Lords respected or resented him. None of them had ever wondered what he did with his time.

"I read," he said, and immediately felt foolish for the mundanity of it.

"You read." She didn't laugh, but something brightened in her expression. "The Reaper, Lord of the Forsaken, terror of the death realms. Reads."

"Extensively."

"What kind of books?"

"History. Philosophy. Poetry, occasionally." He shouldn't be telling her this. It served no strategic purpose. "The living world produces an extraordinary volume of literature about death. Most of it wrong. Some of it surprisingly insightful."

"You read human poetry about death." She was definitely smiling now. "That's either the most predictable thing I've ever heard or the least."

His shadows stirred, restless.

"What about you?" he asked, redirecting before she could dig further. "Before the stealing. What did you enjoy?"

The brightness dimmed. He watched her weigh the question, decide how much to risk.

"Books," she said finally. "My mother had a shelf of them. Novels mostly. Stories about people who lived in big houses and had problems that could be solved by marrying the right person." A pause. "I thought they were ridiculous. I read every single one."

The image of her as a child, curled up with romance novels, was so at odds with the sharp-edged woman across from him that his chest tightened.

"And now?"

"Now I haven't read anything in years. Books are heavy. Hard to steal, harder to carry, not worth much when you sell them." She said it lightly, but her fingers tightened on the glass. "You don't get to keep things when you live the way I did."

The silence that followed held weight. Two people who'd lost things. Different things, in different ways, but the shape of the absence was the same.

"My library is extensive," he said. "You're welcome to use it."

The words came out before he could consider them. An invitation he hadn't planned. His shadows tightened with alarm at his own lack of discipline.

She looked at him for a long moment. Her expression turned careful, searching—trying to determine whether the offer was genuine or another form of control.

"Thank you," she said quietly. Then, lighter: "Any recommendations?"

"Stay away from the third shelf in the eastern alcove. The texts there have a tendency to bite."

"The books bite."

"Everything in a death realm has teeth. Even the literature."

The corner of her mouth curved. Not quite a smile. Close enough to make his shadows stir.

She had finished most of her meal, though she still held her wine glass, turning it slowly between her fingers. The candlelight caught the auburn highlights in her hair, and he noticed she no longer glanced toward the exits every few minutes. Growing comfortable in his presence, even after everything she knew about him.

Foolish. Or brave. He couldn't quite decide which.

She took a sip of the wine, her expression thoughtful. "So you think there's something special about me."

It wasn't a question, but he considered it as if it were. The ward magic responded to her touch in ways that shouldn't be possible for a mortal. The tools had recognized her. His shadows moved around her with protective intent. All of it suggested something deeper than mere coincidence.

"I think you're more than what you appear to be. Whether that's special or just unexpected remains to be seen."

"Unexpected." She seemed to taste the word, rolling it around like fine wine. "I'll take that over 'useful.'"

The corner of his mouth twitched. Barely perceptible, but she noticed.

Her wine glass hit the table with a thunk. "You almost smiled. The Reaper almost smiled at something I said."

"No." But his shadows stirred with amusement.

She laughed. A sound he hadn't heard from her before. It was brief, more of a soft exhale than full laughter, but it changed her face entirely. The wariness melted away, replaced by something lighter, more genuine.

Beautiful. The thought came unbidden and unwelcome, but he couldn't entirely dismiss it.

"After you get comfortable with your abilities," he said, forcing his attention back to practical matters, "we'll have to visit other territories."

"What does that mean?"

"Other ward-lock sites. Survey the damage, attempt repairs if possible." He paused, considering how much to warn her. "It won't be comfortable. Some locations require traveling through unpleasant territories."

"More unpleasant than a realm ruled by the Lord of despair and terror?"

"Different kinds of unpleasant." He stood, and she followed suit. "The Court of Violence, for instance, exists in a state of perpetual war. The Court of the Consumed..." He paused, shadows darkening at the thought of taking her to Vex's domain. "Let's focus on understanding your abilities before we worry about the destinations."

As they moved toward the chamber's exit, he noticed how she walked beside him rather than behind him. Equal footing, as if she'd already claimed the partnership he'd tried to frame as a temporary alliance.

His shadows noticed too, curling with what felt suspiciously like approval.

"I have a question," she said as they entered the corridor.

"Yes?"

"Earlier, when we were working on the ward-lock, your shadows helped me. They moved the tools when I needed them, provided support when the mechanism was unstable." She glanced at him. "Was that intentional?"

"Not entirely."

"What does that mean?"

They had reached the main corridor that led back toward the residential wing. The ribcage architecture rose around them, bone arching overhead. She walked through without the revulsion she'd shown those first days.

Growing bolder. More comfortable. She had no idea what that ease could cost her.

"The shadows are an extension of my will," he said, weighing each word. "They respond to my focus, my priorities. Sometimes those priorities aren't conscious choices."

"Your priorities." She stopped walking, facing him. "Are you saying I'm one of them?"

His shadows moved restlessly at the direct question, coiling around him. She shouldn't ask things like that. Shouldn't force him to examine truths he'd been avoiding.

"I'm saying," he replied, "that magic reflects its user's instincts. Sometimes it recognizes things before conscious thought catches up."

She studied him, and he could see her processing what he'd admitted, what he'd chosen not to reveal—the spaces between his words where truth lived unspoken.

"That's either the most honest thing you've said to me, or the most evasive."

"It can be both."

This time, her smile was unmistakable. "I think I'm beginning to understand you, Dante."

His shadows stirred at the use of his name instead of his title. She'd done it naturally, without thinking, as if the distance implied by "Lord Reaper" or "The Reaper" no longer felt appropriate.

He should correct her. Should reestablish the boundaries that kept them both safe.

"Understanding me may not be in your best interests," he said instead.

"I'll take that risk." Her tone was light, but she held his gaze. "After all, we're partners now. I should probably know who I'm working with."

Partners. There was that word again, the one he'd tried to avoid by insisting on "alliance." But she'd claimed it anyway, reshaping their arrangement with casual confidence that suggested she saw no reason to accept his distinction.

His jaw tightened slightly at the word, even as his shadows seemed to settle with satisfaction.

"Your chambers are this way," he said, gesturing toward the corridor that led to the wing where she had been staying. "Training begins after the morning meal. Don't oversleep."

"I won't." She started down the corridor, then paused, looking back over her shoulder. The bone sconces cast blue light across her features, their skeletal hands cupping flames that flickered as she moved. "Thank you. For dinner, I mean. It was nice. To have someone to talk to."

The honesty of it struck something in his chest that had been dormant so long he'd forgotten it existed. No one thanked him for mere conversation. For the company. As if his presence was something to appreciate rather than endure.

He nodded, not trusting himself to speak.

She continued down the corridor, her footsteps echoing softly against the bone-tile floor until she disappeared.

Dante remained in the corridor for several moments, his shadows stirring restlessly around his feet. They wanted to follow her, to ensure she reached her chambers safely, to wrap around her door like protective sentries.

He forced them back with effort that was becoming increasingly difficult.

This was a mistake. All of it. The dinner, the conversation, the admission that his shadows moved around her with protective intent. He was allowing connection when isolation had served him well for ages.

But the alternative was watching the realms collapse. And somehow, standing in this corridor with the ghost of her smile still lingering in his thoughts, that justification felt less like truth and more like an excuse.

He turned and walked back toward his own chambers, his shadows trailing behind him.

XIX.
DANTE

The ward reports arrived before dawn, but it was Nathaniel who delivered them, not the usual ward-keeper. His chief advisor moved through the study with the ease of someone who'd served for ages, setting the scrolls on Dante's desk.

"Two more failures overnight, my lord." Nathaniel's voice was neutral, but Dante caught the concern beneath it. "One at the boundary between your domain and the Court of Violence, another near the outer reaches where the death realm touches the living world."

Dante read each report twice, his jaw tightening with every detail. The damage patterns were escalating. What had been isolated incidents were becoming coordinated strikes against the entire network. Someone was moving faster than anticipated, targeting vulnerabilities that suggested intimate knowledge of the ward system's architecture.

"The pattern is spreading outward from our domain," Nathaniel observed, moving to stand beside the table where the three-dimensional ward maps hovered. "As if someone is deliberately targeting areas where your influence is strongest."

"Personal, then." Dante's shadows settled around his shoulders, responding to the threat with interest.

"Indeed." Nathaniel paused, selecting his words with care. "There's also... talk in the court. About the human tribute."

Dante's attention sharpened, though he kept his expression neutral. "What kind of talk?"

"The usual speculation when you show interest in anyone." Nathaniel's tone was guarded; years of service had taught him when to tread lightly. "Some are confused by your decision to keep her alive. Others are watching to see if she'll prove different somehow."

"She's proving useful with the ward-work," he said, keeping his tone level.

"Yes, my lord." Nathaniel's expression suggested he knew there was more to it. "Though several courtiers have noted you've been... less dismissive of her presence than you typically are."

Dante's teeth ground together. He'd known this would happen. His court watched everything, noticed every deviation from his usual patterns.

"The human has a rare ability," he said, his voice dropping to that dangerous tone that warned against further commentary. "Her survival serves a practical purpose."

"Of course." Nathaniel inclined his head. "Will you be beginning her training this morning, then?"

"After she's eaten." Dante turned back to the ward maps. "I'll need the instructional materials prepared. The basic texts on ward theory, the practice stones, and the charts showing network architecture."

"I'll have them brought immediately." Nathaniel moved toward the door, then paused. "My lord, if I may. If there is a saboteur, anyone working closely with you becomes a target as well."

"I'm aware of the risks."

"Are you certain she's worth the potential complications?"

A knock interrupted before he could formulate a response.

Both men turned toward the door.

"Enter," Dante called.

The door opened, and she stepped inside.

His shadows moved before he could stop them, reaching toward her in greeting like she was something they'd been waiting for. He pulled them back sharply, but not before Nathaniel's eyebrows rose slightly—a rare display from someone usually so composed.

She'd dressed practically. Dark pants, sturdy boots, a shirt with sleeves rolled to her elbows, hair secured away from her face. Her gaze moved between him and Nathaniel.

"Am I interrupting?"

"Not at all." Nathaniel recovered smoothly, offering her a slight bow. "I was just leaving." He turned back to Dante. "I'll have those materials sent up immediately, my lord."

"See that you do."

Nathaniel moved past her toward the door, then paused. "Miss Brynn. A pleasure, as always."

"Nathaniel." She returned the nod like she'd been doing it her whole life.

The door closed behind him, leaving them alone.

Two chairs had been added to the workspace since yesterday. Simple wooden seats positioned across from each other at the main table, close enough for instruction but maintaining proper distance.

She moved to the table and studied the translucent ward displays. The blue light caught in her eyes.

"You're early," he observed, forcing his attention back to the ward maps.

"You said after the morning meal. I ate." She ran her fingers through the air above the ward displays without touching them, following the network's architecture.

He gestured for her to come closer. "We'll be working here. The training materials will arrive shortly."

She glanced at him, raising an eyebrow. "Was Nathaniel giving you a hard time about training me?"

Perceptive.

"Nathaniel has concerns about the political complications of my keeping you alive," he said.

"Political complications." She studied the ward maps. "You mean people are wondering why the Reaper hasn't killed his tribute yet."

"Among other things."

"What other things?"

He shouldn't answer. Shouldn't encourage this. But something about the way she asked made him respond anyway.

"They've noticed I'm less dismissive of your presence than I typically am."

Her hand stilled above the ward map. A slight flush colored her cheeks, visible even in the blue light. She kept her attention fixed on the projections, but he saw her pulse flutter at her throat.

"Well," she said after a moment, her voice forcibly light, "you haven't tried to kill me yet. That's practically friendly by your standards."

The corner of his mouth twitched. "Get comfortable. We have a great deal of work ahead of us."

She finally looked up, meeting his gaze. Her eyes were brighter than they should be, her lips slightly parted.

"Comfortable," she repeated. "In the Reaper's study. That's asking a lot."

"Yet you're still here."

"So I am." She held his gaze for another heartbeat, then turned away to settle into the chair across from his. "Should I be worried about what you're planning to teach me?"

"We'll start with theory. The network's architecture, how the various magical elements interconnect, the principles that govern ward construction and maintenance."

"Sounds thrilling."

"It will keep you alive." He moved to the other side of the table. "Pay attention. Your instincts during the crisis were good, but instinct alone won't be enough for what's coming."

Her expression shifted. Less playful challenge, more serious assessment. "What is coming?"

"War. Someone is targeting the ward network, and they won't stop until they get what they want. That makes you valuable. Which makes you a target."

"Because I can feel the ward-magic."

"Because you can do more than feel it. You can manipulate it in ways that shouldn't be possible for someone without formal training." He held her gaze. "That makes you dangerous to whoever is behind the sabotage. And it makes you essential to stopping them."

"No pressure, then."

"None whatsoever." His mouth twitched again. "Now, shall we begin? Or would you prefer to trade more verbal barbs first?"

She grinned. "I can multitask."

A knock at the door announced the arrival of the training materials. Servants entered with armfuls of leather-bound texts, practice stones, and rolled charts covered in ward patterns. They set everything on the table silently, then withdrew without meeting his eyes.

She was already reaching for one of the practice stones, turning it over in her hands.

"These are different from the real ward-locks."

"Training versions. Designed with safeguards so you can experiment without catastrophic consequences." He selected the smallest stone from the collection and set it between them. "Before we begin formal instruction, I want to understand exactly how you approached the repair yesterday."

The practice stone glowed faintly, power pulsing within it. She studied it, running her fingers over the carved symbols.

"It felt like a song with missing notes," she said.

"Show me what you mean by that."

She leaned forward, hair falling over her shoulder.

"I don't know if I can recreate it," she said, uncertainty replacing the confidence from moments ago. "During the crisis, I was just reacting."

"Try."

She reached toward the stone, then hesitated. "What happens if I do something wrong?"

"The training stones are designed with safeguards. The worst you'll experience is unconsciousness and a severe headache when you wake up." He positioned himself across from her, ready to observe. "Unlike last night, we have controlled conditions."

"Controlled." She smiled slightly, fingers hovering just above the stone's surface. "Right. Because everything about this situation feels completely under control."

"Touch the stone," he said, his voice dropping to command. "Show me what you can do."

XX.
BRYNN

She looked at the practice stone, then back at him. His eyes were focused entirely on her, watching for any sign of the unusual ability he believed she possessed. The weight of his attention was both intimidating and oddly reassuring. If something went wrong, he was clearly prepared to handle it.

Though what exactly he'd do remained an open question. Catch her? Save her? Or just note how she failed for future reference?

"What do you want me to do exactly?"

"Touch it. Tell me what you sense. Don't try to change anything yet. Just observe."

She reached out slowly, her fingertips touching the warm stone surface. The instant her skin made contact, sensation surged through her. A complex web of information that felt almost like music made tangible.

"It's..." She paused, searching for words for something she'd never experienced before. "Like hearing a melody, but feeling it instead. There are patterns, rhythms, connections that flow in specific directions."

His shadows leaned closer, responding to his focus. She could feel them hovering near her hands. "What kind of patterns?"

"Complicated ones. Like..." She closed her eyes, concentrating on the sensations flowing through her fingertips. "Like a river with multiple currents, but some of the channels are blocked or flowing in the wrong direction."

She explored the stone's magical structure with her senses, following the pathways of power as they wound through its crystalline matrix. The sensation was intimate somehow, like reading the stone's innermost workings.

Unlike the ward-lock she'd repaired, this one felt genuinely hostile, as if it were actively working against itself, fighting its own nature with self-destructive intensity. Even without looking, she could sense the discordant energy it was generating. Like nails on a chalkboard, but magical.

"This feels wrong," she said, opening her eyes. "Angry, almost."

"It's designed to simulate the kind of corruption we've been finding in the damaged ward-locks. Multiple cascade points that amplify instability." He watched her reaction, and she noticed how his shadows retreated slightly from the stone's surface. Even they didn't like it. "Can you sense what's causing it?"

She pressed her palms more firmly against the corrupted stone's surface, immediately feeling the aggressive instability of its magical patterns. The sensation was unpleasant—jagged edges and warped angles that made her fingers ache. But beneath the chaos, she sensed the original structure. Like the ghost of what the ward was meant to be.

"The original pattern is still there," she said slowly. "Buried, but intact. Whoever corrupted this knew exactly what they were doing. They didn't destroy the foundation; they built the instability on top of it."

His gaze sharpened. She felt pinned by that focus, caught under scrutiny.

"Can you undo that kind of sabotage?"

"I think so." She started to reach deeper into the stone's structure, but his shadows wrapped around her wrist before she could commit to the work.

"I didn't say attempt it," he said sharply. "I asked if you could. There's a difference."

He pulled the shadows back, but she could still feel the lingering chill against her skin. Tension was visible in the line of his shoulders. "That corruption could overwhelm you if you approach it wrong. According to conventional theory, attempting to repair this should trigger a contained failure. Enough to knock you unconscious." His voice dropped lower, rougher. "But I'm not willing to test that theory without preparation. You need to understand the fundamentals first."

"What kind of fundamentals?"

"How death magic actually works. How to collaborate with it instead of forcing it." His shadows moved around his shoulders, and she was starting to recognize that as a sign of something. Agitation? Interest? Both? "Most importantly, how to work with guidance instead of relying purely on instinct."

He set the corrupted stone aside and selected a different practice piece from his collection—this one slightly larger and pulsing with steady light. The contrast was immediate. Where the corrupted stone had felt hostile and chaotic, this one felt welcoming. Almost eager.

"We'll start with something that won't fight back," he said, positioning the new stone between them. "Tell me what you sense."

She pressed her palm against the stone's smooth surface. The reaction was immediate but gentler than she'd expected. Power flowed up her arm like warm honey, comfortable and pleasant. She could feel the stone's internal structure, the way magic moved through crystalline channels in steady patterns.

"It feels..." She paused, trying to articulate the sensation. "Contained but not constrained. Like it's holding power rather than trying to suppress it."

Something flickered across his expression. Approval, maybe, or satisfaction. Hard to tell with him. "Go deeper. What else?"

She let her awareness sink further into the stone's magical patterns, trusting her instincts the way she had when picking locks. Sometimes you just had to feel your way through. "It wants to connect to something. Some pathways lead nowhere, like roads cut off halfway to their destination." She frowned, concentrating. "It feels incomplete. Not damaged, just waiting."

"Ward-stones are designed to work in networks," he explained, moving closer to the table—near enough that his scent reached her. "What you're sensing is the stone's resonance patterns searching for compatible connections."

That made sense. She lifted her hand from the stone, spreading her fingers as residual energy dissipated. The sensation was oddly pleasant, like stretching after sitting too long. "Is sensing that level of detail normal?"

"No."

His blunt response made her stomach tighten slightly, but she was getting used to his directness. At least he didn't sugarcoat things or lie to make her feel better. She could work with honesty.

Even if it was occasionally terrifying.

He selected another stone from his collection, this one larger and radiating more actively. "Try this one."

The moment she touched this stone, the difference was noticeable. Where the first had been patient and contained, this one pulsed with complex energy. Multiple patterns flowed through its structure simultaneously, creating interference loops and harmonic resonances that made her fingertips buzz.

Like standing too close to something electrical, but not quite painful. Just intense.

"More active," she said. "The patterns are layered, like multiple conversations happening at once."

"Can you sense how those conversations interact?"

She focused deeper, following the individual patterns as they wove around each other. When one pattern pulsed, it triggered responses in others, which in turn influenced the first, creating feedback loops that fed on themselves. A dance of energy, each partner responding to the other in increasingly complex ways.

"They're not just coexisting," she said slowly. "They're collaborating. Building something together that's more complex than any individual pattern."

"Exactly." The single word carried weight, warmth threading through his tone, making heat spread through her chest.

"Now, without lifting your hand, extend your awareness to the other stones on the table."

She kept her palm pressed against the active stone and reached out with her magical senses. It felt like stretching a muscle she hadn't known she possessed. Gradually, she became conscious of the other stones' presence. Each one singing its own unique song, but all of them trying to harmonize.

"I can feel them," she said, surprised by the clarity. "They're all different, but they want to work together."

"Good." He reached for a piece of equipment she hadn't noticed before—a metal framework designed to hold multiple stones in symmetrical arrangements. "This is a practice ward-frame. It allows stones to connect in stable conditions."

As he placed stones into the framework's holders, she could feel each new connection through her contact with the active stone. The individual songs began to blend, creating harmonies far more beautiful than any single stone could produce. Like an orchestra tuning up, finding their collective voice.

Her breath caught. The harmonies built and built, each stone's voice finding its place in the whole. She hadn't expected death magic to be beautiful.

"Try guiding the energy flow between them," he said, his tone taking on quiet authority. "Gently. Ward magic responds better to persuasion than force."

She focused on the connections, feeling the pathways linking the stones. The magic flowed like water seeking its course, but she could influence its direction with intention. She tried nudging the flow into different patterns, coaxing it along paths that felt more natural.

The response was immediate. The stones' light shifted as energy found new pathways, and she felt the system adjusting to form patterns she hadn't consciously designed. It was adapting to her touch, learning what she wanted before she fully articulated it to herself.

"You're making it more difficult than necessary," he observed, though his tone was thoughtful rather than critical.

She glanced up. He'd leaned forward slightly, gaze fixed on the ward-frame, jaw relaxed rather than tight. "How so?"

"You're working alone." His shadows shifted around his shoulders, and suddenly she could sense their presence in a way she never had before. They weren't just the absence of light; they were entities with their own awareness. "Ward magic was designed for collaboration. The original architects worked in teams."

She met his gaze, her heartbeat quickening at the suggestion. "Are you offering to help?"

His expression tightened, mouth pressing into a harder line. The admission clearly hadn't come easily. "I'm offering to demonstrate proper technique. I can't touch the stones directly without disrupting their balance, but my shadows can provide guidance."

The shadows moved closer to the ward-frame, hovering near connection points without quite touching. She could sense their presence more clearly now. Purposeful, intelligent, waiting for direction. Waiting for his permission to touch what she was working on.

"Let them guide you," he said, command threading through his words. "Don't fight their suggestions."

She relaxed her control over the energy flows and waited. The shadows moved with purpose, positioning themselves at specific points of connection—subtle pressure encouraging the magic to flow more efficiently.

They anticipated her intentions and provided support exactly where needed. The energy flows became smoother, more balanced, creating harmonies far more sophisticated than her solo efforts.

"The shadows can sense magical patterns beyond physical perception," he explained, his voice closer than she'd expected. *When had he moved?* "They're extending your awareness."

One shadow brushed against her wrist as it adjusted a connection point. The cool touch lingered a moment longer than strictly necessary. Or maybe she was imagining that.

Great. Now she was over-analyzing what his magical appendages were doing.

"This feels different," she said, trying to keep her voice even. "Like the magic is eager to work this way."

"Because this is how it was meant to function."

The ward-frame shone more brightly now, the stones singing in harmony. She could feel the system's satisfaction in achieving balance, the way each component supported the others. Rightness hummed through the connections, settling into her bones.

"What happens next?" she asked.

His shadows stilled for just a moment before resuming their work. She could feel his gaze on her.

"Next," he said, the command in his voice making her pulse jump, "we see what you can accomplish when you stop holding back."

Right. No pressure or anything. Just casually unlock long-lost magic in front of the scariest Death Lord while his shadows held her hand.

This was fine. Everything was fine.

XXI.
BRYNN

Brynn's hands still tingled hours after training, white traces shimmering across her knuckles before fading. The ward-magic left marks. Temporary proof she was changing into something that shouldn't have been possible.

She needed answers. And the library had become her refuge.

She'd found this place by accident a couple of nights ago, trying to understand the power humming beneath her skin. Unlike the formal spaces of the palace—the skull-lined throne room, the ribcage corridors, the chambers where death stared from every wall—this room felt different. Softer, somehow. As if whoever had designed it understood that even the inhabitants of a death realm needed somewhere simply to be.

The space curved like the inside of a giant skull, the domed ceiling arching overhead in smooth bone polished to a warm ivory glow. Bookshelves lined the curved walls, built directly into the architecture—each shelf carved from bone, books nestled between them like treasured secrets. The shelves spiraled upward in impossible configurations, some floating in mid-air, suspended by magic that hummed contentedly when she passed.

But it was the details that made it feel like a sanctuary.

Thick rugs covered the bone-tile floor. Deep purples and silvers that muffled footsteps and invited bare feet. The reading chairs were upholstered in worn velvet, the color of twilight, their frames carved from dark wood with only the subtlest bone accents: armrests that curved like cradling palms, feet shaped like curled toes. Someone had chosen comfort over intimidation.

The fireplace dominated one wall. Not the cold blue flames that lit the rest of the palace, but actual fire. Warm. Orange and gold, crackling softly, casting dancing shadows that felt natural rather than alive. The mantel was a single massive jawbone, but it had been carved with climbing roses, the teeth transformed into delicate petals. Death made beautiful. Death made gentle.

Candles floated at reading height throughout the space, their flames steady and warm, responding to her presence, drifting closer when she sat down, hovering over whatever page she was studying. The pale-blue sconces along the walls cast ambient light, but these golden candles felt personal. Attentive.

A reading table dominated the space near the window, its surface scarred. Ink stains, cup rings, the grooves of countless quills pressed too hard during moments of inspiration. The window stretched twenty feet high, a Gothic rose window carved entirely from bone. Intricate tracery spiraled outward from a central medallion, each intersection marked with miniature carved roses. The pale bone glowed in the twilight, making the entire window look like carved moonlight.

Beautiful. Terrible. Just like everything here.

Just like him.

She pushed the thought aside.

The chair she'd claimed as her own, a deep wingback near the fire, had blankets draped over its arms. She hadn't put them there. They'd appeared after her third visit, soft wool in shades of grey. The kind of thoughtful detail that made her chest tight if she thought about it too long.

She flexed her fingers, watching the last traces of white fade. Her body was adapting to forces that should have killed her. Every training session pushed her further from what she'd been, closer to something she didn't have words for yet. The power felt almost comfortable now. Which meant she was in deeper trouble than she'd thought.

This was insane. A thief playing with death magic. Except that wasn't quite true anymore.

She was beginning to understand. Not everything, but enough to recognize patterns in the chaos. Enough to want more. Enough to catch herself watching his hands during demonstrations, memorizing the way shadows moved when his concentration slipped.

Enough to forget why getting close to him was a terrible idea.

The book propped against her knees made her head hurt. Advanced Ward Theory: Principles of Network Stability. Dense technical terminology, diagrams that twisted in dimensions she couldn't quite visualize. But buried in the complexity were concepts starting to make sense. As if some part of her already knew this, was remembering rather than learning.

Energy distribution. Connection efficiency. Resource flow optimization.

Her father's voice echoed: *Business is just understanding what people need and how to get it to them profitably.* Trade routes and supply chains translated surprisingly well to magical theory. The ward network operated on principles she'd learned by watching contracts negotiated, just expressed through power rather than coin.

She closed her eyes against the familiar ache.

The memory brought its familiar companion. Grief wrapped in rage. Dead because someone wanted what they had. Dead because betrayal wore a friendly face.

Dwelling on it wouldn't bring them back. It would just make her sloppy when she needed to be sharp.

She traced one of the diagrams, following interconnected nodes. The fire crackled beside her, warm against her cheek. One of the floating candles drifted closer, as if sensing she needed better light for the detailed illustration.

During training, she could feel these patterns in the magic. The way power wanted to flow in specific directions, how it resisted incorrect channeling, and the singing harmony when everything aligned.

It felt almost like picking a lock, finding the right pressure points and understanding the mechanism's logic.

His shadows helped guide her through the exercises. She'd stopped flinching from their touch, stopped tensing when they wrapped around her wrists to correct positioning. They were extensions of him, and they'd never hurt her. She trusted them more than she should, probably. Trusted him more than smart survival instinct allowed.

But she no longer believed the warning. Whatever else he was—death incarnate, the Reaper—he'd been nothing but patient during training. Harsh when she made mistakes, never cruel. Demanding, never unfair. And he never lost control, even when she could tell he was frustrated.

And the way he looked at her sometimes when he thought she wasn't paying attention...

Not going there. Nothing good comes from noticing things like that.

She shifted in the velvet chair, pulling one of the soft blankets over her lap as she tried to refocus on junction point stability. The fire popped, sending a small shower of sparks up the chimney. Outside the window, the aurora shifted from green to purple, painting the distant spires in an ethereal hue.

The section assumed readers already understood foundational concepts she was still piecing together, like reading financial ledgers when you only knew half the terminology. You could get the general idea, but miss critical details.

Her annotations crowded the margins. Quick sketches showing how she visualized energy flows, questions about terms, connections to observed patterns. Small practical handwriting next to elaborate script. Her mother had insisted on proper penmanship along with mathematics: *A woman in business needs every advantage, including the ability to forge a convincing signature.*

The memory made her smile. Pragmatic to the core. Her mother would've appreciated the irony. All those lessons in reading people and spotting deception now applied to navigating a death lord's court.

The warm flames flickered in response to her mood. Everything here reminded visitors they were far from the living world. Even the comfortable furniture held that slight otherness. Existing in slightly different dimensions simultaneously. But wrong had started to feel like home.

How long had she been here now? Long enough that eternal twilight felt normal. She'd stopped counting days, measuring time instead in training, in books consumed, in the gradual progression from ignorance to competence. Long enough to know which corridors led where, which servants would answer questions, and where he was likely to be at any given hour.

Long enough that this library, with its warm fire and floating candles and blankets that appeared without explanation, felt more like home than anywhere she'd lived in years.

That's the problem. Getting comfortable. Comfortable in the realm of the dead, comfortable with shadows that could kill, comfortable with him. Comfortable noticing the way his voice drops when he's concentrating, or how his shadows curl when he's amused.

The magic in her hands pulsed with her agitation. She controlled her breathing, let the power settle. Control was everything here. Emotion destabilized ward-work. Fear made the magic erratic. And attraction...

She cut that thought off.

Feel the magic, but don't let it feel you—his words during their first real lesson. Master yourself or master nothing.

She returned to the diagram, determined to understand this section before—

"I thought I might find you here."

Her heart slammed against her ribs. The book nearly slid off her knees as she looked up, and she had to catch it with reflexes honed from years of not dropping stolen goods.

He stood at the edge of the firelight, where warm gold met cool shadow. The flames painted half his face in soft light, the other half lost to the darkness that clung to him. How long had he been there? How much had she missed while lost in study? She should've heard him. She was always hyperaware of sounds, movement, and potential threats. That was survival.

Damn it. She needed to get herself together. He made her sloppy.

"Your library is educational." She hoped her voice sounded steadier than she felt, marking her place with one finger. Warmth crept up her neck as she realized how she must look. Curled up in his chair, wrapped in his blankets, surrounded by his books, fire-warmed and comfortable like she belonged here. Like she had any right to his private spaces.

The corner of his mouth shifted. Not quite a smile, but close. That expression she was learning to read, the one that meant she'd amused him against his will. The firelight softened his sharp features, made him look almost approachable.

He moved closer. The temperature dropped, or maybe that was just her awareness of him. The way her entire body tensed with something that definitely wasn't fear. More like how a rabbit might feel watching a wolf approach, except the rabbit wanted the wolf to come closer.

She was losing her mind. That's the only explanation.

His shadows were calmer than usual. Almost relaxed, comfortable in this space, the same way she was. They drifted around him without the tension they carried in court, when he had to maintain perfect control. One tendril reached toward the fire, curling around the warmth like a cat seeking heat.

"You've been spending your evenings here." That low, rough voice that demolished her concentration.

Oh, she was in trouble. So much worse than the magic. Magic might kill her quickly. This would destroy her slowly.

"Well, you said I needed to understand the theory." She gestured at stacked books surrounding her research station, trying to ignore the rapid drumbeat of her heart. "Some of this is starting to make sense. Turns out magical infrastructure has a lot in common with smuggling routes."

His eyebrow lifted slightly. Surprise. The floating candles drifted toward him, drawn by his presence, casting golden light across his sharp cheekbones.

She felt pleased at getting that reaction.

He approached the table. She resisted shifting in her chair. Every step that brought him closer made her hyperaware of the shrinking space between them. Six feet. Five. Four. Her breath wanted to quicken, but she forced it steady.

When he reached her table, he picked up one of the texts she'd set aside. His gloved fingers traced the spine with surprising gentleness. Those hands could drain life with a touch. Watching them handle the book so gently made her chest tighten. He'd been just as gentle during training, his shadows wrapping around her wrists to correct her grip with that same care.

"Graduate-level material." He glanced at her, something flickering in his gaze that caught both the firelight and the blue sconces. Approval, maybe. Or surprise that she was tackling advanced concepts. "Ambitious."

"I learn fast." More defensive than intended. She straightened against the wingback chair, blanket pooling in her lap, her chin lifting the way it did when merchants tried to cheat her. "I understand more than you think. My father always said I had a head for patterns."

She reached for the book in her lap, flipping to the diagram occupying her thoughts. "This section is on junction point stability. The author assumes you know foundational concepts, but if you think of it like—"

She stopped, suddenly aware she was about to explain magical theory to a being who'd been manipulating death magic for longer than she'd been alive. Heat flooded her cheeks.

Great. Lecture the Reaper about wards. That's not arrogant at all. He's going to think she's an idiot.

But he'd moved to stand beside her chair, leaning down to see what she was pointing at. She could feel the cold radiating from him, catch that familiar scent of winter frost and roses beneath something metallic, like the air before a storm. His presence pressed against her awareness like a hand against her spine.

In the firelight, she could see threads in his dark clothes and count the subtle patterns in the shadows clinging to him.

His shadows brushed her arm, and the contact sent electricity racing up to her shoulder. They felt curious tonight, almost playful. Like they wanted to explore her skin. The fire crackled approvingly.

If she turned her head, her lips would nearly touch his jaw. She could see the sharp line of it in her peripheral vision, the elegant angle where jaw met throat. Firelight and shadow painting him in gold and darkness.

Her breath caught. She kept her eyes locked on the page like it was the most fascinating thing she'd ever seen, even though every nerve was screaming awareness of his proximity, even though her body wanted to lean toward that cold instead of away from it.

"Explain," he said quietly, and the rumble of his voice this close turned her stomach over. That commanding tone shouldn't affect her like this—shouldn't make her pulse skip every single time.

XXII.
DANTE

She was brilliant.

He'd known she was clever. Street survival demanded it. But watching her dissect complex ward theory using frameworks she'd built from merchant principles? Translating magical scholarship into trade routes and supply chains like the concepts were interchangeable?

Dangerous.

Not the kind of danger his nature represented. Far more insidious. The kind that made him linger when he should leave, find excuses when distance was necessary.

"The energy has to flow cleanly." Her finger traced pathways in the diagram, and he tracked the movement. Hands that were quick and sure. "Just like goods through distribution networks. Minimize resistance, avoid bottlenecks, use natural channels instead of forcing artificial routes."

Most ward-keepers studied for years before grasping these principles. She'd taught herself in weeks.

Time felt different lately; his existence was divided into moments with her and the spaces without her.

He pushed the thought aside.

This is instruction. Nothing else.

He'd been telling himself that lie for weeks now.

"And here." She leaned closer to the page, and his shadows writhed around his shoulders in response. "Where three channels converge. That's critical. If the flow becomes unbalanced, the whole section destabilizes. Like a trade hub where too many caravans arrive at once. The infrastructure can't handle the volume."

She pulled back, finger sweeping across the full diagram now. "But that's just one junction. Zoom out and every realm has its own command center where the local channels converge and regulate outward." Her finger settled on the central point. "And all of them feed into this. The Mourned Court. Every major channel passes through it eventually. Take that out and the whole network collapses." She sat back slightly, eyes still on the page. "It's like a port city controlling the only deep-water harbor on the coast. You don't need to own every road if you own the one place all the roads lead."

She would have been extraordinary with proper training. Teaching at an academy, shaping young minds. Someone should have recognized her brilliance long before survival forced her into the shadows and locked doors.

The thought came with bitterness. The world had wasted her, made her a thief when she could have been a scholar. Brilliance crushed by circumstance and necessity, reduced to stealing instead of creating.

"Exactly." The word came out rougher than intended. He cleared his throat, forcing his focus back to the diagram instead of the way animation transformed her features. Brightening her eyes, softening the edge she usually carried. Making her look younger. Less haunted. "Most ward-keepers take months to grasp junction dynamics."

She looked up at him, surprise clear. Then pleasure at the praise, quickly masked but not quite fast enough. Like she wasn't used to recognition. Like no one had ever told her she was brilliant.

That shouldn't make his chest ache. Shouldn't make him want to—

His shadows stretched toward her before he caught them, reeling them back with effort that shouldn't have been necessary. They'd grown disobedient around her, reaching without permission, responding to impulses he refused to acknowledge. They wanted to touch, to curl around her wrists the way they did during training. They liked the warmth of her, the way she didn't flinch anymore.

He should step back. Put distance between them. Remind them both what he was. What he'd always be. The Reaper who'd chosen isolation because anything else endangered those around him.

Instead, he reached across the table and selected another text from her stack.

Fool.

"If you understand junction dynamics, this will make more sense." He set the book beside her, acutely aware of how his hand came near hers. The heat radiating from her skin. Warmth that his realm couldn't quite leech away. If he removed his glove, if he let his control slip for just a moment...

He cut the thought off.

"The mathematical models underlying energy distribution. Dry reading, but foundational."

"Everything here is dry reading." But she was already leaning forward to examine the new text, and the movement brought her shoulder closer to his. He could smell her. Warm skin and something bright, like citrus, like sunlight trapped in a realm of eternal dark. Alive. So achingly alive. "Though I suppose ancient magical theory doesn't prioritize entertainment value."

The corner of his mouth twitched. "A shocking oversight from scholars who've been dead for several thousand years."

"You should file a complaint."

"I'll add it to the list." Right below stop finding excuses to extend these evenings and maintain an appropriate distance from the mortal who's somehow become the most interesting thing in his realm.

Right below stop wanting things he couldn't have.

She laughed—not the guarded sound she used with his court. The sound sent an ache through his chest, made his shadows pulse with an emotion he had no business feeling. Pleasure. Warmth. The kind of joy he'd thought his nature had burned away long ago.

He pulled out the chair across from her before he could reconsider, settling into it with the excuse that he needed to see the diagrams properly. Not because her evening research had become something he anticipated. Not because finding her here—absorbed in study with firelight catching in her hair, her clever mind dissecting his realm's magic like she was dismantling a lock—had become the best part of his endless days.

Not because she'd claimed this space as her own, and some part of him reveled in seeing her make herself at home in his domain.

Absolutely not because of those things.

His shadows curled around her chair legs, restless things seeking proximity to her. He let them, just this once, just for tonight. Tomorrow, he'd reinforce control. Tomorrow, he'd remember why distance was necessary.

Tomorrow.

She bent over the new text, bottom lip caught between her teeth. His gaze dropped to her hands as they moved across the page. His mind wandered to what else they could do before he caught himself and redirected. Forcibly.

But he didn't look away when she glanced up and caught him watching. Couldn't quite manage it, even knowing he should. Even knowing every moment like this was a step further down a path that led nowhere good.

"What?" She touched her face self-consciously, and the gesture sent a tightness through his chest. "Do I have ink on my nose or something?"

"No." His voice had gone low and rough. "You're thinking. I can see the gears turning."

"And that's worth staring at?"

Yes. She had no idea how much.

"You approach problems differently than anyone I've trained." True, if incomplete. "It's notable."

Her eyes narrowed slightly, and he could see her trying to determine if he was mocking her. The distrust never entirely left, even after weeks of training. Perhaps mainly because of the training. Intimacy bred wariness in someone who'd survived by trusting no one.

Clever girl. That caution has kept you alive.

"Notable," she repeated. "I'll take that as a compliment."

"You should."

Color crept up her neck. She looked away, but not fast enough to hide it.

He wanted to lean closer. See if the flush went deeper than her throat.

He needed to control himself.

"The mathematical section." He tapped the book, drawing her attention back to safer ground. Something that didn't involve noticing how her breathing had changed, or the way she held herself very still when he spoke in that particular tone. The tone that affected her. Except she never ran. "Start with chapter seven. The notation is archaic, but the principles remain sound."

She looked down at the page, and he watched the moment she forced herself to focus. The effort of will as she pushed past whatever had just passed between them and refocused her mind on the work. Discipline, he recognized. The same kind he employed every moment to maintain control over his nature.

Stronger than she looks. Stronger than she should be.

This mortal thief looked at him and chose to stay. Chose to curl up in his library like she belonged here. Decided to laugh at his dry humor and challenge his assumptions about magic with the audacity of someone who'd never learned proper fear.

Or perhaps she had learned it and learned it thoroughly. And decided he wasn't the thing to fear.

That thought did things to him. Warmth. Foolishness. Something that felt terrifyingly like hope.

She's mortal. Fragile. And he was death itself, wearing the shape of restraint.

But watching her work, seeing intelligence spark in those eyes as she parsed the notation...

Enough. He'd indulged this weakness long enough.

"I should leave—" he started.

The floor trembled beneath them.

XXIII.
DANTE

Books rattled on shelves, and the lights flickered in patterns that set his nerves on edge.

He was on his feet before the second tremor rolled through, his shadows automatically reaching for her arm to steady her as she stood. He released her immediately and moved to the massive windows overlooking his domain. In the distance, where his territory met the neutral zones between courts, a pillar of sickly yellow light rose into the twilight sky.

The ward network was hemorrhaging power. He could feel it like a wound in his own flesh.

Damn it all.

"What is that?" She'd followed him to the window, standing close enough that her shoulder nearly brushed his. Either she didn't understand the danger, or she'd stopped caring.

The latter, most likely.

"Ward-lock failure." The words came out clipped. Distance, severity, and how swiftly the cascade would spread if left unchecked. His mind sorted through the variables with ruthless speed. "Major one."

Another tremor rolled through the palace, strong enough that he felt it in his bones. The barriers were screaming.

"How major?" Her voice held steady through the tremors, and when he glanced at her, she was already reading the situation. Weighing risks and costs as though she'd spent lifetimes making such decisions.

She hadn't. Decades at most. A handful of mortal years learning to survive.

"If it's not contained within the hour, the damage will spread to adjacent sections." He turned from the window, already moving. His shadows raced ahead, clearing the path to his study where the emergency equipment was stored. "The cascade could take down half the neutral zone's infrastructure."

Souls would pour through the breaks. Reality would fracture at the seams. The other Death Lords would scramble to contain the damage, and they would all know it had occurred in his territory, under his watch.

Unacceptable.

"We need to get there."

The words stopped him cold. *We.*

He turned slowly. The casual presumption in that single word made his jaw clench even as his shadows leaned toward her.

"I need to get there." He kept his voice level through considerable effort. "You're staying here."

She'd be safe here. He wouldn't have to divide his attention between repairs and keeping one fragile mortal alive.

Her chin lifted in that stubborn way that meant she was about to make his life harder.

"I'm going with you."

"Absolutely not." The refusal came out as a low growl.

She was already heading for the door, shoulders set with determination that showed she'd made her choice, and arguing would be useless.

Impossible creature.

He crossed the space between them faster than human eyes could track, placing himself directly in her path. He loomed, using every advantage of height and presence. The Reaper. Not some mortal she could sway through sheer determination.

She halted, but she didn't retreat. Just looked up at him with that unflinching gaze that made frustration tighten in his chest.

"You've been training me," she said. "I can help."

"You've had basic instruction." His hands clenched at his sides. The urge to physically remove her to somewhere safe was becoming increasingly difficult to resist. "Field repairs aren't controlled practice in a safe environment. The magic is chaotic. Unpredictable. Lethal."

She needed to understand. Needed to grasp that this wasn't a training exercise where he could halt proceedings if matters went awry.

"And you need someone with ward affinity." She crossed her arms, matching his intensity. "Which I have. You've said so yourself."

She's right. Damn her, she's right.

The repair would proceed faster with her abilities: half the time, perhaps less. Ward-work required attunement she possessed naturally, instincts that took others years to develop.

But the complications...

He couldn't protect her and perform the work at the same time. If the magic destabilized while she was working, if the feedback caught her unprepared...

The memory rose, unwelcome. A talented ward-keeper, screaming as magical backlash tore through her mind. He'd held her, unable to stop the cascade destroying her from within.

His shadows lashed out, striking the wall with enough force to crack stone. The impact echoed through the room.

She didn't even flinch.

"How many people die if the cascade spreads unchecked?" she asked quietly.

Souls would be lost. His people would suffer. The territories of other courts could be compromised. All because he couldn't manage field repairs alone while keeping one mortal woman from harm.

One mortal's safety had begun to outweigh strategic advantage.

He started pacing, agitation making stillness impossible—logic fighting with the desperate need to keep her safe.

Take her: the work proceeds faster, but she remains vulnerable to magical backlash.

Leave her: he works alone in unstable magic, with a higher probability of cascade spreading.

No good options. Only degrees of catastrophic risk.

The rational decision was obvious. Take her because the repair required two people, and she was the only one available with the requisite skills.

The irrational part, the part that wanted to secure her within the palace and handle the danger alone, was the complication.

"You don't understand what you're volunteering for." He turned on her, allowing her to see the full weight of his intensity. "Do you understand what happens when ward-magic goes catastrophically wrong?"

"Tell me."

Always so direct. Never retreating from difficult truths.

It should irritate him. It was becoming one of the things he—

No. Don't complete that thought.

"Active ward-locks tear people apart from the inside." He moved closer, voice dropping to that rough whisper that came when control became physical effort. "The magical feedback stops hearts, drives minds to madness, makes reality unstable. I've held ward-keepers while they screamed, watched their minds fragment into pieces that couldn't be reassembled."

He was close enough now to see her pulse jumping at her throat, to smell warmth and ink and that bright citrus note that clung to her skin.

His hands clenched at his sides.

"I've seen people cease to exist in ways that make death appear merciful."

He needed her to understand, needed her afraid enough to stay safe.

She was quiet for a moment, and he saw uncertainty flicker across her expression. Good. Fear was appropriate.

But then her jaw set, and he knew he'd lost before she even spoke.

"I understand that if we don't try, more people suffer that fate." Her voice was softer now, but no less firm. "Including you, trying to contain the damage alone."

She'd said "including you." Not just the realm, not just the souls. *Him.*

As though his survival mattered to her beyond practical necessity. As though she'd spent any time considering what would become of her if he didn't return from this repair.

His chest tightened. A fracture in the wall he'd spent centuries building, spreading before he could seal it.

He shoved it aside ruthlessly. *This was resource management. Nothing more.*

"I've survived field repairs before," he said, voice cold. Distant. The tone he used when establishing proper boundaries. "Your concern is unnecessary."

"Is it?" She took a step closer, bold when his control was barely maintained. "Because even you have limits. And working alone in that..." She gestured toward the window where the yellow light still pulsed. "...will push them."

She had a point. *Again.*

He would be working at the very edge of his capabilities, racing against time and magical chaos. One error could mean losing not merely the repair but himself to the cascading failure.

And if he fell, no one would remain to keep the barriers stable between life and death.

Yet the thought of leaving her here, waiting and not knowing whether he would return, felt wrong.

Another tremor, stronger than before. Decision made, then.

"If you accompany me..." His voice carried authority now. The tone that made his court tremble. "...you do exactly as I say. No improvising. No testing limits." He moved closer, using his physical presence to emphasize the gravity. "No heroic gestures that complicate an already impossible situation. Is that crystal clear?"

"Understood."

His eyes tightened.

"You're planning to disregard that if you deem it necessary."

She had that look. The one that meant she'd already decided to evaluate the situation herself.

"I'm planning to follow your orders," she said, which wasn't quite a falsehood but wasn't quite the truth either.

They'd reached his study during the argument, her stubbornness carrying her alongside him despite his objections.

He studied her face, searching for uncertainty or false bravado. All he saw was determination that had no business existing in someone so mortal, so fragile, so completely unprepared for what they were about to face.

She was going to be a complication. An enormous complication.

And wasn't that the truth of it? Too late to send her away, too late to maintain proper distance, too late to pretend she was merely another tribute he would eventually kill or discard.

That had changed weeks ago. Perhaps the moment she'd looked at him and refused to flinch.

"Then we leave immediately," he said, voice rough as he turned back to the equipment cabinets. Safer than looking at her. "And hope your beginner's luck doesn't fail you."

He moved, selecting the tools they would require. Specialized containment crystals, emergency ward-repair implements, backup power sources. Each piece of equipment another reminder of how dangerous this would be.

Behind him, he heard her take a steadying breath.

He glanced over his shoulder. She was flexing her hands, a gesture he'd learned meant she was mentally preparing. White traces of magic flickered across her knuckles before fading.

Ready to work. Ready to follow him into magical failure, to confront something that could kill her without hesitation.

Stubborn creature. Reckless. Far too brave for her own good.

And utterly magnificent in her refusal to yield.

His shadows, without his permission, reached out to brush against her shoulder. A whisper of contact, checking, reassuring themselves that she was there.

He pulled them back sharply. This wasn't the time for any of what he was feeling.

"We need to reach the transport circle," he said, slinging the equipment harness across his shoulders. The weight was familiar, grounding. "Stay close once we reach the failure zone. The magic there won't be stable."

Understatement. The magic would be actively hostile, unpredictable in ways that defied natural law.

She nodded once.

She's going to get herself killed.

She's going to get both of them killed.

But he hadn't left her here. Because she was right, and because working alone would be more perilous, and because...

Because the thought of her waiting here, unknowing, bothered him beyond all reason.

Together, they moved toward the door and whatever catastrophe awaited in the neutral zones.

They'd barely crossed the threshold when another tremor struck. Stronger than all the others combined. The palace groaned, and somewhere in the distance, something shattered with a sound like breaking reality.

They were running out of time.

XXIV.
BRYNN

They emerged in the outer reaches of his domain, where the Forsaken truly dwelled.

This far from the palace, the realm showed its true nature. Ruins of unfinished homes dotted the landscape—doorways carved from black stone opening onto nothing, windows reflecting only darkness. Willow trees grew between them, branches hanging down like grasping hands. Memorial stones stood in clusters, names obscured by grime and years of neglect.

The ground held remnants of interrupted lives—a child's toy in the dust. Rusted chains half-buried. Yellowed letters, words lost to time. Each one a small tragedy.

The air tasted of old grief, thick enough to coat her throat with each breath.

She'd thought she understood what his realm was. She'd been wrong.

But even this landscape of sorrow was corrupted now. The failing ward-lock had twisted everything within miles.

The doorways flickered, showing glimpses of final moments—locked rooms where people died alone, abandoned streets, forgotten hospital beds. The willow branches writhed—the memorial stones pulsed with that sickly yellow light, names glowing and fading like dying embers.

Worse than the physical corruption: what moved among the ruins.

Translucent figures drifted at the edges of her vision, drawn to the instability. She caught glimpses of faces. Aching, desperate, reaching. They crowded against some invisible barrier, stretching toward her with terrible need.

Her steps faltered.

This is what he lives with. Every day. Every moment.

"Stay close." Dante moved closer than he usually would, his shadows forming a protective barrier around them both. His voice held an edge she hadn't heard before. "The ward failure is breaking down the containment zones. The Forsaken can see your warmth now."

She nodded, unable to look away. There were so many of them. Dozens were visible from where they stood, and probably hundreds more just beyond her perception.

Her chest tightened.

"They won't hurt you," he said, though his shadows remained ready. "They can't touch the living. But they're drawn to your life. They remember what it was like to be seen, to be acknowledged."

To matter to someone. To not be forgotten.

She forced herself forward, though their yearning pressed against her awareness. One step, then another, past the reaching presences that couldn't quite touch her. Past faces twisted with need and grief and hope that had nowhere to go.

Don't look directly at them. She could fall apart later.

This was what he ruled. Not some abstract concept of death or darkness, but this. Thousands reliving their abandonment eternally, calling out for help that would never come.

"How do you bear it?" The question escaped before she could stop it.

His jaw worked for a moment. Just that one small tell that said more than words could.

"Someone has to."

The answer explained everything and nothing, carrying the weight of ages.

They walked in silence after that, navigating the corrupted landscape. The path toward the failure zone led through terrain that had surrendered to the magical instability. A bridge stood half-finished, its stones floating in mid-air as though construction had stopped. A garden of memorial flowers bloomed and withered in rapid cycles, petals falling upward instead of down.

Reality coming apart at the seams.

As they moved closer to the yellow light, the dead grew more distinct. A woman in a tattered dress, mouth open in a silent scream. A child calling for parents who would never come. An old man wandering in circles, searching for something he'd lost long ago, his form flickering like a failing candle.

She tried not to look at their faces, staying fixed on the path ahead, on the equipment humming against her back as the wardstones got closer to the damaged magic. But their pull was inescapable, the weight of their yearning to be seen, to be remembered.

Her throat tightened. She swallowed hard.

Fix it and get out.

"The tools are responding to the magical instability," Dante said, his voice pulling her back from the edge of being overwhelmed and grounding her. "They're designed to seek damaged ward-work. Unfortunately, that makes them eager to reach areas that could kill you."

"Reassuring," she managed, adjusting the pack's straps. The familiar sarcasm helped center her, gave her something to hold onto besides the crushing awareness of suffering all around them.

They crested a ridge and got their first clear view of the failed ward-lock.

Oh no.

The structure rose from a crater carved into the landscape with unnatural perfection. The ward-lock was a twisted spire of crystalline material that pulsed with that nauseating light, but it was clearly broken. Sections of the crystal were cracked, others were missing entirely, and the remaining pieces floated in positions that defied gravity, held up by failing magic.

Around the pit's edge, hundreds of the dead had gathered in a thick crowd. Maybe thousands. All drawn toward the damaged structure as though it represented escape or salvation or change from their eternal torment.

Her stomach turned. Not from the damage, though that was bad enough, but from the intention behind it.

"Reaper," she said slowly, studying the pattern of destruction. "Look at how it's broken."

He moved closer, and she felt his presence at her shoulder. His expression darkened. He saw it too.

The crater around the ward-lock was perfectly circular, its edges cut as if by a blade. The floating crystal fragments were arranged in precise patterns, creating gaps that would maximize the magical instability while preventing the structure from collapsing entirely. Someone had wanted it to fail slowly, dramatically, causing maximum disruption to the surrounding area.

This was definitely sabotage.

"The damage is too clean," she continued, forcing herself to analyze the technical problem instead of what it meant. "Too specific. This isn't random decay or natural failure."

"No," he agreed, his voice grim. Cold in a way that made her glad she wasn't his enemy. "It's not."

"Strategic sabotage," she said, the words tasting bitter. "Someone who understands ward-magic better than they should."

His shadows writhed at his shoulders, agitated, as if he were furious and trying to control them. "The question is whether we can repair it, or if attempting to do so will trigger whatever they've planned next."

She studied the damaged structure, letting her newly trained senses explore the chaotic magical patterns radiating from it. The energy felt corrupted in ways beyond mere breakage. Unstable, aggressive, like something fighting against its own nature. And beneath it all, the pull of the watching dead made the magic even more volatile.

"Can we fix it?" she asked.

"We have to try." He began unpacking his equipment, and she

recognized the set of his shoulders. Braced for violence, ready for anything. "But this one's worse than the others. The instability is spreading faster, and with this many drawn to it..." He glanced at the crowd surrounding the pit. "Their presence destabilizes the magic further. One wrong move and the entire structure could collapse inward."

Of course it does.

They descended into the crater carefully, the dead drifting aside to create a path. She kept her gaze fixed on the twisted spire ahead, not on the hope in their eyes as they watched the living enter their prison.

The magical interference grew stronger as they approached. The air felt too thick, pressing against her lungs. Her skin prickled with the sensation of being watched by thousands of desperate presences. The ward-stones in her pack vibrated so violently she had to brace the straps to keep them from bruising her shoulders.

This wasn't just another failing ward-lock. This was a cascade point that could trigger failures throughout the entire sector.

If this falls, how much of his realm goes with it?

"I can see the damage patterns," she said, studying the twisted crystal up close. Her training kicked in automatically, analyzing flows and connections even as her pulse hammered. "But they're more complex than what we practiced with. And the energy is fighting itself."

"The sabotage created a feedback loop." Dante's voice was tight. "Every second we're here, it degrades further."

Her mouth went dry. She could see what he meant. The magical patterns weren't just damaged; they were consuming themselves.

"I'll need your shadows from the beginning," she said, unpacking her tools with fingers that tried to tremble. "This isn't something I can start alone."

His shadows moved into position immediately, the familiar touch steadying her racing heart. Grounding. Safe, even here in the middle of chaos. They formed the collaborative framework they'd developed during training, but instead of the controlled guidance from their practice sessions, this felt urgent. Desperate.

The moment she touched the first crystal fragment, pain lanced through her skull.

She gasped, nearly dropping the delicate piece. The backlash was worse than she'd anticipated. Like touching a live wire, electricity crackling along her nervous system. Her vision swam.

"Easy." His voice went rough. "Don't push it."

"I'm fine." She wasn't fine. Every nerve in her body screamed at her to let go, to run. But she forced herself to maintain contact, to push past it. *Find the pattern. There's always a pattern.*

"The primary flow is completely reversed," she said through gritted teeth, studying the mechanism's core while trying to block out the faces watching from just beyond the barrier. "And there's structural damage to the crystal housing. I'll have to stabilize the physical components before I can redirect the energy, but when I move this piece..."

The crystal pulsed violently. Reality rippled around them. She heard Dante's sharp intake of breath as his shadows surged, forming a protective dome just as the ward-lock released a burst of raw magical energy.

The blast slammed into the barrier. For a terrifying instant, she thought it wouldn't hold. The shadows flickered, thinned. Then Dante poured more power into them, and the protection solidified.

Her hands were shaking now, adrenaline flooding her system. "When I realign the primary crystal, the backlash is going to spike."

She took a breath.

"Tension on the secondary array," she said, and his power responded instantly, holding the delicate structure steady. "More. It needs to be completely immobile before I can..."

Another pulse. Stronger this time. The crystal fragments orbited faster, erratic and wild.

"We're running out of time."

"I know!" The snap came out sharper than intended, fear making her voice crack. She steadied herself. *Focus.*

She repositioned the first fragment through the pain screaming along her nerves. The backlash intensified. Her fingertips were going numb, her vision was tunneling at the edges.

"The flow converter needs to rotate..." But his power was already supporting the mechanism, anticipating her need.

Then the primary crystal cracked with a sound like breaking ice.

Raw force exploded outward. The dead surged forward as the containment weakened. And the entire spire began to shudder, reality folding in on itself around them.

"Hold it!" Dante's voice was a command that resonated with power. His shadows exploded in every direction. Some formed a reinforced barrier against the blast; others dove into the collapsing wardlock to physically support the failing structure; still more swept the encroaching dead back before their presence could destabilize things further.

The strain radiated through their connection. She felt him pouring massive strength into maintaining everything at once.

But she couldn't think about that. Her hands flew across the components, making adjustments she barely registered consciously. Training and instinct taking over where thought was too slow. Realigning energy flows. Redirecting the surge. Sealing the cracks with pure force of will and whatever she could channel into the crystal.

The fragment she was holding cracked further. A shard broke off, slicing across her palm. Blood welled, hot and bright.

She hissed but didn't let go. Couldn't let go.

Then his power flowed more firmly through their connection, supporting her grip, sharing the burden.

That helped more than it should.

Together, they forced the energy required into the mechanism, channeling it back into alignment. Her hands and his power, her instinct and his control, working in perfect synchronization.

The repair took minutes that felt like hours. Every second a battle against the destabilizing forces trying to tear everything apart. Her hand burned where the crystal had cut her. But gradually, painfully, the chaos began to settle.

The sickly yellow light shifted to pure, clean blue. Reality settled. The floating stones touched land, and the water flow straightened into its usual pattern. The crystal fragments locked into place with a resonant chime that echoed across the entire sector.

And the dead, no longer drawn by the destabilizing magic, began to drift back toward their assigned zones. Their forms faded from distinct figures into peripheral shadows, then into nothing more than weight on the air.

Still there. Still suffering. Just contained again.

Her chest ached with more than exhaustion.

When it locked into place, her legs went weak. His shadows caught her before she could stumble, supporting her weight.

"Is it holding?" she managed, the words slurring slightly.

"For now." His shadows carefully wrapped her injured hand, applying pressure through the cloth strips he'd torn from his own sleeve. His hands didn't shake, but his jaw was clenched. "That was reckless."

She tried for a smile. It probably looked terrible. "But it worked."

His dark eyes flared with silver at the edges for an instant before he looked away. "This was the fourth failure this week. They're accelerating."

Fourth. In one week.

She looked at the now-stable spire, then at the landscape around them. The doorways had stopped flickering. The memorial stones no longer pulsed. The willow branches hung motionless.

But she could still feel them—the Forsaken. Watching from just beyond perception, waiting in their eternal torment, their need a constant weight on the air.

"How much time do we have before they overwhelm our ability to repair them?" she asked, though part of her didn't want to know the answer.

His shadows shifted restlessly at his shoulders. Agitated. Worried in a way she'd rarely seen.

"Not long enough."

XXV.
BRYNN

The transport circle deposited them back in the castle's east wing with the same disorienting lurch that had carried them to the failure site. Brynn's boots hit stone, and her knees nearly buckled.

She caught herself against the wall, willing her legs to hold. The magical work had drained more than physical strength. Left her feeling hollowed out, scraped clean.

Her hands wouldn't stop shaking.

"Steady." Dante's voice came from too close, and she looked up to find him watching her with an intensity that made her pulse jump.

His shadows were already coiling around her elbow, supporting without quite touching. Cool and solid, sending a shiver through her.

Her body noticed how close he was standing. She was half-dead and covered in grime, and still...

She straightened, pride demanding she stand on her own even as her legs trembled. "I'm fine."

One dark eyebrow rose. He didn't believe her for a second, and the way his gaze swept over her made heat crawl up her neck.

It was practical. Checking if she was about to collapse.

Except his jaw had gone tight, and his shadows hadn't retreated from her arm.

"The immediate crisis is contained," he said finally, dismissing the circle with a wave. The magic dissipated, taking the last of the humid air with it.

She nodded, focusing on slowing her breathing. Here, everything was stable. The shadows fell in normal directions. Reality behaved as it should.

They'd bought time. That was all—a temporary fix for a problem that kept accelerating.

He was worried. About her. The realization settled somewhere warm in her chest.

She filed that thought away for when she wasn't swaying on her feet.

"You need rest," he said, voice dropping to that rough tone that always made her breath catch.

"Probably." She pushed off the wall, testing her balance. Better. Mostly. "Though I suspect rest isn't high on the priority list."

"It is tonight." His gaze lingered on her face. "Tomorrow evening, there's a formal court dinner. Your first."

Tomorrow. Relief loosened a knot in her chest she hadn't realized was there. Time to recover. Time to stop noticing how the cold blue firelight from the wall sconces caught in his dark hair, how his presence seemed to fill the corridor even when he stood perfectly still.

Delirious. That was the only reason she was cataloguing him like stolen treasure, appraising what she couldn't afford.

"Let me guess," she said, brushing futilely at the crystal residue covering her clothes. "They need to see the mortal who can touch ward-stones."

"Word will spread about today's mission. Better they hear it in controlled circumstances." A pause, his attention settling on her face again. "And better you're not dying on your feet when they evaluate you."

Fair point. Though the way he said *dying* suggested he thought she was closer than she'd admit.

"Worried I'll embarrass you by face-planting into the soup course?" She meant it as a joke, but her voice came out rough. Fatigue made her defenses slip.

His eyes darkened. "No."

One word, but the way he said it made her wonder what he was actually worried about. Because it wasn't embarrassment. His shadows wrapped tighter around her arm, almost protective.

Oh, that was worse. That was so much worse than if he just found her useful.

"Will you brief me on who I'll be meeting?" She kept her voice casual, even with the awareness humming under her skin that he was watching her like she might shatter.

"Naia will handle preparations and protocols." He turned toward the main corridor, and she felt the loss of his proximity immediately. Shadows released her arm, trailing back to him. "Rest first. She'll come to you tomorrow afternoon."

"So I have a whole day to dread whatever political nightmare awaits." She managed a smile that probably looked half-dead. "Wonderful."

He paused mid-step, then turned back to face her, and something in his expression made her breath catch. The cold blue firelight carved his profile into sharp angles.

"The court can be..." He seemed to search for words, which was unusual enough to sharpen her attention. "Cruel. Particularly to those they perceive as vulnerable."

"Good thing I don't plan on being vulnerable, then." She lifted her chin, meeting his gaze directly, even though her legs were shaking.

Something flickered in his expression. Almost approval, but edged with heat that sent warmth racing through her.

"No," he said quietly. "You wouldn't."

The way he looked at her in that moment, like he was seeing past everything surface-level to something that actually impressed him, sent a flutter through her chest she had no business feeling.

"Get some rest." He said it like an order, but his tone had gone almost gentle. "You'll need your strength."

Then he was walking away, shadows flowing around him, and she was left leaning against the wall, wondering when exactly she'd started noticing the way he moved. The controlled power in every step. The distance he maintained even when he was clearly concerned.

That control had to cost him something. Keeping everything perfect, everyone at a distance, never letting the mask slip.

She wanted to know what he looked like when that control finally broke.

And that thought needed to go directly back where it came from.

She needed to collapse somewhere horizontal before her legs decided for her.

But she couldn't quite shake the warmth in her chest. Or the memory of his shadows wrapped around her arm, refusing to let go.

Or the way he'd looked at her when he said *You wouldn't.*

Like he knew exactly how dangerous she could be, and didn't mind at all.

XXVI.
BRYNN

The next afternoon, Brynn woke feeling almost human. The exhaustion had faded to soreness, and her hands had finally stopped trembling.

On the wall, the drowning woman had drifted to the bottom, her face peaceful. Eyes closed now, as if she'd finally stopped fighting and found rest.

She was deciding whether to try getting dressed when three sharp knocks sounded at her door. A moment later, Naia entered and went straight to the wardrobe.

"The midnight blue," the ghostly woman said, pulling out the gown and laying it across the bed with care. "Lord Reaper's instructions."

Brynn's pulse quickened. *He'd chosen this? Specified which dress?*

The same dress she'd admired but never worn. Too much like something that announced she belonged here. The silk caught the light like dark water, elegant enough for any court function but cut in lines that wouldn't restrict movement if she needed to run.

Practical. Whether for her comfort or because he expected trouble, she couldn't say. Knowing him, probably both.

And why did that make warmth curl in her chest?

"He was particular about the selection." Naia moved to arrange jewelry at the dressing table. "Specified the color, the cut, even which pieces you should wear with it."

Oh, that was worse. He'd thought about this. About how she'd look wearing it. About the details.

She had a political gauntlet to survive tonight.

"So." Brynn settled into the chair, forcing her thoughts to safer ground. "Who exactly will be evaluating me tonight?"

"Lady Morwyn will be there, of course." The faintest disdain colored Naia's voice as she worked on Brynn's hair with skilled fingers. "She's territorial about Lord Reaper's attention. Old bloodline, significant magical abilities, decades of court influence."

"Territorial." The word lodged somewhere uncomfortable in her chest.

She could still feel his shadows wrapped around her arm yesterday. Still hear that low edge in his voice when he'd ordered her to rest. And now some court beauty with lifetimes of proximity and claim was going to be in the same room, watching them both.

"Let me guess," she said, pushing past the knot in her stomach. "She's been angling for the consort position for the better part of a century?"

"How did you...?" Naia's hands paused in her hair. "Yes, exactly."

Because she'd seen this before. Power attracted ambition like honey drew flies. Women circling wealthy men, playing the long game, building claim through proximity and expectation.

"She has the backing of several factions," Naia continued. "She's also... accustomed to getting what she wants."

"Wonderful." So, a powerful, well-connected woman who'd been circling Dante for decades and probably saw Brynn as an upstart threat. "Anyone else I should worry about?"

"Lord Lucian will likely be there. He's been questioning whether Lord Reaper's recent activities represent the best use of his time and resources." Naia's tone made her feelings about Lord Lucian's opinions clear. "He'll probe to see if you're influencing policy decisions."

Recent activities, meaning saving the realm from magical collapse. Right. Can't have the Lord wasting time trying to prevent reality from tearing itself apart.

"And if I am?" she asked, though she already knew the answer.

"Then he'll either try to win you to his side or eliminate you."

The casual way Naia said *eliminate* sharpened Brynn's instincts. Note the exits, mark potential allies, and watch for poison in the wine.

Nothing she hadn't handled before.

"Noted. Anyone else?"

"Lady Vivienne will be curious about your abilities. She's the court's primary magical theorist. Expect subtle tests of your knowledge and capabilities." Naia arranged a necklace of dark stones around Brynn's throat, the weight cool against her skin. "Master Magnus will want to determine whether you're a temporary novelty or a permanent fixture."

"And how exactly does one make that call?"

"By observing how Lord Reaper responds to you in social settings." Naia's hands stilled, meeting Brynn's eyes in the mirror with unusual directness. "Whether he defends you, includes you in conversations, treats you as an equal or a subordinate."

Heat crept up her neck.

She thought about yesterday. His shadows refusing to leave her arm even after she'd straightened. The way his jaw had gone tight when she'd joked about face-planting into soup. What would the court see when they looked at them together? Would they read the measured distance he maintained as indifference, or notice the tension that crackled whenever they were in the same room?

Would they see how hard it was becoming for her not to lean into those shadows when they touched her?

It was a dinner, not a declaration.

"The court functions on careful balance, miss," Naia continued, her expression turning serious. "Your presence disrupts that balance."

Good. She'd never been fond of other people's balance. Especially when that balance meant keeping her in an assigned box labeled *temporary*.

"Disrupts it how?"

"You're not bound by the same rules as the rest of us. You're mortal. You have no political debts or centuries of allegiances. And now you've proven capable of working magic that most of them can't even perceive." Something like approval flickered in the ghost's features. "That makes you either a valuable ally or a dangerous wild card."

Wild card. She'd been called worse, usually right before pulling off an impossible job.

Though this felt different. Higher stakes. Because it wasn't just about survival anymore.

When had that changed?

"Any specific advice for handling all this political maneuvering?"

"Don't try to out-polite them. They've perfected this over the ages. Be yourself, but be mindful." Naia's expression turned protective. "And remember, miss. Every interaction tonight will be analyzed and assigned meaning. Not just yours. His."

There it was. That weight of expectation.

She wondered if he felt it too. If he was somewhere in this castle right now, thinking about the dinner. About navigating the court's scrutiny.

About her wearing the dress he'd chosen.

When Naia helped her into the gown, Brynn caught her reflection and barely recognized herself. The midnight blue silk moved like it had been made for her, which it probably had been. The off-shoulder neckline bared her collarbones and the elegant line of her throat where the dark stones rested. Her hair fell in artfully casual waves.

Someone who looked dangerous in an entirely different way. Someone who could stand beside a Death Lord and not look diminished.

Not bad for a girl who used to pick pockets for breakfast money.

Her mother would have been proud. Or horrified. Possibly both.

"Ready, miss?" Naia asked, stepping back with satisfaction.

Brynn straightened her shoulders, feeling the weight of the dark stones at her throat. She wasn't just attending as the human tribute. She was walking into a room full of people who would be judging her, trying to determine what her capabilities meant for their schemes.

Let them try. She'd size them up right back, marking every tell, every alliance, every weakness they revealed.

And if Lady Morwyn wanted to play territorial games over a man who wasn't hers to claim?

Well. Brynn had never been good at backing down from a challenge.

Even if she had no right to feel territorial herself.

Even if the thought of watching another woman close to him made possessive heat coil in her chest.

Even if she was walking into this dinner knowing she was in far deeper than she'd ever intended to be.

"Let's go," she said, lifting her chin. "Time to show them what disruption looks like."

And time to see how he looks at you in that dress, whispered a traitorous voice in her head.

She told that voice to shut up.

It didn't listen.

XXVII.
BRYNN

The grand hall had been transformed for the evening's formal dinner.

Long tables filled the vast space, their surfaces polished obsidian set into frames of pale bone. Each was draped with runners of deep purple silk, the same death-woven fabric from the tapestries, showing faint scenes that shifted when she wasn't looking directly at them. Feasts that ended in poison. Celebrations interrupted by massacre.

Additional chandeliers had been hung for the occasion, descending on chains of linked bones to hover over each table. Their cold blue flames reflected off silver place settings and crystal glasses, casting flickering light across the assembled courtiers. Candelabras of twisted bone rose from the center of each table, their flames steady and cold.

The chairs were uniform in their macabre elegance. High backs formed from spread shoulder blades, armrests ending in skeletal hands, seats upholstered in deep purple velvet that matched the silk runners.

Every surface in this court was a reminder of what ruled here.

Brynn paused at the hall's entrance, automatically noting exits and sight lines. Approximately sixty courtiers filled the space, their conversations a low hum of controlled ambition. Everyone was positioned according to some hierarchy she was still learning to read, but the dynamics were clear enough. Those closest to the high table mattered most. Everyone else was audience.

The moment she stepped into the hall, conversations died.

Every face turned toward her, trying to gauge whether she was a threat or an opportunity, worth the effort of crushing or not yet. She kept her expression neutral and walked deeper into the room, letting the midnight blue silk announce that she belonged here, whether they liked it or not.

She'd survived worse scrutiny from people with knives.

Nathaniel materialized through the crowd. Dante's advisor, his translucent form in formal court attire, short dark hair streaked with gray framing light eyes that held quiet authority. "Miss Brynn. Lord Reaper has arranged seating for you at the high table."

Of course he had. Making a statement.

She followed him through the maze of seating, ignoring the stares. Some faces showed curiosity, others blatant scheming. A few looked like they'd already decided she was a problem that needed solving.

The high table sat on a raised platform, extended for the event. Additional place settings of silver and bone, more elaborate candelabras, silk runners embroidered with ward-symbols in silver thread. Her assigned seat was three places to the right of Dante's chair. Close enough to indicate favor, distant enough to avoid scandal. But even at the high table, his chair sat apart. A gap separated his position from the nearest courtier on either side, that invisible boundary no one dared cross.

His chair was unmistakable even from afar: bigger, darker, with a more detailed bone frame than the rest. Clever placement. Calculated. Everything he did was calculated.

"The evening's entertainment should prove enlightening," Nathaniel said quietly as he held her chair. "Lord Reaper thought you should be prepared for the usual dynamics."

Which meant political games disguised as dinner conversation. She settled in and began identifying the players.

To her left sat Master Magnus, the examiner Naia had warned her about. Old even by death realm standards, with silver hair and ice-blue eyes that seemed to notice every detail. The kind of eyes that saw through lies professionally. Beyond him, Lady Vivienne, the magical theorist, already formulating questions about Brynn's abilities based on the sharpness of her gaze alone. Both nodded politely when introduced. Both would discuss her later.

The other courtiers were easier to read. Spirits who'd chosen service over whatever came next, the recently dead given new purpose, and a few who looked solid enough to have been here since the realm's founding. All of them radiated the same careful control that came from existing under Dante's rule.

Conversations flowed around her, and Brynn listened for anything useful about the ward failures. She caught fragments from Lord Lucian's group. "...resources stretched thin..." "...questioning priorities..." His tone carried the authority of someone accustomed to being heard, and others nodded along with his observations about "recent policy changes."

Changes meaning her. Meaning Dante working with a mortal instead of following protocols.

References to "proper leadership" and "traditional approaches" surfaced with suspicious frequency. Some speakers carried the fervor of true believers rather than typical opportunists. People who believed in causes were more dangerous. Causes made people reckless.

Like deliberately sabotaging ward-locks.

A ripple of movement caught her attention. Three women, strikingly ethereal in the way of death realm nobility, directing hungry looks toward Dante's empty chair.

"The Reaper's admirers," Lady Vivienne murmured, following her gaze.

The one in the center had to be Lady Morwyn. Silver-white hair that shimmered in the blue firelight like moonlight, violet eyes with piercing intensity, a gown cut to display her considerable advantages while maintaining propriety. She commanded her group with ease. Every smile, every gesture perfected over decades.

Everything Brynn wasn't.

"Lady Morwyn has been particularly persistent in her attentions," Master Magnus observed dryly. "She believes proximity to The Reaper grants certain privileges."

Brynn filed that away while studying Morwyn more closely. The woman moved like someone accustomed to getting her way, gesturing in ways meant to draw the eye. Professional-level manipulation. Made her street cons look like amateur hour.

Before Brynn could analyze further, the room's atmosphere shifted. Conversations dropped to a more respectful volume. The air grew noticeably cooler. Every spine straightened. The blue flames in the chandeliers flickered in unison.

The Reaper had arrived.

He entered through the main doors, shadows flowing around him. Tonight's formal attire, a fitted black jacket cut close at the shoulders and tapered at the waist, made him look every inch the dangerous lord he was. Her gaze traced the line of it before she could stop herself. The way the fabric moved with him, accommodating rather than constraining.

She forced her attention elsewhere.

His black eyes scanned the room, missing nothing. When his gaze reached the high table, it paused on her.

Just a moment. A brief sweep of darkness over midnight blue silk, lingering at her collar. Her throat.

Heat flooded her face. She held his gaze anyway, because looking away felt like losing something.

His shadows shifted. A tendril curled along the edge of the high table toward her seat, barely visible in the blue firelight. He didn't seem to notice.

Lady Morwyn did.

She intercepted his path like she owned the ground beneath it. "Lord Reaper," she purred, dropping to a tone that suggested private conversations and shared secrets. "You look magnificent this evening."

Her hand hovered near his arm. Close but not quite touching, though the gesture staked a claim in public. Dante's jaw set in the controlled mask he wore for court.

Then she leaned closer and whispered something in his ear. Body language that suggested intimacy, history, expectations. Confidence that she had every right to step within the boundary most others wouldn't dare cross.

Something hot and ugly twisted behind her ribs. Jealousy. She named it for what it was.

Her hands clenched into fists against the skeletal armrests. She forced them open. Forced herself to watch the room instead of that silver-haired head tilted toward his ear. The courtier across from her glanced in Brynn's direction, then quickly away, and Brynn realized her expression must be showing more than she wanted.

She rearranged her face into something neutral. Bored, even. Just a tribute watching court politics she didn't understand or care about.

Even she didn't believe it.

Dante moved toward the head position. Morwyn fell into step beside him as if she belonged there, matching his stride with the ease of someone who'd done it before. She lingered beside his chair as he took his seat, her hand resting on the bone-arch frame in a gesture that announced possession. Ownership. *Mine.*

Brynn stared at her plate. The dark porcelain reflected distorted blue firelight back at her, and she studied it like it contained the secrets of the ward system.

Pathetic. She was being pathetic. He wasn't hers. He wasn't anything to her. He was her jailer with a nicer title, and whatever his shadows did near her chair meant nothing. Shadows didn't have opinions.

She reached for her goblet. Steady hands. She'd take it.

Only when he gave Morwyn a polite but unmistakably dismissive nod did the woman return to her own seat, though not without a final lingering look that promised she'd be back.

The knot behind Brynn's ribs loosened. And that relief was more damning than the jealousy had been.

She took a long drink from her goblet and didn't look at the head of the table. Didn't look at the shadow still curled near the leg of her chair.

Didn't think about what any of it meant.

The meal began. Servants appeared from alcoves carrying food on trays of polished bone, their translucent forms weaving between tables. Brynn ate pale, glowing soup from a bowl carved from a single piece of skull, keeping her attention on the conversations around her. Gathering intelligence. Not thinking about silver-haired women with violet eyes.

She made polite conversation with Master Magnus about ward-magic theory while he probed her knowledge with casual questions, just as Naia had warned. Lady Vivienne listened with the attention of someone taking mental notes.

Let them test. She knew her work was solid.

Once, during a pause, she felt the weight of a gaze and glanced toward the head of the table without meaning to. Dante was watching her. Not the room, not the courtiers. Her.

His black eyes held something she couldn't name. Something that made her breath catch and her pulse trip.

He looked away first.

It was during the second course that the first real test arrived. A courtier from a lower position approached with rehearsed confidence and an elaborate bow that managed to be technically correct while implying condescension. Someone had sent him to probe her defenses.

"Miss Brynn," he said with a smile that didn't reach his eyes. "I hope you'll forgive our curiosity about your unique circumstances."

She set down her fork, its handle carved from a single bone and polished smooth, and gave him her full attention. "What circumstances would those be?"

"Your rapid elevation from condemned prisoner to trusted advisor." His smile was poisonous. "It must be overwhelming to navigate such sophisticated magical concepts when you lack the foundational education most of us take for granted."

Questioning her competence while appearing sympathetic. Several others drifted closer to witness the exchange, waiting to see if she'd crumble under pressure. The blue flames in the nearest chandelier seemed to burn brighter, as if eager for drama.

She had no intention of obliging.

She studied the man for a moment, noting the way his expensive clothes couldn't quite disguise his nervous energy. The slight tremor in his hands suggested he wasn't as confident as he appeared. Someone trying to prove himself by taking down the new player. Probably put up to it by someone more important who wanted to see how she'd respond.

"You're right," she said pleasantly. "I do lack your foundational education."

His smile widened, thinking he'd scored a point.

"For instance," she continued, "I never learned that wearing jewelry enchanted to boost magical perception was considered adequate compensation for natural ability."

His hand moved instinctively to the amulet at his throat. A movement that confirmed her guess. She'd noticed the faint magical signature during their conversation and recognized the enhancement charm from her time studying ward-magic.

"However, I have learned that sometimes fresh eyes can see solutions that decades of 'proper education' apparently missed. Particularly when those traditional approaches have been failing spectacularly."

The man opened his mouth, then closed it again. No recovery from having your competence dismantled so publicly. On the tapestry behind him, a feast scene showed a nobleman choking on poisoned wine. She could have sworn he hadn't been choking before.

He managed a stiff bow and retreated to his seat, leaving the others to reassess their assumptions about the human tribute.

From across the hall, the shadows near Dante's chair had gone very still. When she risked a glance, he wasn't looking at her. He was watching the retreating courtier with an expression that promised consequences.

A shiver traced her spine.

"Well played," Master Magnus murmured. "Though you may have made an enemy."

"I've survived worse enemies than wounded pride."

From across the hall, Lord Lucian observed the exchange with calculating eyes, recalibrating his own approach to her. Good. Let him think twice. Then she saw him lean over to whisper something to the courtier beside him, and her satisfaction dimmed slightly.

That was the real threat. The others were just pawns.

But the courtier had been the opening gambit. A test. The real confrontation came during the fourth course, when Lady Morwyn rose from her seat and approached the high table with purpose.

"Miss Brynn," she said, her words carrying through the hall. "I've been thinking about your earlier comments. About fresh perspectives and their value."

Sharper now. An edge that made conversations falter. Others sensed a more serious confrontation and turned to watch. The entertainment they'd been waiting for.

Brynn's heart hammered, but she kept her expression steady.

"I'm curious. What exactly gives you such confidence in your abilities? Surely someone so new to our realm must feel uncertain about their place here."

A direct challenge to her outsider status. But there was something else in Morwyn's look. A knowing quality that went beyond gossip. Something that made Brynn's instincts scream.

"Uncertainty keeps me alert," she replied evenly. "Complacency kills."

"How refreshingly practical." Morwyn's smile was razor-sharp. "Though I wonder if practicality is enough when wielding forces that have destroyed more experienced practitioners. Do you ever consider the risk you pose to others with your experimental approach to the ward-locks?"

Brynn kept her voice level through force of will. "I consider the greater risk of letting critical systems collapse while experienced practitioners debate whose turn it is to fix them."

"Ah, but there's the question." That intimate tone again. The one she'd used with Dante. Claiming familiarity, claiming understanding. "Whether someone so new to our world can truly comprehend what they're interfering with. There are aspects of life here, of our true nature, that take centuries to understand."

The hall had gone quiet. The temperature dropped, though whether from Dante's reaction or the collective tension, she couldn't tell. His shadows were moving. Not the subtle tendril from before. These rolled outward in slow waves, pooling in corners, darkening the spaces between the chandeliers' reach.

Don't look at him. Don't give her that satisfaction.

Behind Morwyn, the death-tapestry showed a queen being crowned while assassins crept closer in the background.

"Perhaps someone should explain how these arrangements work." Lady Morwyn's words dripped with false pity. "You're a tool, Miss Brynn. Useful for the moment, but tools wear out. They break. They get replaced by better, more experienced models." Her smile was sweet. "Surely you don't imagine you could ever truly belong among your betters?"

Replaceable. Temporary. No permanent place in this world.

In his life.

The worst part was the fear underneath her anger. *What if Morwyn was right?*

She opened her mouth to respond, something cutting about belonging being earned rather than inherited.

She never got the chance.

The temperature dropped so sharply that frost formed on the edges of wine glasses and crept across the tables. Every flame burned lower, the blue light dimming to near-darkness. The shadows surged from the corners, spreading across the floor like a tide.

Every instinct she had screamed danger.

Dante had risen from his chair.

XXVIII.
DANTE

He had been monitoring the evening's conversations with half his attention while conducting his own inventory of loyalties and potential threats. From the head table, he'd caught subtle exchanges between senior courtiers. Glances when certain topics arose, shifts in body language that suggested pre-arranged signals.

Someone was organizing dissent. The question was whether it was connected to the ward sabotage or represented separate political maneuvering.

Lady Morwyn's words carried across the hall, rising to ensure everyone could hear. The attack was public, meant to put the mortal in her place. To remind everyone, especially him, of the vast distance between a temporary tribute and someone who belonged.

Unacceptable.

The temperature had dropped before he decided to act. His shadows responded to the fury behind his control, spreading across the floor.

Tool. Replaceable. Doesn't belong among your betters.

He'd seen the thief's hands clench beneath the table, seen the flash of humiliation quickly masked. Seen her hold her ground against someone far older. The intelligence that had immediately grasped the stakes, the control that had kept her responses even.

He saw far too clearly how those words had cut deeper than a simple insult warranted.

He rose from his chair, the movement creating a ripple of awareness throughout the hall. Conversations stopped entirely as every person present became hyperaware of his displeasure.

They should be afraid.

"Lady Morwyn." He didn't raise his tone. Didn't need to. The shadows carried his words with clarity. "How fascinating to hear your theories on competence."

She turned toward him, confidence melting into a respectful bow of her head. But he caught the flash of satisfaction in her eyes. She'd succeeded in drawing his public attention, forcing his hand. Even if not in the way she'd intended, she'd made him react.

Clever. Foolish, but clever.

"Lord Reaper," she said, violet eyes downcast in a performance of submission. "I was merely expressing concern for the realm's stability."

The lie was elegantly delivered. She cared nothing for realm stability. This was about influence, the ages-old game she'd been playing since long before the thief arrived.

He moved from the head table. His shadows flowed ahead of him, parting the space between the seating, making courtiers lean back instinctively. He walked directly to where Lady Morwyn stood beside the thief's chair—standing over her, claiming that space.

Claiming what she'd tried to dismiss.

"Your concern," he said, "is noted. As is your complete lack of contribution to resolving the crisis you claim to care about so deeply."

Lady Morwyn's composure cracked slightly at the edges. The faintest tightening around her eyes, the minute stiffening of her spine. She hadn't expected him to turn her assault back on her so directly.

She should have.

"In fact, your primary qualification appears to be an impressive catalog of failures disguised as experience." He let that verdict settle over them like frost. Other courtiers shifted uncomfortably, recognizing the implicit threat. If he could dismiss decades of service this easily, none of them were safe. "Tell me, in your centuries of theoretical expertise, how many ward-locks have you personally prevented from collapsing?"

The trap was set and sprung simultaneously. Every person in the hall understood what he'd done. Forced her to admit her uselessness in front of everyone.

Her face went blank as she processed the reversal. "My experience has been more advisory in nature," she managed, strained.

"Advisory." He let the word hang in the air like a death sentence. Let them all hear the contempt in it. "How fortunate, then, that we have someone present who deals in results rather than advice."

The thief had remained still throughout the exchange, unreadable, but her posture suggested readiness. Poised to move if necessary. She grasped the game being played—when to hold, and when to let him handle the threat.

Smart girl. Knows when to let the Reaper defend his territory.

"You look tired." The dismissal was calculated, giving her an excuse to leave with dignity intact. Removing her from the line of fire while showing he'd chosen to do so.

She rose immediately, reading both the dismissal and the protection it offered—her quick intelligence reading between his words.

"Thank you for the enlightening conversation, Lady Morwyn," the thief said with a politeness that somehow sounded condescending.

He caught the flash of rage in Morwyn's eyes before she masked it. Let her be angry. Let her understand what happened when someone targeted what was under his protection.

The territorial claim in that thought surprised him less than it should have.

As the thief moved to stand beside him, close enough that he could feel her warmth, Dante let his gaze sweep the hall once more. The message was clear to everyone present: those who targeted her would be treated as if they had targeted him.

"Master Magnus," he said, addressing his examiner without breaking eye contact with the assembled gathering. "Ensure our court remembers their manners."

The dismissal was unmistakable. The entertainment was over. Anyone who continued this line of challenge would face him directly.

It was done.

As they moved toward the hall's exit, he noted that the thief matched his pace without hurrying, never rushing, never fleeing. She grasped the importance of maintaining a composed facade.

She learns fast. Too fast, maybe.

The corridor offered relative privacy, though ears could still be listening. Servants had excellent hearing when gossip was valuable. Without speaking, he guided her toward the west alcove with a subtle gesture. There were fewer potential eavesdroppers, and the architecture provided natural sound dampening.

Once they reached the alcove's shadows, she began to pace within the space, arms crossed tightly across her chest. Holding herself together through sheer will. Her frustration was evident as she glanced out at the courtyard through the tall windows. Beyond the glass, dark stone pathways and silver fountains intertwined beneath the eternal twilight, a stark contrast to the storm clearly brewing inside her.

He recognized the signs. Adrenaline crash after confrontation, rage, and humiliation held in check until privacy allowed release.

She was quiet for a long moment before finally speaking, and when she did, her words were controlled but laced with anger. "That was more than just politics."

"Yes." No point in pretending otherwise. She was too intelligent for comfortable lies.

"She wasn't just questioning my competence. She was questioning whether you're compromised by working with me." Her analysis cut straight to the point, her eyes narrowing as she stopped to face him. "Personal."

He studied her, noting the way her jaw clenched with suppressed emotion. "Your assessment?"

"She sees me as a threat. Not just professionally, but personally as well." Her arms dropped to her sides, hands forming fists, then flexing as if trying to release the frustration bottled inside her. "The question is how far she'll escalate."

Correct analysis. Morwyn had been circling for decades, building her claim through proximity and expectation. The thief's arrival and his clear favor toward her had disrupted long-laid plans.

Dangerous combination: wounded pride and thwarted ambition.

"She won't get the opportunity."

Something in his tone made her stop pacing and look at him directly.

"What does that mean?"

He found himself studying her. Seeing the emotion that hadn't been visible during the hall confrontation, the way she'd held her ground.

The vulnerability she was showing him now, in private, that she'd never show them.

"It means challenging you was a mistake she won't make again."

The words came out more definitive than he'd intended. More possessive.

She was quiet for a moment, her gaze searching his with unsettling intensity, looking for something. The faint tremor in her fingers betrayed the calm she was trying to project.

"I had it handled," she said, and the determination was genuine. Fierce. She believed it.

"I know." It was the truth. He'd seen her dismantling of the previous challenger, watched her identify weaknesses and exploit them. She could have handled Morwyn too, given time. "But you shouldn't have to."

The words surprised him even as he said them. Her comfort had become more important than politics. Protecting her from assault had become instinctive rather than strategic.

He'd started thinking of her as his to protect.

She looked up at him, her expression softening as the anger melted away, replaced by something that tightened his chest. Vulnerability. Trust. Something dangerously close to affection.

His shadows stirred restlessly, wanting to reach for her. He held them back through the effort of will.

"We should turn in," he said finally, forcing practicality into his tone. "Tomorrow brings another crisis."

Another ward failure, another desperate repair, another opportunity for her to get herself killed while he tried to work and protect her simultaneously.

She nodded, but neither of them moved immediately toward the corridor. The space between them felt charged, heavy with things unspoken.

"Dante," she said, using his name again instead of his title. Softer now, more intimate.

The sound of his name in her mouth affected him in ways he wouldn't name.

"Yes?"

"I'm glad you intervened tonight."

He looked at her, noting how the starlight through the windows caught in her eyes, turning green to emerald. How the midnight blue silk he'd chosen draped perfectly, moving with her. How the anger had given way to confidence. A stark contrast to the uncertainty Lady Morwyn had tried to provoke. How she stood here in his alcove, alone with the Reaper, and showed no fear.

Showed trust instead.

Dangerous.

Her expression shifted. Her pulse jumped visibly at her throat. Her lips parted slightly as her breath quickened.

His shadows stirred without his permission, reaching toward her before he caught them.

Footsteps echoed in the corridor.

He stepped back, realizing he'd somehow moved closer without meaning to. Only inches had separated them.

"Tomorrow," he said, rougher than intended.

"Tomorrow," she agreed, and the way she said it sounded less like acknowledgment and more like a promise.

XXIX.
BRYNN

Brynn could hear hushed voices in the corridor. Servants walking on eggshells, which probably meant the entire castle knew about last night by now.

Wonderful. As if she needed more people staring at her.

She rolled out of bed, automatically checking the room for changes. Same shadows, same view of eternal twilight, same sense that the furniture had been arranged by someone who'd never actually lived in a room. At least the bed was comfortable, even if waking up here still felt surreal.

Three sharp knocks interrupted her morning routine. "Come in."

Naia entered with a breakfast tray that looked suspiciously fancy—real coffee instead of the herbal stuff, fresh fruit, and pastries.

"Let me guess," Brynn said, moving to the wardrobe. "Everyone's talking about last night."

"The entire hall," Naia confirmed, setting down the tray with obvious satisfaction. "Lady Morwyn locked herself in her chambers after the Reaper's intervention."

The way she said 'intervention' made it sound like something far more dramatic than it had been.

She pulled out the midnight blue jacket. Might as well stick with what worked. "How bad is the gossip?"

"Oh, it's not bad gossip." Naia's tone turned distinctly teasing. "More like speculative gossip."

"Speculative about what?" Though she had a sinking feeling she already knew.

"About why the Reaper defended you so decisively. And why you looked so lovely in blue. And whether there might be deeper motivations involved."

Brynn groaned. "They think he's what, courting me? That's ridiculous."

"Is it?" Naia asked innocently, helping with the jacket fastenings. "You did look quite striking last night. And he did seem rather focused on you during dinner."

Right. Because the most powerful Death Lord was secretly hiding romantic feelings for her. That made total sense.

"He was watching to keep me from getting murdered by courtiers with too much wine and too little sense."

"Of course." But Naia's smile warmed. "Though I must say, the midnight blue was particularly effective. You should wear it more often."

Brynn shot her a look. "You made sure that dress was picked, didn't you?"

"I may have given him limited options." Naia's innocence was so exaggerated that it was practically criminal. "If it happened to complement your coloring and catch certain people's attention, well..."

"You're enjoying this entirely too much."

"I've been dead for decades, miss. I take my entertainment where I find it."

Brynn couldn't argue with that logic, even if it meant being the subject of castle speculation. She moved to the breakfast tray, noting how the coffee tasted better than anything she'd had in years. Either the death realm had excellent suppliers, or someone was putting in extra effort to keep her comfortable.

And she had a pretty good idea who that someone might be, which was almost more unsettling than the gossip.

"Any other reactions I should know about?"

"Lord Lucian's asking questions about your training schedule. Lady Vivienne wants to observe your next session. Master Magnus thinks you're fascinating." Naia began tidying the wardrobe. "Oh, and several courtiers are placing wagers on how long you'll survive here."

"How optimistic."

"The smart money's on 'indefinitely,' actually." Naia's smile returned. "After last night's display, people are starting to think you might be more permanent than previous tributes."

Previous tributes who'd died within weeks. The reminder settled uneasily in Brynn's stomach.

She finished her breakfast and checked her appearance one final time. The midnight blue did look good on her. Brought out her eyes, complemented her coloring, made her look like she belonged in a court instead of a prison cell.

THE WALK through the castle confirmed Naia's predictions about servant gossip. Conversations stopped when Brynn approached, resumed in whispers after she passed, and she caught more than one curious stare directed her way. At least no one seemed hostile. If anything, the attention felt more curious than threatening.

A death knight stationed near the main hall directed her to a passage she'd never noticed before. It led to a spiraling staircase that descended far deeper than the castle's exterior hinted was possible.

The air grew cold and stale with each step, thick with the scent of damp stone and old magic—the kind that made her skin prickle with awareness that she was somewhere she shouldn't be.

The staircase ended at double doors carved with the same intricate ward symbols she'd been studying. They swung open at her approach, responding to whatever magical signature she carried now.

The chamber beyond made her stop in the doorway.

It was massive. A vaulted hall that stretched at least a hundred feet in every direction, with smooth stone arches overhead. No bones here. No skulls watching from walls, no ribcage chandeliers, no skeletal hands emerging from shadows. Just clean lines and stone, as if whoever had built this space understood that precision work required clarity, not intimidation.

The absence was almost unsettling after weeks of bone architecture pressing in from every direction, like stepping into a different building entirely.

Ward-stones hung suspended from the ceiling at varying heights, connected by silver chains that hummed faintly. Channels of blue light crisscrossed the floor in complex patterns, linking raised platforms positioned throughout the space. The light here was different too. Warmer, steadier, designed for work rather than atmosphere.

And standing at the far end near the largest suspended ward-stone, adjusting something, was the Reaper.

Her pulse quickened before she'd made it halfway across the threshold.

Get it together. This is just training.

Shadows drifted around him as he moved, responding to gestures too subtle to catch. She suppressed a shiver.

"You're early," he said without looking up from his adjustments.

"Punctuality is a survival skill." She moved closer, forcing herself to sound unaffected even though her heart was doing interesting things in her chest. "This looks significantly more complicated than last time."

"The other day was field repair. Emergency measures to buy time." He straightened, and those dark eyes fixed on her with an intensity that made her breath catch. "Today we work on permanent solutions."

The central ward-stone loomed nearly six feet above the floor, its surface etched with symbols that pulsed with light. Smaller stones cascaded from it at varying heights, each connected by those chains that created an oddly beautiful pattern.

Elegant and probably lethal if mishandled.

"Multiple ward-locks operating in sequence," she observed, following the channels across the floor. "Designed to reinforce each other."

"Precisely. But the synchronization requires..." He paused, his gaze still fixed on her. "More intensive collaboration than our previous work."

The way he said 'intensive' made anticipation tighten low in her stomach.

She studied the raised platforms scattered throughout the hall, noting their positioning relative to the hanging stones. "How much more intensive?"

"The primary controls are here." He stepped onto a platform directly beneath the central stone, where control panels emerged from the floor like metallic petals unfolding. "But the secondary adjustments need to be made simultaneously from various points throughout the hall."

Which meant they'd be working in coordination across a space the size of a small cathedral, with her manipulating delicate mechanisms while he controlled the primary flows. The level of trust required was considerable.

And probably exactly why he'd chosen this exercise.

"And if we're not perfectly synchronized?"

"Catastrophic feedback that will either destroy the ward-stones or drain enough life force to kill us." His tone was matter-of-fact. "Probably both."

Wonderful. Because nothing in this realm could be straightforward.

She climbed onto the nearest platform, examining the crystalline controls that emerged from its surface when she approached. Beautiful mechanisms that responded to touch, their surfaces warm against the chamber's chill.

"How do we maintain coordination across this distance?"

"My shadows will guide you." His expression remained neutral, but something in his voice had shifted. "But they'll need to maintain contact throughout the entire process."

Not the brief touches of their previous training, but a sustained connection while they worked through complex magic that could kill them both.

"How extended?"

"The full sequence takes approximately an hour to complete properly."

An hour. With his shadows wrapped around her hands, guiding her movements, maintaining that constant awareness of his presence and power.

She glanced across the hall at him, noting the way his shadows moved restlessly around the platform like they were already anticipating the contact.

This is fine. This is just magical training.

Except the heat building in her chest suggested otherwise.

"Let's begin with the first configuration," she said, proud of how steady her voice sounded.

XXX.
BRYNN

She positioned herself at the first secondary station. The moment his gloved hands touched the primary controls, ward magic surged through the channels beneath her feet, glowing blue. It carried his signature with it. That dark undercurrent she'd learned to recognize, threaded through the ancient power like he couldn't touch anything without leaving a mark.

"Can you see the energy flows?" he asked.

She studied the crystalline controls in front of her, watching as threads of light began weaving between them. "Yes. There's a pattern forming, but it's..." She frowned, tracking the magical current. "The left side is running stronger than the right."

"Adjust the left crystal to compensate. Quarter turn counter-clockwise."

His shadows reached across the hall before she'd finished processing the instruction.

They wrapped around her wrists with that now-familiar combination of cool silk and barely leashed power, and every coherent thought she'd been holding dissolved. They guided her hands to the correct positions, adjusting her grip in a way that should have felt impersonal.

It didn't feel impersonal.

It felt like his fingers closing around hers. Like he was standing behind her, his chest against her back, his hands covering her hands, showing her how.

She swallowed hard.

When she made the adjustment, the energy flowed in balance, creating a rhythm among all the mechanisms.

But the shadows didn't withdraw.

They remained wrapped around her wrists, their touch firm enough to guide but gentle enough that she could break free if she wanted. Which she absolutely should want. Which any rational person trapped in a Death Lord's realm would want.

Except her pulse was doing something entirely traitorous, and pulling away was the last thing on her mind.

"Better," he said from across the hall, and his voice had dropped to that rough edge that crept in when his control was working harder than usual. "I can't see the individual threads from here. Only the overall power levels. Your eyes are essential for the fine adjustments."

Your eyes are essential.

Not *you're useful*. Not *the tribute serves a purpose*. Essential.

The pressure around her wrists tightened fractionally. Could he feel her heartbeat through the darkness wrapped around her skin?

The thought made heat climb up her throat.

Focus on the work. Not on how his shadows feel. Not on whether he knows what they're doing to you.

"Turn the left crystal one quarter clockwise," he instructed. "Now increase pressure on the central formation."

The shadows guided her movements, their touch steady and sure. She should have been focused on the crystals. Should have been tracking the energy flows with the careful attention they demanded.

Instead, she was cataloguing. The way the shadows pulsed in time with her heartbeat. The way they positioned her fingers with a gentleness that contradicted everything she'd been told about the Reaper. The way they seemed to know where she needed support before she did.

This is training. This is practical. This is—

The tendril curled around her right wrist shifted, tracing a slow path across her inner wrist where her pulse hammered.

She bit the inside of her cheek so hard she tasted copper.

"Hold that configuration while I adjust the primary flows."

His voice was controlled. Perfectly, impossibly controlled. But she'd been watching him long enough to hear the fractures. The slight roughness beneath the command. The way each instruction came with a breath he probably thought she couldn't hear.

She maintained her position, hyper-aware of every point of contact. His magical signature bled through the connection, a dark current running beneath the technical work. She could feel the edge of his concentration, the effort it cost him to keep this impersonal.

Good. Let it cost you something. Because it's costing me plenty.

"Next position."

She moved to the second platform, and his shadows followed without breaking contact. The transition was seamless. His power flowed with her like he'd been moving with her for years. Like their bodies already knew a choreography their minds hadn't agreed to.

This station required more complex work. Three separate energy streams needed to converge at exact points, their flows slightly out of sync.

The shadows split their attention, some guiding her left hand while others directed her right. The dual sensation was almost too much. Darkness on both wrists, both forearms, adjusting and correcting with a focus that made her feel like the only thing in the entire realm.

"The center flow is lagging," she reported, her voice steadier than she deserved. She tested different crystal positions. "Like this?" She rotated one crystal while keeping pressure on the other.

"Exactly."

One word. Low and laced with something that had nothing to do with ward-work.

His approval carried through the shadow connection like warmth pouring down her spine, pooling low in her stomach. She pressed her lips together, refusing to let her breath change where he might hear it.

He said 'exactly' about crystal alignment, not about you. Get it together.

The third position took longer. The energy patterns were more complex, requiring constant adjustment to maintain balance. His shadows had extended up her arms now, tendrils of darkness sliding past her elbows, supporting her movements when she reached for higher controls.

More contact. More surface area of shadow against skin. More of that devastating gentleness that made her forget what she was supposed to be doing.

"Breathe." His voice had gone quieter. A command wrapped in gentleness. "Don't fight the connection."

She realized she'd been holding her breath, trying to maintain some scrap of self-preservation. When she exhaled and let herself sink into the rhythm of the magic, the shadows settled more completely around her arms, and the resistance between them disappeared.

Better. Easier to work when she wasn't fighting his guidance.

Harder in every other way.

Because now there was nothing between her awareness and his. No friction, no barrier, just the seamless slide of his shadows against her skin and the devastating intimacy of moving together without thought.

The fourth position required even more reach. Controls positioned at shoulder height with multiple energy streams weaving together in elaborate patterns. She stretched to grasp the mechanisms, and shadows wrapped around her shoulders, steadying her as she leaned forward.

Large hands. That's what it felt like. Large, careful hands settling on her shoulders, thumbs resting against the curve of her neck.

"There's a knot forming in the upper left quadrant," she said, and her voice came out breathier than she wanted. She cleared her throat. Reached for the controls.

She had to lean farther forward, and the shadows slid from her shoulders to her waist. Anchoring her. The pressure of them spanning her ribs, fingers of darkness curving along the hollow beneath her lowest rib.

Her breath caught. Audibly, this time. No hiding it.

From across the chamber, she heard his breath hitch. Barely perceptible. Covered immediately by the hum of the ward-stones.

But she heard it.

"If this backs up much more, it could cause a cascade failure," she managed, as if she weren't acutely aware of every shadow-tendril pressed against her body.

"Can you clear it?" Strained. He sounded strained.

Good.

She manipulated the crystals, watching as the energy flows shifted and reorganized under her guidance. The shadows adjusted with each movement, anticipating her needs before she'd fully formed them. When she shifted her weight left, they compensated. When she reached higher, they tightened to keep her balanced.

Every small shift she made, catalogued. Memorized. Filed away through darkness.

"Almost... there." The knot dissolved, and the streams resumed their proper pattern. "Got it."

"Well done."

Two words. Spoken low, almost to himself, like praise he hadn't meant to give out loud. The warmth that bloomed through her chest was entirely disproportionate to the compliment.

She caught herself leaning back. Leaning into the shadows still curled around her waist. Barely caught herself. Barely stopped.

He went very still across the chamber. That stillness she was learning meant he'd noticed something he was trying very hard not to react to.

"Steady," he murmured, and the shadow at her waist traced a slow path along the curve of her hip before settling back into its position.

That was not functional.

That was not instructional.

That was his shadow stroking her hip, and he either knew exactly what he was doing or his power had abandoned all pretense of following orders.

She took a breath. Then another. Tried to remember what

breathing normally felt like before his shadows had mapped the geography of her waist.

"Almost finished with this sequence," he said, and something had gone tight in his voice. Like a rope pulled to its limit. "One more adjustment, then I can release you."

Release you. Like she was caught. Like she was something he was holding.

She supposed she was.

When she attempted the final crystal rotation, she noticed something warped in the energy patterns. "Wait." She studied the flows more closely. "There's an instability building in the secondary channels. If I rotate this now..."

"What do you see?"

"A feedback loop starting to form. The energy wants to circle back on itself." She adjusted her grip and found a different approach. "I need to redirect the flow first, then rotate."

She made the adjustment, watching the magical streams realign safely before completing the rotation. The entire sequence settled into a stable pattern.

"Well spotted." Something shifted in his tone. Not just approval now, but genuine respect. The kind that cost a Death Lord something to offer. "That could have been catastrophic."

The shadows lingered.

Resting against her skin. Around her wrists, her forearms, her waist. Holding her like he couldn't make himself let go.

Then they withdrew, slow and reluctant, trailing across her skin like fingers. Leaving paths of awareness everywhere they'd been. Leaving her exposed and strangely bereft in their absence.

She turned to find him watching her from the central platform.

Those dark eyes locked on her with an intensity that made her stomach flip and her knees threaten mutiny. His jaw was tight. His hands, still gloved, were gripping the primary controls hard enough that she could see the tension in his forearms.

"We should take a brief rest before the next configuration," he said, and she heard him draw a careful, measured breath. The breath of a man reassembling his composure from scattered pieces.

You felt it too. Don't you dare pretend you didn't.

"How many more configurations?" she asked, and she didn't bother keeping the edge out of her voice.

His gaze held hers.

"Several. Each one more complex than the last."

More complex. Which meant more contact. Longer contact. Shadows that would need to reach farther, hold tighter, wrap around more of her to guide the increasingly intricate work.

Heat spread through her chest and sank lower.

This is only because it's necessary, she told herself.

But the way he was looking at her, jaw clenched, eyes burning in the blue glow of the ward-stones, shadows coiling and uncoiling restlessly at his feet like they were straining to reach her again already...

That suggested necessity had stopped being the point a long time ago.

"Ready for the second sequence?" he asked. Quiet. Rough.

She moved to the new starting position, already hyperaware of where his shadows would land. Her skin prickled in anticipation, her body remembering every place they'd been.

She looked him in the eye.

"Ready."

His shadows surged toward her before he'd given them permission. She saw the flash of something raw cross his face before his control snapped them back to heel.

But not before the closest tendril had brushed the back of her hand.

Like it couldn't help itself.

Like he couldn't help himself.

She held his gaze and didn't step back.

XXXI.
DANTE

They completed the remaining ward configurations in near silence. The kind that sat heavy between two people refusing to acknowledge what was happening while it continued happening.

His shadows had stopped pretending to be instructional somewhere around the third sequence. By the fifth, they'd been moving with her like they'd known her body for years, anticipating the shift of her weight, the reach of her arms, the rhythm of her breathing. And she'd stopped fighting it. Stopped tensing when they found new skin. Started leaning into the contact like it was something she wanted rather than something she endured.

That was the part he couldn't stop thinking about.

They shouldn't respond to anyone but him. Yet they'd noticed the changes in her breathing, the way her pulse had steadied into trust.

"The systems are stable." He studied the magical flows, fighting the urge to let his power linger on her skin. "These ward-locks should hold for decades, assuming no external interference."

She stepped down from the platform, absently rubbing her wrists where his shadows had maintained contact. Dark traces marked her skin—evidence of a prolonged magical connection that would fade within hours.

Evidence that he'd touched her. That she'd allowed it.

His hands flexed at his sides.

"External interference seems to be the pattern." She didn't move toward the door. Instead, she leaned against the stone railing, her gaze following the streams of energy connecting to the other domains.

He should leave. Put distance between them before his shadows forgot themselves entirely.

He didn't move.

She was quiet, studying the energy flows. Then: "I've been watching these patterns for weeks now. Five separate realms." Her eyes tracked the streams. "Why not one place where all the dead go?"

"Because different deaths create different wounds." He moved closer, gesturing at the energy flows. "Souls in incompatible states destroy each other. They need separation to heal."

She turned to face him, and he realized he'd closed the distance to mere feet. Near enough that his shadows drifted toward her of their own accord.

"And then what? They just stay here forever?"

"Rebirth." The word came out rougher than intended.

Her eyes widened. "What?"

He shouldn't continue. But she was looking at him with that gaze that never flinched, and he explained anyway.

"Once a soul has processed its death, it may choose to return to the living world. New life. No memory of what came before."

She absorbed that in silence, her brows drawing together slightly. "So death isn't the end."

"Not usually. The death realms are waypoints. We process the transitions, give souls time to heal before they begin again."

"But if someone dies here..."

"For souls already claimed by the realms, death here is final. The cycle ends permanently." His voice flattened. "For mortals, it's different. Your soul would pass to whichever realm claims you."

"And which realm would that be for me?"

He didn't answer. Couldn't. Because the thought of her soul passing to any realm but his...

She seemed to read the answer in his silence. Her gaze dropped to the dark traces on her wrists. His magic's mark on her skin. When she looked up again, her shoulders had squared, chin lifting.

"The tribute system." Her voice sharpened. "If death is just part of a natural cycle, if the realms exist to help souls heal... where exactly do living sacrifices fit into this cosmic balance?"

There it was.

He could deflect. Offer explanations about strengthening barriers, maintaining balance.

He couldn't lie to her.

"They don't."

His shadows thickened, agitated by his own admission. By the truth he'd never spoken aloud to any tribute before.

"The tribute system is archaic. A relic from when the barriers were new and humans feared what existed beyond death. It began as a partnership. Mortals helping strengthen barriers." He paused. "The wards haven't required sacrifice to function for ages."

Silence.

She didn't move, but her eyes narrowed. "You're telling me I was sent here, chained, marked for death, for nothing?"

"For politics." The admission tasted like ash. "The human kingdoms fear what would happen if they stopped. We allow them to believe refusing would bring catastrophe."

She studied him with that gaze, and he wondered what she saw. Whether the truth made him more or less monstrous in her eyes.

"Have any tributes survived?"

"No."

She was quiet, processing. He watched her work through conclusions that tightened his chest.

"You could stop it. Refuse them."

"I could." He'd considered it countless times, always finding reasons to maintain tradition instead. "But the other Death Lords would continue. If I alone refused, the human kingdoms would perceive weakness. Send their tributes to other domains where survival is even less likely."

"So you maintain it because you're all too proud to be the first to blink."

His shadows reached for her again, drawn by the challenge in her voice, the fearlessness that never failed to affect him. "Yes."

She pushed off the railing, moving closer. Near enough now that he could count the rapid beat of her pulse at her throat.

"At least you're honest about it." Her voice had dropped, intimate. "Most would dress it up in noble purpose."

"I've lived too long for lies."

She held his gaze, her lips pressing into a thin line before relaxing. Then she nodded once. "Good to know where you actually stand."

"Does it change anything?"

"I'm still trapped either way." But her tone carried less bitterness than it had weeks ago. "At least now I know the truth."

His shadows curled around her wrist. That same place they'd maintained contact during the ward-work, where his magic had left traces. He should pull back. Should maintain distance.

Her breath caught. Barely audible, but he noticed it.

The tension between them shifted. Still present, but no longer sharp with anger. His chest felt tight, his shadows restless against her skin.

Far more dangerous than fury.

"I should prepare for tomorrow." Though part of him wanted to keep her here, keep this unexpected honesty flowing between them. Keep her near enough to touch. "We're visiting the other courts. They won't be as forthcoming."

She held his gaze for another heartbeat, her chin lifting slightly. Defiance or decision, he couldn't tell. His shadows tightened fractionally around her wrist, possessive.

Then she pulled back, and the loss of contact felt like tearing.

"Try to get some rest, Reaper." She paused at the threshold and glanced back. "You look like you haven't slept in decades."

His lips twitched. "More like centuries."

Her answering smile was brief but genuine before she disappeared from view.

He watched the empty doorway, his shadows reaching after her.

Unable to accept the increasing distance, unable to retreat to the isolation that had kept him safe.

XXXII.
BRYNN

Brynn found Dante in his private study before dawn. He stood hunched over his desk, surrounded by maps and intelligence reports spread across every available surface. His sleeves were rolled up to his elbows, revealing forearms corded with muscle as he moved documents around.

Her steps faltered.

Black gloves still covered his hands, but something about seeing him like this, shirt pushed back, absorbed in work, made her pulse do something inconvenient. She'd seen him unleash his power. Watched him command an entire court with a single word. But this felt more intimate somehow. The Reaper doing paperwork. The most feared Death Lord in existence, frowning at supply reports like they'd personally offended him.

She had bigger problems today than his forearms.

She paused in the doorway. The maps showed a territory she didn't recognize. Desert stretches broken by mountain ranges, scarred dunes, fortress cities carved into cliffsides. Red markers dotted the landscape like blood drops.

"We're visiting Seraphina today." He didn't look up. "Her court feeds on violence. Everyone there died brutal deaths. War, murder, accidents. They'll see you as a weakness to exploit."

That rough tone stirred irritation and something less convenient inside her.

"I can handle myself, Reaper."

He went still. Papers stopped moving under his hands. When he looked up, those dark eyes held an edge that hadn't been there yesterday.

"Not there." Weight pressed into each word.

Brynn stepped into the study. His shadows shifted as she approached, darkness bunching around his boots like muscles tensing for a fight. One tendril curled toward her ankle before snapping back to his side.

Even his shadows couldn't decide what to do with her.

"Then explain instead of issuing orders."

His fingers curled into the parchment, crumpling the edges. The muscle along his jaw tightened.

"Seraphina believes strength is the only thing that matters. She's been hostile to cooperation between courts from the beginning." He straightened to his full height, and the room shrank. "Recent ward failures near her territory give us reason to investigate, but she won't welcome scrutiny."

Brynn studied the tension in his shoulders. The way he held his body like a blade angled toward the door. There was history here. Conflicts that predated her by eons.

"Hostile how?"

He gathered several reports into a neat stack, movements sharper than necessary. "She believes the old ways were better. Each court isolated, ruling through strength alone." He tapped one of the red markers. "She'll use anything she can find to drive a wedge between us. To prove that cooperation makes me weak."

The way he said it, the weight on certain words, pauses where there should have been none, made her wonder what he wasn't telling her.

"What aren't you telling me?"

His gaze snapped to hers. Approval flickered across his face before he could hide it. Like she'd passed a test she hadn't known she was taking.

"She and I have disagreed on policy for as long as anyone remembers." His voice dropped lower, into that register that made her stomach tighten. "Don't let her goad you into anger. That's when she's most dangerous. And don't trust anything she tells you about the other Death Lords." A beat. "Or about me. She has her own agenda."

There. That hint of vulnerability beneath the command. Whatever Seraphina might reveal, he was worried about it. About what Brynn might learn. What she might believe.

The question sat on her tongue. What could Seraphina possibly tell her that he hadn't? But she swallowed it. Not now. Not when he looked like that, coiled tight, every line of his body braced for something worse than a diplomatic visit.

"When do we leave?"

"Within the hour." He moved to a cabinet and withdrew traveling gear. Dark leather armor designed to blend with shadows, reinforced with wards that shimmered faintly in the low light.

This wasn't diplomacy. This was walking into enemy territory armed.

"Thief."

The way he said it pulled her attention back like a hand on her wrist. Quiet. Almost intimate. Nothing like the cold dismissal it had been weeks ago.

His gaze held hers. "Whatever happens there, whatever she says, you're under my protection. Don't let pride make you forget that."

Her chest went tight. Not from fear. From the way his voice roughened on *protection*, like the word cost him something.

He was worried. For her. And she liked that way too much.

"I won't do anything reckless," she promised.

One dark eyebrow rose. His expression suggested he doubted every word, but the corners of his mouth softened. Not quite a smile. Close enough to count.

"Good." He held her gaze a beat longer than necessary. Then turned back to his maps.

The shadows continued their restless dance around the room, coiling and uncoiling. One drifted toward the doorway where she stood, hovering near her hip before retreating.

Hunter preparing for battle. Death Lord bracing for conflict.

Whatever waited in Seraphina's court had even the Reaper on edge.

Brynn adjusted the leather armor across her shoulders and told herself the flutter in her stomach was nerves.

She was a terrible liar.

XXXIII.
BRYNN

An hour later, dressed in the leathers he'd provided, reinforced with magic she could feel humming against her skin, Brynn met Dante in the east corridor. His shadows moved with more purpose than usual, coiling and uncoiling around him like something caged.

He turned without greeting.

Brynn stepped into his path. "Before we go, I need information I can actually use. Not just warnings."

He stopped. Those dark eyes studied her face with the same intensity he'd use to gauge a threat.

"The desert kills the weak before they reach her gates." His voice dropped. "She'll judge every word, every gesture. Looking for something to exploit."

Brynn absorbed this, filing the patterns away. Court politics, but with actual murder instead of social ruin.

"What about her personally?"

"Intelligent. Ruthless." His expression darkened, shadows deepening around his eyes. "She pushes boundaries until something breaks."

"Noted."

They stepped into the transport circle together. His shadows wrapped around her immediately, darkness pressing close with an urgency that felt almost possessive. Reality dissolved, her stomach flipping, but she'd learned not to fight the sensation.

The world reformed.

Heat slammed into her, stealing moisture from her lungs. They stood on sandstone under merciless light. Sweat formed on her skin immediately, the leather clinging to her body in ways that would become unbearable within minutes.

"The sun burns mortal skin in minutes." Dante's shadows spread overhead, creating a canopy above her. "That's the least dangerous thing here."

She stood inside his shadow like it was the most natural thing in the world. His darkness shielding her from the sun while the rest of him radiated tension. Something about that made her chest ache in a way she refused to examine.

Brynn turned slowly, taking in Seraphina's domain.

Endless desert stretched in all directions. Red sand broken by jagged mountains rising like bone against a cloudless sky. What first appeared as wind-sculpted dunes revealed itself as something else entirely. Too-straight ridgelines. Dark metal glinting in sunlight.

Buried weapons. Thousands upon thousands of swords, spears, and axes driven blade-first into sand. Marking where warriors fell and stayed.

"Battlefield burials." Her throat was already dry.

"Every grain has tasted blood." Something in his tone suggested he'd witnessed some of those battles personally.

Ahead, a massive mesa dominated the landscape, its cliffs rising hundreds of feet from the desert floor. The fortress wasn't built atop the mesa. It was carved directly into the rock face, hollowed from stone like a wasp's nest burrowed into wood.

Multiple levels descended into the cliff, each tier deeper than the one above, creating an inverted pyramid of carved chambers and passages. Windows punctured the red stone at irregular intervals. Black openings that could hide archers or worse. Watchtowers jutted from the cliff face like fingers, their positions seemingly random until her eye caught the pattern.

Every tower commanded overlapping sight lines. No blind spots. No approach that wasn't covered by multiple vantage points.

Whoever had designed this hadn't been thinking about beauty. They'd been thinking about killing fields.

The only entrance sat at ground level. A single canyon cutting through the mesa's base, forcing visitors into a passage between towering walls. Chokepoint turned killing field.

Dark spots marked the desert between their position and the fortress. What might have been oases except for the trenches surrounding each water source. Fortified. Defended. Even survival required conquest here.

"She's turned everything into warfare." Brynn stayed within his shadow-canopy, examining the efficiency while every survival instinct screamed at the hostility of this place.

"Seraphina was a general before becoming a Death Lord." Something shifted in Dante's voice. Not quite admiration. Respect between equals who understood what it took to command the dead. "Every soul serving her died in battle and chose to continue fighting in death."

They began the trek across sand toward the canyon entrance. With each step, the scale became clearer. The mesa was enormous, large enough to house thousands. The carved fortress descended deep into stone, layer upon layer of chambers invisible from the surface.

Brynn was acutely aware of how exposed they were. Two figures crossing open desert toward a fortress designed to destroy armies. Dante walked beside her without urgency, his shadow-canopy shifting to track the sun's angle, adjusting to keep her covered. The care in it, the unconscious precision, made warmth tighten behind her ribs.

She focused on the fortress instead. Easier than focusing on him.

As they approached, warriors appeared on the cliff face. Figures moving along walkways and through windows, watching their approach with open interest. Not hidden. Making their presence known.

This was a fortress that wanted you to see its defenses. Wanted you to understand that assault was impossible.

The canyon mouth loomed ahead. Stone walls rising on either side, the passage barely wide enough for three people abreast. Murder holes pocked the cliff faces above. Arrow slits. Platforms where defenders could rain death on anyone trapped in the corridor.

"You can't assault this." Her voice came out rougher than intended, lungs protesting the heat. "You can only walk into a trap or be invited."

"Exactly." His shadows tightened around her as they entered the canyon. One tendril pressed against the small of her back, guiding her forward. His hand would have rested in the same spot, if he could touch her.

She didn't pull away.

The passage stretched for hundreds of feet. An eternity of exposure while walls blocked any escape. Heat radiated from stone that had baked under the desert sun for millennia. Sweat ran down Brynn's temples.

Then the canyon opened.

The courtyard beyond was carved directly from the mesa's interior. A circular space hollowed from rock, open to the burning sky above. Bloodstone paved the ground, its surface polished to a brightness that gleamed like fresh wounds.

Carved doorways punctured the walls at ground level, passages leading deeper into the fortress. Walkways and balconies spiraled up the interior, each level connected by staircases carved from the cliff. Warriors lined every level, watching.

Weapons covered every available surface. Not stored but displayed. Swords mounted on walls within arm's reach. Spear racks positioned at intervals. Axes, maces, and morning stars arranged like artwork but clearly functional. Every decoration doubled as an armory.

The design was efficient in a way that made her skin prickle. The courtyard walls funneled desert winds, creating ventilation despite the enclosed space. The circular design eliminated corners where attackers could take cover. The multiple levels provided firing positions at every height.

Warriors moved along the upper walkways. Men and women who carried themselves with the confidence of those who'd never known defeat. Every single one had died in battle and chosen to continue fighting in death.

Every single one had their eyes on Brynn, and none of them were being subtle about it.

She kept her spine straight. Let them look.

"The Reaper." One guard called down from a second-level balcony, voice carrying across stone. "And his... *companion*."

The pause before the word was surgical. Designed to diminish.

Dante's shadows darkened visibly. The temperature plummeted even through the blazing heat, and the guard's smile faltered for just a moment before he recovered it.

Brynn filed that reaction away. The Reaper's shadows responded to insults aimed at her the same way they responded to direct threats. Interesting. Dangerous. Something she absolutely should not find as satisfying as she did.

"Lady Seraphina awaits in the throne room." The guard's composure had returned, but his eyes kept flicking to the shadows pooling at Dante's feet. "She's looking forward to seeing your mortal."

Your mortal. Like she was a pet. A possession.

Brynn held the guard's gaze until he looked away first. Small victory. The only kind available when you were walking into a fortress designed to break armies and all you had was a sharp tongue and borrowed leather armor.

Dante moved toward the carved doorway. His shadows followed, pulling away from her. Desert sun hit her full force for three brutal seconds before the darkness lurched back, wrapping around her without his permission.

He didn't turn around. But his shoulders went rigid.

She followed him into the fortress without a word.

XXXIV.
BRYNN

The walls were lined with weapons mounted in glass cases. Swords with nicked blades, war hammers dark with stains, spears still bearing fragments of the armor they'd pierced. Tattered banners hung from iron brackets, their fabric torn and bloodstained, displaying heraldry of dead armies.

Every single display was a trophy. A kill. A conquest.

The Death Lords really committed to their aesthetics. She'd give them that.

Brynn took it all in. The spacing of the displays, the positioning of certain weapons for quick access even behind the glass, the corridor designed to intimidate while remaining functional.

The heat wasn't helping. Sweat still clung to her skin beneath the leathers, making her aware of how exposed she felt here. How mortal. Seraphina wasn't just showing off. Every visitor would understand exactly what kind of power they faced before reaching the throne room.

Dante walked beside her, close enough that his shadows brushed the edge of her boots. She didn't know if that was intentional or if his darkness was doing that thing again—reaching for her when he wasn't paying attention.

She told herself she wasn't paying attention either.

But she'd noticed his hands. Gloved fingers flexing once when they'd crossed into Seraphina's territory, then going deliberately still. Like he was reminding himself to stay controlled.

She wondered what it cost him. All that restraint, all the time.

The throne room opened before them like a cavern carved from red stone. Columns of marble supported the vaulted ceiling, but between them, two-handed swords had been driven point-first into the floor, their crossguards forming archways. Shields hung on the walls like coins, some split clean in half, others bearing the dents and gouges of last stands.

The air tasted of metal and old blood.

Brynn's mouth had gone dry. The Forsaken court was unsettling in its beauty, all impossible architecture and living shadows. This was different. This was a room that wanted her to know exactly how many ways she could die in it.

The throne was built from stacked weapons. Broken blades, shattered axes, splintered spear hafts welded together into a seat of metal and conquest.

And sitting at the center, looking entirely comfortable on her throne of broken weapons, was Seraphina.

Up close, she was even more imposing than she'd appeared from a distance. Six feet of violence, watching their approach with the calm of someone who'd carved her legend in blood and wasn't finished yet.

Brynn forced herself to breathe normally, to keep her expression neutral even though every nerve in her body wanted to step backward. She'd walked into hostile territory before. Noble estates, guilds that would kill her if they caught her. This was just another threat to navigate.

Except this one could probably snap her neck while carrying on a conversation.

Dante's shoulder shifted almost imperceptibly. Angling toward her. Putting himself a half-step ahead without making it obvious.

She shouldn't have found that comforting. She definitely shouldn't have felt her spine straighten because of it.

"Reaper." Seraphina's voice carried across the throne room

without effort. The kind of command that came from years of shouting orders across battlefields. "Still collecting strays, I see."

Heat flooded Brynn's face before she could stop it.

Seraphina noticed. The corner of her mouth curved.

Brynn locked her jaw and gave nothing else away. But beside her, Dante went still. Utterly, completely still. The kind of stillness that preceded violence.

His shadows spread an inch wider across the floor.

He didn't rise to it. "Seraphina." His voice stayed level. "Ward failures have been reported across multiple territories. We're investigating to determine the scope and cause."

No pleasantries. No pretense that this was a friendly visit.

Brynn stayed silent, studying Seraphina's face for micro-expressions, tells, anything useful. But part of her attention kept drifting to the shadows pooling at her feet. They'd curled around her ankle now.

She doubted he'd noticed. His focus was fixed on Seraphina, his profile sharp as cut glass in the red-tinted light. Jaw set. Eyes cold.

He looked like what he was. Death, wearing a beautiful face.

She needed to stop noticing his face.

"Ward failures." Seraphina rose from her throne. She was taller than Brynn had estimated, her presence filling the space in a way that pressed against the walls. "And you brought *this* to inspect magical infrastructure older than her entire bloodline?"

The dismissiveness made Brynn's jaw clench.

She kept her mouth shut. Her nails found her palms.

Darkness pooled deeper at Dante's feet, gathered tight.

"She's proven exceptionally skilled at reading ward-magic patterns." His voice stayed level, but an edge crept underneath. The kind of tone that made her pulse skip even when it wasn't directed at her. "Her evaluations have been invaluable."

Invaluable.

The word shouldn't have meant anything. It was a political defense, nothing more. A Death Lord protecting his asset in front of another predator.

It still landed where it shouldn't have.

"Invaluable." Seraphina descended the steps from her throne, and

Brynn watched her move with the kind of lethal grace that reminded her, uncomfortably, of someone else. "You always did have interesting definitions of value, *Dante*."

His actual name instead of his title. Familiar. Intimate.

Cold slid through Brynn's chest.

You always did. How long had they known each other? What history lived in that casual use of his name, in the way Seraphina's eyes swept over him like she knew exactly what was underneath that controlled exterior?

Her nails pressed harder into her palms.

Beside her, Dante's gloved hand twitched. Once. The barest movement. If she hadn't been watching—if she hadn't been so pathetically aware of his every movement—she would have missed it.

But she was. And she didn't.

She wondered if Seraphina had made that hand twitch for different reasons, once.

The thought burned more than it should have.

Seraphina moved closer, and Brynn had to actively fight the urge to step back. Every instinct screamed at her to maintain distance, to not let this woman into her space.

But retreating would be weakness. And weakness here meant blood.

"A mortal." Seraphina circled them slowly, examining Brynn from different angles like she was evaluating a weapon. "Who thinks she understands forces that predate her species by millennia." Her eyes raked over Brynn with cold appraisal. "Tell me, little thief. What qualifies you to judge my wards?"

The question was a trap. Answer too confidently, and she'd be arrogant. Too humbly, and she'd confirm Seraphina's verdict that she was worthless.

Brynn met her gaze directly, forcing herself not to look away even though those eyes made her skin crawl. "I read patterns. Ward magic has patterns."

"Patterns." Seraphina's smile widened, showing teeth. "How delightfully simple." She stopped circling, standing close enough that Brynn could see the individual scars on her arms. Dozens of them, maybe hundreds. Each one a story written in violence. "And if I asked you to demonstrate this pattern-reading on my person, would you see anything interesting?"

The threat was subtle but unmistakable.

Brynn's fingers twitched at her sides. She was standing within arm's reach of a Death Lord who could end her before Dante's shadows crossed the distance.

The shadows at her ankles tightened.

"We all have documented failures in our courts now." Dante's voice cut through the tension, drawing Seraphina's attention away. "We're trying to understand what's happening and whether the incidents are connected."

He shifted as he spoke, positioning himself between them. Subtle enough to look casual. Deliberate enough that Brynn felt the wall of cold air that always surrounded him brush against her arm.

His hand grazed hers as he moved. Gloved fingers against her bare wrist. Brief. Barely there.

Stay calm. I'm here.

She couldn't possibly know that's what it meant. Could be accidental. Could be nothing.

Her heart stuttered anyway.

She shouldn't have noticed. Shouldn't have felt her shoulders drop a fraction as his shadow fell across her.

The pressure eased just enough for her to breathe.

"Connected." Seraphina's focus shifted entirely to Dante now. "You think the failures aren't random?"

Brynn watched her face. Was that surprise? Concern? Or was she asking because she already knew the answer?

But she also watched the way Seraphina looked at him. The assessment in those eyes. The familiarity.

She hated that she noticed. Hated that she cared.

"That's what we're trying to determine." Dante's shadows spread across the floor, slow and deliberate. "Which is why we need access to your ward-stones. To document the damage and compare it to what we've found elsewhere."

Seraphina studied him for a long moment. Her gaze moved from

Dante to the shadows pooling at his feet, then slid to where those shadows curled around Brynn's boots.

Amusement flickered in her expression.

Wonderful. The terrifying war goddess found her entertaining. That couldn't possibly end badly.

"Access to my defensive infrastructure." Her smile turned sharp. "How convenient for the Reaper to map my vulnerabilities."

There it was. The real concern. Not ward failures. Trust. Or the complete absence of it.

Brynn watched the two Death Lords face each other, both radiating power that pressed against her. This wasn't just about wards. This was old grudges and ancient politics stretching back long before she was born.

And somewhere in those centuries, Seraphina had learned to call him by his real name.

None of that was Brynn's business. None of it should matter to her at all.

"Your vulnerabilities are already exposed if the wards are failing." Dante's voice carried steel. "We're offering to help you understand why."

"Help." Seraphina laughed. Sharp, humorless. "From the Death Lord who's spent the last hundred years in isolation?" She stepped closer to him, close enough that Brynn could see the way his jaw tightened, the way the muscle flexed beneath pale skin. "Forgive me if I'm suspicious of your sudden interest in my domain's security."

Two Death Lords circling, deciding whether to fight or concede. Brynn's every instinct told her to put distance between herself and whatever was about to happen. But moving would draw attention back to her. And Seraphina's attention was the last thing she wanted.

"If the ward network is degrading, it affects all of us." His shadows had gone still now. "Whatever's causing this won't stop at court boundaries."

Seraphina's expression shifted. Skepticism giving way to calculation. "You're genuinely concerned."

"Yes."

Silence stretched between them. Brynn barely dared to breathe.

Finally, Seraphina stepped back. "Your pet can examine my wards." Her gaze cut to Brynn. "But if she breaks anything, I'm keeping her."

"No."

The shadows at Brynn's feet surged outward, spreading across the stone. They coiled up her calves, wrapped around her waist, pulled her half a step closer to him, before they seemed to catch themselves and went still.

Brynn's heart slammed against her ribs.

He still hadn't looked at her. His eyes stayed fixed on Seraphina, cold and lethal. But his darkness had just claimed her in front of another Death Lord, and from the way Seraphina's smile widened, she'd noticed every bit of it.

"Interesting," Seraphina murmured.

Dante's jaw tightened further. That muscle jumping again.

The shadows retreated slowly, settling back into their usual pool around his feet. But Brynn could still feel the echo of them against her skin.

She risked a glance at his profile. At the tension in his shoulders, the rigid set of his spine. He had to know what he'd just revealed. Had to know Seraphina would file it away and use it later.

He'd done it anyway.

Her chest tightened in a way she couldn't explain.

"Fine." Seraphina's smile was all teeth and promise now. "Let's see what your little thief can do, then."

XXXV.
BRYNN

They were moving through corridors barely wide enough for two people, forced into single file past alcoves where guards could hide. Holes gaped in the ceiling above. Positions for archers.

Every step deeper felt like walking into a throat that could swallow them.

"Efficient," Brynn observed.

"War teaches efficiency." Seraphina shrugged like she'd designed these traps personally. "Pretty corridors don't stop enemies."

Dante said nothing. He'd fallen into step behind her when the corridor narrowed, close enough that the cold radiating off him brushed against her back.

She caught the way his eyes moved over every feature, every potential threat. Assessing. Calculating. His shadows stayed tight against his boots, coiled and ready.

At least one of them was focused on the actual danger here.

They passed through doors into a chamber that felt different from the rest of the fortress. The walls were carved with symbols that pulsed with energy. Ward-magic, old and powerful, hummed against her skin like static.

At the center stood a ward-stone nearly eight feet tall, its crystalline surface shot through with veins of red that matched the desert stone outside.

Even from the doorway, Brynn could see fractures spiderwebbing across the surface in patterns that made her skin prickle.

"There." Seraphina jerked her chin toward the stone. "See what your expertise makes of that."

Dante positioned himself where he could observe both the stone and Seraphina. The same way he'd positioned himself in the throne room.

"When did this damage first appear?" His voice was cool, professional.

"When do you think?" Seraphina's smile turned edged. "Your pet claims to understand this magic. Let her tell us."

Pet. Brynn's jaw tightened, but she let it go. Not worth the ammunition. And rising to the bait would only prove Seraphina right about her.

She approached the stone, aware that every movement was being judged. Scarring radiated from several points across the matrix, forming a web that she recognized immediately.

She'd seen this signature before. In the Forsaken domain, in the emergency repairs they'd made. The saboteur's work.

But admitting that now would be foolish.

"The damage suggests stress over time." She let her hand hover along the crystal surface. Not touching, not revealing how much she actually understood. "But I'd need to examine the residue to determine specifics."

"Would you now?" Seraphina moved closer. "And what makes you think I'll let you put your mortal hands on my ward-stone?"

"Because you brought us here to survey the damage," Dante said, his voice carrying an edge that made the guards by the door shift their weight.

Brynn glanced at him. The tension along his jaw. The stillness in his body. Fighting his instincts. Letting her handle this but coiled to intervene.

She looked away before Seraphina could read anything in her face.

"I brought you here to see if your little thief could recognize what she was looking at." Seraphina's tone was designed to provoke. "So far, she's managing basic observations. Impressive for a mortal, though."

Impressive for a mortal. High praise from someone who collected corpses as décor.

Brynn kept her focus on the ward-stone. Her fingers curled against the crystal.

"The damage is unusual," she said. "I'd need to touch the stone to understand more."

"Unusual how?"

She chose her words with care. "The breaks follow lines in the structure rather than spreading randomly. It suggests targeted stress points."

"Targeted." Seraphina's laugh held no humor. "Such an interesting word choice. Are you suggesting someone deliberately damaged my ward-stone?"

The trap was set. Admitting their suspicions to a potential saboteur would be foolish, but refusing to answer might end their investigation before it started.

She could feel Dante's attention on her back. Waiting. Trusting her to navigate this.

"I'm suggesting the damage warrants examination," she said, threading the needle between truth and caution.

"How diplomatic." Seraphina studied her for a long moment. "Very well. Touch the stone. But know that if you damage it further, the consequences will be painful."

"Threaten her again."

Three words. Dante's voice had gone so soft it was barely audible, but the temperature in the chamber dropped ten degrees. His shadows spread across the floor, no longer coiled but *reaching*, and the guards by the door took an involuntary step back.

Brynn's heart slammed against her ribs.

He hadn't moved. Hadn't raised his voice. But the Reaper had just made it very clear what would happen if Seraphina touched her.

Seraphina raised an eyebrow but said nothing more.

Brynn placed her hands flat on the crystal surface, forcing her attention back where it belonged. Ward-magic hummed against her palms, familiar now after days of training. But underneath that familiarity, wrongness pulsed through the stone.

The fractures followed too precise a pattern. Targeting exactly the right points to cause disruption while appearing natural.

Sabotage. No question.

She wasn't about to announce that conclusion.

"The signature is complex," she said. "There are layers of different energies here."

"Layers?" Seraphina stepped closer to the stone. "What kind of layers?"

"I'd need more time to analyze them properly. And ideally, I'd want to compare this to your other ward-stones."

"Would you?" A flicker crossed Seraphina's face, gone before Brynn could read it. "And in the process, you'd gain intimate knowledge of my defensive network. How convenient."

The accusation hung in the air.

"If we wanted to attack your domain, we wouldn't announce ourselves and request a tour," Dante said. He'd pulled his shadows back under control, his voice level again.

"Wouldn't you? The best way to learn an enemy's weaknesses is to offer help while gathering intelligence."

Seraphina trailed her hand across the fractured surface. She wasn't examining it—she already knew every crack.

Dante's shadows went rigid against the floor.

"We aren't your enemies," he said. His voice was level. The power crackling around him was not.

"Enemies often hide behind friendly faces." Seraphina circled the stone, trailing her fingers along the crystal. "Tell me, Reaper. How do I know this investigation isn't a cover for sabotage?"

"Because your ward-stones have been failing faster than what you reported at the council," Brynn pointed out, trying to pull the tension back from the edge before it snapped.

The words were out before she could catch them.

Idiot. She'd just handed Seraphina ammunition to deflect suspicion.

Seraphina went still. "Faster." She repeated the word like she was turning it over, examining its edges. "I reported failures at the council meeting, yes. But I never mentioned their rate. Or that they'd been accelerating." Her smile widened. "How do you know that?"

The blood drained from Brynn's face.

The council had disclosed that all courts were experiencing ward failures. But the speed, the escalation, the pattern of increasing frequency—Seraphina hadn't shared that. They only knew because of what they'd found in the Forsaken domain and pieced together from the sabotage patterns.

She'd just revealed they knew more than they should.

"The residue on your stone suggests recent damage layered over older breaks," she managed, keeping her voice steady through sheer force of will. "That implies acceleration."

"Does it?" Seraphina pressed closer. "Or did someone tell you what to look for before you arrived?"

Brynn's pulse quickened. She kept her expression steady.

"The way the energy still resonates. Older damage would have settled differently. This feels fresh. Within the past few weeks."

An educated guess. She committed to it anyway.

"Interesting." Seraphina's tone gave nothing. "And you base this on what training, exactly?"

"I'm a fast learner."

"Indeed you are. Fast enough to identify sabotage. Fast enough to recognize targeted damage." She was closer now, close enough that Brynn could feel the heat radiating off her skin. "One might wonder where you learned such things."

They were losing ground. Seraphina wasn't just being evasive. She was turning the investigation back on them.

Making *them* the suspects.

"Perhaps we should examine your other ward-stones," Dante said, reclaiming the room. "A broader sample would provide better data."

"I don't think so."

"If you're not willing to cooperate—" His voice dropped.

"Oh, I'm perfectly willing to cooperate," Seraphina interrupted, pleasant as poison. "But cooperation requires trust. And trust, Reaper, must be earned."

She moved toward the chamber exit. "When you're ready to share what you really know about these failures, and who you really suspect, perhaps we can have a more productive conversation."

Seraphina had revealed almost nothing while extracting information they hadn't meant to give. Whether innocent or guilty, she was playing a game several moves ahead of them.

And they'd just shown her their hand.

XXXVI.
BRYNN

As they followed her out of the chamber, the corridors felt even more oppressive on the way back. Every shadow potentially hiding a guard, every alcove a reminder of how deeply they'd walked into enemy territory.

Dante's expression gave nothing away. His shadows did. Darkness writhed around his boots, coiling and snapping in patterns she'd learned meant he was fighting his temper.

"Your investigation techniques need work," Seraphina said conversationally as they climbed the stone steps. "Too eager, too revealing. Fatal when dealing with enemies."

"Are you our enemy?" Dante asked, his voice quiet in that way that made the air feel thinner.

"That depends." Seraphina paused at a junction, glancing back. "Everyone who enters my domain is evaluated for threat level." Her gaze fixed on Brynn. "Your little pet here... she's more interesting than I expected."

Brynn kept her expression neutral, but her nails bit into her palms. She'd proven herself capable, and this Death Lord still couldn't find a better word than *pet*.

They reached the main level of the fortress, where corridors branched off into different sections. Seraphina gestured toward what appeared to be guest quarters. Comfortable spaces with excellent views of what was probably an execution ground.

"You'll need to rest before traveling in this heat," she said. "The desert doesn't forgive weakness."

"We can manage—" Brynn started.

"Can you?" Seraphina's smile cut. "How refreshingly confident."

A guard approached Dante, murmuring about escort protocols and the safest route through the desert. He turned to address the warrior, his attention diverted by logistics.

Seraphina waited exactly long enough for his focus to shift before stepping closer to Brynn.

Too close.

"You think you know him, little thief?" Her voice dropped to barely above a whisper. "The great Reaper?"

Brynn held her ground through the chill running down her spine.

"I know enough."

"Do you?" Seraphina tilted her head. "Tell me, has he mentioned the last human who got too close?"

Brynn forced herself not to react. Her fingers curled tight.

"What are you talking about?"

"He hasn't told you." Seraphina's laugh was soft, merciless. "How interesting. The great Reaper, keeping secrets from his pet."

Brynn glanced toward Dante, still engaged with the guard.

He was hiding something. She just didn't know what yet.

"He doesn't scare me," she said, lifting her chin.

"He should." Seraphina's expression shifted. The mockery fell away, and what replaced it was worse. It looked almost like pity. "We all should. You're playing with forces that have destroyed everything they've touched."

Brynn studied her face, trying to separate truth from manipulation. Seraphina held her gaze without flinching.

"You're trying to turn me against him."

"I'm trying to save your life." Seraphina's voice dropped lower. "The wards aren't the only things breaking. Ask him about the tribute he became attached to. And what happened when she started asking the wrong questions."

She'd assumed this was unprecedented. All of it. The way his shadows curled toward her when he wasn't paying attention. The way his voice roughened when he said *thief*, like the word had changed shape in his mouth. The way he'd spread his darkness over her in the desert without thinking, adjusting it to track the sun so it never left her skin exposed.

She'd assumed she was the first person to stand this close to him and not run.

The suggestion that someone else had stood exactly where she was standing. That he'd watched someone else with that same intensity. Shielded someone else with those same shadows. Said someone else's name in that same low, rough voice.

And that person was probably dead now.

Because of him.

Her nails carved crescents into her palms. She kept her face still, kept her breathing even, kept every single thing she was feeling locked behind her teeth. Because if Seraphina saw what those words had done, she'd won.

"You're lying."

"Am I?" Seraphina stepped back, her voice returning to normal volume as Dante finished with the guard. The shift was seamless. Performer to audience in a single breath.

Dante's attention snapped to them. His shadows tightened, darkness pooling between him and Seraphina.

"Is there a problem?"

His voice was neutral. The warning underneath was not.

"No problem." Seraphina's mouth curved. "Just sharing history with your companion. The desert has so many fascinating stories."

She watched Brynn as she said it. Watching to see if the seed had taken root.

"What kind of stories?" Dante's voice could have frozen the desert outside.

"Oh, the usual tales of mortals who ventured too deep into our realm." Seraphina gestured toward the guest quarters. "Most don't end well, I'm afraid. The death realm has a way of consuming those who don't belong."

Her tone shifted to something light, pleasant, hollow. "Rest well. The journey back to your court will be... illuminating."

As Seraphina disappeared down a corridor, Brynn felt Dante's focus settle on her.

"She told you something."

Of course he'd noticed.

Brynn met his gaze. Seraphina's words sat in her chest like swallowed glass.

Ask him about the tribute he became attached to. Ask him what happened when she started asking the wrong questions.

She wanted to demand the truth. Wanted to ask if any of this was real or if she was just history repeating itself. If the way he looked at her meant what she thought it meant, or if someone else had stood exactly where she was standing and believed the same thing.

But the questions wouldn't come. Because asking meant hearing an answer. And she wasn't ready for what that answer might break.

"Nothing important," she said.

Dante studied her face for a long moment. His shadows reached toward her, tentative, and she stepped out of range before they could touch her.

A flicker crossed his expression. There and gone.

She turned toward the guest quarters and didn't look back.

XXXVII.
DANTE

The guest quarters Seraphina provided were luxurious in the way a gilded cage was luxurious. Stone furniture, art depicting battles, a sleeping alcove through an archway draped with silk. Everything designed to impress while reminding visitors they were surrounded by violence.

Dante's shadows spread through both spaces immediately, probing for passages, listening devices, magical surveillance. Finding nothing didn't ease him. Seraphina was too skilled for crude methods.

The stone walls still radiated heat from the day's sun. Comfortable for his kind. Punishing for mortal flesh.

"The heat's getting to you," he said, watching Brynn sink into one of the chairs with less grace than usual.

Her face was flushed. She moved stiffly, carefully, like her muscles were staging a revolt the desert crossing had cost more than she'd admit.

"I'm fine."

The deflection was automatic. So was the way she leaned back against the chair as if sitting upright had become a negotiation.

His gaze caught the tremor in her hands. The way she hadn't looked at him since they'd left Seraphina.

Whatever had shifted during that whispered conversation was worse than exhaustion.

"You're not fine." He moved to the window, positioning himself where he could watch both the courtyard below and her reflection in the glass. "And before you argue, I mean physically. The heat, the realm. Your body isn't meant for this."

"My body has handled worse."

The edge in her voice made power prickle along his shoulders. Whatever Seraphina had whispered was working through her like venom.

"What did Seraphina tell you?"

"Nothing worth repeating." She didn't meet his eyes. She focused instead on the art across from her. Cavalry charging through fallen enemies.

The woman who'd argued strategy with him this morning wouldn't even look at him now.

Seraphina had found her mark.

"Whatever she said—" He stopped. Watched her shoulders tense. "I'm not going to tell you to dismiss it. But without knowing what it was, I can't tell you which parts were true and which were designed to cause damage."

"I don't want to talk about it."

He studied her profile. The set of her jaw. The way she gripped the armrests like they were the only solid things in the room.

She wasn't ready. Pushing now would only drive her deeper into silence.

"All right." He leaned against the wall, creating distance even when everything in him pulled toward closing it. "The investigation didn't go as planned."

She took the safer topic like a lifeline. "No. She revealed nothing useful."

"While extracting information we hadn't intended to share." He kept his voice even. "Interrogation disguised as cooperation."

"Do you think she's the saboteur?"

"I think she's hiding something. Whether it's guilt or knowledge of who's responsible remains to be seen." He gave her room. "We'll need to investigate the other courts before drawing conclusions."

Brynn nodded. Her fingers stayed white-knuckled on the armrests. The flush in her cheeks had deepened.

"You need rest," he said, gentling his voice in a way he hadn't done for anyone in longer than he could remember.

"I need—" She stopped herself, throat working. "Yes. Rest."

Not what she'd been about to say. His shadows followed her movement as she stood, drawn by an instinct he couldn't suppress.

"I'll watch the chamber. Sleep while you can."

She moved toward the sleeping alcove, each step slower than the last. He watched her longer than he should have.

Then she paused halfway.

Her shoulders rose and fell with a breath that seemed to cost her something. One hand lifted toward the curtain, then dropped. She turned just enough for him to see the curve of her throat, the stubborn line of her jaw.

If she would just turn around. Just look at him. Just say whatever was eating her alive.

The space between them felt like it had its own gravity. Ten feet of stone floor. She was right there.

Her fingers curled into a fist at her side.

Please.

She continued forward without looking back, disappearing behind the silk barrier, and his chest gave way.

He stood motionless, staring at the curtain that now separated them. Thin silk. He could see the shadow of her moving behind it. The suggestion of her form as she crossed to the bed.

He took up a position where he could monitor both the entrance and the alcove. Close enough to protect. Far enough to honor the distance she'd demanded.

His shadows spread through the room, alert for disturbance. Some settled around the outer chamber, dutiful and focused. Others drifted toward the silk curtain, ignoring his commands, straining toward her.

He reined them back. They crept forward again.

From the alcove, the rustle of fabric. The creak of the bed frame as she turned over. She was trying to get comfortable. He needed to stop listening.

Another exhale. This one shakier.

His hands curled into fists against his thighs.

She was lying there awake. Alone with whatever doubts Seraphina had planted. And he couldn't reach her. Not because of distance. Because she'd drawn a line, and he would not cross it.

His shadows pooled at the threshold. Not touching the curtain. Pressing close to the boundary she'd drawn but not breaching it. One tendril curled under the edge. Just barely. Just enough to feel the air on the other side, warmer with her presence.

He should pull it back.

He didn't.

Minutes stretched. The fortress quieted around them. Guard shifts changing, conversations fading, the desert settling into evening stillness. Through that single shadow-tendril, he felt the moment her breathing changed.

The irregular pattern smoothing out. Exhaustion finally claiming what willingness couldn't provide.

She was asleep.

His shadows slid under the curtain without permission, pooling around the bed. Not touching her. He had that much control left. But close. Close enough to feel her warmth. To stand guard over her sleep even when she wouldn't let him guard anything else.

He didn't pull them back.

Behind silk curtains, she slept. Trusting him with her safety even when she wouldn't trust him with her thoughts. She could have demanded separate chambers. Insisted on walls instead of curtains, guards instead of him.

She still believed he wouldn't hurt her. She just didn't believe anything else right now.

The shadows lengthened across the floor as evening claimed the fortress. He remained motionless. He did not go to her. It was the hardest thing he'd done in a very long time.

XXXVIII.
DANTE

The eternal twilight wrapped around Dante like a familiar cloak, the cool air a relief after the punishing heat of Seraphina's domain.

He found no comfort in their return.

Brynn hadn't spoken since waking. She'd emerged from the sleeping alcove with shadows under her eyes and a blankness to her expression, accepted the travel rations he'd procured without comment, and followed him to the transport circle like a prisoner being escorted.

And now she was further away than ever.

The journey had passed in silence that felt like suffocation. Every attempt at conversation met with monosyllables. Every glance he stole showed him the same closed expression, the same distance.

Now she stood apart from him in the circle's aftermath, posture rigid, eyes focused somewhere over his shoulder rather than meeting his gaze. The wall she'd constructed had been reinforced by hours of whatever thoughts had been churning behind that mask.

"We should debrief," he said. Testing. Hoping for any crack in the distance between them.

"Fine."

One word. Flat. Final.

His shadows stirred restlessly around his boots, straining toward her despite his efforts to keep them contained. They remembered last night's closeness—her warmth, her scent, the steady rhythm of her breathing as she slept. They wanted it back.

He understood the feeling entirely too well.

She walked toward the main palace without waiting for him, her stride purposeful but stiff. The Forsaken Court's chill raised goosebumps on her bare arms. His hands flexed with the urge to pull her against him.

As if he could. As if touch was something he was allowed.

He matched her pace easily, his longer stride requiring no effort. "The other courts will need to be investigated. Thessa's domain, then Caelum's. Vex's, eventually."

"I assumed."

His jaw tightened.

This was the woman who'd spent their journey to the Violent Court asking questions about Death Lord politics, who'd insisted on understanding every nuance of their investigation strategy. Who'd leaned close to study maps with him, close enough that her scent had wrapped around his senses and made concentration nearly impossible.

Now she walked beside him like a stranger fulfilling an obligation.

They reached the main entrance, where servants bowed as they passed. Brynn acknowledged them with polite nods but didn't engage. No observations about the architecture. No questions about the servants she'd been slowly befriending. No glances at him to share some private observation, the way she'd started doing in recent weeks.

Nothing.

Just distance that formed a wall he couldn't breach.

The silence pressed against his skin as they climbed the staircase toward the residential levels.

She stopped at the landing where their corridors diverged, finally turning to face him.

Her expression was composed. Distant. The face of someone addressing a superior they didn't trust.

But her eyes—

For a heartbeat, before her jaw set and the anger rose to cover it, he saw hurt—the kind she'd never let him see if she could help it.

Something cracked in his chest.

"I need to rest properly. In my own chambers."

The words were reasonable. The tone was ice.

"Wait." The word came out rougher than intended.

He should let her go. Should respect the distance she was demanding. Should remember that he was the Reaper, that caring about mortals only led to grief, and that whatever Seraphina had poisoned her with was probably deserved.

He stepped closer instead.

Her breath caught. His shadows surged toward her. He barely managed to rein them back before they wrapped around her.

The way she'd let them, once before yesterday.

"Whatever Seraphina said—"

"I told you." She cut him off, but her voice wavered on the last word. "It's nothing important."

Another step. Close enough to count her eyelashes. Close enough to see the flutter of her pulse beneath the delicate skin of her throat.

Close enough to touch, if he dared.

"You haven't looked at me since yesterday." The words felt like pulling teeth. "You've barely spoken. Something she said changed things between us, and I can't—"

He stopped. Swallowed the rest. He couldn't fix what he didn't understand. He couldn't defend against accusations he hadn't heard. He couldn't stand this distance when he'd only just learned what closeness with her felt like.

She was staring at him now. Finally, *finally* meeting his eyes, and what he saw there made his breath catch in response.

Hurt. Confusion. Anger, yes. But beneath it, something that looked almost like longing. Like she wanted to close the distance between them as badly as he did.

Like she was fighting herself as hard as he was fighting himself.

"Please." He couldn't remember the last time he'd used that word. "Tell me what she said."

Her lips parted. The lower one trembled, just slightly, and his gaze dropped to it without permission. The soft pink of her mouth, the way her tongue darted out to wet her lips—

His shadows slipped their leash.

One tendril curled around her wrist before he could stop it. Just touching. The way they'd touched her during training, when she'd let them guide her movements and hadn't pulled away.

She didn't pull away now, either.

Her pulse jumped beneath the shadow's grip. He felt it like it was his own heartbeat, racing and ragged. Her breath came faster, chest rising and falling in a rhythm that made him want to step closer still, to press her against the wall and chase whatever she was hiding until she gave it up.

For one endless moment, they stood there. His shadow on her wrist. The space between them was charged with everything they weren't saying.

Her mouth opened. Her eyes softened.

She was going to tell him.

He could see it: the wall cracking, the words rising in her throat. Whatever Seraphina had said, whatever poison had been planted, she was going to let him in. Let him defend himself. Let him—

Her gaze dropped to the shadow wrapped around her wrist.

And the wall slammed back into place so fast he almost felt the impact.

She yanked her arm free. His shadow recoiled, wounded, and the loss of her pulse beneath his touch felt like amputation.

"Goodnight, Reaper."

The title landed like a blade between his ribs. Twisted. Buried to the hilt.

She barely used it anymore. Only when she was angry. When she wanted distance. When she wanted to remind them both what he really was.

She turned and walked away. Every line of her body rigid. Every step carrying her further from him.

He didn't follow.

His shadows writhed at his feet with something that felt like grief and want and rage all tangled together. The phantom sensation of her pulse still throbbed against the tendril that had touched her.

The click of her door closing echoed off the stone walls.

He stared at the empty corridor long after the sound faded. The tightness in his chest didn't ease. It deepened.

Dante tried to focus on reports from the other courts, analyzing patterns that might reveal the saboteur's identity.

His shadows crept toward the door without permission, straining in the direction of her chambers. He called them back. They went reluctantly, and he felt their displeasure like an ache behind his ribs.

Or perhaps that was his own.

Near midnight, he gave up pretending to focus. The maps and documents from their investigation lay scattered across his desk, marked with notes in his handwriting and her more casual script.

Their partnership, visible in ink and parchment.

He stared at a notation she'd made about ward harmonics, remembering the way she'd leaned over the desk to write it. Close enough that he caught the scent that haunted him now. Close enough that his shadows had curled toward her without permission and she'd swatted them away with a distracted hand, like they were nothing more than overeager pets.

She'd smiled when she did it. A small, private thing meant just for him.

He could go to her. Demand answers. Use the authority that came with his position to force the truth from her lips.

The thought made his stomach turn.

He couldn't stay here.

His sanctuary waited through the private entrance of his chambers.

The midnight garden was the one place in his domain where nothing recoiled from him. He'd found the black roses long ago—a wild tangle in a forgotten corner, its blooms so saturated with death magic that it thrived under his touch when everything else withered.

He'd built the garden around that single miracle.

Now they climbed the stone walls, blooming in reverse, from withered darkness into velvet softness. Death to life, over and over. Deep moss cushioned his steps. Night-blooming jasmine scented the air. At the center, a fountain of black stone, its water flowing soft and quiet.

No servants came here. No courtiers sought audience. Even his shadows behaved differently in this space, settling around him like a cloak rather than reaching restlessly for something they couldn't have.

He lowered himself onto the worn stone bench and let the quiet wrap around him.

Here, he didn't have to be the Reaper. Didn't have to calculate the danger he posed or maintain the iron control that kept everyone safe from his nature.

Here, he could just exist.

But even the roses couldn't quiet his mind tonight.

Goodnight, Reaper.

The words echoed through him. She'd wielded his title like a weapon, and the worst part was that he understood. She was angry. She wanted distance. She wanted to remind herself, and him, that whatever had been building between them wasn't safe.

That *he* wasn't safe.

His hands curled into fists against his thighs.

He'd been alone so long he'd made peace with it. The distance kept people safe. He hadn't minded.

Until her.

The roses bloomed in their quiet defiance. And Dante sat in his sanctuary and ached for something he'd never thought to want.

XXXIX.
BRYNN

Her chambers felt smaller than usual, the walls pressing in. Brynn paced from the windows to the wardrobe, her mind churning with Seraphina's words.

She'd claimed exhaustion to escape Dante's questions, but sleep was impossible. Every time she closed her eyes, she saw Seraphina's knowing smile, heard that sympathetic voice: *You're not the first mortal to catch his attention. You're just the latest.*

Just the latest.

The words burned through her like acid, eating away at every moment she'd thought was meaningful. Every glance. Every time his shadows had reached for her, and she'd felt chosen.

Hells, she was an idiot.

She'd seen him lose control when he was worried about her. Watched his expression tighten when she was in danger. Felt his shadows wrap around her wrists during training, gentle despite everything he was, adjusting her grip with touches that lingered longer than necessary. She'd replayed those touches at night. Pressed her fingers to her wrists where his shadows had been and let herself imagine.

Now she wondered how many women had done the same thing.

Treasured the same almost-touches. Mistaken his loneliness for something meant specifically for them.

She rubbed at her wrists, like she could scrub away her own stupidity.

She read people for a living. She'd survived by never being fooled. And she'd fallen for the oldest trick in existence: a powerful man making her feel like she mattered.

For the first time since her parents' deaths, since she'd learned that everyone could be bought or manipulated or simply taken away, she'd stopped calculating exit strategies. She'd actually let herself think she'd found somewhere she belonged.

And the woman before her had probably thought the same thing. And that woman was probably dead.

The laugh that escaped her was ugly and broken.

She needed answers. If Dante wouldn't volunteer them, she'd demand them.

The study was empty, maps spread across his desk like he'd left in a hurry. The receiving rooms deserted. She thought back to their conversations, the way he'd spoken about preferring solitude, retreating from court demands.

The gardens.

She'd glimpsed them from her windows. Beauty growing in perpetual twilight, places where death magic created instead of destroyed. If he had anywhere truly his own, it would be there.

Brynn grabbed a cloak and headed for the door.

The main corridors still held traces of court life: shadow-guards stationed at intersections, the low murmur of servants behind closed doors, cold fire flickering in iron sconces. But as she moved deeper into the western wing, those signs fell away. The sounds of the palace dimmed until she could hear her own breathing.

The architecture changed. Grand halls built for intimidation gave way to narrower passageways where the stonework was finer, more deliberate. Carved details she'd never seen in the public spaces: vines twisting through the dark stone, petals unfurling along archways. Not decoration for visitors. Personal. Shaped for himself over centuries of solitude.

The ward-stones hummed differently here. Lower, steadier. Like the palace breathing in its sleep.

She passed through a gallery where tall windows overlooked the inner grounds. Aurora light rippled across the sky outside, casting shifting colors over the stone floor. Purple bleeding into silver, then deepening to close to blue. She'd grown accustomed to the realm's eternal twilight, but here, without the court's cold fires and obsidian mirrors competing for attention, the light was almost gentle.

A strange word for anything in the Forsaken Court.

Every step felt like crossing a line. Like walking toward answers that might shatter whatever fragile hope she was still clinging to.

Good. She needed it shattered.

At the far end of the corridor, a partially concealed archway opened onto something wilder. Not the manicured grounds she'd seen from her chambers. A place that had been allowed to grow.

The door opened with barely a whisper.

She stopped on the threshold.

Black roses climbed the walls in tangled profusion, thorns catching the aurora light like dark glass. Jasmine hung heavy in the still air, its sweetness threading through something earthier underneath: wet stone, cold soil, the green smell of things growing where they shouldn't be able to. A fountain at the center spilled water over tiered basins of dark stone, so quiet she could hear individual drops striking the surface of the pool below.

Midnight peonies bloomed in clusters along the pathways, their petals so deeply purple they looked black until the light shifted and revealed their true color. Dark-leafed trees grew along the far wall, their branches reaching both upward and downward, roots and canopy mirroring each other. Between them, pale flowers she couldn't name glowed faintly, scattered through the darker foliage like fallen stars.

Nothing here flinched or withered. Everything existed alongside a presence that destroyed most living things.

He'd built this. The man who wouldn't let anyone within arm's reach had spent centuries coaxing life from a realm defined by its absence.

The thought hit harder than she expected, and she shoved it aside. She hadn't come here to be moved. She'd come here for answers.

And there, on a worn stone bench near the fountain, sat Dante.

Her breath caught before she could stop it, and she hated herself for the reaction.

He looked different here. The rigid control he wore like armor had softened, his shoulders less tense, his posture almost open. Aurora light caught the sharp planes of his face, silvering his dark hair. Without the court distance, without the careful restraint, he looked younger.

More like someone capable of breaking her heart.

Her eyes traced the line of his throat above the dark collar of his shirt. The elegant sprawl of his fingers against his thigh. The slow rise and fall of his chest.

She still wanted him. Even now. Even standing here with Seraphina's poison working through her blood, something in her refused to catch up with what her mind already knew.

The anger was easier. She grabbed hold of it.

He looked up at her, surprise flickering across his features before his expression went carefully blank. That neutral distance he wore with everyone else.

The distance he hadn't kept with her in weeks.

Its return fed her anger. Of course. Of course he was retreating into the Reaper now.

"I've been looking for you." Her voice came out brittle. "She said I wasn't the first mortal to catch your attention."

He went still on the bench.

"She told me to ask about the tribute you became attached to. About what happened when she started asking the wrong questions."

The tribute you became attached to. Not her. Someone before her. Someone who'd probably stood in this garden and looked at him the way she was looking at him now.

She caught the tightening around his eyes. A flicker that might have been pain before the blankness settled back.

"You don't want to know."

His voice scraped over her skin. That low, rough tone that made her stomach clench even when she was furious with him.

"Yes, I do." She stepped closer against every instinct telling her to protect herself. "I need to know."

She needed to know if she was real. If any of it was real. Or if she was just the latest version of a pattern he'd been repeating for centuries.

His jaw tightened. His fingers curled against his thigh.

The space between them held its breath.

Brynn wrapped herself in anger because the alternative was falling apart, and she waited.

XL.
DANTE

The sound of the entrance opening made his shadows recoil.

No one knew about this place. No one had ever—

She stepped into his sanctuary, vibrating with rage.

But underneath it—hurt. The brittle edge of someone who'd trusted him and now wondered if that trust had been misplaced.

The thief had found his refuge. And she'd come armed with questions.

He stood from the bench as she approached, his mask slamming into place even though every instinct screamed that it was already too late. She'd seen too much. Knew too much.

"She said I wasn't the first mortal to catch your attention."

The words came out sharp, her voice tight with emotion she was barely controlling. Her hands were clenched at her sides, knuckles white, and even in her fury, she was beautiful in a way that made his shadows ache toward her.

He forced them still.

"She told me to ask you about the tribute you became attached to. About what happened when she started asking the wrong questions."

Elizabeth.

The name dragged up memories he'd buried so deep he'd almost convinced himself they'd stopped hurting. Seraphina had found that weakness and wielded it perfectly.

And now Brynn stood before him with devastation written in the rigid line of her shoulders, the too-bright shine in her eyes, the way she held herself like she was bracing for another blow.

She thinks she's just another in a pattern.

"You don't want to know." His voice came out rough, a warning she wouldn't heed. Had never heeded, from the first moment she'd looked him in the eye and refused to flinch.

"Yes, I do." She stopped just outside the circle of the fountain's light. "I need to know."

She wasn't just angry. She was hurt in ways that had nothing to do with political games, and that cracked him open.

She'd let herself feel something. And now she was standing in his garden, wondering if any of it had been real.

"Seraphina has her own agenda," he said. "Whatever she told you—"

"Don't." The word cracked like a whip. "Don't you dare try to deflect this. I'm not some naive child you can distract with warnings about political games."

His shadows writhed at the anger in her voice. They wanted to wrap around her, soothe the rage radiating from her skin. He held them back through sheer will.

"Tell me about her." Brynn stepped closer to the fountain's edge, into the light that made her eyes flash. "Tell me about the woman who was here before me."

The woman who was here before me.

The guilt nearly drove him to his knees. Because she did matter. She mattered in ways Elizabeth never had. Ways he hadn't let himself look at too closely because that would mean admitting how far gone he already was.

"Her name was Elizabeth." The words scraped out of him.

He watched her expression shift. Her anger flickered, surprise that he was actually answering. Then it blazed higher.

"What happened to her, Dante?"

The use of his name instead of his title undid him. She was demanding answers from him as a person. Not the Reaper. She wanted truth from Dante.

He turned away, moving to the fountain's edge because he couldn't face her while saying this.

His hands gripped the stone hard enough that cracks spider-webbed beneath his fingers.

"She was curious. About everything. The court, the realm, how things worked here. She asked endless questions." He forced himself to breathe through the tightness behind his ribs. "And I was lonely."

The admission tore open a wound that had never properly healed. Lifetimes of isolation, of keeping everyone at arm's length. Lifetimes of being the thing that made even other Death Lords uneasy.

"When someone finally treated this place like a fascinating new world instead of a nightmare, when someone asked questions out of curiosity rather than terror..."

His voice broke slightly.

"I made the mistake of thinking I could have that."

He could feel her moving closer behind him. Her scent reaching him now, warm citrus cutting through the jasmine and night-blooming flowers.

Too close. And he could never make himself tell her to stop.

"She didn't quite grasp how dangerous it all was," he continued, staring at the aurora overhead. "Like she didn't understand that the biggest danger was standing right beside her."

"What happened?" Brynn's voice came from directly behind his left shoulder now. Close enough that his shadows strained toward her with longing he couldn't suppress.

His hands clenched harder on the stone.

"I let my guard down. Started spending time with her, showing her parts of the court that were meant to stay hidden. I told myself it was harmless. She was just curious, and I was just..."

Lonely. So lonely, he'd let himself believe he could have something that was never meant for him.

"She tried to touch you," Brynn said quietly instead.

"We were talking in the library one evening. She was excited about something she'd discovered in one of the texts. Animated and happy."

He made himself say the rest.

"She reached out without thinking. Grabbed my hand to pull me over to show me what she'd found."

The garden seemed to hold its breath.

"I wasn't prepared. For lifetimes, I'd maintained constant vigilance around innocents. But in that moment of happiness, of connection..."

He turned back to face her.

"My power drained her life before I could stop it. She collapsed in my arms, and I watched the light leave her eyes. She was gone in seconds. Just gone."

Silence stretched between them.

Brynn's expression had shifted. The anger was still there, in the tension around her eyes, the set of her jaw. But compassion had joined it.

He didn't deserve it.

"That's why you won't let anyone close," she said softly. "Not because you don't know what you're capable of. Because you found out what happens when you forget, even for a second."

Yes.

"And you've spent your whole existence punishing yourself for it."

"It wasn't letting my guard down." The words came out sharp, desperate for her to understand. "It wasn't a simple mistake. I'm not human. I never was."

His shadows darkened around them.

"I'm the Reaper. I harvest life with my touch. That's not a curse or a transformation. That's what I was born to be."

"And what has all that isolation done to you?" Her voice was quiet but intense, cutting through his defenses. "What has believing you're nothing but a monster done to the being underneath?"

The question hit a wound he'd buried so deep he'd thought it could never surface.

"I don't matter. Only their safety matters. Only making sure I never forget again what I'm capable of."

"You're wrong."

She stepped closer. Close enough that he could count the brown flecks in her eyes. Close enough that her scent wrapped around him and her body heat reached him through the cool garden air.

"Elizabeth's death was a tragedy. But it wasn't murder, Dante. It was an accident."

"An accident that killed someone who trusted me." The words came out stripped of everything but raw truth.

"An accident that taught you to be even more careful." She moved forward again, and his heart stopped. "You think I don't see how you calculate every gesture, every moment of proximity? You've spent lifetimes learning that vigilance."

"That's what I am." The desperation bled through. "Death waiting for someone to make a mistake."

"Your nature is choosing restraint every single day. Your nature is carrying guilt to protect people you barely know."

"Don't." Rough, raw. "Don't make me into something I'm not."

"I'm not making you into anything."

Her hand moved slowly, telegraphing her intent, giving him time to pull away. To maintain the distance that kept her safe.

He couldn't move.

"I'm seeing what you really are. What you've always been underneath the guilt and fear."

Her fingers hovered inches from his face, and every instinct screamed at him. Half to retreat. Half to close the distance himself and damn the consequences.

His shadows slipped their leash. One tendril curled toward her wrist before he caught it and yanked it back with a shudder.

Her pulse beat visibly in her throat. Steady. The rhythm of someone who'd made a decision.

"How can you be so certain?" The question came out desperate. "How can you trust that when I can't even trust myself?"

"Because I've watched you choose safety over everything else, every single day."

Her hand was so close he could feel the heat of her skin.

Her eyes locked with his. The anger was still there, banked now rather than blazing, but beneath it he saw trust that made his ribs ache.

Trust. Despite everything Seraphina had said. Despite every reason she had to doubt him.

"You're not going to hurt me, Dante." Her voice was soft but certain. "You won't let yourself."

XLI.
BRYNN

The shadows wove between them, tendrils that moved with purpose, creating a barrier she hadn't asked for. She could feel their touch against her outstretched hand, substantial enough to push back against her skin.

Even his power was trying to protect her from him.

Or protect him from her.

She should lower her hand. Should step back, rebuild her walls, remember that she'd come here furious and convinced she was nothing special—just the latest in a pattern of mortal women foolish enough to catch the Reaper's eye.

But she'd watched his face as he told her about Elizabeth. Watched centuries of guilt crack open, raw and so painfully genuine that her anger had faltered.

He wasn't a monster incapable of caring. He was someone who'd cared too much, lost everything, and spent lifetimes punishing himself for one moment of weakness.

And he was looking at her now with eyes full of want and terror, like she was simultaneously the thing he needed most and the thing that could destroy him.

She knew that feeling.

Idiot, the survival part of her brain hissed. *He just told her that he killed the last woman who got close. And here she was, hand extended, inviting a wolf to feed from her palm.*

She didn't lower her hand.

"Trust yourself," she said softly, her fingers hovering inches from his face. Close enough that she could feel the temperature difference between his skin and the air. Close enough that she could see the way his pupils had dilated, how badly he wanted to believe her. "You're not the same person who made that mistake."

His breathing went ragged. She watched conflict play across his features—the rigid control cracking, desperation surfacing beneath.

His shadows writhed between them, reaching for her even as they pushed her back. Wanting her. Fighting themselves the same way he was fighting himself.

His eyes closed.

Pain crossed his features. For a moment, she thought he might let her touch him.

Might finally trust himself enough to take the risk.

Her heart pounded so hard she could feel it in her throat. Her arm ached from holding it up so long, trembling with the effort, but she refused to lower it.

His shadows stilled. The barrier between them wavered, thinning until she could almost feel the coolness of his skin through the darkness.

His eyes snapped open.

And she saw the moment he made his choice.

The shadows surged upward, impenetrable, and the impact hit her. She staggered back, her outstretched hand meeting nothing but cold, unyielding darkness where his face had been.

"I can't."

Two words. Broken. Final.

"I'm sorry."

She opened her mouth to argue, to plead, to rage. But before she could form a single syllable, he disappeared.

He vanished into shadow and darkness, using his power to flee what terrified him more than any enemy ever could.

Brynn stood frozen, hand still outstretched toward empty air. The garden pressed in around her. The beautiful garden he'd created while convincing himself he was only capable of destruction.

Slowly, she lowered her arm.

Her fingers were trembling.

He ran.

The anger came first. Easier than the hurt threatening to crack her chest open.

"Coward," she whispered to the empty garden.

The word echoed off the stone walls, swallowed by roses that bloomed backward.

She pressed her hands against her eyes, breathing through the tightness in her chest.

She'd let herself believe that maybe—*maybe*—she was different.

Stupid. She was so stupid.

The tears came without permission, furious and unwanted, and she hated herself for every single one. Hated that she'd let him close enough to hurt her. Hated that even now, standing alone with his rejection ringing in her ears, part of her understood why he'd run.

She wiped her face roughly, pulling herself together with the same grim determination that had gotten her through her parents' deaths, through years on the streets, through every betrayal and loss.

She was good at surviving.

This would be no different.

Brynn looked around the garden one last time. The roses. The fountain. The bench where he'd sat looking so lost before she'd arrived.

A place where even the Reaper could be something other than death.

And he'd fled it rather than let her touch him.

"Coward," she said again, but her voice broke on the word.

She wasn't sure if she was talking about him or herself.

XLII.
BRYNN

One week of this bullshit.

Seven days since Dante had fled his own garden like a startled cat, leaving her standing among black roses with her hand still reaching toward empty air. Seven days of meals sent to her room, polite excuses about "Lord Reaper's schedule," and pretending she wasn't checking every shadow for signs of him.

Brynn threw herself into the chair by her window, glaring out at the eternal twilight. Somewhere in this sprawling palace of bone and shadow, the most feared Death Lord in existence was hiding from her.

Hiding. From a mortal thief who barely came up to his shoulder.

The coward.

She'd marked every slight. Servants maintaining distance when delivering messages. Formal notes replacing conversation—*Lord Reaper requests, Lord Reaper requires*—as if they hadn't progressed past that months ago. The complete absence of shadows curling around doorframes when she passed through corridors.

He was everywhere and nowhere. His power hummed through every stone, wrapped around every ward-lock she touched, but the man himself had vanished like smoke.

And wasn't that just perfect. She'd finally started to think maybe there was something real between them. Then the moment things got complicated, the moment she'd seen past his control to the lonely man underneath, he'd run.

Should've known better. People with power always did this: they used you when it suited them, discarded you when things got messy. Her parents had trusted a partner who smiled and promised loyalty right up until he'd framed them for treason.

The formal knock at her door interrupted her brooding.

She didn't bother getting up. "What?"

A death knight in livery entered, his translucent features neutral. "Lady Brynn, Lord Reaper requests your presence in his study. There are matters requiring your attention."

Matters requiring your attention. Delivered like she was some minor functionary instead of the woman who'd seen him break apart a week ago.

"Does he, now?" Brynn stood slowly. Anger was better than hurt. Anger kept you sharp. Hurt made you vulnerable. "And what sort of matters require my particular expertise?"

The knight's expression didn't change. "I was not informed of the specifics, my lady. Only that your presence is requested immediately."

"Tell his lordship I'll be along shortly."

The moment the door closed, she moved to her wardrobe with intent.

If Dante thought he could summon her like a servant after a week of silence, he could damn well wait. She took her time, braiding her hair with care that would've made her mother proud, checking her lockpicks out of spite. The leather corset she'd been saving for no particular reason. The one that made her waist look small and everything else look... not small. The belt with the silver buckle that caught light and drew the eye. Fitted leather pants instead of practical work clothes.

Maybe he'd notice exactly what he'd been running from.

Petty? Absolutely. Satisfying? More than it should be.

The corridors felt familiar after all this time in the palace, but the servants' behavior had shifted. Still polite, still deferential, but with a wariness that hadn't been there before.

She passed a cluster of courtiers near the grand staircase. Their conversation died the moment they saw her. One of them, a beautiful death-touched woman who'd been trying to catch Dante's attention for weeks, smiled with too many teeth.

"Lady Brynn," the woman said, voice dripping with sweetness. "How lovely to see you. We were just discussing how alone Lord Reaper has been lately."

Brynn smiled back. "Were you? How fascinating that you have so much time to discuss your lord's private affairs instead of attending to your own duties."

She kept walking before any of them could respond, but felt their stares like knives between her shoulder blades.

The court had noticed. And they were pleased about it.

She found his study door ajar and didn't bother knocking. She pushed it open, letting it hit the wall with a satisfying thud.

Dante stood behind his massive desk, maps spread across its surface.

Her traitorous heart stuttered.

He wore full court formal—black silk and leather that emphasized every line of his body, the high collar framing his jaw, the fitted cut making his shoulders look impossibly broad. His dark hair was swept back from his face, revealing the sharp angles of his cheekbones, the sensual mouth set in a hard line.

He looked like the feared Reaper. Like death incarnate wrapped in elegance and power.

He looked *devastating*, and she hated herself for noticing.

She needed to stop. He'd been hiding from her for a week. She was supposed to be angry.

She was angry. Furious. But her body hadn't gotten the message. Her pulse was doing something stupid, and her mouth had gone dry, and some pathetic part of her was watching the way his black eyes absorbed the candlelight and gave nothing back.

When he looked up, his expression was blank. The eyes that had looked at her with something almost like vulnerability seven nights ago gave away nothing.

Then his gaze swept over her, and whatever he'd been about to say died in his throat. He went still. His fingers curled against the desk.

Good. He'd noticed.

"Thank you for coming," he said, as if she'd had a choice. His voice came out rough. He cleared his throat.

Her spine straightened at his tone. The commanding one. The one that made her want to either obey or defy him, and she wasn't sure which urge was worse.

"Did I have a choice?" She settled into the chair across from his desk without invitation, crossing her legs slowly. His gaze flicked down, just for a heartbeat, before jerking back to her face. "Because that message sounded remarkably like a summons."

"We have appointments with two more courts." He gestured to the maps like this was a normal strategic meeting. Like they hadn't stood in his garden with almost no space between them. "The investigation requires—"

"Right to business, then." Brynn leaned back, studying him. Looking for tells. Weak spots. Places where his control cracked. "No acknowledgment of the fact that you've been treating me like I've got some contagious disease."

His jaw clenched. There, a tell.

"I haven't been—" The words came out clipped. "I've been managing court affairs."

"Is that what we're calling it?"

His hands flexed on the desk's edge, fingers digging into the wood hard enough that she heard it creak. The shadows at his feet darkened before he yanked them back under control.

"The investigation—"

"Has been sitting idle while you hide." She leaned forward, forcing him to either meet her eyes or obviously look away. "So either tell me where we're going and why, or admit you've been sulking."

The shadows spread across the floor despite his efforts. His dark eyes blazed with an intensity that made heat curl low in her stomach.

"Careful, thief." The word came out low, edged with warning.

"Or what?" She held his gaze, refusing to back down even though her pulse was racing for all the wrong reasons. "You'll ignore me for another week?"

Silence.

The shadows writhed at his feet. His chest rose and fell with slow, controlled breaths.

When he finally spoke, his voice was dangerously soft. "We're visiting The Lingering Court today. Tomorrow, The Mourned."

"That's it? That's all you're going to say?"

"What would you have me say?"

The truth. That something happened in that garden. That he felt it too. That he'd been hiding because he was terrified of what was between them.

But she couldn't force those words out. Couldn't make herself that vulnerable when he was standing there behind his desk like it was a fortress wall.

"Nothing," she said finally. "Clearly."

Pain flickered across his expression before the mask slammed back down.

"You're needed because you're the only one who can read the ward damage patterns." He turned back to the maps, shuffling papers with unnecessary force. "Your abilities are essential to—"

"Don't." The word came out sharper than intended. "Don't reduce this to my abilities. Don't pretend the last few weeks have been purely professional."

His shoulders went rigid. He didn't turn around. Didn't look at her.

The silence stretched, heavy with everything neither of them was saying.

"Right." She stood, moving slowly around the desk, closing the gap between them. Crossing into the space no one else dared enter, the twelve feet of distance that everyone in this court knew to maintain.

His shoulders went tight as a bowstring.

"Anything else I should know?" She stopped close enough to see the tension in his jaw, the rapid pulse beating in his throat. Close enough that she could smell him. The same scent that had haunted her for a week. "Special protocols for dealing with ghosts and peaceful deaths?"

He didn't step away. Didn't move at all. But she could see the effort it cost him, the way every muscle in his body had locked down.

"Thessa's domain can be disorienting." His voice came out strained. Rough. He lifted his hand to point at the map, keeping several inches between their fingers like even that proximity was dangerous. "Stay close. Don't wander off. Don't touch anything without permission."

"You mean stay close like I have been?" She let the bitterness bleed through. "Oh wait. That was you running."

His head turned toward her.

The air between them ignited.

She could see silver flecks in his dark eyes, the way his pupils had dilated until there was barely any color left. Could see the muscle jumping in his jaw, the tendons standing out in his neck, the tight grip he had on the desk's edge.

His gaze dropped to her mouth.

Her breath caught. Her heart slammed against her ribs. Every rational thought in her head went silent, drowned out by the sudden, desperate want that flooded through her.

Neither of them moved. Neither of them breathed.

The moment stretched. His shadows crept toward her feet, reaching for her despite his rigid control. His lips parted. His body swayed forward, barely, like he was fighting gravity.

Then he stepped back.

He put the desk between them again like a barricade, and the loss of his proximity hit her like a slap.

"The investigation." His voice came out hoarse. "We have work to do."

Her hands were trembling. She curled them into fists at her sides.

"Of course." She stepped back as well, pride the only thing keeping her upright. "And tomorrow's visit?"

He grabbed onto the subject change like a drowning man clutching a rope. "Caelum should be cooperative. Reasonable." His finger jabbed at another section of the map, gaze fixed firmly on the parchment. "He deals with natural deaths, peaceful crossings."

Brynn nodded, filing away the information while studying his profile. The rigid set of his shoulders. The way he wouldn't meet her eyes. The rapid rise and fall of his chest betrayed how affected he actually was.

"When do we leave?" she asked, proud that her voice didn't waver.

"Within the hour."

"Fine. I'll meet you at the transport chamber."

She was halfway to the door when his voice stopped her.

"Wait."

The word came out rough. Almost unwilling. Like it had escaped against his will.

She turned back slowly, hope flickering to life in her chest.

He stood behind his desk as if it were a shield. The shadows had gone still. Too still. His hands were braced against the wood, and for just a moment, he looked like a man at war with himself.

"The investigation is important." He wasn't looking at her. "The realm's stability depends on finding the saboteur."

Of course. Back to safety. Back to what he could control.

A bitter laugh escaped her. "Of course it is. Wouldn't want anything personal to interfere."

His mouth opened. His gaze met hers, and she saw something raw flash across his expression.

For one heartbeat, she thought he might actually say it. Whatever was choking him. Whatever had made him flee the garden. Whatever kept making him look at her like she was simultaneously salvation and damnation.

But he didn't.

"One hour," he said finally. "The transport chamber."

Not what she wanted to hear. But apparently, all he was capable of giving.

"I'll be there."

She turned back toward the door, refusing to let him see how much his distance actually hurt.

XLIII.
BRYNN

Brynn studied the intricate patterns carved into the stone floor, tracing the way death magic had been woven into every line and curve. Easier to focus without him here. Without that current of power that followed him everywhere.

Footsteps echoed in the corridor.

She didn't need to look up to know he'd arrived. The shadows in the room responded instantly, deepening and shifting toward him like they were drawn to their master. The temperature dropped. The air seemed to tighten.

Her pulse jumped anyway.

"Ready?" he asked, his tone clipped.

She looked away before her eyes could linger. She'd done enough of that in the study.

"Yes," she replied, stepping into the circle's center. Her voice came out steadier than she felt.

He joined her, maintaining distance even in the confined space. His shadows wrapped around both their feet, creating the boundary that would hold them together during transport while keeping them safely apart.

Always apart. Always that same measured distance.

She bit back the word she wanted to throw at him. He didn't deserve the satisfaction of knowing how much his silence cost her.

"Thessa's domain operates on different principles than the other courts," he said as power began building around them. "Time moves strangely there. Hours can pass in minutes, or minutes can stretch for what feels like days. Don't trust your internal sense of duration."

"Noted." She didn't trust herself to say more without the frustration bleeding through.

The circle flared, and reality dissolved around them in a rush of cold and darkness. For a moment that lasted both forever and no time at all, they existed in the space between realms—suspended in possibility, surrounded by whispers in languages that predated speech.

She was acutely aware of his presence beside her. Even in the void between worlds, she could feel him. The weight of his power, the tension in his body, the measured inches he maintained between them.

Then the world reformed, and her breath caught.

They stood in a city that looked like a nightmare and an elegant dream. Tall, narrow buildings with elaborate stonework stretched into fog so thick it seemed solid, their steep-pitched roofs disappearing into perpetual mist. Wrought iron balconies hung like frozen lace from every window, and gas lamps flickered with fire.

The cobblestone street beneath their feet gleamed like polished bone. Every footstep echoed with sounds that didn't belong to anyone visible, and the air felt thin and cold, making each breath a conscious effort.

But it was the scent that hit her first. Old flowers mixed with something that reminded her of libraries where books slowly crumbled to dust. The smell of things preserved long past their natural time.

"Stay close."

Two words. Low and rough and edged with authority that expected obedience.

Her body responded before her mind could override it. Shoulders squaring, breath catching, want flickering to life in her chest, no matter how she tried to smother it.

Not this again.

His shadows spread outward, creating a visible barrier around them both.

"The spirits here aren't malicious," he continued, "but they're persistent. They may try to draw you into their unfinished business."

She could see them now. Translucent figures in clothing from every era moving through the streets. Their movements had a hypnotic, repetitive quality that made her want to follow their patterns.

A woman in an elaborate gown stood at the corner, hands raised as if adjusting a mirror that wasn't there. She repeated the same gestures over and over. Patting her hair, touching her throat, smoothing her skirts. Her mouth moved in silent words.

"She's getting ready for a party," Dante said quietly, and Brynn hated how his voice softened with compassion. Hated that even now, even when she was angry with him, glimpses of the man beneath the Reaper made her chest ache. "One that happened sixty years ago. She's been preparing for it ever since."

Her throat tightened.

Trapped in a single moment. Unable to let go. Repeating the same actions forever because moving on meant acknowledging what was lost.

She glanced at Dante before she could stop herself.

Is that what he's doing? Trapped in the moment Elizabeth died?

Near a lamppost, a man in a soldier's uniform marched ten steps forward, stopped, saluted an empty space, then turned and marched ten steps back. His boots struck the stones in perfect rhythm.

"He's delivering a message," Dante continued. "Orders that might have saved his regiment, if they'd arrived in time."

The weight of repetition pressed against Brynn's mind. These weren't just ghosts. They were souls caught in the most critical moments of their existence, playing them out forever because they couldn't accept that the moment had passed.

"How do you resist it?" she asked, watching a child chase the same ethereal butterfly in a circle.

"Focus on what's real now, not what was real then." His voice carried the weight of experience. "They can pull the living into their patterns if you're not careful."

She tried counting her heartbeats to track the passage of time, but even that felt unreliable. Her pulse seemed to slow and quicken without rhythm. Steps that should have taken seconds dragged on for minutes. Conversations felt rushed even when spoken slowly.

Around them, the spirits began to take notice. Not threatening, but curious in a way that made her skin crawl. Their movements slowed as the living visitors passed, and she caught fragments of their words:

"...told him I would write, but the letter's still on my desk..."

"...if I'd just left five minutes earlier..."

"...she never knew how sorry I was, how sorry I am, how sorry..."

The repetitive nature of their words created an almost musical quality, a chorus of regret that seemed to harmonize with the fog. Brynn found herself slowing to listen, to understand what each spirit was trying to resolve.

A cool tendril of shadow wrapped around her waist.

Her breath caught.

The shadow wrapped around her middle like a possessive hand, pulling her back from the spirits. It pressed against her ribs, curled around the curve of her hip, held her with an intimacy that made her pulse stutter.

Cool pressure that felt almost like a caress. Almost like being claimed.

She looked back at Dante.

He stood frozen, every line of his body rigid. His eyes were fixed on where his shadow wrapped around her like he couldn't quite believe what his power was doing.

Like he couldn't make himself call it back.

The shadow tightened.

Her mouth went dry.

For a moment, neither of them moved. The air between them crackled.

Then he yanked it back, his hands flexing at his sides.

"Don't listen too closely," he said, voice hoarse. "Their regrets are contagious. You start thinking about your own mistakes. That's how they pull you in."

It was too late for his warning. She was already thinking about her parents—the words she'd never said. The life stolen from all of them. The grief felt suddenly fresh, as if it had happened yesterday.

The thought stopped her in her tracks. She was surrounded by spirits of the dead, had been living in the death realm for weeks, and she'd never once asked about seeing her parents.

What did that say about her?

The shadows around them thickened in response to her distress, forming a stronger barrier between her and the spirits. She noticed how they moved like anchors, keeping her grounded instead of drifting into the past.

"This way," Dante said, guiding her toward a massive Gothic mansion that held steady while the landscape shifted around it. His voice was still rough. He still wasn't looking at her directly.

She followed in silence, hyperaware of the space between them. Of the tension radiating from his shoulders with every step.

As they approached, the spirits' movements became more organized near the palace. Less frantic. Even the cobblestones seemed more solid.

"Thessa's influence," Dante explained, and she heard the relief in his voice at having something safe to discuss. "She helps them find resolution when they're ready, but she doesn't force it."

The iron gates recognized his authority and rearranged themselves, metal flowing like water to create a passage. The courtyard beyond defied logic. Water cascaded from floating pools, staircases spiraling in impossible directions.

"Remember," he said as they climbed the front steps. "Don't let yourself get caught. Stay focused on our purpose."

"I understand," she said, and let him hear the edge in her voice.

The massive doors swung open before they reached them.

A figure materialized from the shadows between the portraits. More solid than the spirits outside, but still translucent. She wore robes that seemed woven from mist.

"Lord Reaper. I am Maren, Lady Thessa's servant. She has been expecting you both."

They followed Maren through corridors that stretched and shrank according to a mysterious logic.

The door opened onto a salon where silver furniture reflected light from an unseen source. Mirrors lined the walls, showing not reflections but scenes from different moments in time.

Lady Thessa sat in a chair that seemed to exist across multiple moments at once, her gown shifting between translucent and solid.

"Lord Reaper. And the living one who walks among the dead." Her voice came from everywhere at once. "I have been expecting you."

"We're investigating the ward failures," Dante said.

"Ah, yes. The unraveling." She gestured to the mirrors, and Brynn glimpsed a complex web of glowing lines. The ward network overlaid with damaged sections, crumbling boundaries. "Spirits whisper of visitors who come before the breaking. Of questions asked about designs meant to endure."

Dante's attention sharpened. "Visitors from which courts?"

Thessa's form flickered. "Violence came seeking patterns of destruction. Consumption came seeking vulnerabilities. Mercy came seeking knowledge of transitions."

All three courts. All with reasons that could be innocent or damning.

"When did they visit?" Brynn asked, earning a sharp look from Dante.

Thessa's gaze fixed on her with unnerving intensity. "Time moves strangely here. Was it yesterday? A year ago? Tomorrow?" Her smile was unsettling. "They each came asking questions. Some more pointed than others."

"That's not particularly helpful," Dante said, frustration edging his tone.

"Violence asked about ward resilience. How much damage they could withstand. Consumption asked about power redistribution when boundaries fail. Mercy asked about peaceful transitions. Whether failing wards could be guided into gentler configurations."

"All reasonable questions for Death Lords concerned about the system's integrity," Dante said.

"Indeed. Or reasonable questions for one who wishes to exploit it."

Brynn leaned forward. "Did any of them ask about the same specific wards?"

"Perceptive." Thessa's smile was approving. "All three showed particular interest in the secondary anchor points. The keystones that support the primary wards but are less obviously protected."

Brynn studied the layout in the mirrors. "These are all secondary anchors. If they fail, the primary wards will be strained, but the system won't collapse immediately."

"No. But when weakened sufficiently..." Thessa made a gesture, and the map showed wards failing in sequence. "The boundaries will thin. Souls will wander. The courts will bleed into each other."

"Creating chaos," Dante said quietly.

"Or opportunity. For one who wished to reshape the boundaries." Thessa's form flickered. "Violence seeks to expand through conquest. Consumption seeks to devour all it touches. Mercy seeks what it believes is best for all, whether others agree or not."

"Three different motives," Dante said. "And you've given us just enough to suspect everyone while confirming nothing."

"The truth lies not only in destruction, but in what remains untouched." Her voice grew distant. "Sometimes what is preserved tells as much as what is destroyed."

The room started to shift around them.

"Or perhaps," Thessa's voice echoed as she faded, "the truth is something none have considered."

Maren materialized beside them. "Lady Thessa needs rest. I will show you back to the courtyard."

They followed in silence. Brynn felt Dante's awareness of her like heat against her skin. The distance he maintained, the way his shadows kept drifting toward her before he pulled them back.

The courtyard had shifted again. The floating pools now reflected scenes from the investigation: Seraphina's fortress, Vex's golden halls, Caelum's perfect paradise.

"The way back to your realm is there." Maren pointed to a gate that hadn't existed before. Then she paused, studying Brynn with disconcerting intensity.

"A word of advice?"

Brynn waited.

"Those who linger here teach us that holding onto the past prevents embracing the future." Maren's gaze flicked meaningfully toward Dante, then back. "But they also teach us that some things are worth holding onto. The trick is knowing which is which."

Her eyes held Brynn's for a long moment.

Then she dissolved into mist, leaving them alone in the courtyard.

Brynn looked at Dante. He stood with his back to her, shoulders rigid, shadows pooling at his feet.

"She's talking about you," Brynn said quietly. "The spirits in their loops. Unable to let go."

His shoulders tensed further. He didn't turn around.

"I know," he said finally, his voice rough.

And he walked through the gate without looking back.

XLIV.
BRYNN

The familiar weight of the forsaken realm settled around them. But instead of the usual sense of returning to something that might become home, the Forsaken Court felt oppressive tonight. Too quiet. Too empty.

Coming back to a place that wasn't hers. To a man who kept her at arm's length, no matter how close they stood.

They walked toward the main palace without speaking. The weight of Thessa's domain still pressed against her mind. All those spirits caught in their worst moments, unable to let go.

Just like him.

The thought had been building all day, whispered by every ghost they'd passed. She'd been living in the death realm for weeks. Surrounded by spirits, souls, the dead. And she'd never once asked the question that now felt unavoidable.

"My parents," she said abruptly, stopping in the middle of the corridor. "Are they here?"

Dante went very still.

Dread crossed his face.

"Can I see them?" The question came out quieter than she'd intended, but she pushed on. "I know they're dead, but I've been living among the dead and I never even thought to ask—"

"Don't." The single word came out sharp. Almost desperate.

"Don't what? Don't ask about my own family?"

"Don't ask questions you don't want answers to." He turned to face her fully, and she saw exhaustion there, and guilt.

Her stomach dropped. "What does that mean?"

He ran a hand through his hair, a gesture so human it caught her off guard. "It means some knowledge only brings pain."

"They're my parents. I have a right to know."

"Do you?" The question was harsh. "Do you have a right to knowledge that will destroy any peace you might find in this place?"

The corridor felt like it was closing in. Servants had vanished, sensing the dangerous undercurrent in their lord's voice.

"Tell me," Brynn whispered.

"No."

"Tell me what happened to them."

"I said no." His voice carried that edge she'd heard him use on courtiers who overstepped, the tone that reminded everyone exactly who they were dealing with.

But she wasn't everyone else.

"You don't get to decide what I can handle." She moved toward him instead of backing away. "You don't get to shield me from my own life."

"Your life ended the night you were marked for tribute." He held her gaze. "Everything since then has been borrowed time."

The cruelty of it stole her breath.

"Then tell me about their deaths," she said quietly. "If my life is already over, what's left to shield me from?"

For a moment, she thought he might break. His shadows reached toward her before recoiling.

"Time changes everything in the death realm," he said finally, his voice barely above a whisper. "Even love. Even memory. Even the people we once were."

"What does that mean for them?"

His eyes closed briefly. "It means the parents you remember, the ones who loved you... They don't exist anymore. Death changed them. The betrayal that killed them, the way they died believing the worst..." He shook his head. "They're trapped in that final moment of despair, reliving it endlessly. They wouldn't recognize you. Couldn't recognize you. All they know now is the pain of believing their daughter turned against them."

The words drove the air from her lungs.

She'd expected them to be unreachable.

Not this.

"They think I betrayed them?" Her voice came out thin. Broken. "They died believing I was part of what destroyed our family?"

"The betrayer was thorough." His voice gentled in a way that made her chest ache. "Made it look like the whole family was involved. Your parents' final moments..." He stopped, shaking his head.

"Tell me."

"They were calling your name. Asking why you'd done it, why you'd turned against them. The betrayal broke their hearts before it killed them."

The floor felt unsteady beneath her feet.

All this time, she'd carried the grief of losing them. The anger at their betrayer. The guilt of surviving when they hadn't.

She'd never considered that they might have died hating her.

"So they exist," she said when she could speak again, "but they're not... them."

"They're echoes." His voice was soft now, almost tender. "Broken echoes of their worst moment, played forever. And seeing you would either mean nothing to them, or it would cause them pain beyond imagining."

Her parents weren't just dead. They were imprisoned in their own anguish. Forever believing she'd destroyed them.

"That's why you didn't tell me," she whispered.

"Yes."

They stood in the corridor, separated by mere feet but feeling like worlds apart. She felt tears prick at her eyes and blinked them back furiously.

The weight of it was crushing.

"I'm sorry," he said quietly, and she heard genuine pain in his voice. "I'm so sorry."

She nodded, not trusting herself to speak.

Then she made the mistake of looking up at him.

His expression held something she hadn't seen before. Recognition. Like he knew exactly what it felt like to lose someone and never get them back. To be surrounded by the dead and still be completely alone.

For a moment, standing there in the aftermath of devastating truth, she thought maybe they could comfort each other. Maybe this shared understanding of loss could bridge the distance he'd been maintaining.

"Dante—" she started, moving toward him.

His expression shuttered immediately. The vulnerability vanished behind cold blankness.

"The investigation," he said, his voice going flat. "The spirits mentioned visitors asking about ward construction."

She actually laughed, a broken, disbelieving sound. "Are you serious right now?"

"Thessa deals in riddles. Her information could point anywhere."

No. She wasn't going to let him do this. Wasn't going to let him use her grief as another barrier between them.

"Stop," she said, her voice shaking. "Just stop."

"The pattern is building—"

"I don't care about the pattern!" The words came out sharper than intended, but she was raw, and he was retreating like none of this mattered. "My parents are trapped in a nightmare of thinking I destroyed them, and you're talking about ward construction?"

His jaw tightened. "I'm trying to—"

"You're trying to avoid." She closed the distance between them, watched him force himself not to back away. "You've been avoiding me for a week. You ran from your own garden rather than acknowledge what's happening between us. And now you're using my grief as another excuse."

"There's nothing happening between us beyond the investigation."

She stepped back.

"Nothing?" Her voice came out small, and she hated herself for it.

"Nothing," he confirmed, and his tone was so flat, so final, that she almost believed him.

Almost.

But his darkness was writhing around his feet. His hands were clenched so tight the leather of his gloves creaked. And there, just for a second, something flickered in his dark eyes that looked like agony before he buried it.

"You're lying," she said quietly.

"I'm keeping you alive."

"From what? From caring about someone? From letting someone care about you?" She held her ground. "Or are you just keeping yourself safe?"

His shoulders went rigid. "You don't understand—"

"Then make me understand!" Her voice broke on the words. "Make me understand why you looked at me in that garden like I mattered, then spent a week pretending I don't exist. Why did you just hold me together through the worst news of my life, then immediately shut me out?"

"Because this—" He gestured sharply between them. "—can't happen. Won't happen."

"Why not?"

"Because I could kill you!"

The words exploded out of him. His control shattered, his whole body rigid, shadows erupting in violent tendrils.

"Because my nature is death." His voice broke into a near-shout. "And no matter how careful I am, no matter how much I want—"

He stopped abruptly, jaw working.

There it was. The truth he'd been hiding behind formality and a week of silence.

Her heart was slamming against her ribs. "How much you want what?"

She watched him fight with himself. Watched the war play out across his features, in the way his body strained toward her even as he held himself back.

For one breathless moment, she thought he might actually answer.

He exhaled. Straightened. When he spoke again, he was the Reaper once more.

"It doesn't matter what I want. All that matters is keeping you alive long enough to fix the wards. After that, you can return to the living world."

The dismissal broke something in her.

"That's it?" Her voice came out barely above a whisper. "That's all I am to you? A tool for fixing your ward problem?"

"Yes."

But his shadows strained toward her.

"We'll continue tomorrow," Dante said finally, his voice hollow. "The Mourned Court. Dawn."

"Fine. Tomorrow."

XLV.
DANTE

Dante didn't go to his chambers.

Instead, he found himself in his study again, standing before maps and reports that suddenly meant nothing. His hands were braced against the desk, head bowed, as he breathed through the wreckage of the last hour.

The look on her face when she'd understood about her parents. The way she'd needed comfort and he'd given her ward construction.

Pathetic.

His shadows shifted restlessly around his feet, straining toward the door. Toward where she'd gone. He yanked them back, but they fought him, responding to wants he refused to acknowledge.

He could still smell her. Sunshine and citrus. It didn't belong here. Neither did she. His body remembered how close she'd been. How easy it would have been to close the distance instead of widening it.

There's nothing happening between us beyond the investigation.

The lie tasted like poison even in memory.

He moved to the window, looking out over his domain. The twilight seemed heavier tonight, the aurora less vibrant. Even the realm was responding to his turmoil.

He'd finally said it—finally admitted the fear that drove every retreat. And instead of understanding the danger, she'd looked at him like he was breaking her heart.

Maybe he was.

You're already caught in your own pattern. Unable to move forward, unable to let go.

His hands clenched on the windowsill hard enough that the stone cracked beneath his grip.

She was right. That was the worst of it. She'd seen exactly what he was doing and refused to let him hide from it.

A soft knock interrupted his spiral. He didn't turn around.

"Enter."

Lord Aldric materialized from the shadows. The Bone Knight, who had served as his captain for multiple ages. One of the few bound souls who had earned something approaching trust.

"My lord. There are instabilities throughout the domain." Aldric's hollow voice carried concern. "The ward-keepers report fluctuations. Souls experiencing unusual dreams. The borders with adjacent realms showing weakness."

When a Death Lord's control slipped, the realm felt it.

"And the Weeping Marshes have gone silent," Aldric continued. "The souls there have stopped their mourning for the first time in recorded history."

Dante's jaw tightened. His personal crisis was destabilizing the entire domain. The souls felt his turmoil and responded, their eternal torments disrupted by his loss of control.

"Have the ward-keepers check all boundary stones. Anyone experiencing unusual phenomena should report immediately."

"Yes, my lord." Aldric hesitated. "Should we postpone tomorrow's diplomatic visit?"

"No." The word came out sharp. "Tomorrow proceeds as planned."

Aldric bowed and faded back into the shadows, but not before Dante caught the knowing look in his eyes.

Alone again.

He returned to his desk, forcing himself to focus on tomorrow's visit to the Mourned Court. After Seraphina's hostility, Caelum's gentle nature should feel like a reprieve.

The thought of taking her into any Death Lord's domain still sent a ripple of unrest through his realm.

He tried to settle into his usual meditative state. But his mind kept returning to the corridor. To the moment she'd stepped toward him, voice breaking, asking him to try.

And he'd retreated. Again.

His shadows slipped their leash, creeping toward the door before he caught them and forced them back. They wanted her. His power wanted her. Some fundamental part of him pointed toward that door like a compass needle seeking north.

A week since the garden. A week since she'd stood before him with her hand outstretched, reaching for his face, telling him he wouldn't hurt her. Telling him to trust himself.

And he'd vanished rather than let her touch him.

A week of seeing that moment every time he closed his eyes. Her hand suspended in the space where he'd been. The look on her face when she'd realized he was gone.

A week of telling himself it was mercy when it felt like cruelty.

At least she's alive. At least she's safe from him.

Even if the look in her eyes when she'd walked away had gutted him.

He moved back to the window. In his garden below, the black roses were dying. Actually dying, when nothing in his realm had truly died in lifetimes. Petals fell like dark snow, littering the ground.

His hands curled into fists at his sides.

She didn't understand. Couldn't understand what it meant to watch someone die from your touch. To learn through grief that your nature didn't allow for connection.

But even as he told himself that, he knew it wasn't the whole truth.

He wasn't just afraid of killing her.

He was afraid of what it would mean to try. To hope. To let himself want something he'd spent lifetimes convincing himself was impossible.

And she'd seen that. Had looked right through his excuses to the cowardice underneath.

He returned to the maps, forcing himself to focus on routes and protocols. But underneath it all, one thought kept circling:

She was the first person in centuries who'd made him feel like something other than a monster.

And he'd treated her like she was nothing.

He blew out a breath. Let the mask fall back into place.

Even if it killed something in him to maintain it.

The instability pulsed through his realm one final time. In the Weeping Marshes, the souls began their mourning again. But the wails had taken on a new quality.

They were mourning for him now.

XLVI.
BRYNN

Brynn had barely slept.

She lay in the massive bed, staring up at the carved bone. Every time she'd closed her eyes, she'd seen her parents' faces. Not as she remembered them, warm and loving, but twisted with betrayal in their final moments.

They had been calling her name. Asking why she'd done it.

The memory surfaced on its own, the one she'd buried so deep she'd almost convinced herself it wasn't real.

The alley behind their house. Deep shadows stretching between buildings. She'd just returned from the market district, hours of negotiations leaving her mind racing with numbers and trade agreements. Late getting home. Her parents would be worried.

Voices from the back entrance. Harsh. Unfamiliar. Mixed with her parents' tones.

Her father's voice was trembling with fear she'd never heard before.

She'd pressed against the wall, straining to listen.

"Where is she?" A cold voice.

"She's not here." Her father, too quick, pitched too high. "She's just a girl. She wouldn't understand—"

"There has to be some mistake." Her mother's voice cracking.

"It's already too late."

Her father let out a sound like the air had been punched out of him.

Then her mother screamed his name.

Then nothing.

Brynn had stood frozen, hand pressed over her mouth to keep from making a sound. Her mind refused to process what she'd heard. Couldn't be real. Couldn't be—

"Find the girl." The cold voice again, unhurried. "She can't have gone far."

Boots on stone. Coming toward the alley.

She ran.

She'd told herself she would circle back. Would find help. Would explain everything once she understood what was happening.

She never saw them again.

Brynn pressed her face into the pillow, fighting the sob building in her chest. She'd cried enough last night. Had broken down alone in her room, learning that her parents weren't just dead. They were caught in that accusation forever.

And she couldn't even try to reach them. Could only carry the knowledge that somewhere in this realm, they existed in eternal anguish, calling out for the daughter they believed had destroyed them.

Maybe she should have let him keep this truth from her.

No. She shook her head against the pillow. She'd needed to know. Had a right to know.

Even if it was destroying her.

And then he'd given her ward construction. She'd been reeling from the worst news of her life, and he'd pivoted to investigation strategy like she was just another item on his agenda.

Nothing between them. Just a tool for fixing wards.

She'd offered him everything. Had stood there breaking and asked him to try. And he'd looked her in the eye and told her she was nothing.

Fine.

If that's what he wanted, that's what he'd get. She could be nothing. Could be exactly the cold, professional tool he'd reduced her to.

The twilight outside had shifted from deep purple to pale lavender. Soon, servants would arrive with schedules and formalities, and she'd have to face the day.

Face him.

She rolled over, catching a faint trace of roses from the garden on her pillow.

She needed to stop. He'd made his choice perfectly clear.

A sharp knock cut through her thoughts.

"Come in," she called, grateful for the interruption.

A death knight entered, hollow eye sockets fixed on her with neutral precision. "Lady Brynn. Lord Reaper requests your presence in the transport chamber. Today's diplomatic visit to the Court of the Mourned will proceed as scheduled."

Court business. Of course.

"Tell Lord Reaper I'll be there," she said flatly. No warmth. No questions about whether he'd slept. He didn't deserve her concern.

When the door closed, Brynn moved to her dresser. The mirror showed her exactly what she expected: red-rimmed eyes, pale skin, evidence of a sleepless night written clearly on her face.

That wouldn't do.

If he wanted to pretend last night hadn't happened, fine. She could play that game better than he could. She'd been performing since she was twenty years old, fleeing into the night with nothing but the clothes on her back.

She splashed cold water on her face, working to erase the signs. Chose her clothing with care: a deep blue dress formal enough for diplomacy but practical enough for trouble. Secured her tools—lockpicks in hidden pockets, ward-sensing instruments strapped against her thigh where the long skirts would conceal them.

Her reflection looked composed. Professional. Like a woman who felt nothing at all.

Exactly what she needed.

A softer knock interrupted her preparations. "Brynn? May I come in?"

"Enter."

Naia slipped through the door, translucent form carrying a breakfast tray far too elaborate for the early hour. "Lord Reaper requested I bring you something to eat before your departure." She set it down with a meaningful look. "He was quite insistent about making sure you were properly prepared."

He'd sent breakfast.

A week ago, that might have meant something. Now it just felt like an obligation.

"How thoughtful," Brynn said, and let the sarcasm show.

Naia's eyes flickered with surprise at her tone. "Brynn—"

"I'm fine." The words came out sharp. She softened slightly. Naia wasn't the one she was angry at. "Sorry. Didn't sleep."

"I can see that." Naia studied her face, playfulness fading into concern. "I heard about your parents. I'm so sorry."

The sympathy almost cracked her armor. Brynn blinked hard, forcing everything back down.

"It was a long time ago," she managed.

"That doesn't make it easier." Naia moved closer, translucent hand hovering near Brynn's shoulder without quite touching. "For what it's worth, Lord Reaper looked wrecked this morning. Whatever happened between you, I don't think he's sleeping any better."

Her chest wanted to twist. Wanted to soften. Wanted to ask if he was alright.

She didn't let it.

"That's his problem," she said coolly. "We have work to do."

Naia's eyebrows rose slightly, but she didn't push. "At least eat something first. You'll be no good to anyone if you collapse."

Brynn forced down a few bites to appease her. Everything tasted like ash.

A harder knock came before she'd finished. "Lady Brynn? Lord Reaper is ready to depart. Your immediate presence is required."

Required. Not requested.

Irritation prickled through her. After everything, he still thought he could summon her like a servant.

She grabbed her travel cloak and headed for the door.

The corridors felt different today. Servants moved too quickly, glancing at shadows. The stones beneath her feet hummed with unsteady energy.

Something was wrong with the realm.

She filed it away. Not her problem. She was just here to fix wards.

When she reached the transport chamber, Dante was already there. He stood with his back to the entrance, studying reports a death knight delivered in hushed tones. Formal attire. Long sleeves covering every inch of skin.

His shadows writhed around his feet, more agitated than she'd ever seen them.

He dismissed the knight and turned.

She faltered mid-step.

He looked terrible. Shadows beneath his eyes. Jaw tight enough to crack. He looked like a battle fought and lost all night.

For one treacherous moment, she wanted to go to him. Ask if he was alright. Bridge the distance between them.

Then she remembered his voice, flat and final: *Nothing happening between us.*

She put her walls back up.

"Lord Reaper," she said, and watched him flinch at the formal address. He'd earned it.

His shadows reached toward her instantly, fighting his control, desperate to close the distance he wouldn't cross.

Nothing between them, he'd said. While his power betrayed him with every breath.

She ignored it.

"Thief." His voice was neutral, but she caught the slight roughness. The way his eyes searched her face before he shuttered his expression.

"You required my presence. I'm present." She kept her voice level. Gave him nothing.

Something flickered in his eyes. Hurt, maybe. Or frustration. A muscle ticked in his cheek.

Now he knew how it felt.

"The Mourned Court awaits," he said after a pause. "Reports

suggest Caelum's domain remains stable despite the ward failures. We should be able to conduct a thorough investigation."

"Then let's go." She stepped into the transport circle's outer ring without waiting for him, positioning herself as far from him as the space allowed.

He joined her after a moment, and she felt his gaze on her. She kept her eyes forward.

"About last night—" he started, voice low.

"Is there something about the investigation you need to discuss?" she cut him off, keeping her voice calm and distant, exactly like him.

His shadows surged toward her feet. She felt the cool brush of them against her ankle and stepped away.

His shoulders stiffened.

"No," he said finally. "Nothing."

"Then we should proceed."

His shadows spread around both their feet, creating the boundary for transport. He stood close enough that she could feel the hum of power rolling from him.

Her own body wanted to sway toward him. She stayed still.

He'd wanted distance. Here it was.

As power built around them, she kept her gaze fixed straight ahead. But she felt his eyes on her the whole time. Felt his shadows pressing against her ankles like they were begging for contact that his hands wouldn't allow.

The circle flared, and reality dissolved around them.

XLVII.
BRYNN

When the world reformed around them, she couldn't stop the sharp intake of breath.

They stood on a hilltop overlooking paradise.

Rolling hills stretched toward snow-capped mountains piercing blue sky. The light held at perpetual golden hour, warm sunlight with hand-painted clouds drifting overhead. After weeks of eternal twilight, the warmth on her skin was startling.

"This is..." she started, then stopped.

"Beautiful," Dante finished quietly. "Caelum's domain reflects his purpose. Natural deaths, peaceful crossings."

She didn't look at him. Didn't acknowledge that he'd completed her thought.

Below, waterfalls tumbled from mountain heights, their spray creating rainbow prisms. The sound wasn't just rushing water. It was musical, almost orchestrated. Wildflowers bloomed everywhere, and trees bore both blossoms and fruit simultaneously.

The air tasted of mountain pine and something impossibly pure. Each breath loosened something in her chest, and for the first time since learning about her parents, the crushing weight eased slightly.

Deer moved through the landscape without wariness. Birds with jewel-toned feathers sang in complex harmonies. Butterflies drifted through gardens where souls tended flowers or created art that glowed with inner light.

A child laughed nearby, running to embrace a soul that knelt with open arms. Parent and child reunited in eternal peace.

Then her chest cracked open.

Her parents should be here. Should have died surrounded by love instead of lies. Should have found rest instead of—

She looked away, blinking hard.

"Focus on the present." Dante's voice cut through her spiral.

"I'm fine," she said flatly. "Let's go."

She started down the path without waiting for him, needing distance. Needing not to feel the pull of his presence when she was supposed to be angry.

None of that anger reached the rest of her. Even furious, even hurt, she was aware of him behind her. The weight of his attention on her back, the cool brush of his shadows near her ankles.

She walked faster.

A path of smooth stone led toward a palace that grew from the mountainside. White marble spires rose in flowing lines, columns catching the light, terraced gardens cascading down slopes.

Dante caught up to her easily, his longer stride erasing the distance she'd tried to create. "The approach is designed to calm visitors. Caelum believes meaningful conversation requires tranquility."

"Does it work?"

"More than most Death Lords would prefer." An edge crept into his voice. "Difficult to maintain proper suspicion."

As they walked deeper into the realm, her shoulders dropped. The sunlight, the music of water, the contentment radiating from every soul. It combined to create an overwhelming sense of rightness.

How could she distrust a place where souls painted and laughed and rested?

Dante's shadows wound tighter at his feet.

The palace gates came into view, wrought from silver and pearl rather than iron and bone. Graceful architecture reached toward the sky.

"Remember," Dante said quietly as they approached, "we're here to investigate sabotage."

"I remember why we're here," she said coolly. "I don't need reminders."

The gates opened, and a figure emerged from the gardens.

Lord Caelum approached along the terraced path, and Brynn found herself struck again by how perfectly he belonged here.

Tall and classically handsome, he moved with grace that seemed native to this realm. His hair caught the light like spun bronze, his robes woven from soft clouds.

His smile reached his eyes.

"Lord Reaper," he said, extending both hands. "And Lady Brynn. Welcome to my domain. I only wish your visit came under better circumstances."

"Caelum." Dante's nod barely qualified as acknowledgment.

Caelum's smile never wavered. "The ward failures have been devastating. I've lost three boundary stones just this week." He turned to Brynn, eyes holding genuine interest. "But you're the one everyone's been talking about. The one who can actually read the damage patterns."

"I'm still learning," she said, though pride warmed in her chest at the recognition.

"Modest as well as skilled." He gestured toward the palace. "Come, we shouldn't conduct serious business standing in the gardens. I have refreshments prepared, and a workspace where you can examine what I've gathered."

He led them through gates that opened at their approach. They passed souls engaged in peaceful activities. An old man teaching children to paint with glowing colors, a woman tending flowers that sang softly when touched.

"Your domain is remarkable," Brynn found herself saying.

"Thank you. It's taken ages to achieve this level of harmony." His pride carried satisfaction without arrogance. "When souls arrive here, they've earned their rest. My role is simply to provide the environment where they can find it."

The words found the wound she'd been protecting.

"Death doesn't have to be an ending," Caelum continued gently. "For those who lived with love and kindness, it can be a beginning."

She blinked hard, forcing the grief back down.

Dante's gaze cut to her.

She didn't look at him.

He remained silent during the walk, but she caught him watching Caelum with an intensity that seemed misplaced. His jaw was tight, his shoulders rigid even in the realm's tranquility.

They entered the palace, and the interior was as flawless as everything else. Marble that seemed to glow from within. Chambers that felt exactly the right size. Furniture that invited relaxation.

Caelum led them to a study lined with books and scrolls, where a table held extensive research materials.

"Please, sit," he said.

The chair adjusted as she settled, perfectly supporting her back. After weeks of threatening furniture in Dante's realm, the comfort was almost shocking.

"I've prepared refreshments, but first, let me show you what I've discovered. You're not the only ones who've noticed the pattern. These aren't random failures. Someone is targeting the wards." Caelum moved to the table, sorting through documents. "The pattern is quite clear once you know what to look for."

"I've documented over twenty separate incidents of ward damage across the death realm." He spread out a detailed map marked with notations. "When you plot them geographically and temporally, a pattern emerges."

Brynn leaned over the map, her abilities immediately recognizing the significance. Incidents scattered across domains, but clusters appeared near boundary points exactly where the ward network was most vulnerable.

"These here," she said, pointing. "They're all within days of each other."

"Yes." Caelum's expression held approval that made her sit straighter. "And if you look at the timing..." He produced a scroll with meticulously recorded dates and times. "Someone with knowledge of our diplomatic schedules would know when defenses might be distracted."

Dante leaned forward, studying the map. "Explain the border incidents."

Caelum hesitated, seeming reluctant. "I've been tracking diplomatic visits, trying to understand if there's a correlation. The pattern that emerged is... troubling."

He pointed to several incidents near his domain's boundaries. "These all occurred within hours of scheduled diplomatic meetings. But not just any meetings."

"Which ones?" Brynn asked, though the reluctance in his tone made her stomach sink.

"Lady Seraphina's visits." His expression shifted to something sad, almost grieving. "I didn't want to believe it at first. Seraphina and I have worked together for ages. But when I mapped her travel schedule against the incidents..."

He produced another set of documents: travel records, witness statements, magical resonance readings showing traces of violent death magic at damaged sites.

"This is comprehensive," Brynn said, impressed. After days of chasing cryptic warnings, concrete proof felt like a gift.

"I've always believed in meticulous record-keeping." Caelum's modesty seemed genuine. "When you're responsible for souls' eternal rest, attention to detail becomes essential."

"Why would she target the wards?" Dante's voice carried an edge.

His shadows had spread across the floor, creeping toward the table.

Caelum sighed. "I've given this considerable thought. Seraphina has always been dissatisfied with the current balance. She believes the other courts have grown too soft, too willing to show mercy." He gestured to the realm around them. "She's made comments before about how natural deaths are wasteful. That souls should serve the realm's power rather than finding rest."

The explanation made sense. Brynn remembered Seraphina's aggressive demeanor, the violence radiating from her presence: the desert fortress, the scarred warriors, the philosophy of strength through conflict.

"Violence has always been her solution," Caelum continued. "I think she may be trying to weaken the ward system so violent deaths become more common, expanding her domain's influence at the expense of courts like mine."

He produced what appeared to be intercepted correspondence. "My sources have reported meetings between Seraphina and unknown parties. Discussions about 'necessary changes' and 'acceptable losses.'"

Dante took the documents, scanning them intently. "These are authentic?"

"I wish they weren't." Caelum shook his head. "I've known Seraphina since the courts were first established. To think she would endanger everything we've built..." His voice carried genuine pain. "But the evidence is undeniable."

Brynn studied the materials spread across the table. After days of dead ends, someone was finally being helpful.

"What do you recommend for next steps?" she asked.

"Confrontation would be dangerous." Caelum's expression turned thoughtful. "Seraphina is powerful, and if she's truly orchestrating this, she'll have contingency plans. I think our best approach is to present this evidence to the other Death Lords, build consensus before taking action."

"Agreed," Dante said, though his tone suggested he agreed with nothing. "Confrontation would be premature."

"Exactly. We need unity when we act." Caelum's expression grew grave. "The stability of the entire death realm depends on maintaining trust between the courts."

Trust. The word landed differently now.

She glanced at Dante without meaning to. His jaw was tight, his whole body radiating tension despite his neutral expression.

She looked away.

"Your abilities really are impressive," Caelum said, turning to her fully. "I've worked with ward magic for my entire existence, but I've never seen anyone read the patterns the way you do. The way you immediately recognized the significance of the border clusters..." He shook his head in admiration. "Remarkable."

Heat rose to her cheeks. After last night, she'd needed to hear that.

"Thank you," she managed.

His shadows spread further across the floor, pressing against her boots.

She shifted her feet away.

"It must be exhausting work, though," Caelum continued. "All that exposure to damaged magic..." He glanced toward Dante, and something flickered in his eyes. "And working in the more intense courts can't make it easier. The emotional weight of some domains affects everyone differently."

Brynn felt Dante go rigid beside her.

"If you ever want a change of pace," Caelum added easily, "my archives have extensive ward documentation. It might be interesting to compare historical patterns. And..." He paused, his smile turning gentle. "If you ever need somewhere to think, to process everything you've learned recently, my domain is always open to you. Sometimes we all need refuge from darker places."

The offer hit her unexpectedly hard.

Somewhere bright and warm, where souls found rest instead of torment. Somewhere she wouldn't have to see Dante's distance or feel the weight of her parents' suffering.

Somewhere she could breathe.

"That's very generous," she said, and meant it.

Dante's hand twitched at his side.

"The offer's always open." Caelum's voice was warm. Welcoming. Everything Dante's wasn't.

"The evidence is useful," Dante said abruptly, gathering the documents. "We should review it more thoroughly back in my domain."

"Of course." Caelum seemed unbothered. "I only wish I had discovered the pattern sooner. Perhaps we could have prevented some of the damage."

As they prepared to leave, he walked them back through the

gardens toward the transport point. The souls they passed still moved with serene contentment, and the realm continued to radiate beauty.

Brynn found herself walking slower, reluctant to leave. The golden light felt like a balm after weeks of twilight. The peace felt like something she'd forgotten she needed.

Caelum paused as they reached the hilltop. "Keep me informed of your progress. If you need anything. More evidence, witnesses, or just..." He looked at Brynn specifically. "A respite from the investigation's weight. My door is always open."

"We will," Dante replied curtly, already turning toward the transport circle.

Caelum bowed to Dante in farewell, then turned to Brynn. His eyes held warmth and what might have been concern. "It's been a pleasure talking with you, Lady Brynn. I hope when this crisis passes, you'll consider visiting again under happier circumstances. You deserve rest after everything you've endured."

The words shouldn't have affected her so much.

But after crying over her parents' fate, after Dante's rejection, after carrying so much alone, having someone acknowledge that she deserved rest felt like absolution.

She glanced at Dante.

He was watching her. His face was a mask, but his shadows wound tight around his boots.

"I'd like that," she said to Caelum, letting her voice warm in a way she hadn't allowed it to warm for Dante all day. "Very much."

Pain cracked through Dante's expression. His shadows whipped around his feet, agitated and wild.

Caelum's smile brightened. "I look forward to it."

Dante turned sharply toward the transport circle without a word.

She followed, but slowly. Taking her time, making him wait.

As they stepped into the transport circle, the realm began to fade. The light dimmed, the warmth receded, and Brynn felt reality settling back onto her shoulders like a familiar weight.

She kept her gaze fixed straight ahead.

But she felt his eyes on her the whole time.

The golden light disappeared.

The eternal twilight of the Forsaken realm closed around them once more.

XLVIII.
DANTE

Dante stood on the opposite side of the circle from Brynn, watching her face as they materialized in his palace. She hadn't looked at him once during the transport. Hadn't spoken. Had given him exactly the cold distance he'd claimed to want.

It was unbearable.

The familiar chill of his realm's twilight felt stark after Caelum's manufactured paradise. Dante dismissed the attending servants with a gesture, his shadows coiling restlessly around his feet.

The visit had left him on edge. Caelum's evidence had been too perfect, his hospitality too warm, his offer to Brynn too pointed.

My domain is always open to you. You deserve peace after everything you've endured.

Caelum had seen her vulnerability. The grief she carried, the exhaustion from sleepless nights. He'd offered her exactly what she needed most.

Refuge. Light.

Everything Dante's domain couldn't provide.

He led her toward his study without a word, holding the door open when they arrived. She swept past him without acknowledgment, and even that small rejection cut deeper than it should have.

Maps and reports cluttered his desk, but now they had Caelum's documentation to add. Evidence that painted a clear picture of Seraphina's guilt.

Too clear.

Brynn moved to the desk, spreading out the documents. "This is exactly what we needed." Her voice carried the first optimism he'd heard in days. Optimism she'd shown Caelum, not him. "Concrete proof, witness testimony, a clear timeline."

Dante settled into his chair, studying her face rather than the evidence. She looked less exhausted than she had this morning. The golden light had brought color back to her cheeks and eased the tension in her shoulders.

Made her smile at someone who wasn't him.

"Caelum was very thorough," he said slowly.

"Aren't you pleased?" She looked up, challenge in her eyes. "His documentation gives us everything we need."

"Answers every question we might ask." He leaned back, shadows shifting around him. "Perhaps too neatly."

Brynn straightened, arms crossing. "You think he's lying?"

"I think he had explanations ready for everything. Convenient evidence pointing clearly at Seraphina."

"And that's suspicious?" Frustration sharpened her voice. "We finally have proof, and you're dismissing it because it answers our questions?"

His jaw tightened. Maybe he was looking for problems where none existed. Maybe his instincts were being clouded by the way Caelum had looked at her. The way she'd responded to his warmth.

The way she'd relaxed in that paradise like she'd finally found somewhere she belonged.

"His offer was inappropriate," he said finally.

"What offer?" Her frustration shifted to confusion. "The archive access?"

"He offered you a place in his domain." The words came out rougher than intended.

"He offered me access to research materials." Her voice went cold. "And maybe a chance to be somewhere that isn't drowning in eternal twilight and suffering souls. Somewhere I'm actually wanted."

The accusation hit harder than it should have.

"And you think that makes his evidence suspect?" she continued, eyes flashing. "Because he treated me like a person instead of a problem? Because he was kind to me?"

His shadows recoiled.

"Or maybe," Brynn said, stepping closer, wielding her anger like a weapon, "you can't stand that someone else showed me basic consideration. Maybe watching me smile at him reminded you that you've done nothing but push me away since the moment I arrived."

"That's not—"

"You told me there was nothing between us." Her voice cracked. "You said I was just a tool for fixing wards. And now you're angry because someone treated me like I matter?"

He had said those things. Had watched her face crumble and said them anyway, telling himself it was protection when it was cowardice.

And now she'd found someone who offered her everything he refused to give.

"Do you want to go there?" he asked quietly.

She stopped. "What?"

"To his domain." His shadows went completely still. "Would you be happier there?"

She stared at him. "I don't understand why you're asking me that."

He looked away, focusing on the maps rather than her eyes.

"If you would be—" His hands clenched against the chair's edge. Wood creaked under his grip. "I won't..."

Won't what? Won't stop her? Won't beg her to stay? Won't admit that the thought of her choosing Caelum's light over his darkness felt like dying?

"You won't what?" Her voice had softened slightly.

Every instinct screamed at him to take it back. To demand she stay. To stop being such a coward and tell her the truth.

But Elizabeth's dying eyes flashed through his mind. The betrayal as his nature drained her life.

He couldn't do that to Brynn. Couldn't risk her.

Even if letting her go felt like self-mutilation.

"I won't stop you," he managed finally.

The silence was deafening.

She stood frozen, something shifting in her expression—hurt and anger and something else he couldn't read.

"Dante—"

A sharp wail cut through the air. Ward-stones throughout the palace began screaming, crystal shattering over and over, echoing with increasing urgency.

Dante was on his feet instantly. His shadows exploded outward, his hand moving toward Brynn without thinking. Reaching to pull her behind him. To shield her.

He stopped himself just in time.

"Major breach," he said, moving toward the door. "Stay here."

"Like hell," she replied, already following.

The palace erupted into chaos. Death knights surged from the shadows, hollow eye sockets igniting with pale fire. Servants darted into passages.

"My lord!" Lord Aldric materialized beside them. "Multiple attackers are exploiting the ward chaos. They've breached outer defenses!"

"How many?"

"Unknown. They're masking their numbers—"

Aldric's voice was swallowed by the first attacker barreling around the corner—humanoid but flickering between shadow and substance, wielding blades that drank light.

Dante reacted instantly, positioning himself in front of Brynn. His power tore through the attacker's form, dispersing it.

But there were more coming. He could feel them, dozens of hostile presences converging with coordination.

Another rounded the corner, human-shaped but moving with inhuman speed.

Its eyes were fixed on Brynn.

Every instinct he possessed blazed to life.

His shadows lashed out, striking the creature with enough force to send it stumbling. The air chilled as his restraint began to slip, frost forming on the walls.

"Stay behind me," he growled.

He felt her press against the stone wall, her breath quick and sharp in the frigid air. The sound made his instincts snarl.

They'd come into his domain. Into his palace.

They were hunting her.

Two more attackers emerged, flanking with coordination that suggested planning. His shadows spread wider, eager for the hunt. The temperature dropped another ten degrees.

Another wave. Five this time, tight formation. One broke away, darting down a side corridor.

"They're trying to flank us," Brynn warned.

He was already moving. Death magic erupted in a pulse. Glass exploded throughout the corridor, and he heard her gasp as his shadows surged around her, keeping shards from touching her.

The attackers before him vanished as his power cut through them.

But there were more.

"Dante!" Her voice cut through, urgent, but he could barely hear it over the roar of his own power.

His perception expanded, magic weaving through the palace like a web. Dozens of hostile presences. Coordinated. Coming for her.

His restraint began to fracture.

Waves of power poured off him. He barely registered her calling his name again. The sound felt distant compared to the threats.

An attacker breached the eastern wing. His magic reached out, obliterated it.

Another closed within fifty feet of where she stood.

His restraint snapped completely.

Power erupted, shaking the palace's foundations. Every shadow in his domain responded, rushing toward him. Temperature plummeted so drastically that the air crystallized.

Windows blew out. Stone cracked. Metal twisted under the strain.

He no longer fought individual attackers. He hunted every hostile entity at once, consciousness stretching across every inch of his domain like the wrath of death.

But it wasn't enough.

As long as a single threat lingered, his nature demanded more. More power. More destruction. More death.

Stone fractured beneath his presence. Air thickened with pressure.

He could hear her calling his name from somewhere far away, but it was distant, irrelevant compared to the hunt that consumed him.

Hunt. Kill. Protect.

Nothing else mattered.

His power surged outward, searching every corner of the palace. Walls shuddered as it hunted for threats that no longer existed.

Every movement became a potential enemy. Every sound a target.

Something shifted in his peripheral vision. Too close to what he guarded.

His attention snapped toward it, power gathering to destroy—

Warm hands pressed against his face.

The sensation cut through everything.

Human skin against his.

His eyes flew wide. Chaos faded as clarity returned in a rush.

Brynn stood before him, her palms cradling his face, warmth radiating despite the freezing air. Her eyes were wide with fear, but not of the attackers. Of him.

Of him.

She was touching him.

Skin to skin.

And she was alive.

"Dante." Her voice shook. "It's me. It's over. Come back."

His hands came up without thinking, covering hers. His gloved hands over her bare ones, feeling the pulse of life beneath her skin.

No death magic responding. No drain. No destruction.

Just her heartbeat.

"How...?" The word emerged broken.

"I don't know." Wonder mixed with fear in her eyes. "But you're not hurting me."

He stared at her. At the impossible reality of her touching him and living.

Nothing between us, he'd told her. *I could kill you.*

Every excuse. Every wall. Every rejection.

Beliefs. Certainties he'd held for his entire existence. The fundamental truth of his existence: his touch meant death.

Except for her.

"I could have killed you," he said, voice breaking. "I couldn't hear you. Couldn't stop—"

"But you didn't." Her hands stayed steady. Grounding him. "You came back to me."

He leaned into her touch, trembling with the effort of believing it was real.

"This isn't possible," he whispered.

"And yet." Her thumb moved across his cheekbone, and his breath shattered. "Here I am."

The corridor lay in ruins around them. Ice and broken glass, cracked stone and twisted metal. Evidence of what he became when his nature was unleashed.

But her pulse didn't race. Her eyes held his.

"Brynn," he said.

"All those times you pushed me away." Her voice cracked. "All those times you said you'd hurt me. That there couldn't be anything between us."

He closed his eyes against the truth of it.

"I believed it," he managed.

"I know." Her voice softened slightly. "I know you believed it."

He pressed his forehead against hers, hardly believing the contact was possible. No death. No destruction. Just this. Her skin against his, her breath mingling with his own.

"I thought I'd lose myself," he whispered. "Thought you'd be caught in it—"

"I'm right here." Her grip tightened. "I'm not going anywhere."

I won't stop you, he'd told her minutes ago. Had been ready to let her go to Caelum's paradise because he'd believed his nature made him too dangerous.

Footsteps echoed through the ruined corridors.

Reality crashed back in.

"My lord." Aldric's form flickered into view. "Vex and Seraphina. They felt your power. They're coming."

Dante stepped back from Brynn. Her hands fell away.

Cold rushed in where warmth had been.

But if the other Death Lords saw her touching him. Saw that she'd survived direct contact with his unleashed power—

"How long?" he demanded.

"Minutes."

Not enough time.

He scanned the destruction: frost-cracked stone, broken glass—evidence of what he became when anyone threatened what was his.

"You were behind shadow-barriers," he said, voice rough. "The entire time. You never saw me lose restraint."

"But I wasn't—"

"You were." His eyes met hers. "Or they'll dissect you to find out how you survived. They'll want to know why a mortal can touch The Reaper and live."

Her face went pale. "Understood."

He forced himself to step further away, establishing distance between a Death Lord and his tribute.

Vex appeared first, gold eyes sweeping over the wreckage. "Impressive work. Though perhaps excessive?"

Lady Seraphina followed, blood-red hair catching the dim light. "Your power shook the Violent Court's war-stones. What required such enthusiasm?"

"A coordinated assault on my domain." Dante kept his voice cold. "Multiple infiltrators using ward-chaos as cover."

"All eliminated?" Vex's smile showed too many teeth. "No survivors for questioning?"

"None."

"Pity." Seraphina's gaze shifted to Brynn. "Your tribute appears remarkably intact for someone caught in The Reaper's fury."

"Shadow-barriers," he said flatly. "Standard protocol."

"How fortunate." Vex stepped closer, gaze fixed on Brynn. "Most mortals don't survive proximity to uncontrolled death magic. She must be remarkably resilient."

Dante went very still. Vex was fishing.

"Strange that assassins would target your domain specifically," Seraphina continued. "What could they want here that other courts lack?"

"Ward archives. The most comprehensive research in the death realm."

"Research." Seraphina's smile turned sharp. "How scholarly."

Her disbelief was apparent, as was Vex's.

"Well," Vex said finally, "crisis resolved. But perhaps restraint might serve better in the future. Such displays attract attention from those who prefer the status quo."

"Noted," Dante replied.

"Excellent." Vex's form began dissolving. "It would be unfortunate if these incidents became regular."

Once they left, silence filled the ruined corridor. Dante waited, extending his senses to ensure they were truly gone.

Then he turned to face her.

She'd moved closer now that they were alone.

"They don't believe you," she said quietly.

"They suspect something. Just not what."

"Yet."

She was right. Eventually, someone would wonder why The Reaper had lost himself so completely protecting a mortal tribute.

"This makes you dangerous," he said. "The first mortal to touch me and live. The moment they know, they'll want to claim you or eliminate you."

Her chin lifted. "What if I don't give them the chance?"

"They'll take it anyway."

"So we hide it."

"We hide it," he agreed.

But they both knew some secrets were too big to contain.

"We should get some rest," he said finally.

She nodded, but neither of them moved.

XLIX.
DANTE

The wreckage surrounded them. Broken glass, scorch marks, the smell of spent death magic. His guards had been dismissed. The other Death Lords had retreated.

And his face was still burning where she'd touched him.

"Come with me." The words were out before he could stop them.

She nodded.

He led her through the shadows, bypassing corridors where servants might see. They emerged in his private chambers, the one place no one entered without invitation. Not his servants. Not his guards. Not anyone, in centuries.

Until her.

The hearth still held embers from this morning. He waved a hand without thinking, and flames leapt up, casting warm orange light across the room. A strange contrast to his nature: this pocket of warmth he'd carved out for himself in a realm of cold. His one indulgence.

She looked around. Taking in the space. Seeing him in the books stacked by the chair, the worn blanket he'd never replaced, the bed that suddenly seemed to dominate the room.

His gloves were still on.

He looked down at his hands. Black leather, butter-soft from years of wear. His constant companions. His barrier against the world.

Against her.

Slowly, he reached for the first glove. His fingers fumbled with the button at his wrist. Ridiculous. He'd done this thousands of times. But his hands wouldn't cooperate, trembling too badly to work the simple fastening.

She crossed the room.

He went still as she stopped in front of him. Close enough that he could see the firelight dancing in her eyes. Close enough that her warmth ghosted across his skin.

Her hands rose to his.

"Let me."

He should say no. Should maintain this last barrier between them.

He turned his wrist toward her instead.

Her fingers worked the button free. Gentle. Unhurried. Like they had all the time in the world. Like undressing the most dangerous creature in the death realms was something she did every day.

She tugged the glove off, finger by finger, and set it aside. Reached for his other hand.

He watched her work the second button. Watched her slide the leather free.

His bare hands hung at his sides.

Brynn looked up at him.

Then she raised her hand. Palm up.

He stared at it. Such a simple gesture. Such an ordinary thing, to offer your hand to someone. People did it every day in the mortal world. Casually. Thoughtlessly. Never understanding what a gift it was.

His hand met hers.

The first thing he noticed was the texture. The calluses on her fingers, rough from years of lockpicks and rope. He'd forgotten that skin had texture, that each person's hands told a story.

The second thing was warmth.

Such an inadequate word. Her hand was alive. Heat radiated from her palm into his, and his body didn't know how to process the information. His nerve endings were screaming, overstimulated, trying to interpret the sensation they'd forgotten how to understand.

His fingers trembled. He couldn't stop them.

She stepped closer.

His breath stopped. Actually stopped, lungs forgetting their function, because she was right there and she wasn't dying and he could feel her pulse thrumming against his palm—

Her free hand rose toward his face.

He flinched.

The reaction was involuntary, a lifetime of conditioning snapping through him. *Don't let them close. Don't let them touch—*

She paused. Waited.

Patient. So impossibly patient with the Reaper who'd forgotten how to be touched.

He forced himself still. Forced his eyes to meet hers. Managed a nod that felt like surrender.

Her fingertips brushed his cheek.

The sound that escaped him—

He didn't have a name for it. Something between a gasp and a groan, wrenched from somewhere beneath his ribs. His eyes slammed shut. His whole body shuddered.

Her thumb stroked along his cheekbone.

His knees almost buckled.

Just that. Just her thumb, tracing a slow arc across his face, and he was shaking so hard his teeth should have been chattering. The apex predator of the death realms, undone by a thumb on his cheekbone.

Pathetic. Weak.

He didn't care.

Her fingers slid along his jaw. Exploring. Learning the shape of him through touch, and the intimacy of it was so piercing that it felt like she was reaching directly into his chest.

He'd forgotten what this felt like, to be known through someone's hands. To have another person map your edges and choose to stay anyway. He'd told himself for so long that he didn't need it, that he'd evolved beyond it. That touch was a weakness he'd outgrown.

Lies. All of it.

He was starving. Had been for centuries without realizing it. Now her hand was on him, and he didn't know what to do with it.

"Dante." Her voice, soft. "Open your eyes."

He couldn't. If he opened his eyes, he'd have to see her looking at him. Have to witness whatever was on her face: pity, perhaps, or worse, the dawning realization of how broken he truly was.

"Please."

He opened his eyes.

She was looking at him like he was something rare.

The breath that left him came out ragged. He couldn't think. Couldn't do anything but feel.

His free hand rose toward her face. Hovering. Not quite brave enough to close the distance.

What if this is the touch that kills her? What if the first one was a fluke—

She leaned into his palm.

Her cheek was soft. He could feel the tiny muscles shifting as she pressed into his touch. Could feel the heat of her blood beneath her skin. Could feel a person choosing to be close to him.

His thumb traced her cheekbone. Reverent. Terrified.

She didn't die.

His hand curved around the side of her face, fingers sliding into her hair. Silk and softness, and his hand was shaking so badly he was probably pulling it, but she didn't complain. Just watched him with those steady eyes while he fell apart.

"You're shaking," she whispered.

He tried to laugh. It came out broken. "I can't stop."

"Does it hurt?"

"No." *Yes.* "It's just...a lot."

That was the understatement of the century. His entire body felt like an exposed nerve. Every point of contact was a universe of sensation. Her hand in his, her cheek against his palm, her fingers still resting on his jaw. Too much and not enough, and he didn't know how to hold it all.

She stepped closer.

Her body pressed against his.

A low growl rumbled through his chest.

His arms wrapped around her. Instinct, not thought. Her head tucked under his chin. Her arms circled his waist. Her warmth bled into him.

His face buried in her hair. Smoke from the attack. Warm citrus underneath that was just her, and he was breathing it in with desperate gasps because he didn't know how long this would last, didn't know when she'd realize what a terrible idea this was—

She held him tighter.

Her fingers dug into his spine, holding tight, like she was afraid he'd disappear. Like she was claiming him just as much as he was claiming her.

His shoulders were shaking. His breath came ragged and uneven. He was coming apart in her arms and couldn't stop it.

He should pull back. Compose himself. Pretend he hadn't just buried his face in a mortal woman's hair like she was the only thing holding him together.

He buried his face deeper instead.

Her hand came up to cradle the back of his skull. The gesture undid him all over again.

His arms tightened around her. Probably too tight. He couldn't gauge pressure anymore, couldn't remember how hard it was when you weren't trying to kill someone. But she didn't complain. Just held on while he learned how to let himself be held.

Minutes passed. Maybe hours. His body slowly stopped trembling, the overwhelming flood of sensation settling into something he could almost bear.

She didn't let go.

Eventually, she pulled back. Just far enough to look at him.

He braced for it. The pity. The discomfort. The realization that she'd just witnessed the Lord of the Forsaken break and needed to extract herself politely.

"Hi," she said softly.

"Hi."

"Was that okay?" she asked.

The question almost broke him again. *Was that okay?* As if she'd done something wrong. As if giving him the first genuine touch he'd experienced in longer than he could remember could ever be anything less than—

"Okay," he repeated. The word came out hoarse. "You're asking if that was okay."

Uncertainty flickered across her face.

He caught her hand. Pressed her palm to his cheek. Held it there while he looked at her with everything he'd spent so long learning to hide.

"That was the single most..." He stopped. Started again. "I don't have words. For what that was."

"Good," she said. "Words are overrated anyway."

His lips twitched—almost a smile.

He guided her toward the settee near the hearth without letting go, unwilling to break contact now that he finally had it.

She curled into his side before he could overthink it.

Her head found his shoulder like it belonged there. Her hand settled on his chest, over his heart. Her legs tucked up, body fitting against his.

His arm wrapped around her.

They sat in silence. The fire crackled. His shadows drifted in lazy spirals, utterly content.

His free hand found hers. Their fingers interlaced.

He studied the way their hands fit together. Her small fingers between his long ones. Her warmth against his cold. Her calluses against his smooth palms.

He memorized it.

"Stop thinking so loud," she murmured against his shoulder. "I can hear you catastrophizing from here."

"I don't catastrophize."

"You absolutely do. I can feel your whole body tensing up."

She wasn't wrong. He forced his muscles to relax. Forced himself to stay present instead of spiraling into all the ways this could end badly.

Her thumb traced circles on his chest. Idle. Soothing. Like

touching him was natural. Like she'd been doing it for years instead of minutes.

His arm tightened around her.

At some point, her breathing evened into sleep.

He closed his eyes and listened to her breathe and let himself exist in this moment without trying to hold onto it.

She leaned against his side. Her hand over his heart.

Her fingers twitched in sleep, curling tighter into his shirt.

He pressed his lips to the top of her head.

His shadows curled around them both.

For the first time in centuries, the Reaper slept peacefully.

L.
DANTE

He woke to warmth.

For a disorienting moment, he couldn't place it. His chambers were always cold, the hearth always dying overnight, the chill of the Forsaken court seeping through stone walls that had never known summer. But something was different. Something was—

Brynn.

She was still tucked against his side, one hand curled into his shirt, her breath slow and even against his collarbone. At some point in the night, she'd shifted, wedging herself more firmly into the space between his body and the arm of the settee, as though determined to claim every available inch of contact.

His arm was still around her. Numb from the elbow down. He didn't move it.

This was the part where it ended. He knew how this worked. She'd touched him and survived, yes, but it had been the adrenaline, the chaos of the assassination attempt, some temporary alignment of magic that would correct itself by morning. She'd pull away and he'd feel nothing but cold air where she'd been, and the brief, impossible mercy of her skin against his would become another thing he'd lost.

He held himself still. Didn't breathe too deeply. Stayed in the space between sleeping and waking where she was warm against him and nothing had gone wrong yet.

Her breathing changed.

He felt her awake gradually. The shift in her body, muscles tensing as consciousness returned. The slight catch in her rhythm when she registered where she was. Who she was pressed against.

He braced himself.

She yawned against his chest.

Then she settled deeper into his side, her hand sliding from his shirt to his forearm. Her thumb traced a lazy circle against the inside of his wrist, like this was something they did. Like she'd touched him a hundred times before and would touch him a hundred times again.

His throat closed.

"Your arm is numb, isn't it?" she said, her voice rough with sleep.

"Completely."

"You should have moved me."

"No."

She tilted her head up. Her hair was a disaster, pressed flat on one side, wild on the other. A crease from his shirt collar ran across her cheek. Her eyes were half-closed, squinting against even the dim twilight.

"Stop looking at me like that," she mumbled. "I haven't even had tea."

"Like what?"

"Like I performed a miracle. I fell asleep on your shoulder. People do that."

People do that. Three words that carved straight through him. Normal people, with normal lives, fell asleep on each other's shoulders every night without it being the most significant thing to happen to them in hundreds of years.

She sat up and stretched, arms overhead, spine arching. His arm flooded with returning sensation, pins and needles crawling from elbow to fingertips. He flexed his hand.

She reached over and took it.

Wrapped her fingers around his and held on while she rubbed sleep from her eyes with her free hand.

"Still works," she said, and the corner of her mouth curved.

"Apparently."

She looked at him, and whatever she found in his face made her go still.

"You thought it wouldn't," she said quietly. "You thought you'd wake up and I'd be gone."

He couldn't answer that. Couldn't explain the particular cruelty of hope when you'd spent centuries without it.

She squeezed his hand. "I'm still here. And you're not getting rid of me before breakfast."

She stood, then wandered toward the window, stepping directly into a stack of books he'd left on the floor.

"Those are in the way," she informed him.

"They've been there for decades."

"Then they've been in the way for decades."

He felt his mouth twitch. The unfamiliar pull of muscles that had been dormant too long. She noticed and pointed at his face.

"There. Right there. You almost smiled."

"I don't smile."

"You *almost* smile. Which is worse, honestly. It's like watching someone get to the edge of a sneeze and not follow through."

He should not have found that charming. He found it devastating.

"Come on," he said, rising from the chair. "Let's go get food."

She followed him through to his private dining room, but halfway down the corridor, her hand found his. Her fingers slid between his like they belonged there, and she tugged him to a stop.

"What?" he asked.

"Nothing." She was looking up at him with an expression he couldn't quite read. "I just wanted to do that."

His shadows curled around her wrist in response, and she laughed—a soft, surprised sound.

"They're very clingy this morning."

"They're not the only ones." The words came out before he could stop them.

Her eyebrows rose. "Was that a joke? Did the Reaper just make a joke?"

"No."

"It was. You made a joke about being clingy. I'm marking this day in history."

"I take it back."

"Too late. It's already marked." She started walking again, pulling him along by their joined hands. "The day the Lord of the Forsaken admitted to being clingy. They'll write songs about it."

"They will not."

"Ballads, Dante. Mournful ballads about the Reaper who just wanted to hold hands."

His teeth clenched against the retort he wanted to make, but warmth was spreading through his chest. A feeling that was very close to happiness.

The dining room was familiar territory now, after weeks of working meals and strategy sessions. But everything felt different this morning. She pulled him toward the table, then turned and leaned back against its edge, tugging him closer by their still-joined hands until he stood over her.

"Hi," she said softly.

"Hi."

His free hand rose to her face. His thumb traced along her cheekbone, and she leaned into the touch, her eyes fluttering half-closed.

"I could get used to this," she murmured.

"Don't." The word came out rougher than he intended. "Getting used to me is dangerous."

"So you keep saying." Her hands slid up his chest, fingers curling into the fabric of his shirt. "And yet here I am. Undestroyed."

"The day is young."

She laughed again, and he found himself leaning down, drawn by the sound, by the warmth of her, by the impossible reality of her hands on him and his hands on her and neither of them dying from it—

The servant materialized in the doorway.

Brynn jerked back instinctively, trying to pull her hand free. They'd agreed to keep this quiet. To protect her from becoming an even bigger target than she already was.

Dante's hand tightened on hers.

She shot him a warning look. *What are you doing?*

He didn't let go.

The spirit stood frozen, translucent form flickering. Its eyes darted from their joined hands to their proximity to the way Dante's other hand was still curved around Brynn's jaw.

"Breakfast," Dante said flatly. "For two."

The servant's form flickered again before retreating so quickly it nearly left a vapor trail.

Brynn let out a breath. "We agreed—"

"I know."

"You're the one who said it was dangerous for people to know—"

"I know."

"Then why—"

"Because I couldn't." The admission came out rough, almost angry. His shoulders went rigid, shadows coiling with agitation. "You tried to pull away and I couldn't make myself let go."

She stared at him. The Reaper, Lord of the Forsaken, who had built his entire existence around restraint, couldn't let go of her hand.

"The entire palace will know by midday," he said, releasing her fingers at last. "I'm sorry. That was selfish."

"Dante." She caught his hand before he could pull away completely. "I don't care."

"You should. This paints a target—"

"I already have a target on my back. Someone's already tried to kill me." She squeezed his fingers. "At least now I get something good along with the danger."

He looked at her for a long moment. The walls he'd spent decades building were crumbling, and he couldn't find it in himself to care.

"You're reckless," he said quietly.

"So are you, apparently." She smiled.

His thumb brushed across her knuckles once before he stepped back. "Sit. Eat. We need to talk about what happens next."

"So commanding." But she was smiling as she took her usual chair, and when he sat beside her instead of across from her, she immediately hooked her ankle around his under the table.

They ate like that. Shoulders brushing, legs tangled, her stealing food from his plate just to see if he'd let her.

He let her.

Halfway through the meal, she set down her fork and asked, "Any word on who sent the assassin?"

"My shadow-guards are hunting." He reached for his glass.

"But you have suspicions." She waved her fork. "Beyond the obvious—same person behind the ward failures, same person behind the knife in my direction."

"The timing was too precise to be a coincidence. They knew exactly when the wards would destabilize." He took a sip of water. "Which means access to information most don't have."

She nodded slowly, tearing a piece of bread between her fingers. "So we're looking for someone with inside knowledge. That narrows it down to what—the other Death Lords and their inner circles?"

"Essentially."

"Flattering company." She stole another piece of fruit from his plate, her knee pressing more firmly against his. "Any theories on which of your fellow Death Lords might want universal chaos?"

He set down his glass, considering. "All of them benefit in some way. Seraphina gains power when violence increases. Vex feeds on the desperation that comes with instability." He traced a finger along the table's edge. "Caelum positions himself as the reasonable alternative whenever chaos makes the other courts look dangerous. Instability benefits his reputation as the merciful option."

"And Thessa?"

"The Lingering court profits from souls that refuse to move on. Chaos creates more of them."

She was quiet for a moment, chewing thoughtfully. "We've visited Seraphina, Thessa, and Caelum. We still need the Consumed court."

His hand stilled on his glass.

Her eyes narrowed.

"You don't want to take me there."

"Vex is different from the others." He chose his words carefully. "His power works through desire. Through obsession. He finds what you want most and uses it against you."

"You think I can't handle it?"

"I think you're remarkably resistant to most forms of manipulation." He released his glass and leaned back in his chair. "But Vex doesn't manipulate the way others do. He gets inside your head. Shows you things. Makes you want things you shouldn't want."

"Things like what?"

Like me, he didn't say. *Like staying in this realm forever. Like abandoning everything you were for the promise of something that will never satisfy you.*

"Things that feel true until you realize they've consumed you," he said instead.

She turned in her chair to face him. "You're worried about me."

"Yes."

"Because of Vex, or because of what he might show me?"

"Both."

She grabbed his hand again and squeezed. The contact still sent a jolt through him.

"I survived the Violent court," she said. "I survived your court. I survived someone literally trying to kill me last night." Her thumb traced across his knuckles. "I can handle one manipulative Death Lord with an obsession problem."

"You don't know what he's capable of."

"Then tell me." She squeezed his hand again. "Brief me. Prepare me. But don't try to protect me by keeping me ignorant. That's not how this works."

That's not how this works. As if they had an established dynamic. As if "this" was something with rules and expectations that she had every right to invoke.

He supposed it was. He supposed she did.

"The Consumed court looks beautiful," he said finally, his thumb moving absently against her palm. "Perfect, even. Midnight light, endless luxury, everything designed to appeal to your deepest desires. But it's all hollow. The food never satisfies. The wine never fills you. The pleasures never end because they never actually complete."

"Sounds exhausting."

"It is. That's the point. Vex feeds on the wanting, not the having.

His entire realm is designed to create desire that can never be fulfilled."

"We go together," she said. "We stay together. We don't let him separate us." Her grip tightened on his hand.

He should say no. Should insist she stay here, where his shadows could protect her, where Vex's influence couldn't reach.

But she was right. They needed to investigate the Consumed court. And she'd proven, again and again, that she was stronger than he gave her credit for.

"Deal," he said.

She smiled—that sharp, satisfied smile that meant she'd won and she knew it. "Good. When do we leave?"

He glanced toward the window, where the eternal twilight was brightening toward its approximation of midday.

"This afternoon. I want my shadow-guards to finish their hunt first. If there's any information about last night's attack, I want it before we walk into Vex's domain."

"Reasonable." She stole one last piece of fruit from his plate, popping it into her mouth with exaggerated satisfaction. "That gives us a few hours."

"For what?"

"I don't know." She leaned back in her chair, her ankle still hooked around his under the table. "I've never had a few hours with nowhere to be and nothing trying to kill me. It's a novel experience."

He was in over his head.

He'd grown familiar with the sharp ache of want over recent weeks. This was different. Quieter. The realization settling into his bones that this woman, stealing his food and teasing him about ballads, had become essential.

Not because he needed her to fix the wards.

Because he needed *her*.

"We could stay here," he said, and his voice came out rougher than he intended. "A few hours of nothing trying to kill you sounds like something worth protecting."

Her expression softened, the sharpness giving way to warmth. "Yeah?"

"Yeah."

She smiled again, but this one was different. Gentler. She tugged on his hand, pulling him closer, and when she leaned up to press her lips to his cheek—soft and quick and over before he could fully process it—his entire world narrowed to that single point of contact.

"Okay," she said quietly. "Let's do that."

They stayed at the table. Her legs tangled with his. His hand in hers.

She trusted him. He could see it in the way she leaned into his side, the way she'd stopped bracing for impact every time he moved.

He wasn't sure he deserved it.

He held her hand anyway.

LI.
BRYNN

Dante's hand brushed hers as she passed him the transport documents, and neither of them pulled away.

His fingers were gentle against her knuckles, the contact so light it could have been accidental. But they both knew it wasn't. They'd been doing this for hours now, finding excuses to touch, testing this impossible thing they'd discovered. She could touch him. And live.

Her pulse stuttered as his thumb traced a slow path across the back of her hand. Such a small thing. Such a devastating thing. The Lord of the Forsaken, the Reaper, was stroking her hand like she was something worth protecting instead of something that should shatter at his touch. His shadows curled around her ankles the way they always did now, another way for him to reach for her.

"The transport circle is ready," he said, his voice dropping low enough to make her stomach flip.

"Then we should go."

She didn't move. Neither did he. His dark eyes held hers, and she watched want flicker in their depths. Uncertainty. The same war she felt every time they stood this close.

She was in so much trouble. But the warning had lost its edge somewhere along the way. She'd been in trouble since the moment she'd looked at the Reaper.

Dante's jaw tightened, and he slowly pulled his hand back. He reached for his gloves on the table and tugged them on, one finger at a time.

"We should go."

Cold air rushed into the space where he had been. She missed it immediately.

They stepped into the transport circle together, his shadows wrapping around them both for the journey. Even that felt different now. Personal rather than merely practical. The darkness pressed close, carrying his scent, his presence, surrounding her in a way that made her hyperaware of every inch of space between their bodies.

"Remember," he said quietly as the magic built around them, "Vex feeds on desire. Don't let the environment influence your judgment."

The warning should have prepared her. It didn't.

Rolling hills stretched before them, covered in grass that shimmered like spun silk under a star-strewn sky. Crystal towers rose from the landscape, catching pale moonlight. The darkness felt warm rather than cold, designed for whispered secrets and stolen moments. The pull of it wrapped around her like silk, tugging at something low in her chest.

She forced herself to look away, focusing on Dante instead. His jaw was tight, shadows gathered defensively around his boots, his shoulders carrying tension she'd learned to read over weeks of watching him. He didn't want her here. Not because he thought she couldn't handle it, but because he was worried about what this place might do to her.

She should have found it patronizing. Instead, she stepped closer to him as they walked, using his presence as an anchor against the realm's seductive pull. His shadows responded immediately, tendrils of darkness brushing against her wrist, her hip, her shoulder. Greeting her. Claiming her. She wondered if he knew they did that, wondered if she should tell him.

She definitely wasn't going to tell him how much she liked it.

The courtiers they passed were all beautiful, their movements graceful and inviting, but their eyes gave them away. Hollow, searching, never finding what they wanted. She'd seen that look before, on street corners in the human realm, on the faces of gamblers who'd lost everything and kept betting anyway—the look of people chasing something that would never satisfy them.

The grass that had looked lustrous from a distance proved brittle underfoot, crumbling to ash with each step. The scent in the air was intoxicating. Sweet incense, exotic spices, fine wine. But underneath lurked something stale. Overripe fruit. Beautiful rot. This whole realm felt like an elaborate setup. The kind of deal that seemed too good until you read the fine print and realized you'd signed away your soul.

"The gates," she murmured, keeping her voice low.

Dante glanced at her, one eyebrow raised.

She nodded toward the entrance. "Brass with gold leaf. The gems are clouded. It's all fake."

Approval flickered across his face. "Everything here is," he said quietly. "Beautiful promises that deliver nothing."

The massive doors swung open, and a figure emerged.

Lord Vex moved without seeming to hurry, yet covered the distance between them faster than should have been possible. When he smiled, it was too perfect, and he was focused entirely on her rather than Dante.

Cold slithered down her spine.

"Lord Reaper," Vex said, his voice smooth as honey wine, but his gaze never left Brynn's face. The intensity felt invasive, as if he were storing away information. "And the famous ward-reader, Brynn."

He said her name like he was savoring it. Like he had any right to it. She kept her expression neutral, but her hand drifted closer to Dante's without conscious thought, and his shadows immediately curled around her wrist in response.

Dante's voice came out flat. "Vex." Only one word, but the temperature dropped several degrees.

Vex's smile didn't waver as he led them through halls lined with mirrors and gold leaf. He kept up steady commentary, but she felt his attention returning to her again and again, studying her reactions, the way she moved, the distance she kept from Dante. *He's reading me. Like a mark.* She knew this game. She'd played it herself a hundred times, identifying weaknesses in potential targets, figuring out what they wanted most so she could use it against them. The difference was that she'd stolen jewelry and coins. Vex looked like he wanted to steal something far more personal.

The mirrors didn't show reflections. They showed desires.

She caught a glimpse of herself in one polished surface, and her breath stopped. Wealth. Belonging. Dante reaching for her without hesitation, without fear, his hands on her face and his mouth—

She jerked her gaze away, heat flooding her cheeks. The mirrors knew what she wanted most. And they weren't subtle about it.

Vex's receiving chamber dripped with luxury, every surface designed to overwhelm and seduce. He gestured for them to sit, his gaze fixed on her with unnerving focus. "Now then. Let's discuss these troubling ward failures, shall we?"

He moved to a cabinet and retrieved some documents. But as he spread them across the table, her stomach dropped.

These weren't reports about ward damage. They were about her.

Maps showing everywhere she'd traveled since arriving in the death realm, marked with dates. Detailed sketches of her working with ward-tools, drawn from angles that suggested the artist had been watching from hiding. Notes describing her magical responses, her reactions to different types of death magic, and observations about her body language during conversations she'd thought were private.

Her hands went cold against the table.

"Your abilities really are remarkable," Vex said, settling into an ornate chair. "The way you responded to those ward-tools in the human realm. Immediate resonance, wasn't it? Your blood sang to them before you even understood what they were."

She remembered the moment in the vault when the tools had called to her, when ancient magic had responded to her touch, before she'd even arrived in the death realm.

"How do you know about that?" The question came out smaller than she'd intended, and she hated herself for it.

"I make it my business to understand anything that interests me."

His smile sharpened. "And you, sweet thing, have been fascinating from the moment you arrived."

Dante had gone still beside her. She could feel the tension radiating from him, his shadows spreading slowly across the floor, frost beginning to form at the edges of the windows.

He was getting ready to kill someone. She probably shouldn't have found that as comforting as she did.

"I believe in being thorough." Vex reached for another document. "For instance, I know you've been experiencing headaches after working with particularly damaged ward-stones. The pain settles behind your right eye, doesn't it? Feels like pressure building until you think your skull might crack."

She'd barely mentioned the headaches to anyone. Had tried to hide them. How did he know about the specific location, the exact sensation?

"Vex," Dante said, his voice dropping low enough to promise violence.

"Oh, but there's more." Vex's attention remained on her. "I know the connection feels different in different domains. Stronger in some places, weaker in others. I even know..." He leaned closer, and his scent hit her. Rich and sweet on the surface, but with vinegar underneath. "...that when you held those tools for the first time, they *called* to you. Not just responded. Called. Like they'd been waiting for you specifically."

Her chest tightened. She could still remember that moment. The way the tools had hummed when she touched them, as if they'd been sleeping and her presence had awakened them. The feeling of rightness, of coming home to something she'd never known she'd lost. She'd never told anyone about that feeling. Not even Dante. *Especially* not Dante, because some part of her had been afraid of what it meant.

The temperature plummeted. Ice crept across the windows, audible cracks forming, and the air thickened under the pressure.

"Keep your distance, Vex." Dante's voice was steel wrapped in frost.

"Distance?" Vex finally looked at him, molten eyes bright with amusement. "I'm just showing interest in her remarkable abilities. Such passion, Lord Reaper. One might think you have a personal stake in this."

Her cheeks burned, but she couldn't tell if it was embarrassment or something else entirely.

Vex turned back to her, moving his chair closer with a scrape that made her flinch. "Such a strong connection to ward magic. Almost like you're *meant* for it."

The frost spread faster now, crawling across every surface. Dante's power responding to his anger, whether he wanted it to or not. The rigid set of his shoulders, the way his hands curled into fists, the dark glow building in his eyes.

"That's enough," Dante said.

"Is it?" Vex rose, moving around the table toward her. "I find her responses to the magic quite intriguing. The way it bends to her will, almost like she's commanding it rather than channeling it. Don't you?"

Dante stood abruptly, his shadows surging outward. "Step away from her."

Her pulse jumped in her throat, and she didn't know if it was fear of Vex or reaction to the possessiveness in Dante's voice. Both. Definitely both.

Vex stopped behind her chair, and she could feel unnatural heat radiating from him, warmth that felt hungry rather than comforting. His voice dropped to a murmur. "Such a strong connection to power that should be foreign to you. Makes one wonder what else is hiding in that blood of yours."

Frost from Dante's side. Heat from Vex's. She was caught between two forces that could destroy her, and some hysterical part of her brain noted that this was becoming a theme.

She should start keeping a list. Ways her life had gone sideways. "Caught between Death Lords" could go right under "framed for parents' murder" and "sent as tribute to the realm of the dead."

"Now, Vex." Dante's voice carried the tone he used when he was moments from unleashing his full power.

"Protective, aren't we?" Vex's hands settled on the back of her chair, bracketing her without quite touching. "Tell me, does she know why those tools responded to her so readily? Why the magic answers her touch like she belongs to it?"

His words stirred doubt in her chest. Did Dante know something about her abilities that he hadn't shared? She glanced at him, and for a fraction of a second, she saw it, guilt flickering across his expression. Or fear. Before she could be certain, it was gone, replaced by cold fury.

The ice crept faster across the windows. The crystal walls began to crack under the temperature strain.

"Careful, Reaper," Vex said, his smile turning hungry. "We wouldn't want any accidents. You know how... fragile mortals can be."

"We're done here." Dante's voice was flat, final. "Brynn. We're leaving."

She started to rise, but Vex moved faster.

His hand closed around her wrist before she could pull away, his grip burning hot against her skin. He yanked her back, spinning her to face him, and his other hand came up to cup her jaw, forcing her to meet his eyes.

"Such a waste," he breathed, his thumb stroking across her cheekbone. "All that power sleeping in your blood, and he keeps you ignorant. Keeps you dependent. Don't you want to know what you really are?"

She couldn't move. Couldn't breathe. His touch felt foreign, draining, like he was trying to drink the warmth from her through the contact.

"Ask him about your bloodline," Vex whispered, his lips close enough that she could smell that sickly-sweet rot on his breath. "Ask him how long he's known. Ask him why he hasn't—"

The shadows slammed into Vex.

One moment, his hands were on her face, his body too close, his words crawling under her skin. Next, he was across the room, slamming against the crystal wall so hard the entire structure cracked. Dante's shadows wrapped around his throat, his chest, his limbs. Pinning him, while frost exploded across every surface in the chamber.

Dante stood between them now, and she couldn't see his face, but she could see his shoulders heaving. The shadows pouring off him were violent, writhing, hungry.

"You touched her." He advanced on Vex. "You put your hands on her."

Vex wheezed against the pressure on his throat, but somehow he was still smiling. "Struck a nerve, did I?"

The shadows tightened. The crystal behind Vex's head cracked further, spiderwebbing outward.

"Dante." Her voice came out steadier than she felt. Her wrist was still burning where Vex had grabbed her, and her jaw ached from his grip. "Let's go."

He didn't move. The shadows kept tightening.

"If you kill him, there will be consequences," she said, hating that she had to be the reasonable one when every part of her wanted to watch Dante tear him apart. "Political consequences. For you. For your realm."

A long moment passed. The shadows trembled.

Then Dante's hand found the small of her back, and he pulled her against his side, positioning his body between her and Vex even as the shadows slowly, reluctantly loosened.

Vex slid down the wall, gasping, but his gaze found hers over Dante's shoulder. "Ask him," he rasped.

Dante's shadows swept around them both, pulling them into transport magic before Vex could say anything else.

LII.
BRYNN

Solid ground hit her feet and Brynn's knees nearly buckled. The familiar chill of twilight felt like a sanctuary after Vex's false paradise. But her skin still crawled where he'd touched her. His hands on her wrist, her jaw. His breath against her face. All of it repulsive, like poison seeping through her skin.

Dante dismissed the servants with a gesture before they could speak. Then he turned to her, and the rawness in his expression made her breath catch.

"Come," he said quietly, extending his hand.

She stared at his palm. Such a simple offer. But after everything Vex had said, after the questions now circling in her mind...

She tentatively placed her hand in his.

His gloved fingers closed around hers, and relief flooded his features so intensely it made her throat tighten. This touch felt right. Warm where Vex's had burned. Safe, where Vex's had felt like a violation.

That was the problem, wasn't it? He always felt safe.

He led her through corridors toward chambers she'd seen only once before. His thumb brushed across her knuckles as they walked, and her pulse jumped at even this small contact. Her body didn't seem to care about what he was keeping from her. Her body only knew that his touch made her feel whole in ways she couldn't explain.

When they reached his private chambers, she recognized the warm orange fire instead of the cold blue. The worn reading chair by the hearth. The deep rugs she'd sunk her feet into just days ago.

His shadows pooled in the corners, calmer here than anywhere else.

"Sit," he said, gesturing toward the chair. "Let me make sure he didn't hurt you."

She sank into the worn velvet, and when he moved toward her, she couldn't help the way her body responded. Pulse quickening. Breath shallowing. Even now.

"I'm fine," she said, but her voice wavered.

"Humor me."

He knelt beside her, and the sight of the Reaper on his knees still made her heart ache, even through her anger. His fingers traced along her arms where Vex had grabbed her, and she shivered.

When he found the bruises darkening on her wrist, his jaw went rigid.

His thumb brushed over one of the marks, feather-light, and she had to close her eyes against the contrast. Vex's grip had burned. Dante's touch soothed. Her body wanted to lean into him, wanted more of that gentle contact.

When he finished his inspection, he sat back on his heels and met her eyes. The silence stretched between them.

"He didn't hurt me," she said quietly. "But you heard what he said. About my blood. About the ward-tools calling to me." She pulled her hand from his grip, and his fingers twitched like they wanted to chase hers. "Was he right?"

Guilt flickered across his face. Or fear. Gone before she could be certain.

"Vex was trying to manipulate you—"

"That's not what I asked." She stood abruptly. Needing distance. Needing to think without his presence clouding her judgment. "He said you've been hiding secrets about what I am. About why ward magic feels like remembering instead of learning."

Dante rose slowly, and she watched his expression shutter. The same way it always did when she pushed too hard.

"The ward-tools are old. They respond to magical sensitivity—"

"Stop." The word cut through his deflection. "Stop managing me. Stop deciding what I can handle. You were there. You heard everything he said." She met his eyes. "So tell me which parts were lies."

He ran a hand through his hair. The Lord of the Forsaken, always so controlled. Coming undone.

"What aren't you telling me about who I am?"

For a long moment, he just looked at her. Then his posture shifted. Resignation, maybe. Or surrender.

"You want it?" His voice came out rough. "All of it?"

"Yes."

He turned away, bracing both hands against the windowsill, head bowed. She watched his shoulders rise and fall with a breath that seemed to cost him something.

"The ward system was built by individuals," he said finally, still facing the window. "Souls with the ability to work the boundary magic between life and death. They called themselves the Architects."

She tracked the rigid line of his shoulders but didn't speak.

"When they faded, their knowledge went with them. Or so everyone believed." He turned to face her, and his composure had cracked open. "But there have always been theories that the bloodline survived. That occasionally, a soul would be born with the old gift, dormant and unrecognized."

He paused. Swallowed.

"When you arrived as tribute, and I saw the way the ward-tools responded to you, I started looking into it. I've spent centuries in these archives. I know what Architect magic looks like in the old texts. And what you do, the way the wards respond to you, it's not just sensitivity. It's something deeper."

"You're saying I have this bloodline."

"I'm saying I believe you do. I've studied every record I could find since you came here. The way you interact with ward magic, it matches descriptions of the old Architects almost exactly. Your ability isn't learned. It's inherited."

The words didn't make sense. Couldn't make sense.

"That's impossible."

"Is it?" He took a step toward her, and she took one back. Hurt flashed across his face, quickly suppressed. "You said it yourself. The magic feels natural. Instinctive. Because it's in your blood. Your ancestors built these barriers, and that ability passed down through generations. Most of the time dormant. But in you..."

"I pick locks. I steal things. I don't build magical barriers between realms."

"Because you never knew what you were." His shadows reached toward her, then recoiled when she flinched. "Your abilities were suppressed until you touched those ward-tools and awakened what was already inside you."

She moved to the window. Putting distance between them.

Her mind was racing, trying to slot this new information into everything else she knew. But part of her was also cataloguing what he'd said. *I started looking into it. I believe you do. I've studied every record.* He wasn't confessing to a secret he'd carried from the beginning. He was telling her something he'd been piecing together.

That distinction mattered. She wasn't sure yet how much.

"How long?" she asked. "How long have you suspected?"

"Since the first time you worked the wards and they responded like they recognized you." His voice was hollow. "I've been researching since then. Digging through records that haven't been opened in millennia. Trying to be certain before I told you something that would change everything."

"And are you? Certain?"

"As certain as I can be without asking you to submit to tests I wasn't willing to put you through."

She pressed her forehead against the cool glass. Felt her breath fog against it.

He'd been investigating. Not hiding a confirmed truth, but chasing a theory he wasn't ready to burden her with until he understood it himself. She could see the logic in that. Could almost forgive it.

Almost.

"There's more," she said. It wasn't a question. She could hear it in the weight of his silence.

When she turned, the look on his face confirmed it. He'd gone pale. His hands were clenched at his sides, and his shadows had gone completely still around his feet.

"I need to tell you something about your family," he said. "And I want you to understand that I'm not certain. I may be wrong. But you deserve to hear what I've found."

Her shoulders went rigid. Her pulse thudded in her ears.

"What about my family?"

He turned to the nightstand and pulled out a stack of documents. Old parchment, newer notes in his angular handwriting. He set them on the edge of the bed between them but didn't push them toward her.

"After I began to suspect what you were, I started investigating why someone with this bloodline would end up as a street thief instead of trained in their abilities." He spoke carefully. "I looked into your family. Your father's business, his reputation, the circumstances of his arrest."

She couldn't breathe.

"The charges against your parents never made sense. I had my people examine the records from the mortal realm. Trade logs, court documents, witness accounts. The evidence that convicted them was fabricated. Professionally. By someone with resources and reach far beyond a rival merchant."

"I already knew they were innocent." The words came out scraped raw. "I've always known."

"I know." His voice dropped. "But I don't think their murder was random. Or motivated by simple greed."

The room tilted.

"What are you saying?"

"I'm saying that someone discovered what your bloodline carried. The Architect gift. And they wanted it eliminated, or they wanted your family's collection of old relics that might have been connected to the original ward-cores." He gestured at the documents. "I can't prove it yet. The trail goes cold in several places. But the pattern fits. The timing of the accusations, the speed of the conviction, the thoroughness of the asset seizure. Someone powerful orchestrated this."

No.

Her knees didn't buckle. She locked them in place through sheer will, gripping the back of his chair until her knuckles went white, vision blurring at the edges.

All this time. All this time, she'd wondered why. What her parents had done to deserve their fate. She'd blamed herself for years, convinced that if she'd been smarter, faster, better, she could have saved them.

And it might have been because of something none of them understood. A gift sleeping in her blood.

"How long have you known this part?" she whispered.

"I've suspected for weeks. The research has been ongoing." He took a step toward her, then stopped himself. "I didn't tell you because I didn't want to give you grief built on a theory. I wanted answers first. Proof. Something real."

"That wasn't your decision to make."

"I know."

She turned to face him, and the pain in her chest wound tight, a knot she couldn't reach to undo.

"You should have told me the moment you suspected. All of it. The bloodline, my family. Even if it was just a theory." She heard the tremor in her voice and hated it. "I've spent ten years not knowing why my parents died. Ten years blaming myself. And you had pieces of the answer and sat on them because you wanted to be sure?"

His shadows curled inward. He looked like she'd struck him.

"I was trying to protect you from uncertainty—"

"I've lived in uncertainty my whole life!" The words burst out, and the flames in his hearth flickered. "I don't need you to hand me neat answers tied up with ribbon. I need you to trust me with the messy parts. The parts you haven't figured out yet. That's what partners do."

The word hung between them. Partners.

"You're right." He dragged a hand across his face, and when it dropped, he looked exhausted. Every one of his centuries showing in the lines around his eyes. "I told myself I was being careful. Thorough. But the truth is, I was afraid."

"Afraid of what?"

"That you'd look at me differently." The words came out barely audible. "That you'd wonder if I only valued you because of what you are. What you can do." He met her eyes, and the raw honesty there nearly broke her. "I wanted you to know that what I feel for you has nothing to do with bloodlines or abilities. That I would choose you even if you had no magic at all."

Her chest constricted.

She wanted to go to him. Wanted to close the distance and let him hold her and pretend this conversation didn't matter.

But it did matter.

"I believe you." Her voice cracked. "But you still should have told me. You don't get to decide what I can handle. Not about my own identity. Not about my family."

He flinched at the word family. His hand came up to the back of his neck.

"I know. I'm sorry."

She wiped the tears from her cheeks. She hadn't even realized she was crying.

"I need time," she said. "To think."

She moved toward the door. Her hands were shaking.

"Brynn." His voice stopped her at the door. She didn't turn around. "I should have trusted you with all of this sooner. That's on me. I never wanted to hurt you."

She stood there for a long moment. Hearing the desperation underneath his careful words. Feeling his shadows hovering at the edges of her awareness, reaching for her and then pulling back.

"I know," she said quietly. And she did. That was what made this hurt so much. She wasn't angry because she thought he'd used her.

She was angry because he'd made choices about her life without her. Because he'd decided what she needed to know and when.

She opened the door.

"I just need time."

She left before he could say anything else. Before the look on his face could convince her to stay.

LIII.
BRYNN

Days had passed since she'd walked out of Dante's chambers, and Brynn had perfected the art of avoiding him entirely.

The library had become her sanctuary. Volumes on ancient magic, death realm history, and the souls who'd built the barriers between worlds. She'd devoured them all, searching for anything about who she supposedly was, though the books on the ward architects were frustratingly scarce.

Now she sat at her dressing table while Naia worked behind her, the servant's deft fingers arranging her hair into something elegant. Brynn could see the exhaustion in her own eyes. Too many restless nights, too many hours reading until the words blurred together. Too many dreams where he reached for her and she let him.

She hated those dreams most of all.

"You've been spending an awful lot of time in that library," Naia observed, her voice carrying that teasing tone she used when she wanted to pry without seeming to pry. "Find anything interesting in all those dusty tomes?"

"Research," Brynn said. "I wanted to understand what I apparently am."

"And do you? Understand, I mean?"

Brynn met Naia's eyes in the glass. "I understand that everyone knew more about my identity than I did. Including him." She paused, swallowing past the tightness in her throat. "I understand that my parents were murdered because of what I am. That my entire life has been shaped by something I never knew about."

She stopped herself, blinking back the tears that threatened.

Before Naia could respond, a firm knock echoed through the chamber.

They both went still. Brynn's servants always announced themselves with gentle taps and deferential voices. This knock held authority that made her stomach tighten with recognition.

She knew that knock. Had heard it outside her door every morning for the past couple of days, followed by his voice asking if she was well, if she needed anything, if she would please talk to him.

She'd ignored him every time. And every time, she'd pressed her hand to her chest afterward, trying to push down the ache that bloomed there at the sound of him walking away.

"Brynn," came Dante's voice through the door, formal after days of silence between them. "I need to speak with you."

Her hands clenched in her lap.

"I'm not dressed for receiving visitors," she called back.

"This concerns court business. It's urgent."

Court business. Of course. Not an apology. Not an explanation. Another decision made, another announcement delivered. Another thing he'd decided she needed to know only when it suited him.

The pattern was exhausting.

Naia raised an eyebrow at Brynn's reflection, clearly sensing the tension crackling in the air. After a moment, Brynn nodded toward the door, her jaw tight.

If he wanted to play this formally, she could do that.

"Very well. Come in."

The door opened, and Dante stepped inside.

The sight of him caught her off guard.

Dark circles under his eyes, hair disheveled as if he'd been running his hands through it repeatedly. His jaw was tight, his shoulders rigid beneath his dark clothing. He looked like he hadn't slept since their confrontation. Like he'd been holding himself together through sheer force of will, and the seams were starting to show.

Her heart clenched at the sight, and she hated it. Her body swayed toward him before she caught herself. Even now, even after everything, some part of her still wanted to go to him. Smooth the lines from his face. Let him hold her until the world made sense again.

No. She forced herself to stay seated, fingers digging into her palms.

His dark eyes found hers, and want flickered in their depths. Regret. A desperate hunger that made her pulse jump through her fury.

Then he looked away, and his expression shuttered.

"Lord Caelum has called for a Gathering of Souls," he said, his voice neutral. Like they were strangers discussing business instead of two people who'd touched each other's faces and whispered confessions in the dark. "Tomorrow evening. All the Death Lords will attend, along with their courts. He believes a show of unity will help stabilize the political situation after the recent unrest."

Brynn studied him, taking in the rigid posture. His shadows shifted restlessly at his feet, straining toward her before he yanked them back.

"I see," she said coolly. "And my attendance is required?"

"As my..." He paused.

The silence stretched. Part of his court. His tribute. His partner.

None of those words fit anymore. They both knew it.

His hand came up to rub the back of his neck—the same gesture she'd seen in his chambers, when he'd been trying to hold himself together. He caught himself doing it and dropped his arm, but not before she noticed.

"Your presence would be expected."

Not as his partner. Not as someone important to him. Not even as his tribute.

Just... expected. Like any other courtier.

The dismissal stung more than it should have. And underneath the sting, the hurt grew teeth.

He'd kept her identity secret. Her parents' murder. Everything about who she was. And now he couldn't even bring himself to claim her publicly. To acknowledge what she meant to him in front of others.

"Then I'll attend," she replied, keeping her voice as neutral as his. She could feel Naia watching them both with fascination. "Whatever is required."

"The gathering begins at sunset. I'll send word about the arrangements."

"Fine."

For a moment, he lingered in the doorway. His dark eyes met hers again, and she watched his control waver, saw the raw ache beneath the mask. His hands clenched at his sides. His shadows strained toward her one more time, desperate tendrils reaching across the floor.

His mouth opened slightly, like he wanted to say something. Something real. Something that mattered.

Say it. She stared at him, willing the words out of him. Say something that isn't court business or duty or decisions you've already made without me.

Then the moment passed.

He pulled back. Straightened his shoulders. Rebuilt the walls she'd watched crumble just seconds before.

"Thank you," he said quietly, and left without another word.

The door closed behind him with a click that sounded like defeat.

The silence that followed felt thick. Brynn realized she'd been holding her breath and forced herself to exhale slowly. Her pulse was still racing, her body still warm from just being in the same room as him.

Hells, she was predictable. And furious about it.

Naia turned to look at Brynn with genuine curiosity.

"Well," Naia said finally, her translucent form settling onto the chair beside the dressing table. "What did you do to him? He looks absolutely dreadful."

"I didn't do anything to him," Brynn replied, though the words felt hollow even to her own ears. "He did it to himself."

"Hmm." Naia's expression was skeptical. "Him coming to your door every morning only to be turned away, and you looking like you haven't slept in days... Are you quite sure about that?"

Brynn turned away from the mirror, unable to look at her own reflection anymore. Unable to see the hurt and anger and longing written so clearly on her face.

"He lied to me, Naia. About everything that mattered." Her voice cracked no matter how she fought it. "How am I supposed to trust that?"

"I'm not saying you should," Naia said gently. "I'm just observing that you're both miserable. And that perhaps misery isn't the punishment you think it is."

Brynn shrugged. She wasn't going to think about that right now.

Her mind shifted to the gathering. A political event. All the Death Lords in attendance, along with their courts. A place where appearances mattered, where every gesture would be scrutinized and interpreted.

An idea began to form. Petty and vindictive and deeply satisfying.

He wanted to keep her at arm's length? Fine. Let him try to ignore her when she made herself impossible to overlook.

"Naia," she said slowly, her voice gaining strength as the plan came together. "How quickly could the palace tailors work? If I needed something made by tomorrow evening?"

Naia's eyebrows rose with interest, her translucent form brightening. "That would depend on what you had in mind. Something simple could be managed, but anything elaborate..."

"Not simple," Brynn interrupted, turning to face her fully. Her heart was beating faster now, adrenaline chasing away the exhaustion. "Elaborate. Beautiful." She met Naia's eyes. "I want everyone at that gathering to see exactly who I am. Not his tribute. Not someone to be managed and kept in the dark. An Architect."

Naia's smile turned positively wicked. "Oh, my dear. Now you're speaking my language."

"Can you arrange it?"

"Leave it to me," Naia said, rising gracefully. "I know exactly who to speak to. And I have some ideas that I think you'll find... satisfactory." She paused at the threshold, glancing back. "This is going to be absolutely delicious."

As Naia slipped out, Brynn turned back to the mirror.

She was done being managed. Done being protected. Done being kept in the dark while he decided what she could and couldn't handle.

At the Gathering of Souls, everyone would see exactly who she was.

Including him.

LIV.
BRYNN

The knock came at sunset.

Brynn had been ready for an hour, standing before her mirror while Naia made final adjustments to the creation they'd conspired to bring into existence.

The gown captured twilight. Fabric that shifted between deep purple and midnight blue depending on the light. Thousands of tiny crystals sewn across the bodice and down the skirt like scattered stars, the beading tracing constellations, ward-symbols woven into the decoration that only those who knew what to look for would recognize.

The neckline was lower than anything she'd worn before. Elegant but daring, revealing the curve of her collarbones and the hollow of her throat. The bodice fitted her perfectly, emphasizing curves she'd kept hidden beneath practical clothing for so long. The skirt was impractical as hell, trailing behind her and pooling at her feet, but it looked devastating.

"Confidence," Naia said, her eyes bright with anticipation, "You've survived Death Lords, ward failures, and court politics. One ball won't break you."

"No," Brynn agreed, smoothing her hands over the bodice. The crystals were cool under her palms, grounding. "It won't."

The knock came again, more insistent this time.

"My lady," came a servant's voice through the door. "Lord Reaper awaits your presence in the main hall."

Let him wait a little longer.

"Tell him I'll be there momentarily," Brynn called back, taking one final look at herself.

She drew in a steadying breath, felt the beading press against her ribs. Her reflection looked back at her. The woman in the mirror looked like someone who belonged here.

She moved toward the door.

The corridors of Dante's palace hummed with more activity than usual. Servants hurried past, their translucent forms carrying supplies and messages. She caught glimpses of his death knights checking weapons and armor before departure, their hollow sockets burning with pale fire.

The Gathering of Souls was clearly a significant event. One that required extensive security even for a Death Lord.

The throne room stretched before her: tooth mosaic floor, skull-lined walls burning with cold blue flame, shadows moving with their own purpose. Tonight, the space was filled with members of Dante's court preparing for departure.

And there, at the center of it all, was Dante.

He stood in conversation with Aldric and two of his military advisors, dressed in formal black with silver threading along the collar and cuffs. The tailored cut emphasized his broad shoulders and commanding presence, making him look every inch the Death Lord he was. His dark hair was arranged, his expression controlled as he listened to Aldric's report.

He looked powerful. Untouchable. Composed.

Her pulse quickened at the sight of him. She crushed the reaction down, let a small, satisfied smile curve her lips instead.

Not for long.

Around him, courtiers draped in midnight velvets and bone-white silks waited in elegant clusters. Lady Morwyn stood near the transport circles, her silver gown catching the ethereal light. When she spotted Brynn, her expression turned cold before she turned away.

All of it stopped when Brynn entered the hall.

The silence began with the servants closest to the doorway, their tasks forgotten as they turned to stare—one by one, the quiet spread through the hall. Courtiers fell silent mid-sentence, advisors lost their train of thought, even the death knights' hollow sockets flickered with what might have been surprise.

She felt the weight of their attention.

And she held her head high, letting them look.

Dante, still speaking to Aldric about security arrangements, didn't immediately notice the sudden quiet. "...ensure the perimeter remains secure during the gathering. I want reports every—"

He stopped mid-sentence. Some instinct made him turn, perhaps sensing the shift in the room's energy, possibly feeling the weight of the silence.

When he saw her, the words died on his lips.

His hand, which had been gesturing as he spoke, froze in midair. The shadows at his feet went utterly still.

Then they surged toward her.

Not subtle tendrils this time. A wave of darkness that swept across the black floor, straining toward her like they were desperate to touch, to claim, to close the distance he couldn't. He yanked them back, his jaw clenching, but they kept reaching.

So much for the legendary composure of the Lord of the Forsaken. His shadows were practically wagging like an eager hound, and he looked about as subtle as a dragon at a garden party.

Brynn began walking across the hall, her steps confident despite her racing heart. The crystals caught the light with every movement, making her shimmer. She could feel eyes following her progress, could hear the whispered conversations starting behind her.

But she kept her focus on Dante's face.

His gaze dropped to the beading on her bodice. Traced the patterns there. Recognition flashed through his expression as he realized what he was seeing. Ward-symbols. Architect markers. An identity claimed in crystal and thread for everyone to see.

His throat worked as he swallowed.

"Good evening," she said when she reached him, her voice carrying clearly in the sudden quiet. "I hope I haven't kept you waiting."

"No," he said, his voice rough. He seemed to realize everyone was staring and cleared his throat, only partially succeeding at composure. "You... no. We were finalizing arrangements."

But his eyes kept returning to her. To the way the dress emphasized her figure, to the elegant neckline that revealed the curve of her throat, to the beading that made her look like she was carved from the night sky.

And underneath her satisfaction, her own body was betraying her just as badly. Her skin felt too warm. Her pulse wouldn't slow. Standing this close, she could smell him.

She wanted his hands on her. Hated that she wanted it. Hated that even now, even furious, some part of her just wanted him to reach for her.

She stepped back before she did something stupid.

"The tailors did excellent work," she said, keeping her voice light. "Naia had very specific ideas about what would be appropriate for such an important gathering."

"Appropriate," he repeated, the word coming out strained. His hands clenched at his sides, and she could see him fighting the urge to reach for her. "Yes. Very... appropriate."

The repetition was almost painful, like he couldn't think of anything else to say. Like she'd broken something in his brain.

She barely suppressed a smile.

Aldric cleared his throat, breaking the moment. "Perhaps we should proceed? Lord Caelum will be expecting us, and the diplomatic considerations—"

"Of course." Brynn smiled at the gathered court, noting how several of the nobles were still staring at her. Lady Morwyn's expression had shifted from cold dismissal to grudging respect.

"You look..." Dante started, then stopped. The words escaped without permission, dragged out of him by some force he couldn't control.

"Yes?" she prompted, tilting her head to look up at him.

He was struggling. She could see it. The way his throat worked, the way his jaw had gone tight, the tremor in his shadows that kept straining toward her hem. The Lord of the Forsaken, always so composed, coming apart at the seams in front of his entire court.

"Beautiful," he finally managed, his voice dropping low enough that only she could hear, like it cost him something to say it. "You look beautiful."

The word landed somewhere beneath her ribs and *stayed* there, warm and unwanted.

No. Absolutely not. She was not doing this.

She was supposed to be punishing him, not melting because he'd managed a single compliment. She had *standards*. She had *grievances*. She had a very detailed mental list of every lie he'd told her.

None of that seemed to matter when he looked at her like she'd stolen the breath from his lungs.

But she wouldn't give him the satisfaction that he still affected her.

"Thank you," she replied, her smile polite. "You look very... lordly."

His jaw tightened slightly. She'd given him nothing. That was the point.

"Shall we go?" she asked, smoothing her skirts. "I understand Lord Caelum is expecting us. We shouldn't keep him waiting."

For a moment, he just looked at her. Desperation flickered in his expression, a silent plea he wouldn't voice in front of his court. His hands trembled with the effort of holding himself back.

Then he gestured toward the transport chamber, maintaining the distance between them.

"After you," he said, his voice neutral again.

She moved ahead of him, acutely aware of his presence behind her. Of the space between them that felt charged with everything they couldn't show publicly. The touch breakthrough they had to hide, the fight that remained unresolved, the desire that simmered beneath everything else.

As they approached the transport circle, she caught Dante's eye one more time.

He looked like a man in pain. His shadows strained toward her despite the audience, betraying every feeling his face tried to hide. The tight set of his jaw. The hunger in his eyes he couldn't mask, no matter how hard he tried.

She allowed herself a small, satisfied smile.

Then the world dissolved into light.

LV.
BRYNN

The Court of the Mourned had outdone itself, transforming paradise into something even more breathtaking than before. But Brynn barely noticed the enhanced beauty around them: the additional waterfalls creating new rainbows, the flowers blooming in wilder patterns, the light somehow more welcoming.

Her focus was entirely on the man walking just far enough behind her. Close enough to appear to be escorting her, far enough to maintain distance.

His shadows reached for her ankles before he yanked them back.

Every time they did it, want and fury twisted together in her chest until she couldn't tell which was winning.

"Lord Caelum certainly knows how to make an impression," she observed as they approached the white marble palace, making polite conversation that completely ignored the tension crackling between them.

"He does," Dante replied, his voice neutral. But she caught the way his eyes flicked to her exposed shoulder when she turned her head, the tightening of his jaw. The way his hands clenched at his sides like he was physically restraining himself.

Her skin warmed under that gaze. She hated how much she wanted him to stop restraining himself.

The palace terraces were already crowded with hundreds of beings in their finest attire. She'd never seen so much otherworldly beauty gathered in one place: warriors from Seraphina's desert courts, in armor that gleamed like bronze; ethereal spirits from Thessa's domain, who seemed to fade in and out of visibility; golden-eyed courtiers from Vex's realm, radiating hunger and dangerous beauty.

And all of them turned to look as Dante's party arrived.

"Welcome!" Lord Caelum's voice carried across the terrace as he approached their group, his arms spread wide. Tonight, he looked particularly magnificent in flowing white and gold robes, his ageless features radiating warmth. "My friends, what an honor to have you join our celebration of unity and cooperation."

He embraced Lady Seraphina warmly, clasped hands with Lady Thessa, and even managed a brief touch with Lord Vex, despite the other Death Lords' reluctance to get too close.

With Dante, he offered no acknowledgment at all—turned away as if the Lord of the Forsaken weren't standing three feet behind her.

The slight was obvious. Cold flickered in Caelum's eyes before the warmth returned so quickly she almost thought she'd imagined it.

Interesting. The Lord of Peace and Mercy snubbed another Death Lord in front of the entire gathering. So much for tonight being about "unity and cooperation."

Then Caelum turned to her, and his honey-brown eyes seemed to light up.

"And the remarkable Lady Brynn," he said, taking her hand and bringing it to his lips. "You look absolutely radiant tonight."

From the corner of her eye, she saw Dante take a half-step forward before stopping abruptly. His hand had moved toward her before he'd caught himself, clenching into a fist at his side.

"You're very kind, Lord Caelum," she replied, letting her hand linger in his just a moment longer than necessary.

Dante's shadows spread across the terrace before he wrestled them back.

A hand-kiss. That's all it had taken. She hadn't even *started* yet.

"Please, just Caelum," he said, his eyes crinkling with warmth.

"Tonight is about friendship, not formality. I want everyone to feel completely welcome and at ease."

"Shall we join the festivities?" Caelum motioned toward the dance floor, where music was already starting to play. "I believe they are about to start the first set."

As they moved up the pathways toward the main terrace, Brynn walked between Caelum's easy charm and Dante's simmering tension. Conversations paused as they passed, courtiers from all the realms taking note of her transformation. Taking note of how she walked beside Caelum rather than behind Dante. How she smiled at the Lord of the Mourned's conversation while maintaining distance from the Lord of the Forsaken.

She could feel Dante's gaze on her back. Could practically hear his restraint fraying with every step she took away from him.

But her heart ached anyway.

"Lady Brynn," a familiar voice called out, and she turned to see Lady Vivienne approaching, one of Dante's court members, the magical theorist who'd always shown interest in her abilities rather than just her proximity to power. "You look absolutely magnificent tonight. That dress is remarkable. The way the crystal work channels light is quite sophisticated. Is that ward-pattern I see woven into the beading?"

Brynn smiled, pleased that someone had noticed the craftsmanship beyond just the surface beauty. "Thank you. The tailors were very accommodating of my specific requests."

"Indeed, they were." Lady Vivienne's expression grew thoughtful as she glanced toward where Dante stood speaking with Lord Vex and Lady Seraphina, his posture rigid. "I must say, the dynamics tonight are quite fascinating to observe. So much tension beneath the surface of diplomacy."

The comment was neutral enough, a scholarly observation rather than gossip. But Brynn caught the subtle curiosity underneath. Lady Vivienne was always studying patterns, analyzing relationships, and power structures.

"Yes," Brynn replied, keeping her tone equally neutral. "It's remarkable how much can be communicated through what isn't said."

Lady Vivienne's smile turned knowing, and she opened her mouth to respond—

But then the music shifted to something graceful and inviting, and the moment passed.

"Lady Brynn," Caelum appeared at her elbow. "Would you honor me with the first dance?"

She glanced toward Dante, who was still deep in conversation with the other Death Lords. His back was to her. She doubted it was an accident.

Fine.

"I would be delighted," she said, placing her hand on Caelum's offered arm and letting her voice carry just enough for Dante to hear if he was listening.

As Caelum led her onto the dance floor, she caught the exact moment Dante's conversation faltered. His shoulders went rigid, and she saw his head turn slightly. Not enough to look directly at her, but enough to track her movement across the terrace.

Enough to see her hand resting on Caelum's arm, her smile warm as the Lord of the Mourned said something charming.

Caelum was an elegant partner, leading her through the steps with grace while maintaining appropriate distance. Nothing scandalous, nothing that would cause talk. Just a Death Lord dancing with a visiting guest in courtly fashion.

But it was enough.

"You seem troubled tonight," Caelum observed as they moved through a turn that brought them momentarily closer together. His honey-brown eyes were concerned. "I hope everything is well in the Forsaken Court?"

"As well as can be expected," she replied, letting a note of weariness color her voice. A hint of vulnerability. "Though I confess, court politics can be exhausting when you're still learning the rules."

"I imagine they can be, particularly for someone still learning their place in a world that doesn't always welcome outsiders." His eyes were understanding and compassionate in a way that felt genuine. Almost too genuine. Like he'd been waiting for exactly this opening. "It must be difficult, never quite sure where you stand."

"You're very perceptive," she said, letting herself sound grateful even as unease prickled at her neck. How did he know she wasn't sure where she stood?

"The offer of sanctuary in my realm still stands, you know." Caelum's voice was earnest. "Should you ever find yourself in need of a place where you're truly valued for who you are, not what you can do."

She let her hand tighten slightly on his shoulder. "That's incredibly generous of you. More generous than I probably deserve."

"Nonsense." Caelum's expression was sincere. "Someone with your gifts, your intelligence, your courage, your remarkable abilities, deserves to be treasured, not hidden away like a secret shame."

The words found their mark. But how had Caelum known where to aim?

She filed the question away and smiled.

As the dance ended, she let herself lean slightly closer to Caelum, her voice dropping. "Thank you. For the dance, and for understanding. It means more than you know."

When she turned from Caelum's arms, she found Lord Vex waiting with a casual bow and a smile that was all sharp edges beneath its beauty.

"Might I claim the next dance?" he asked, his gold eyes bright with interest and what might have been amusement. "I find myself quite curious about the woman who's caused such discussion among the courts."

Brynn hesitated.

Their last encounter flooded back. His hands on her shoulders, her jaw, his breath too close, his words crawling under her skin. The memory made her stomach clench with anger and fear.

But she refused to let him see her flinch. Not here. Not in front of everyone.

She glanced toward Dante.

He was standing with Aldric now, apparently deep in conversation. His expression was neutral, his posture controlled.

But his whole body had tensed when Vex approached. Wound tight. Ready to move.

He was watching.

Her pulse quickened at the intensity of his gaze.

"Of course," she said, taking his offered hand and ignoring the way her skin crawled at the contact. "I'd be honored."

Vex didn't dance. He circled. Every movement brought him closer, testing how much she'd allow. That lazy smile never wavered.

She kept her expression pleasant, but she didn't let herself relax into the dance. Didn't let her guard drop for a second.

"You're playing a dangerous game," he murmured as they moved through the steps, his voice low enough that only she could hear.

"I don't know what you mean," she replied innocently, keeping her tone light.

"Of course you do. You're far too intelligent to pretend otherwise." His smile was knowing, almost approving. "The question is whether you're prepared for the consequences when he finally breaks. When that control he's so proud of shatters completely."

She let her gaze drift over his shoulder to where Dante stood.

His conversation with Aldric had died. He wasn't even pretending to listen anymore. His dark eyes were fixed on her with an intensity that made the air feel heavier.

His hands were clenched so tight she could see his knuckles from across the terrace. His jaw was rigid. And his shadows were spreading across the floor, straining toward them.

This was what she'd wanted. To make him feel it. To make him understand what he was losing.

But hells, the way he was looking at her. Like she was the only thing in the room. Like he might burn down this entire paradise just to get to her.

"Perhaps he needs to break," she said quietly. "Perhaps some things are only valued when there's a real risk of losing them."

Vex's laugh was low and appreciative. "Clever. Ruthless, even. But be careful, sweet thing. Predators are most dangerous when cornered. Most unpredictable when they realize what they're about to lose."

She should have bristled at the endearment. But somehow, in this context, it felt less possessive and more observational. Like he was acknowledging the game she was playing rather than trying to claim her as his own piece on the board.

"I can handle dangerous," she said.

"Can you?" Vex's gold eyes glittered. "I wonder if you know what you're really provoking. What happens when a Death Lord stops holding back."

The words sent a shiver down her spine.

As the song ended, she stepped back from Vex with a polite smile, relief washing through her at putting distance between them even as she kept her expression serene.

She found herself facing a small line of potential partners. Word had spread through the gathering that the mysterious Lady Brynn, the one who'd transformed from uncertain tribute to something that commanded attention, was accepting all invitations to dance.

Several courtiers from various realms were eager to discover what the fuss was about.

She glanced once more toward Dante.

He hadn't moved. His eyes still burned with that desperate, barely leashed hunger.

She held his gaze for a long moment.

Then she turned away and accepted the next offered hand.

LVI.
DANTE

From across the terrace, Dante watched Caelum spin Brynn through a waltz, their movements graceful.

Separate. Cordial. Untouchable.

It was the performance they'd both committed to for the investigation's sake—the distance that was supposed to protect her from becoming a target. He understood the necessity. Had agreed to it himself.

He took a sip of wine, the taste bitter on his tongue, and tried to focus on anything else. The political conversations happening around him. The orchestrated displays of unity. The subtle power plays between courts.

But his eyes kept drifting back to her.

Always back to her.

She crossed the floor, the crystal beading on her dress catching the light with every step. Twilight fabric shifting between purple and midnight blue. Starlight scattered across darkness.

His colors. His realm's aesthetic. The Forsaken Court wrapped around her body like an embrace.

She'd come here furious with him, determined to punish him, to prove she didn't need him. And she'd dressed herself in him without even realizing it.

The knowledge hit him somewhere deep in his chest. Made it hard to breathe.

She looked like she belonged among the Death Lords and their courts, not as a tribute or a tool, but as something powerful in her own right. She looked like what she was: descended from those who'd built the barriers between worlds.

And she was dancing with everyone except him.

He'd done this to himself. Kept her in the dark. Made choice after choice for her without asking. This was exactly what he'd earned.

The truth didn't make it hurt any less.

The dance ended with a graceful spin, Caelum's hand at her waist steadying her. He bowed over her hand, pressing his lips to her knuckles in a gesture that lingered just a fraction too long.

She smiled in response.

Not the guarded mask she'd worn around Dante for days. The polite distance, the forced neutrality. This was warm. Unguarded.

His jaw clenched hard enough that he felt his teeth grind together.

He'd done this. He'd done this. He'd done this.

Vex approached before she'd fully stepped away from Caelum, offering his arm with that charming smile that always hid his true intent. Dante saw her tense, clearly remembering their last encounter.

But she still took Vex's arm after only a moment's hesitation.

Dante's hands curled into fists at his sides.

Vex's hand claimed her waist, pulling her into the dance. The touch was possessive, his fingers spread across the small of her back. Right where the fabric met the curve of her spine.

The bastard held her far too close. His lips brushed her ear as he murmured words that Dante couldn't hear, but could see the effect of. Her shoulders relaxed slightly, a reluctant laugh escaping her throat.

That sound cut straight through him.

Bright and musical and rare. He could count on one hand the number of times she'd laughed in his presence. Each one had felt like a gift, something precious she'd chosen to share with him.

Now she was offering it to Vex. Vex, who'd cornered her, threatened her, and put his hands on her against her will.

And Dante couldn't do a damn thing about it because he'd forfeited the right to protect her when he'd proven himself unworthy of her trust.

"You look like you're planning someone's funeral," Seraphina observed, materializing beside him with a goblet in hand. Her red hair caught the light, and her expression was one of amusement rather than concern.

"I'm always planning someone's funeral." The words came out rougher than intended.

"Mm." She followed his gaze to where Vex was spinning Brynn through another turn, his hand still splayed across her back. The movement made the beading on her dress shimmer. Made the fabric shift against her curves in ways that made Dante's blood run hot. "Though usually not quite so personally. Usually, you don't look like you want to tear someone apart with your bare hands."

His shadows had begun to writhe around his feet.

Several nearby nobles edged away, recognizing the warning signs.

The music swelled, and Vex dipped her low. Too low, his face hovering inches from hers, his grip spanning her back with intimate familiarity. The neckline of her dress gaped slightly, revealing the hollow of her throat, the curve of her collarbones.

For a heartbeat, they stayed frozen in that pose, and possessiveness unfurled in his chest like something feral waking.

She was wearing his twilight. His starlight against her skin. *His.*

"Interesting," Seraphina murmured, her voice cutting through his spiral. "I don't think I've ever seen you this close to losing control in public. Not in all the time I've known you."

"I'm perfectly controlled." The lie rang hollow.

A crystal wine goblet on a nearby table developed hairline cracks with an audible sound.

Seraphina glanced at the fracturing glass, then at Dante's grip on his own goblet. His hands were trembling. He couldn't make them stop.

"You sure seem like it," she said dryly, taking a step back.

The song ended. Vex released her with obvious reluctance, his hand trailing down her arm in a final possessive gesture that made Dante's vision blur at the edges.

"You could always cut in," Seraphina said, her voice neutral, though she gave him a knowing look. "Claim a dance like any other courtier seems free to do."

"This is a diplomatic function." The words ground out between clenched teeth. "I can't show favoritism. Can't make it obvious that she's—"

Important to him. The only thing that had broken through the isolation in ages. The woman wearing his colors while she refused to look at him.

"Since when has that stopped you from doing what you want?" Seraphina murmured, swirling her wine with amusement at his predicament.

Before he could respond, another partner cut in—a warrior from Seraphina's court built like a mountain, all broad shoulders and protective instincts—one of her elite guards, a man who'd died in battle defending others.

And he held Brynn like something he wanted to keep.

The warrior leaned down to murmur something in her ear, his head bent close to hers. Whatever he said made her throw her head back with delight, exposing the graceful line of her throat. The laugh was unguarded, beautiful.

And it wasn't for him.

Dante's wine glass exploded in his grip.

The sharp sound of shattering crystal cut through the music and conversation. Several courtiers jumped, startled. Dark wine stained his gloves, dripped onto the marble at his feet. Crystal shards glittered among the spreading liquid.

He barely noticed.

All he could see was another man's hands on her skin. Another man making her smile. Another man earning what Dante had thrown away with his secrets and his arrogant certainty that he knew what was best for her.

"Reaper." Seraphina's voice was sharp now, cutting. "You're making a scene. People are staring."

He looked around, awareness returning slowly.

A wide circle of space had formed around him. Shadows writhed across the terrace in aggressive patterns, spreading outward. Frost was forming on the ground despite the warm night air.

Every conversation within twenty feet had died into silence. Nobles from various courts stared at him with expressions ranging from alarm to fascination.

On the dance floor, Brynn looked up. Their eyes met. The corner of her mouth twitched upward.

Then she turned back to her partner. She leaned closer to the warrior, letting his bulk shield her from Dante's gaze. Using him as a barrier.

The dismissal was clear and cutting.

His restraint snapped.

"That's it." The words emerged as a low growl, causing nearby courtiers to flinch. "I'm done watching."

He was already moving before rational thought could stop him. Political considerations, the investigation, and maintaining appearances. None of it mattered anymore.

Not when she was in another man's arms. Wearing his twilight. His starlight. His colors, while she gave her smiles to everyone else.

He cut through the crowd, and courtiers scrambled out of his path. His shadows spread before him like a wave, and the temperature dropped further with each step.

"Try not to kill my warrior!" Seraphina called after him, her tone more amused than concerned. "He's one of my favorites, and they're difficult to replace!"

The warrior noticed his approach first, his instincts recognizing a threat. To his credit, he didn't immediately release Brynn. Instead, he straightened to his full impressive height, easily six and a half feet of solid muscle, and positioned himself slightly in front of her.

Shielding her. From Dante.

As if Dante were the danger. As if Dante were the one who couldn't be trusted.

Except he was. He'd proved that when he kept things from her.

He ignored that thought.

"Evening, Lord Reaper," the warrior said slowly, his voice flat, though his posture said otherwise.

Dante's response was a low snarl that barely resembled words. His shadows reached for Brynn without his permission, curling around her ankles possessively, wrapping around the hem of her dress like they were trying to claim her back.

Brynn stepped out of the warrior's embrace, moving around him to face Dante directly. Her chin lifted, and her eyes flashed with challenge and anger.

Hells, she was magnificent. Even furious. Even looking at him like she wanted to tear him apart.

Especially then.

"Something wrong?" she asked, her voice carrying clearly in the sudden quiet that had fallen over the gathering.

Everything. Everything was wrong.

"We need to talk," he managed, his voice rough. The effort of not throwing her over his shoulder and dragging her away from every male who dared look at her was making his hands shake. "Now."

"I'm busy." She raised an eyebrow, her tone as frigid as the ice spreading from his feet. "Dancing. At a diplomatic gathering. Or did you not notice?"

The casual dismissal, delivered for all to hear, stung.

"Besides," she continued, her voice dropping to something more dangerous, "don't you think you've made enough decisions about what I need without asking me first? Enough choices about my life without my input?"

Her words found their target. Around them, the entire gathering had gone silent. The other Death Lords were watching now. Caelum with concern that didn't quite reach his eyes. Vex with open interest. Seraphina with amusement. Lady Thessa had materialized from somewhere, her form bright with curiosity.

"We're leaving," Dante said, his voice low and unyielding. Final. "Now."

"I'm in the middle of a dance," she replied, each word enunciated. Her politeness was laced with steel.

"The dance is over."

"But I'm enjoying myself." Her chin lifted slightly higher in challenge. "I'm having a wonderful time, actually. Meeting new people. Dancing. Being treated with honesty and respect for once."

"Enjoying yourself?" The words came out as a growl that made several nearby nobles take another step back. "You're dancing with every man here while treating me like I'm—"

He caught himself before he could finish that sentence.

But the damage was done—the vulnerability exposed.

Her eyes went wide, then narrow with understanding. With satisfaction.

"Like you're what, exactly?" Her voice was quiet. "Like you're someone who lies to me? Someone who makes decisions about my life behind my back? Someone who keeps me ignorant about my own identity while everyone else knows?"

She took a step closer, and he could see the anger and hurt burning in her eyes.

"Because that's exactly what you are, Dante. That's exactly what you've proven yourself to be."

His name. His actual name, not his title. But spoken with such contempt, he flinched. She'd whispered that name against his skin when they'd touched. Had said it with wonder when she'd realized she could survive his power. Had breathed it like a prayer in his chambers when everything had been different.

Now she wielded it like a weapon.

And it cut deeper than any blade.

Before he could respond, before he could find words that wouldn't make this worse, Caelum appeared at her elbow.

"Is everything alright?" he asked, his voice all concern and warmth. His hand settled gently on her arm in a protective gesture. "You seem distressed, my dear. Should we perhaps find somewhere quieter to—"

The casual endearment. The protective touch. The way he was

standing close to her, positioning himself between her and Dante—the flash of cold satisfaction beneath his mask of concern.

It was the final spark in a powder keg.

Dante's control didn't crack. It detonated.

Shadows exploded outward like a supernova of darkness, claiming the entire terrace. They spread across the marble in waves, swallowing the light. The temperature plummeted so fast that frost formed instantly on every surface. Every piece of glass within fifty feet—goblets, windows, decorative crystals—developed stress fractures with sharp cracking sounds.

Several courtiers fled outright. Others froze in place, afraid that movement would draw the Reaper's attention.

"Get your fucking hands off her," Dante snarled, his voice carrying the authority of death. "Now."

Caelum's hand fell away immediately, and he stepped back, raising his hands. His expression was pure wounded innocence, but Dante caught it again—satisfaction flickering in his honey-brown eyes. The slight curl at the corner of his mouth before he smoothed it away.

He'd wanted this reaction. Had been pushing for it all night.

But Dante couldn't think about that now. Couldn't think about anything except her.

In the sudden, ringing silence that followed, Brynn stared at Dante. Her expression was a complex mix of emotions. Shock at his public loss of control, satisfaction at finally breaking through his composure, and fury that he'd done it here, now, in front of everyone.

"There," she said quietly, but her voice carried in the silence. "Was that so hard? Actually showing what you feel instead of hiding behind control and political distance?"

He understood then. She'd been waiting for this. Testing him. Pushing him to finally show what he felt instead of maintaining that facade and proving that he cared enough to break his own rules.

"We're going home," he said, his voice rough. "Now."

For a moment, she just looked at him. Taking in his loss of control, the shadows still writhing around them both, the desperate need he could no longer hide.

Her expression was unreadable.

"Fine," she said finally, her voice deceptively calm. The kind of calm that preceded storms. "Let's go home and discuss how you just humiliated me in front of every Death Lord in existence."

The promise of the reckoning to come was clear in her tone. This wasn't surrender. This was her choosing the battleground.

Without waiting for his response, she turned and walked toward the edge of the terrace where he could open a transport portal. Her spine was rigid with anger, her movements sharp.

The twilight dress flowed behind her.

Every eye in the gathering followed her progress.

He followed, shadows billowing around them both as the entire gathering watched in fascinated silence.

This was far from over.

LVII.
DANTE

Dante kept a firm hold on Brynn's elbow as they materialized back at his palace. Firm enough that she couldn't just walk away from him again.

He could feel the fury radiating off her. But he wasn't ready to unleash his own. Not yet. Not where his people could witness whatever was about to happen between them.

Their footsteps resonated on the floor. Hers were pointedly loud, a defiant statement echoing through the halls, while his were quiet.

"I suppose dragging me away like property was your idea of diplomacy?" The words dripped with sarcasm. "Very lordly of you. Very controlled."

He said nothing. Couldn't trust himself to speak yet.

Because if he opened his mouth, he'd tell her exactly what it had felt like to watch Caelum's hands on her. To hear that bastard call her *my dear* like he had any right. To watch her smile at every male who'd touched her while she'd barely looked at Dante all evening.

A shadow-servant pressed itself against the wall as they passed, wisely giving them a wide berth. Even his bound servants could sense the storm building between them.

"Oh, wonderful. The silent treatment." Her voice sharpened with frustration. "Because that's exactly what this situation needs. More of your dramatic silences and brooding."

His jaw clenched. The shadows trailing behind them grew thicker, darker, writhing as they responded to his emotional state.

A pair of his courtiers rounded the corner ahead, their conversation dying mid-sentence as they took in the scene: their lord gripping the tribute's arm, shadows billowing like storm clouds, the air around them crackling with tension.

They immediately found somewhere else to be.

"Every Death Lord in existence just watched you lose control like a jealous—" She cut herself off, but the unfinished word hung between them like a challenge.

Jealous what? He wanted to snarl at her to say it. Call him what he was.

But he kept walking, kept silent.

"Are you planning to speak to me at all," Brynn continued, her voice rising slightly with each word, "or just grunt like a caveman who's claimed his prize and is dragging it back to his cave?"

A decorative vase on a side table developed hairline cracks that spread. The cold flames in the wall sconces flickered and dimmed.

"I can walk by myself, you know." She tried to pull free, but his fingers tightened fractionally, making it clear she wasn't going anywhere until they reached his chambers. "I'm not actually property, despite tonight's performance suggesting otherwise."

Wasn't she? The thought was dark, possessive, and he didn't try to fight it anymore. Wasn't she his? Hadn't she been his since the moment she touched his face and didn't die?

They passed the great hall where court was usually held. The massive oak doors were closed, but he could hear whispered conversations of courtiers within—no doubt discussing tonight's spectacle.

The Reaper's loss of control.

His public claim of the human tribute.

Let them talk. Let them gossip and speculate and draw whatever conclusions they wanted. None of it mattered compared to getting her alone.

"This is ridiculous," Brynn muttered, but her voice had shifted slightly. Lost some of its sharp edge. "I can't even look at you right now."

Her tone made him glance down at her. Her jaw was set in stubborn lines, her chin lifted in that defiant angle he'd come to know meant she was fighting tears or anger or both.

But there was vulnerability beneath the defiance now. A fragility that hadn't been there before. As if his silence was cutting deeper than his public possession had.

As if being shut out by him hurt worse than being claimed by him.

His hold on her elbow gentled fractionally before he caught himself. *No. Don't soften. Not yet.*

They turned down the corridor leading to his private wing. Here, the shadows were always thicker, always moving with awareness. They reached for her automatically, curling around her ankles and wrists like they were greeting her. Like they'd missed her.

She shivered at the contact, and he caught the way her breath hitched. Not from fear. Want. The recognition made his blood run hotter.

"You're being childish," she said, but her voice had lost its bite. "Whatever I did, we should discuss it like adults. Like—"

"Not. Here." The words came out as a low growl, the first he'd spoken since they'd left the terrace.

She went quiet at that, perhaps finally hearing the dangerous edge in his voice. The promise of exactly what kind of discussion they were going to have once they were behind closed doors.

His chambers were at the end of the corridor, past shadow-guards who straightened to attention and tried very hard not to stare at their lord dragging his tribute past them with violence in every line of his body.

The heavy wooden door, carved with intricate scenes of death and rebirth, loomed ahead.

"Dante." Her voice was quieter now, almost tentative. Uncertainty creeping in beneath the anger. "I—"

His name. His actual name, from her lips. Not the title, not "Lord

Reaper," but *Dante*. After she'd wielded it like a weapon at the gathering, used it to cut him in front of everyone.

Now it sounded different. Softer. Almost like she was reaching for him.

It nearly broke him.

"Save it," he said without looking at her, reaching for the door handle. "Whatever you're going to say, whatever explanation or excuse you have, save it for when we're alone."

The door swung open to reveal his private sanctuary. He guided her inside, finally releasing her as he turned to face her for the first time since they'd left the gathering.

The moment the door sealed shut behind them, Brynn put space between them. Quick steps backward until she was in the center of his chamber, arms crossed defensively over her chest.

The firelight caught her figure, played across the curves he'd watched other men admire all evening. His hands clenched into fists at his sides.

"Now you can explain what the hell that was about," she said, her jaw set in that stubborn way that made him want to either throttle her or kiss her senseless. Both. Definitely both. "What gave you the right to drag me away from a diplomatic gathering like—"

He didn't answer immediately. Just looked at her, really looked at her—taking in the flush of anger on her cheeks. The defensive set of her shoulders, even as she stood her ground against the Reaper, who was barely containing himself.

She was magnificent. Beautiful and fierce and completely, utterly his.

"You're going to stand there and glare at me?" Her voice rose slightly, frustration bleeding into anger. "After what you just did? Do you have any idea how humiliating that was? How—"

She started to pace, gesturing sharply as the words poured out of her in a rush. Her movements were agitated, catching light with each step.

"Every Death Lord there watched you drag me away like some kind of primitive, like I was property you were reclaiming. Like I had no say in the matter. Like my choices don't matter at all because you decided—"

He moved.

One moment, she was in the center of the room, ranting about his behavior, her hands gesturing wildly. The next he was there in front of her, crowding her space with his body. He backed her up until her shoulders hit the stone wall with a soft thump.

His hands slammed against the wall on either side of her head, caging her in with his body without quite touching her. Close enough that she could feel the heat of him, the violence radiating from him.

But not touching. Not yet.

The effort of holding himself back made his arms tremble against the stone. Made his breath come ragged. Every instinct screamed at him to close the distance, to claim her mouth, to show her exactly who she belonged to.

"Stop. Moving." His voice came out low and dangerous, finally unleashing everything he'd been holding back all evening. All the jealousy and possessiveness and desperate need he'd been trying to control.

Her eyes went wide, her breath catching audibly. Her pulse hammered visibly in her throat, fast and frantic.

She was pressed against his wall, caged by his arms, surrounded by his shadows, and her body was responding to him, anger be damned. He could see it in the flush spreading down her neck. In the way her lips parted. In the slight sway toward him before she caught herself.

She was just as affected as he was.

And they both knew it.

Between them, the air crackled with tension that had nothing to do with anger and everything to do with the fact that they were finally, finally alone.

LVIII.
BRYNN

Brynn's breath caught as he loomed over her, his dark eyes burning with anger. She could feel the tension radiating off his body, could practically taste his rage in the air between them.

This was the first time she'd seen him truly angry. Not cold, not controlled, not wearing that mask of deadly calm he usually maintained.

This was pure fury.

It should have terrified her.

Instead, it sent heat racing through her veins like wildfire.

"Don't you dare try to intimidate me after what you just—"

"Intimidate you?" He let out a harsh laugh, but there was no humor in it. His face was inches from hers now, close enough that she could see the silver flecks in his dark eyes. "Thief, if I wanted to intimidate you, you'd know it."

The endearment-that-wasn't sent a shiver down her spine. He hadn't called her that in days—not since their fight, not since she'd walked out. Hearing it now, rough with emotion and possession, made her chest tighten.

Don't react. Don't give him the satisfaction.

Her jaw set defiantly even as her heart was hammering against her ribs.

"Then what DO you want, Reaper?"

She spat his title at him, the same way he'd used "thief". A reminder of what they were supposed to be to each other. Lord and tribute. Death Lord and mortal. Nothing more.

His gaze dropped to her lips for just a heartbeat before snapping back to her eyes. Hunger flashed in their depths.

"What do I want?" he repeated, his voice rough. "I want to know why you let them touch you."

"Touch me?" She blinked, then laughed—a sharp, cutting sound. "They were dancing with me. It's what people do at gatherings. Perhaps you've forgotten, given how long you've spent brooding in corners."

His jaw tightened. "That warrior had his hands on your bare skin."

"On my waist. During a waltz." She tilted her chin up, meeting his glare with one of her own. "Should I have made him hover away like your terrified courtiers do with you?"

He went very still. "Caelum was calling you 'my dear.'"

"Caelum was being polite. A concept you might try sometime."

"And Vex—" His voice dropped to a growl. "You danced with Vex. After what he did."

That landed. She felt her composure slip for just a moment before she caught it.

"I handled Vex just fine. I didn't need you swooping in to—"

"You shouldn't have had to handle him at all!" His palm slammed against the wall beside her head, making her flinch. "He touched you. He cornered you in his own court and put his hands on you, and tonight you let him hold you like nothing happened—"

"Because I refuse to let him think he has any power over me!" Her voice rose to match his. "Because, unlike some people, I don't need to be protected from every perceived threat!"

"This isn't about protection!"

"Then what IS it about, Dante?" She shoved at his chest, but he didn't budge. Solid as stone, caging her against the wall. "Because it looks like you're angry that I dared to have a good time without your permission!"

His shadows surged across the floor, climbing her ankles, her calves. She kicked at them instinctively, but they just wound tighter.

"Tell your shadows to back off."

"No."

"Dante—"

"They go where they want." His shadows curled tighter around her ankles. "And apparently, they want to be wrapped around you. Can't imagine where they got that idea."

Heat flooded her cheeks. From anger, she told herself—only anger.

"You're being ridiculous. I danced with people at a party. That's not a crime."

"You were punishing me." He leaned closer, and she pressed back against the wall, heart pounding. "Every smile you gave them. Every laugh. You were making sure I saw. Making sure I suffered."

"And what if I was?" She met his stare without flinching, even as the shadows crept higher, teasing the hem of her dress. "What if I wanted you to feel even a fraction of what I felt when I found out you'd been lying to me for weeks?"

"I never lied to you."

"Oh, spare me—"

"I never lied." His hands pressed harder against the wall, bracketing her completely. "Every word I've ever spoken to you has been true."

"You kept my own identity from me! You knew what I was, who I was, and you said nothing while I stumbled around in the dark!"

"To protect you—"

"To control me!" She shoved at his chest again, and this time he shifted back half a step. Not much, but enough that she could breathe. "You made decisions about my life without asking. You treated me like I was too fragile to handle the truth. That's not protection, Dante. That's manipulation."

His mask cracked. She saw it, the flash of pain beneath the anger.

"And tonight," she continued, pressing her advantage, "you dragged me out of that gathering like I was property. Made a scene in front of every Death Lord in existence. Do you have any idea what that looked like? How it felt?"

"I don't care how it looked."

"Of course you don't! Because you never think about what I might want. You just decide what's best and expect me to fall in line like everyone else in your court."

His shadows had gone still around her legs. The air between them crackled with tension.

"Is that what you think?" His voice was quiet now. Dangerously quiet. "That I see you like everyone else?"

"I think you see me as something to manage. Something to protect whether I want it or not. Something to keep in the dark because you've decided I can't handle the truth."

"Brynn—"

"No." She held up a hand, cutting him off. "You don't get to 'Brynn' me right now. Not after weeks of cold shoulders and making decisions behind my back. You wanted to know why I danced with them tonight? Why I smiled and laughed and let them touch me?"

She stepped forward, into his space, close enough to feel the heat radiating off his body.

"Because they asked. Because they treated me like a person with choices instead of a problem to be solved. Because for one night, I wanted to feel like I mattered to someone who wasn't trying to control me."

She watched each word land. Watched him flinch.

But the satisfaction felt hollow. Bitter on her tongue.

His shadows had retreated, pooling around his feet. His fingers curled at his sides.

When he finally spoke, his voice was raw.

"You're right."

She blinked. Whatever she'd expected him to say, it wasn't that.

"What?"

"You're right." He ran a hand through his hair. "I made choices about your life without asking. I kept things from you that you had every right to know. I told myself it was protection, but it was control. Fear disguised as care."

She couldn't speak. Could barely breathe. Because the Reaper, the terrifying Death Lord who'd made her life hell for weeks, was actually admitting he was wrong.

"I was terrified." His voice cracked on the word. "Terrified of you becoming a target before you were ready. Terrified of every ambitious Death Lord trying to claim you. Terrified of losing you before I even had you."

His eyes met hers, and she saw it, the vulnerability beneath—the loneliness beneath the control, the desperate, aching want that mirrored her own.

"I should have told you. I should have trusted you to handle it instead of deciding for you. I was wrong, and I'm sorry, and I know that doesn't fix anything. But I didn't lie to you—"

"That's semantics," she said, but her voice had lost its edge.

"Maybe." He exhaled slowly. "But a lie would have meant I was trying to deceive you. What I did was try to protect you from truths I thought would hurt you. It was wrong. It was arrogant. It was exactly the kind of controlling behavior I despise in others, and I did it to the one person who deserved better from me."

Damn him. Her eyes were burning. She blinked hard, refusing to let the tears fall.

"You still did it," she whispered. "You still kept me ignorant while everyone else knew."

"I know."

"You still watched me struggle with questions about myself and said nothing."

"I know."

"And tonight—" She had to pause, had to swallow past the lump in her throat. "Tonight you humiliated me in front of everyone."

His expression shifted. The vulnerability didn't disappear, but hunger rose alongside it.

"Tonight," he said slowly, "I watched every male in that room put their hands on you."

His shadows began to move again, sliding across the floor toward her.

"Watched them hold you close. Heard them make you laugh. That bright sound you so rarely give to anyone." His voice dropped lower. "And I couldn't do a damn thing about it. Because I'd destroyed any right to claim you."

The shadows curled around her ankles—cool silk against her heated skin.

"Do you have any idea what that was like?" He stepped closer, and she didn't retreat. Couldn't. "Watching you give them all the warmth you've been denying me?"

"You deserved to suffer," she breathed.

"I did." His agreement was instant. "I deserve every moment of it. But that doesn't mean it didn't tear me apart."

The shadows climbed higher, teasing the hem of her dress, and want curled through her anyway.

"Good." The word came out breathless. "Maybe now you understand how it felt. Being kept outside. Being shut out."

"I understand." His hand lifted, hovering near her face but not quite touching. "I've understood since the moment you walked out. Since I've spent every night alone, knowing you were hurting because of the choices I made."

She was trembling. Hating herself for it. Hating him for making her feel this way when she was still so angry, still so hurt.

"Tell me something." His voice dropped to a low growl. "Did you like it tonight? Having their hands on you?"

"That's not—"

"Did it make you feel the way you're feeling right now?" His eyes were dark with intensity. "Heart pounding? Breath catching?"

She pressed her lips together, refusing to answer. But the trembling gave her away—pulse racing, skin flushed, heat coiling tight in her core.

"No," she finally admitted. The word escaped before she could stop it.

"No." Satisfaction flashed in his gaze. "And why is that?"

The shadows slid higher still, and a sound escaped her that she couldn't suppress.

"Why didn't their touches affect you the way mine does?" he pressed. "Tell me."

She held out for another moment. Another breath.

Then the shadows found a particularly sensitive spot, and the truth spilled out in a gasp.

"Because it wasn't you."

LIX.
DANTE & BRYNN

Brynn

That was all it took for his mouth to find hers.

This wasn't anything like the restrained touches they'd shared in the days after the breakthrough, when every brush of skin had felt like testing a live flame. This was a claim. Primal and unyielding, all the wanting he'd been leashing finally unleashed.

She kissed him back with a desperation that should have embarrassed her. Weeks of tension, of longing, of fighting the pull between them while her anger burned and his secrets festered. All of it surging into this fierce collision of mouths and teeth and need.

His tongue swept against hers, tasting her, claiming her, and heat pooled between her thighs so fast it made her dizzy.

"Finally," she gasped against his lips, not meaning to say it aloud.

He swallowed the word whole. Made it his.

His shadows swirled around them both, wrapping possessively around her waist, sliding up her arms, cool silk touching every inch of exposed skin while his hands stayed braced against the wall on either side of her head. The dual sensation, darkness touching her everywhere while he touched her nowhere, sent shivers racing down her spine.

One tendril traced along the neckline of her dress, dipping beneath the fabric to stroke the swell of her breast. Her breath caught.

"You're mine," he growled against her mouth, teeth grazing her lower lip hard enough to sting. "Say it."

"Make me."

The sound that rumbled through his chest was barely human. Predatory and satisfied and hungry all at once. It vibrated through her where their bodies pressed together, and she felt an answering clench low in her belly.

One hand tangled in her hair, tilting her head back to expose her throat. The other gripped her waist hard enough to bruise, dragging her body flush against his.

She could feel him through their clothes. Hard. Wanting. The thick ridge of his cock pressed against her stomach, and hells, she wanted to touch it.

The kiss turned consuming. Teeth and tongue and the dark, dangerous taste of him flooding her senses. She was drowning in it. Wanted to drown in it. Wanted to feel him everywhere.

"I've wanted this," he murmured against her throat, his mouth trailing fire down the column of her neck, "since the moment you talked back to me."

"Then stop talking," she managed, her voice embarrassingly breathless, "and take what you want."

His control cracked. She saw it happen. That iron restraint she'd been fighting against for weeks, finally giving way.

His shadows wrapped around her thighs, lifting her effortlessly until her legs wrapped around his waist. The movement pressed his cock directly against her core, and they both groaned at the contact.

Even through layers of fabric, she could feel him, hard and thick and straining toward her. Her hips rolled instinctively, grinding against him, and the friction made her moan.

"Dangerous words, thief," he warned, voice dropping to that low, rough tone that made her pulse pound. His hips rocked forward, pressing harder against her, and pleasure sparked through her nerve endings.

"Good thing I'm not afraid of danger, Reaper."

She sank her teeth into the spot where his neck met his shoulder, had been wanting to do that for longer than she'd ever admit, and his sharp intake of breath was deeply satisfying.

He pressed her harder against the wall, his mouth finding hers with renewed intensity. Her hands fumbled at his jacket, fingers clumsy with urgency, and he let her work it off his shoulders. Let her yank at his shirt until her palms pressed flat against his bare chest.

The sound he made was half growl, half prayer.

Her nails raked down his chest, leaving trails of fire. Her fingers found his nipple and pinched, and his hips jerked forward involuntarily, grinding against her heat.

"Your turn," he managed, and his shadows danced around her, finding the complicated laces at the back of her gown.

His realm's aesthetic wrapped around her body like he'd chosen it himself. And now the fabric was loosening, slipping, pooling at her waist until she was left in nothing but a thin chemise.

Through the sheer fabric, he could see everything. Her nipples were already hard and straining against the material. The flush spreading down her chest. The way her breath came too fast.

"Perfect," he breathed.

His shadows slid beneath the chemise before she could respond, cupping her breasts, teasing her nipples with cool touches. She gasped, arching into the sensation.

"Your shadows," she managed, "they're—oh—"

"They know what I want." His eyes were dark, watching her face as his shadows circled her nipples, rolling them between incorporeal fingers. "They've wanted to touch you like this for weeks. I've had to hold them back."

She pulled him closer. "Don't hold back."

His mouth descended on her collarbone, trailing down to the edge of her chemise while his shadows continued their work. She was making sounds she couldn't control, little gasps and moans that seemed to drive him wilder.

"Dante." His name slipped from her lips like a prayer.

He paused. "Say it again."

"Dante."

He kissed her then, softer than before. A brief moment of tenderness that made her chest ache. Because she'd said his name like it meant something. Like he meant something.

Then he was carrying her toward the bed, shadows swirling around them both.

She expected him to lay her down gently.

Instead, he threw her onto the mattress.

She landed with a bounce, skirts tangled around her thighs, the silk sheets a shock against her flushed skin. Before she could catch her breath, he was on her.

"Mine," he growled, hands already tearing at the remnants of her dress.

The expensive fabric ripped under his fingers. Her hips jerked toward him.

"Prove it."

Her hands raked down his chest, desperate for more of him. But shadows wrapped around her wrists, yanking them above her head and pinning them to the mattress.

She was trapped. Held down. Completely at his mercy.

Her cunt clenched.

His mouth descended on her throat, teeth grazing hard enough to mark. "You like this," he said against her skin. "Being held down. Helpless."

"I don't—"

One shadow slid up her inner thigh, and her protest died in a moan.

"Liar." His voice was filled with dark satisfaction. "Your body tells me the truth even when your mouth won't. I can smell how wet you are."

Oh hells. Her face flamed, but her hips tilted toward that teasing touch, seeking more contact.

"All that defiance, all that fighting," he continued, his mouth trailing down to her collarbone. "You were just waiting for someone strong enough to make you yield."

"I don't yield to anyone."

"No?" His shadow pressed directly against her core, rubbing through her soaked underwear, and she couldn't stop the sound that escaped her. "Then why are you dripping?"

Damn him. "Dante—"

"That's not an answer."

He tore the chemise away, leaving her bare except for her stockings and the ruined scrap of fabric between her legs. His eyes raked over her, hungry and possessive.

"Look at you. Spread out on my bed like an offering."

She should have felt vulnerable. Exposed. Instead, the way he was looking at her, like she was the most desirable thing he'd ever seen, made her feel powerful.

"Are you going to look all night, or are you going to do something?"

His smile was predatory. "Demanding little thief."

Then his mouth found her breast, and she stopped thinking.

Dante

SHE WAS GOING to be the ruin of him.

The way she looked right now: flushed and wanting beneath him, hair spread across his dark sheets, her body arching toward his mouth. It was taking every shred of his control not just to take.

His teeth caught her nipple, tugging with just enough pressure to ride the edge between pleasure and pain. She cried out, spine curving off the bed, and the sound went straight to his cock.

More. He needed more of those sounds.

He sucked her nipple into his mouth, tongue swirling, while his shadow continued to rub maddening circles against her cunt through her underwear. The fabric was soaked through. He could feel her heat even through the material.

"Dante, please—"

"Please what?" He switched to her other breast, biting down just hard enough to make her gasp. "Tell me what you want, thief. Use your words."

"I want—" She broke off in a moan as his shadow pressed harder. "I want your mouth."

"You have my mouth."

"Lower."

His cock throbbed at the demand. His demanding little thief was finally asking for what she needed.

He kissed his way down her body, taking his time. Mouth tracing over her ribs, her stomach, the jut of her hipbone. His shadows kept her wrists pinned while new ones spread her thighs wide, holding her open for him.

He tore away her underwear and just looked at her.

Her cunt was slick and swollen, glistening in the firelight. Pink and perfect and *his*. He'd thought about this more times than he'd ever admit. Wondered what she'd taste like, what sounds she'd make, whether she'd be loud or quiet when she came.

"Beautiful," he murmured, and his breath against her sensitive flesh made her whimper. "Do you have any idea how long I've thought about this? Tasting you?"

"Dante, please, I need—"

"I know what you need."

His tongue traced a slow line up her slit, and she nearly came off the bed.

She tasted like heaven.

Sweet and musky and *his*, and he couldn't get enough. His tongue explored every fold, every dip, learning what made her breath stutter and what made her moan and what made her thighs tremble around his head.

"Oh hells—" Her hips bucked, seeking more contact. "Dante, please—"

He pinned her hips with one hand, keeping her still while his tongue circled her clit. The little bud was swollen and sensitive, and when he sucked it into his mouth, she screamed.

That's it. He wanted to hear her.

His shadows held her thighs wide, preventing her from closing them, from escaping the relentless assault of his mouth. He could feel her building toward orgasm. The way her breathing turned ragged, the way her hands fought against the restraints.

He pulled back.

"No!" She actually sobbed with frustration. "Dante, don't you dare—"

"Tell me who you belong to."

"I'm going to kill you—"

He pressed his tongue flat against her clit and gave one long, slow lick. Then stopped again.

"Who do you belong to, thief?"

"You, damn it! I'm yours, I'm yours, now please—"

He rewarded her with two fingers sliding inside her cunt while his mouth returned to her clit with renewed intensity. She was tight—so fucking tight—and hot and drenched, her walls clenching around his fingers like she was trying to pull him deeper.

"That's it," he murmured against her flesh, working his fingers in and out. "Good girl. Take what you need."

The endearment made her clench harder. He filed that away for later. Many, many uses later.

He curled his fingers, finding that spot inside her that made her back arch, and sucked hard on her clit. She shattered.

Her orgasm crashed through her, her whole body shaking, her cunt spasming around his fingers while she screamed his name. He kept his mouth on her through every pulse, drawing it out, wringing every last shudder of pleasure from her body.

Only when she went limp did he finally pull back, releasing her wrists from their bindings. She reached for him immediately, hands fumbling for his waistband with urgent need.

"Need to touch you," she breathed. "Need—"

He let her.

Her hands were shaking, her whole body still trembling with aftershocks, but she worked his pants open and wrapped her fingers around his cock.

Hells. He was so hard it hurt. Her grip was so warm and eager, stroking him with clumsy urgency.

His head fell back, a groan tearing from his throat.

"That's it," she breathed, echoing his earlier words. "Good Reaper. Take what you need."

His eyes snapped to hers, blazing. "Careful, thief. That mouth is going to get you in trouble."

"Promises, promises."

She stroked him again, twisting her wrist at the head, and he nearly lost control. Pre-cum leaked from the tip, and she used it to slick her movements, her thumb rubbing over the sensitive head until his hips jerked involuntarily.

She pushed him onto his back, and he let her, surrendering control for the moment. His cock jutted up between them, flushed dark with need, and she wrapped both hands around him just to watch his face.

"Brynn—" Her actual name, rough with desperation. "If you keep doing that, I'm going to—"

"Going to what?" She stroked him faster, harder. "Come for me? I want to see it. Want to feel you lose control."

"Not yet." He grabbed her hips and flipped them, pinning her beneath him again, breathing hard. "Not until I'm inside you."

The words made her pupils dilate. She was still slick from her orgasm, her thighs wet with it, and when his length slid against her folds, they both groaned.

They moved together, urgency mounting. He dragged through her arousal, the head catching against her entrance with every roll of their hips. She was grinding against him shamelessly, coating him with her slickness.

"Please," she breathed. "Dante, I need—I need you inside me—"

"I know, thief. I know."

She pushed against his shoulders, and he let her flip them again, let her straddle him. The head of his cock pressed against her entrance, and she started to sink down—

Every instinct screamed at him to let her. To thrust up into that tight heat and claim her completely.

Instead, his hands caught her waist.

Brynn

"Not yet."

She stared at him in disbelief. "What?"

His jaw was clenched, every muscle in his body taut with restraint. She could feel him trembling beneath her. Could feel his cock twitching against her entrance, straining to be inside her.

And he'd stopped.

"Not when we're still angry," he managed, his voice wrecked. "Still fighting."

"I don't care about fighting right now—"

"I do." He cupped her face in his hands, making her look at him. His eyes were dark with want, but underneath was tenderness. It made her chest ache. "When I take you completely, it won't be out of jealousy or anger. It will be because you're mine, and I'm yours, and we'll both choose it with clear heads."

She stared at him, chest heaving, her body screaming at her to ignore him and sink down anyway.

But his thumbs were stroking her cheekbones. And his eyes were so earnest, so vulnerable beneath the hunger.

"You're ridiculous," she whispered, but her voice came out soft instead of angry.

"Probably." He pressed a kiss to her temple, her cheek, the corner of her mouth. "But you deserve more than a claim made in anger for our first time together."

The wall she'd built since walking out of his chambers cracked. Then crumbled.

He pulled her down against his chest, both of them still breathing hard, skin slick with sweat. She let him arrange her against him, let herself be held even with everything still hanging between them.

His cock was still hard against her thigh. She knew he had to be aching. But he just held her, one hand stroking slowly up and down her spine.

"I'm still furious with you," she murmured against his shoulder.

His lips twitched. "I wouldn't expect anything less."

"You made a scene at the gathering. Humiliated me in front of everyone."

"You were trying to make me jealous." His voice was dry. "It worked."

She narrowed her eyes and smacked his shoulder. "You're not supposed to admit that."

"Would you prefer I lie?"

She huffed a breath that was almost a laugh.

"This doesn't fix everything," she said.

"No." He pressed his lips to her hair. "But it's a start."

She should pull away. Retreat to her own chambers and process everything that had just happened. Rebuild the walls he'd demolished with his mouth and his shadows and his infuriating restraint.

Instead, she burrowed closer against him.

His heartbeat was steady beneath her ear. His shadows curled around them both like a blanket, cool and possessive and oddly comforting. The fire crackled low in the hearth, casting light across the ceiling.

She was still aroused. Her body was still humming with unsatisfied need, but underneath it was something that felt like hope.

No one had ever wanted her to mean something before. She'd been a thief to use, a tribute to sacrifice, a bloodline to exploit. But Dante... Dante wanted to wait until they chose each other. Until it was real.

"Dante?" she murmured.

"Hmm?"

"When we do this properly..." She traced idle patterns on his chest, feeling his muscles twitch beneath her fingers. "I want all of it. The shadows, the control, everything. I want to know what it's like when you don't hold back."

His whole body went taut beneath her. When he spoke, his voice was rough. "You don't know what you're asking for."

"Then show me." She lifted her head to meet his eyes. "Show me what it's like to be claimed by a Death Lord."

The look in his eyes made her shiver. Hungry and possessive and full of promise.

"Careful what you wish for, thief," he murmured. "I have centuries of restraint to unleash."

"I'm counting on it."

His laugh was low and warm, and his arms tightened around her.

LX.
DANTE

The alarms woke him instantly.

One moment, he was asleep with Brynn's warm weight tucked against his side, her head resting on his chest, her breath gentle against his skin. Her fingers were still curled loosely against his ribs, exactly where they'd fallen when exhaustion claimed them both.

Mine, he'd thought as he drifted off. *Finally mine.*

The next moment, magical alarms were shrieking through the palace, their pitch climbing until even his hearing struggled to bear it.

Ward-stones flashed emergency crimson throughout his domain, painting the walls in blood-red light. His shadows recoiled from where they'd been wrapped protectively around them both, responding to the crisis before his mind fully caught up.

Brynn jerked awake beside him, going from relaxed to instantly alert—years of survival instincts overriding sleep in a heartbeat. "What is that?"

"Ward failure." He was already on his feet, power crackling through the air as he felt the damage rippling through his realm like cracks spreading. "Multiple failures. Simultaneous."

Not an accident. Not natural decay.

This was an assault.

Someone had been waiting. Planning. Striking at the exact moment when they'd let their guard down.

"How many?" Brynn was moving, reaching for the first thing she found—his shirt, discarded hours ago in their urgent need for each other.

She pulled it on, and his heart clenched.

The black fabric hung loose on her frame, the hem falling to mid-thigh, the shoulders slipping to reveal her collarbone. She looked small in it. Fragile, even with her jaw set in determination.

She looked like his.

And he might be about to lose her.

"All of them." His voice came out rough as the full scope hit him through his connection to the ward network. Every alarm screaming. Every boundary failing. "Every court. Every major barrier between realms."

Her face went pale. He watched understanding dawn in her eyes—that sharp mind he'd come to rely on, cutting straight to the truth.

"Someone used our..." She swallowed. "They used us being distracted. They waited until—"

She didn't finish. Didn't need to.

Guilt twisted through him.

From the receiving hall beyond, transport circles blazed to life, the formal summons binding all Death Lords for realm-threatening crises. Emergency protocol. Mandatory attendance.

"You're bringing me." She was already moving toward the door, reaching for the ward tools she'd left on his dresser, strapping them to her thigh.

"Protocol says—"

"Protocol can burn." Her eyes flashed as she met his gaze. "I'm the only one who can read the ward damage patterns accurately. You need me there."

She was right. They both knew it.

But every instinct he possessed screamed against bringing her into a room full of panicked Death Lords when everything was falling apart. Panicked beings made dangerous choices. And she would be the most vulnerable thing in that room.

"Stay close to me," he commanded, shadows already wrapping around her—thicker than usual. Possessive in their need to shield her. "And if I tell you to run—"

"I won't leave you to face this alone." She stepped closer, and her hand found his chest. Right over his heart, where she'd pressed her palm last night.

The touch burned through him.

"We're stronger together," she said quietly. "Remember?"

The words landed deep, warming places that had been cold for so long. He wanted to pull her back to bed and forget the world was ending. Wanted to keep her safe in his quarters while he dealt with whatever threat was coming.

He couldn't have either. Not when the realms were collapsing.

The transport circle flared crimson—no more time.

He pulled her against him for one brief moment, breathing in her scent. Still carrying traces of him, of them, of what they'd allowed themselves to have. Her heartbeat raced against his ribs. Fast with fear, but unwavering in resolve.

"Together," he said roughly against her hair.

Then they stepped through into chaos.

LXI.
DANTE

The Bone Temple was unraveling.

Dante felt it the moment they materialized at the crest of the hill—the corruption radiating from the ivory spires that had stood since before any of them claimed their thrones. The cathedral built for darker prayers was crumbling.

Where the air had once tasted of nothing, neutral space waiting to be filled, it now crackled with unstable magic. The barriers between realms were bleeding into each other, and this place that existed between all of them was bearing the cost.

Overhead, the sky churned with contradictions. His eternal twilight warred with Seraphina's blazing desert sun. Thessa's perpetual mist tangled with Vex's star-strewn darkness. Caelum's golden light flickered through it all like lightning in a storm.

The once pristine ivory walls now had red cracks running through them, pulsing like infected wounds.

Dante's hand found the small of Brynn's back, keeping her close. She was still wearing his shirt under a hastily donned coat, and some possessive part of him took satisfaction in that even now. His shadows spread around them both, restless and agitated in a way he couldn't control.

The last time they'd stood here, she'd been six feet behind him. A tribute he barely tolerated. Someone he'd commanded to stay silent unless directly addressed.

Now she walked beside him, and he couldn't imagine her anywhere else.

The central chamber was already crowded when they descended. The vast circular space with its vaulted ceiling felt smaller somehow, oppressive with failing magic and the tension of panicked beings.

The five-pointed star inlaid in the floor still marked each throne's position, but the metals had lost their luster. His black marble reflected chaos instead of twilight.

The other Death Lords had already arrived.

Seraphina stood in full battle armor, her red hair bound with razor wire, every weapon she owned strapped to her frame. She looked ready to march into war the moment they identified a target.

"Reaper." She acknowledged him with a sharp nod, then her eyes flicked to Brynn. Approval crossed her fierce features. "Architect."

Brynn straightened beside him. The recognition was intentional—a warrior acknowledging another's earned place. The last time they were here, Seraphina had barely glanced at her.

Vex paced along the chamber's edge like a caged animal, his usual languid grace replaced by something twitchy and frantic. He looked diminished: skin too pale, movements too jerky, eyes too wide.

He kept looking at Brynn. Quick, darting glances that made Dante's jaw clench. His shadows darkened visibly around her, and Vex's gaze skittered away—someone losing their power, looking for anything to cling to. He wouldn't find it here.

Thessa drifted near the center star, her form more translucent than usual. She was seeing multiple timeline possibilities—he could tell by the way her eyes moved, tracking futures that hadn't happened yet.

Her expression was haunted and tired in a way he'd never seen. Whatever she was seeing made even the Lady of the Lingering afraid.

And Caelum.

Caelum stood at the head of the chamber in white and gold robes that seemed to emit their own light, untouched by the chaos. His composure was intact. Not a hair out of place. Not a trace of panic in his brown eyes.

Everyone else was afraid. Everyone else was scrambling. But Caelum looked like he'd been expecting this.

Suspicion hardened in Dante's chest.

"Thank the depths you're here," Caelum said, relief seeming genuine enough to make Dante's instincts scream louder. "I've been tracking the damage progression. We have perhaps forty-eight hours before complete collapse."

Brynn tensed at his side.

"Tracking?" Seraphina's hand moved to her sword hilt. "Since when do you monitor our individual ward systems? That's not part of your domain."

Dante watched Caelum's face. There was a slight tightening around his eyes.

"Since I realized someone was systematically weakening them." Caelum's expression shifted to grave concern. "I should have acted sooner. But I hoped I was wrong."

Caelum gestured, and the air above the star shimmered. Magic coalesced into a three-dimensional map of the entire ward network.

Hundreds of connection points. Thousands of smaller wards. Through sixty percent of them, angry red pulsed like spreading infection.

Brynn leaned forward, drawn by the map. Her eyes tracked the damage, reading a language only she could understand and already working the problem while the rest of them were still reeling.

"Show me the attack patterns." Her voice cut through the tension. "The sequence. Which wards failed first."

She stood among beings who'd existed for millennia and commanded information like she belonged here.

Caelum's expression flickered before the mask returned. "Of course."

The map shifted, revealing the damage's progression. Red spread across it, each failure triggering the next.

Dante's eyes drifted back to Caelum.

"You have a solution," Vex said. "You wouldn't have called us without one."

"I do." Caelum moved toward the map. "We pool our power, all of us, and channel it through a single focus point to reinforce the core ward-stones."

Simple enough. And Dante already knew the answer.

"Through you," he said quietly.

Every eye turned to him.

Caelum's smile was gentle. "I have the most experience with peaceful transitions. My power is naturally suited to healing rather than destruction." His eyes met Dante's. "Unlike some of ours."

The dig beneath the diplomacy. Brynn's fingers brushed against his, barely a touch, but he felt her tension. She saw through him too.

"I'll need her abilities as well." Caelum's attention shifted to Brynn with that warm expression that made Dante's shadows writhe. "The ward-architect bloodline will be essential."

Every instinct Dante possessed rejected the idea.

"And then?" Thessa's voice carried distant whispers. "After you channel our power through yourself?"

"Then we pray it's enough." Caelum paused. "I won't lie, if I lose control of that much combined death magic..."

He didn't finish.

But Dante heard what he wasn't saying. If it failed, Caelum died a martyr. If it succeeded, he held the power of all five courts. Either way, he won.

His shadows wound tighter around Brynn.

LXII.
BRYNN

She could feel Dante's tension through the hand at her back. It matched her own growing suspicions.

Something about this felt rehearsed. The concerned friend who reports the theft they committed. The helpful partner bleeding the business dry. She knew this game.

Caelum's magical map rotated slowly above the center stone, all those red warning lights pulsing in perfect synchronization.

The sabotage patterns didn't look random; they looked structural —planned with the kind of intentionality that took years to develop, and the type of intimate knowledge that should have been impossible for anyone outside the ward-keeping bloodline.

"The attacks began months ago," Caelum was saying, gesturing to different sections. "Small failures at first, easily overlooked as natural decay. But they've escalated dramatically in recent weeks."

Right around the time she and Dante had started fixing things. Right around the time someone would have realized she could undo what they'd been building.

She felt Dante's shadows stir against her ankles. He'd caught the same timing.

"How did you detect the pattern?" She kept her voice neutral.

"These ward-stones are distributed across individual realms. You shouldn't have visibility into other courts' infrastructure."

Across the circle, Seraphina's hand drifted toward her sword hilt.

"I wasn't monitoring anything inappropriate," Caelum assured her, his smile warm. "I was simply... worried. As the lord responsible for peaceful transitions, I thought it prudent to investigate on everyone's behalf."

"Since when?" Seraphina demanded. "You've never given a damn about barrier maintenance before. That's Reaper's nightmare, not yours."

"Since the stability of all our realms became threatened." Caelum's expression shifted to wounded sincerity. "I had hoped to resolve this quietly. But the saboteur has forced my hand."

"And who is this saboteur?" Vex demanded, his diminished power making his voice sharp. "You seem remarkably well-informed about their methods."

Caelum's expression grew grave.

"I'm still investigating. But given the specificity of these attacks, it has to be someone with intimate knowledge of the ward network. Someone with access to all our realms." He paused. "Someone we trust."

The temperature in the circle dropped. Vex's eyes darted between the other Death Lords. Thessa's form flickered, becoming more translucent.

Behind her, Dante's power drew tighter. She could feel his shadows wanting to surge forward, to tear answers from Caelum's throat. But he held still. Waiting. Trusting her.

The realization steadied her.

If she was right, she needed proof. Something he couldn't explain away.

Her abilities had been growing stronger since she'd stopped fighting what she was. She could see deeper into the magical structures now. Read flow patterns others might miss.

And suddenly she understood.

"These breaks," she said slowly. "They're not random attacks.

Someone knew exactly which supports to remove to cause maximum cascade failure."

"Yes!" Caelum's approval came too quickly. "Which is why we need your talents to identify which core supports remain intact."

But that wasn't what she was seeing.

Her fingers trembled as she traced one of the red zones, following power flow patterns that were becoming clearer with every second.

Every break had been designed to force power through specific junction points. Points that would naturally channel everything through a single domain if repairs followed someone's well-thought-out plan.

He wasn't trying to destroy the wards. He was trying to own them.

"The Mourned Court," she said quietly.

Dante went very still behind her.

"All the remaining stable channels lead back to your realm, Caelum. Every single one."

Silence.

Vex stopped pacing. Seraphina's hand closed fully around her sword. Thessa solidified completely.

"Of course they do." Caelum's voice remained calm. "My domain has always served as the primary stabilizing force. The original architects built it that way, a fail-safe. Natural deaths, peaceful transitions. My power is fundamentally different. Less volatile."

He gestured to the channels.

"It's why my power is best suited to channeling repairs. The system naturally consolidates through my domain during a crisis."

The explanation was almost believable.

She felt Dante's shadows stir against her skin.

"You said the attacks started months ago," she continued, keeping her tone curious. "But I've been tracking ward instabilities as part of my training. Some of these damage patterns are much older. Years, at least."

A pause. Barely a heartbeat.

"You're mistaken," he said, but the warmth had cooled. "The recent attacks—"

"I'm not mistaken." She met his gaze directly. "I know these ward-stones intimately now. This damage didn't start months ago. It's been building for decades."

"What are you suggesting?" Vex's voice had gone quiet, dangerous.

"I'm suggesting that whoever did this has been planning for a very long time. And they know the ward network better than any outsider should." She paused. "They know it the way someone who's been actively managing it would. Someone with operational access, not just theoretical knowledge."

Something flickered behind Caelum's eyes. The mask slipped, just for a second.

"You have a suspicious mind, child." She bristled at the word. "I suppose it comes from your background. But sometimes the simplest explanation is correct."

Dante's shadows tensed against her skin. She felt his attention sharpen.

The other Death Lords were watching. Seraphina's hand hadn't left her sword. Vex had gone still. Thessa was solidifying further.

They weren't dismissing her.

"Let me prove my intentions," Caelum said smoothly. "Let me walk you through exactly how we can stabilize the network."

He offered proof because he still thought he could convince them.

"All right," she said. "Show me."

The map rotated, and she studied not just the damage patterns but the way Caelum gestured. The ease with which he manipulated controls that should have required specialized knowledge to even perceive.

He was too comfortable. Moving through these systems like second nature.

She needed him to slip further. To reveal something only the saboteur would know.

"To repair these junction points," she said slowly, "we'd need to understand how the damage was done." She kept her voice curious, unthreatening. "How would someone even access these deep ward-layers? They're supposed to be sealed."

Dante's hand pressed slightly firmer against her back. He'd caught what she was doing.

"The interior channels can be accessed through the tributary nodes." Caelum gestured to the map, warming to the subject. "You'd need to destabilize the outer shell first. A precise sequence of pressure points that creates a temporary gap without triggering the alarm wards. Then you redirect the bleed-off through secondary channels to mask the intrusion while you work."

The words kept coming like he'd done it a hundred times.

Her blood went cold.

Dante's shadows wrapped tightly against her ankles, and she knew he'd heard it too.

"That's not repair methodology," she said.

Caelum's mouth was still open, ready to continue. He stopped.

"I asked how to fix the damage." She met his eyes. "You just told me how to cause it."

Across the circle, Seraphina's sword slid halfway from its sheath.

Vex had gone absolutely still.

LXIII.
DANTE

One second they were discussing repairs. The next they were staring at a man who'd just revealed intimate knowledge of techniques he should never have encountered.

And Brynn had caught him perfectly.

She hadn't accused him of anything directly. Hadn't made claims she couldn't prove. She'd just asked technical questions and let him damn himself with his own expertise, his own arrogance. Dante's shadows stirred with pride. She'd seen through Caelum when the rest of them were still scrambling.

"You've been managing the ward network," Dante said. "Personally. Actively. For years."

Caelum's composure cracked at the edges. "The situation required—"

"Required what?" Vex cut in, his diminished power crackling with fury. "Required you to learn sabotage techniques? Required you to systematically redirect ward energy through your realm? Required you to position yourself as our only salvation?"

"You don't understand." The words came out sharper than his usual tone, irritation bleeding through the practiced compassion. "The current system is fundamentally flawed. Broken. Do you know how many souls arrive at our domains traumatized by violent deaths? How many spend eternity reliving their final moments of terror?"

His voice rose. Passion replacing performance.

The true believer was emerging from underneath the gentle savior.

"So you decided to fix it?" Seraphina's blade cleared its sheath entirely. "By destroying it first?"

"By healing it." Caelum's eyes blazed with conviction. "By creating something better. A system where every death is peaceful, every transition guided by compassion instead of abandoned to chaos and suffering."

The temperature around the stone circle dropped as Dante's shadows responded to the threat. Not just to them personally, but to everything they were bound to protect.

To the fundamental nature of death.

"Under your control," Brynn said quietly—cutting straight to the heart of it. Dante's hand pressed harder against her back.

"Under proper guidance." Caelum looked directly at her, and something hungry flickered behind his eyes. Something possessive that made Dante's shadows surge protectively. "You have the power to rebuild the entire network from its foundations. To create barriers that guide souls to appropriate rest instead of trapping them in cycles of suffering."

"Wait." Vex had gone very still. "You want all of us to channel our power through you. Every Death Lord, all our domains' energy, flowing through a single point."

"You'd have control over everything," Seraphina said. "Every soul. Every death. Every transition."

"I'd heal everything." The fervor was unmistakable now. "No more violence. No more terror. No more suffering."

"Under your definition of peace," Dante said quietly.

He'd been to Caelum's realm. Had seen those contented souls drifting through paradise.

Had noticed something off about them that he couldn't quite name. They looked empty. Content but hollow, like puppets with their strings cut.

"According to someone who actually understands what true peace means." Absolute conviction. "I have spent millennia perfecting the art of gentle death. I know how to ease a soul's transition, how to guide them to contentment. Imagine if every death could be like falling asleep in safety, welcomed by love instead of fear."

Around the circle, power began to stir.

"The souls in your realm," Thessa said suddenly, her voice carrying echoes of distant revelation. "Something about them feels... off. Different."

"They're content," Caelum said, real irritation bleeding through. "Free from the burdens that plagued them in life."

Dante's shadows recoiled instinctively, his power recognizing something wrong even before his mind could articulate it.

"No," Brynn said, her voice level, though tension radiated off her. "I won't help you remake death in your image. I won't help you force your version of peace on everyone."

Pride swelled in Dante's chest even as fear threaded through it. Because she'd just painted a target on herself. Just made herself the obstacle standing between a madman and his paradise.

The line drawn. The choice made.

Caelum went still. Then his head tilted, and the gentle guide vanished like he'd never existed.

Dante had seen that look before—in the mirror, long ago, before he'd learned to control what he was. But he had never looked at her like that, never seen her as something to possess.

"I had hoped you would understand the gift I'm offering," Caelum said. Nothing soft remained in his eyes. "But I see now that your attachment to suffering runs too deep for reason. That your connection to him has corrupted your ability to see clearly."

Golden light erupted from Caelum, wrapping around Brynn before she could react. Before Dante could reach her.

She cried out as the light yanked her backward toward the transport circle.

Her feet left the ground.

His shadows exploded outward.

But even as he moved, even as his power lashed out to shield her, he knew he was too late.

Her hands grasped at nothing.

She reached for him.

"BRYNN!"

The word tore from his throat.

He lunged forward, shadows grasping, straining, trying to wrap around her and anchor her to this realm. To him. His hand stretched toward hers across the shrinking distance.

Their fingers brushed for one heartbeat.

Then she was ripped away.

Light seared his vision. When it cleared, she was gone.

The silence that followed was broken only by the wail of emergency alarms and the distant sound of barriers failing throughout the realms.

Dante stood frozen, his hand still extended toward empty air. His shadows writhed around him in anguished chaos, stretching toward something that was no longer there.

LXIV.
BRYNN

Consciousness returned in fragments.

Golden light wrapping around her, Caelum grabbing her. Dante's shadows exploding outward too late. The bone temple. The transport blazing beneath her feet. Their fingers brushing before—

Then nothing but spinning darkness and the sensation of falling through layers of reality.

Pain lanced through her skull. Her head had struck something during landing. Everything hurt.

Her arms wouldn't respond—pulled overhead, wrists burning with what felt like acid and ice mixed together. Every instinct screamed to pull free, to run, but her body wouldn't obey.

She tried reaching for the ward-sense that had become second nature, the connection to death magic that hummed in her blood since she'd started training with Dante.

Pain exploded through her arms. White-hot, searing, making her gasp aloud.

The restraints were designed to neutralize her abilities.

The smell hit her next, forcing her eyes open despite the throbbing in her skull: hot metal and ash, with that sweet-rot smell of old meat that made her gag. Like the slaughter district in summer.

The sky above had blood-red clouds roiling across a dark purple expanse, lit from below by furnace fires that turned everything the color of old copper. Ash fell like snow, stinging where it touched exposed skin.

She was chained upright against a pillar of dark metal, arms stretched overhead, feet barely touching scorched ground. The metal pulsed with heat against her back, like standing against the chest of some massive beast.

Old instincts kicked in through the fear. Years of casing vaults had taught her to think when panic screamed at her to freeze.

Except what she saw made her stomach drop.

This wasn't a chamber. It was a factory floor stretching farther than she could see through haze and heat distortion. Massive furnaces lined what might have been streets, their iron doors glowing cherry-red.

She was already sweating, shirt sticking to her back beneath the outer layer.

Dante's shirt. She was still wearing it under the coat. Fabric that still smelled like him, like safety.

Between the furnaces, pipes ran everywhere—overhead and underfoot, a maze of metal and glass. Through the transparent sections, amber light flowed like honey, pulsing toward a central point beyond her sight.

Gears the size of houses turned with grinding sounds that made her teeth ache. Steam vented from valves with shrieks that sounded almost like voices. Hundreds of them. Maybe thousands.

Her stomach twisted. The sweet-rot smell suddenly made horrible sense.

He was processing them. Souls. Refining them like materials.

"Good. You're awake."

Her whole body went rigid.

Caelum stepped into view, and he wasn't the serene guide from the paradise realm anymore. He moved with jerky energy. His white and gold robes were still immaculate, somehow clean amid the filth, but his eyes burned with fervor. The eyes of someone who'd stopped pretending sanity mattered.

"I was beginning to worry the transport had damaged you." He circled her pillar slowly. "That would have been wasteful. You're far too valuable to lose."

"Where—" Her voice came out raw, throat burning from ash. "What is this place?"

"My refinery." Pride colored his voice as he gestured broadly. "The heart of my operation. Where I've been building real power for millennia while the other Death Lords squandered theirs on sentiment."

The wailing suddenly made sense. This was production—manufacturing on a massive scale.

He stepped closer, hands trembling with excitement.

"Do you know how frustrating it's been? Watching you tour the other courts, seeing you with him. The Reaper. That monster who hoards his power for nothing."

"Dante doesn't—"

"He wastes everything!" The shout echoed off metal, fury twisting his features. "All that death magic, all that potential, and he just sits there surrounded by his suffering souls while the rest of us share scraps!"

Monster. He'd called Dante a monster.

"I've been planning this for decades," Caelum continued, words spilling faster. "Positioning pieces. Sabotaging the wards slowly enough that no one noticed."

His laugh was sharp, brittle.

"And then you arrived. The ward-architect bloodline awakened after being dormant for so long. At first, I thought you'd ruin everything." His eyes fixed on her with renewed intensity. "But then I realized you were the key I didn't know I needed."

He stopped directly in front of her. Close enough that she could smell meadow flowers beneath the industrial reek.

The contrast made her stomach heave.

"You were supposed to see it," he said quietly. "The superiority of my vision. I showed you paradise. And you chose him instead."

"Whatever you're doing here, it's not peace." The words came out stronger than she felt.

"It's better than peace." He grabbed her chin, forcing her to meet his eyes. His fingers were cold, wrong in the furnace heat. "It's purpose. Let me show you."

He released her and stepped back, spreading his arms.

"Every soul that dies peacefully comes to me first. Thousands over the ages. The other Death Lords guide them onward, help them rest, waste all that potential on sentiment."

His lip curled with disgust.

"I extract what matters. Their essence, their power. What remains after extraction serves me. Perfect order from the chaos of individual will."

"You're torturing them."

"They're resources." He said it so simply. Like discussing harvesting wheat. "And I use every part. Nothing wasted. Watch."

He gestured, and smoke cleared. Through the gap, she could see glass chambers large enough to hold a person, metal arms ending in needle-like probes descending like spider legs, gears and pistons working in perfect unison.

The scale of it was obscene.

A translucent form was strapped into the nearest chamber. An elderly man, features filled with fear. She could see his mouth moving. Pleas, probably. Maybe prayers.

The machine came to life.

The probes descended, piercing his chest. Light began flowing through the tubes immediately, streaming out of him in ribbons.

His mouth opened in a cry that cut through all the others.

His soul was being pulled out piece by piece while he was conscious.

"The extraction takes time," Caelum said conversationally. "Hours to days, depending on the soul's strength. I've refined the process considerably. It used to be messier."

The old man's form dimmed as more essence was pulled from him. His features began to smooth, becoming less distinct—less individual. The fear in his eyes faded slowly because the capacity to feel was being extracted along with everything else.

First fear went. Then pain. Then confusion. Then awareness. Then nothing.

"When complete, they emerge perfected," Caelum continued. "No pain, no fear, no wants or needs beyond serving their purpose. They're happy, Brynn. Free from the burden of choice."

"They're nothing." Her voice was barely a whisper. "You've erased everything that made them who they are."

"I've freed them from the prison of self. The illusion of individual consciousness causes all suffering. Remove it, and what remains can serve something greater."

He actually believed this. Actually thought he was saving people.

The machine completed its work with a pneumatic hiss. The old man drifted free, expression serene now. Completely blank.

The same look she'd seen on souls in Caelum's paradise. Those souls had already been processed. Already nothing.

Guards were bringing forward another form. A woman, fighting and wailing. She saw what was waiting. Understood what was about to happen.

"I've processed millions," Caelum said softly. "Every peaceful death for ages. With your abilities, I could accelerate everything. Decades compressed into years."

He turned back to her, genuine conviction in his eyes.

"You could help me reshape the entire death system. Make every death peaceful, every soul content in service. Don't you see how beautiful that would be?"

"No." She forced the word out. "I won't help you erase souls. I won't help you turn people into nothing and call it peace."

Dante's realm was cruel. But his souls were still themselves. Still able to be reborn.

Disappointment crossed Caelum's features.

"You will," he said quietly. "Eventually. They all do."

He gestured to one of his shell servants, a young man with blank eyes and a serene smile. The hollow soul drifted forward with automatic obedience, moving to adjust controls on nearby machinery.

Caelum turned back to her and smiled.

"Take her to holding," he ordered.

Cold hands locked around her arms. They released her restraints, and her legs gave out.

They hauled her upright, supporting her weight entirely. Dragged her through the facility, past extraction chambers and rivers of pipes carrying stolen essence. Past souls being drained, their cries echoing.

They descended metal stairs into deeper levels where the heat was less intense but more oppressive. The wailing faded with each level, replaced by silence.

The chamber they entered made her inhale sharply.

Soldiers. Hundreds. Maybe thousands. Standing in perfect formation in the crimson light. Arranged in ranks stretching beyond sight into darkness. All armed, all armored, all ready.

All wearing the same blank expression.

He was weaponizing them. Victims turned into soldiers.

The shells dragged her through ranks that didn't move, didn't acknowledge them, didn't exist beyond their programming. Toward a cage carved into the far wall. Simple bars of dark metal, barely large enough to stand in.

They shoved her inside. The bars sealed with a hiss of magic.

Caelum appeared outside.

"Consider carefully," he said softly. "Partner or resource. Queen beside me or a hollow shell in my army. The choice is yours, but the outcome is inevitable."

She stayed silent.

He turned and walked back through his army, white robes pristine among the weaponized shells.

The bars burned when she touched them, magic searing her palms. She pulled back with a hiss.

Around her, the silent army waited. Above, the extraction chambers continued their work. She could still hear the cries faintly, distant but constant.

She sank down in the cramped cage, back against the wall. Drew her knees up to her chest.

She pressed her face against his shirt, breathing in the fading scent of him.

He would come. He had to come.
She'd just found him. They'd just finally—
She squeezed her eyes shut against the tears threatening to fall.
He would come.
The machinery hummed above. The army stood silent below.
And she was trapped between them with time running out.

LXV.
BRYNN

Time lost meaning in the cage.

Crimson light that never changed. An army that never moved. Machinery humming above, occasionally punctuated by screams that made her flinch every time.

She'd tried the bars twice more. Both times, they seared her hands badly enough that she'd bitten back cries of her own. Her wrists were raw, her palms blistered.

No escape that way.

She'd mapped every inch of the cage, noted every soldier in her line of sight, counted the levels between her and the extraction chambers above.

Information without application. Strategy without opportunity.

He'd come. The way he'd screamed her name as she was ripped away. The way his shadows had reached for her. He'd come.

But Caelum had hidden this place for centuries. How long would it take?

Footsteps on metal stairs.

She jerked upright, ignoring the protest from stiff muscles. Multiple sets, moving in synchronization that marked shells.

Four hollow guards appeared first. Then Caelum descended into view.

His expression made ice spread through her chest. He looked pleased. Excited. Like someone about to unwrap a gift they'd been anticipating.

"I've been thinking about you," he said, gesturing for the guards to open the cage. "About your rather impressive survival skills. Ten years on the streets, no resources, no family. Yet somehow you not only survived but thrived enough to attempt that vault robbery."

Her pulse was already racing as the cage opened and cold hands dragged her out. Her legs barely supported her weight after hours—maybe days—cramped in that space.

"Take her to the center. I want her properly secured for what comes next."

They hauled her up through the silent army, toward the factory floor. But not to the extraction chambers. Instead, they brought her to a single chair surrounded by open space and golden light pouring down from above. Restraints built into the arms and legs. No walls. No shelter. Just her, with thousands of empty faces turned toward her.

She thrashed against their grip. It took several of them to shove her down and lock the restraints around her wrists and ankles.

Caelum circled slowly, studying her.

"Do you know what I find most interesting about you, Brynn? It's not your abilities. It's that you ended up with the one Death Lord I couldn't easily reach."

Her stomach dropped.

"Let me tell you a story about patience." He pulled over a stool and sat at eye level. "Your father was a merchant. A collector of antiquities. What he didn't know was that many of those relics were actually Architect tools. Individually inert, but collectively, they formed a guide to the original ward-cores."

Her father's study. All those dusty objects he'd cherished, arranged with careful labels in his neat handwriting.

"I tried to buy them first. Generous offers through intermediaries. But your father refused. Called them family heirlooms."

Her fingers curled against the armrests. The metal dug into her blistered wrists, and she welcomed the pain. It kept her anchored.

"So I took a different approach. Fabricated charges of smuggling. I had agents in the merchant guilds, the customs houses, even the crown prosecutor's office."

The trial had happened so fast. Arrested and convicted within days.

"But your father's collection was only part of what I wanted." He leaned forward. "I'd been tracking Architect bloodlines for centuries. Most are dormant. Useless. But occasionally, a soul is born with the gift close enough to the surface that the right catalyst could awaken it."

He paused.

"Your parents had a daughter. And my sources confirmed the markers. Faint, but present."

Cold dread pooled in her gut. He'd known about her since before her parents died.

"I framed your parents. Seized the collection. But I let you live. Because if you died, your soul would pass through to the death realms untrained. And do you know what happens to an Architect soul when it crosses over without awakening?"

She said nothing.

"It fragments. The gift disperses across the realms, lost forever."

He met her eyes.

"You were useless to me dead. So I had my people tracking you for years. Your movements, your criminal career. I needed you alive until I could claim you."

Ten years of looking over her shoulder. And he'd been watching the whole time. Not hunting her. Guarding his investment.

Bile rose in her throat. She swallowed it down and tested the left restraint, twisting her wrist slowly. The metal didn't give. But the motion steadied her.

"Most Architect bloodlines need a catalyst to trigger the dormant ability." He gestured, and a shell guard stepped forward carrying something wrapped in velvet. "So I provided one."

He unwrapped it slowly.

The ward-tools—the ones she'd found in Lord Edmund's vault. The ones that had started this entire nightmare.

Her breath stuttered.

"Lord Edmund was my pawn. I gave him these tools, then made sure rumors reached the right ears. A vault filled with treasures, poorly guarded, ripe for theft."

The job that had seemed too perfect.

"I made sure you heard those rumors specifically. The tools were bait, designed to test whether the gift had awakened."

Every choice she'd thought she was making. Every step she'd believed was her own.

"Here's where things should have been simple." His tone shifted to genuine irritation. "Edmund was supposed to have you marked as tribute. At the ceremony, I would claim you. The Reaper despises tributes—barely participates, claims whoever's left, ignores them until they expire."

He turned to face her.

"I would have had you in my court within hours. You would have been grateful. I would have trained you, and you would have helped me willingly."

The scope of it staggered her. Decades of positioning, all leading to a single moment.

"But the Reaper showed up. For the first time in decades, Dante attended personally. And before I could act, he looked at you and claimed you himself."

Real anger underneath the golden warmth.

"You were pulled into the one court I couldn't easily access. Under the protection of the one Death Lord powerful enough to keep you from me."

The mask slid back into place.

"I adapted. I offered to take you off his hands. He refused. I tried to persuade you that my court was safer. But you formed a genuine attachment to him."

He shook his head.

"He kills everything he touches. His realm is built on suffering. And you chose him. Again and again."

He leaned close.

"Do you know why you can touch him? It's your blood. The ward-architects built the original barriers between life and death. Their magic was designed to work alongside death magic. You're not immune because of some grand destined love. You're immune because your ancestors engineered themselves to be."

She said nothing. Let the silence speak for itself.

He gestured at the facility around them.

"I never wanted to steal power. At the council meeting, I proposed the Death Lords consolidate domains under unified leadership. Mine. If they'd agreed, none of this would have been required."

He pointed at her.

"But you strengthened the wards I'd been destroying. You gave them confidence the crisis could be resolved without me. A mortal stumbling through the death realms, and she ruined decades of work."

He rose from the stool and stood over her.

"Help me willingly, and you keep everything. Your abilities, your memories, your sense of self. Rule beside me as a true partner."

She would never.

"Before you answer, consider this. If you refuse, the Reaper will tear apart the death realms searching for you. His domain will collapse. And I'll extract your abilities by force."

He stepped back.

"Your choice, Brynn. Help me build paradise. Or watch everything you love burn while I take what I need anyway."

One of the shell guards placed something on her arm. Small, metal, cold. One of the ward-tools.

Magic surged through her as the tool responded to her bloodline. But it felt corrupted, twisted.

Pain exploded through her arm.

Like something hooked into her bones and pulled, dragging magic out through her blood by force.

She screamed.

"The tools can extract more than essence," Caelum said over her screaming. "They can pull at specific abilities. This is a very mild application."

Bone-deep agony that made thought impossible.

Dante—

His name was all she could hold onto. His face. His voice. The way he'd held her just hours ago.

Caelum removed the tool.

The pain stopped instantly. Left her gasping, shaking, sweat pouring down her face.

"That was perhaps thirty seconds. Full extraction takes hours. Sometimes days."

He set the tool down and knelt in front of her.

"Choose, Brynn. But choose quickly."

The tool descended toward her arm.

LXVI.
DANTE

His shadows had never left her.

They'd been on her since the first touch, a protective instinct he hadn't acknowledged until it was too late to stop. Threads wrapped around her wrist, woven through her hair. Barely visible, but there.

When Caelum's transport circle activated, those shadows went with her.

Dante felt it instantly. The pull. Her being ripped from his realm. From his side. The bond snapping taut like a fishing line caught on something massive and sinking fast.

Hours ago she'd been in his arms. He'd tasted her, felt her come apart beneath him, held her while she fell asleep.

And now she was gone.

The stone circle still crackled with residual magic. The other Death Lords converged.

"The transport signature is scrambled," Thessa whispered. "Layered. Hidden beneath—"

"I know where she is."

His voice came out flat.

He could feel her through the connection. Her terror. Her confusion. The way her heart raced when she was trying to be brave.

Seraphina moved closer, understanding the danger in his stillness. "We'll help you—"

"No." His shadows darkened. "Go back to your realm. He'll use the chaos to expand if we all leave."

"Reaper—"

"If I'm not back in a couple of hours, assume I've failed." He turned toward the portal. "Then burn his paradise to the ground."

He didn't wait for agreement. Just followed the thread connecting him to her, tearing open a pathway through reality.

The transition fought him. Reality buckling, twisting, trying to keep him out. Not a normal passage between realms. Something hidden, fortified, built in the spaces between spaces.

When he finally forced his way through, the refinery slammed into him like a fist.

Extraction chambers stretched endlessly. Souls strapped inside, screaming as golden light was torn from their chests. The machinery hummed, processing them one after another.

This was what Caelum meant by peaceful paradise. This was where he'd been taking them. All those contented souls. This was what he'd done to make them that way.

His shadows recoiled from the concentrated despair before surging outward, feeding on it. But the thread connecting him to Brynn was what mattered. That was what pulled him forward.

Alarms shrieked.

Figures poured from the processing chambers, shells in armor. His shadows tore through them without slowing. More appeared. Dozens, then hundreds. He carved through them, but they kept coming. Each wave more organized than the last.

Victims, not soldiers. Souls Caelum had erased and turned into weapons. And Dante was destroying what remained of them to reach her.

The facility sprawled endlessly. Levels stacked on levels, corridors branching in every direction. Processing floors filled with chambers. Shell soldiers guarding every passage.

The thread pulled him deeper. Stronger with each level he descended.

A blade found his shoulder. Another his ribs. Minor wounds, but accumulating. Dark ichor welled against his skin before his shadows surged to compensate.

His power was draining, the army learning with each wave, finding the hairline gaps that widened as exhaustion mounted.

Then the thread pulled harder. More insistent.

He moved faster, abandoning caution. His shadows exploded outward, clearing entire corridors. The facility groaned under the weight of his power—metal buckling, support beams cracking.

The thread blazed with pain.

Her pain.

Then he heard it.

Her scream.

The sound of her being tortured.

The thread flared with her agony, sharp enough to make him stagger. Last night, that voice had been gasping his name, laughing against his chest.

Now she was screaming because he wasn't fast enough.

Exhaustion didn't matter. Nothing mattered but getting to her.

He tore through the next door and found himself facing a massive chamber. Thousands of shell soldiers in perfect formation, stretching beyond sight.

And beyond them—

Brynn.

Strapped to a chair, arms locked in glowing restraints. Blood on her wrists where she'd fought them. Her face was pale with pain.

And Caelum standing over her with a twisted ward-tool pressed to her arm, golden light pulsing as it tore at her abilities.

While she screamed.

Their eyes met across the distance.

Relief flashed across her face. Then terror. Then Caelum's hand tightened on the tool, and her back arched with fresh agony.

Another scream. Weaker this time, her voice breaking.

The army flooded forward, thousands of shells moving to block his path. To slow him down while their master continued torturing what belonged to Dante.

Every bit of restraint. Every ounce of control he'd maintained while searching, while conserving power.

It meant nothing now.

Dante stopped holding anything back.

His shadows exploded outward with enough force to crack the floor beneath him. The temperature plummeted to impossible depths, frost spreading across every surface. His form flickered between solid and something else entirely.

The shells between them dissolved. Hundreds gone in seconds. The army tried to reform, tried to block his path, but they were hollow copies facing the genuine thing.

Through the gap his power had created, he saw her clearly now.

Tears on her cheeks. The tool was still pressed to her arm, still glowing.

She was still wearing his shirt under that coat. Still carrying pieces of him with her. And Caelum was trying to tear those away too.

But the shells kept coming. Wave after wave, synchronized to overwhelm through sustained assault. From every angle simultaneously. He met them with unleashed power, shadows tearing through dozens at a time.

Metal screamed. Armor shattered. Bodies dissolved.

But there were thousands.

For every dozen he destroyed, two dozen more stepped into the gap. The army was adapting, exploiting the fractures in his defenses that grew wider as his power drained.

More blades found marks through the gaps—his shoulder, his forearm, his thigh. Cuts were accumulating with each passing moment.

His power was still vast, still devastating everything close to him, but even he had limits. He'd never tested them. Never had reason to push this far.

Never had something he couldn't bear to lose.

A spear grazed his neck, just enough to draw blood.

The shells pressed closer, sensing weakness. More disciplined strikes, tighter formations. Learning that he could be worn down.

He was tiring, and Caelum, watching from beside her chair with that tool still in his hand, knew it.

"Ah, there we are." Caelum's voice carried across the chaos, calm through the carnage. "The Reaper, come to save his thief. How predictable."

He gestured casually, and the army shifted, creating a corridor between Dante and the chair. An invitation. Or a dare.

"Please." Caelum rested his hand on the back of her chair, dangerously close to her shoulder. She flinched but couldn't pull away. "Let's discuss this reasonably. You're powerful, Reaper, perhaps the most powerful of all the Death Lords. But you're in my realm now. Fighting my army. Destroying victims who've already suffered enough."

"Each one was someone's beloved," Caelum continued, almost gently. "Someone's child, parent, lover. And you're unmaking them by the hundreds just to reach one mortal girl."

She wasn't just one mortal girl. She was everything.

His shadows writhed around him. The temperature dropped another ten degrees. Frost crept across the floor, climbing the legs of the nearest soldiers.

"Let her go." A growl more than words.

"Or what?" Caelum's smile widened. "You'll fight through my entire army? Destroy thousands more while I watch? You've already killed hundreds, Reaper. How many more will you obliterate before you admit you can't win through force?"

He spread his hands in a gesture of reason.

"Even the Reaper himself eventually tires. And I..." He gestured at the endless army, at the chambers humming above. "I have soldiers without end. All the time in existence. All the patience required to wait for you to exhaust yourself."

He was right. Dante could feel it: the drain, the wounds, the power that had been infinite an hour ago now scraping against its edges.

He couldn't fight forever. But he didn't have to fight forever. He just had to fight long enough.

The army stood motionless. Above, the chambers hummed and souls screamed.

Caelum's expression turned thoughtful.

"So let's be civilized. Find a solution that satisfies us both."

His eyes gleamed.

"We both want Brynn alive. Whole. Herself. The question is whether she remains that way... or becomes fuel for something greater. Her essence, purified, serving eternal paradise. Isn't that better than a brief mortal life?"

Caelum didn't understand. He couldn't.

Dante would trade every century of his existence for one more night with her.

Caelum touched the chair near her shoulder. She jerked away, and Dante's shadows surged forward before he forced them back.

"What do you say, Reaper? Shall we discuss terms? Your strength and her abilities could be valuable to my vision. If you'd only see reason."

His shadows expanded.

"There's no negotiation."

The temperature plummeted. Frost formed on everything—armor, weapons, the chair she was strapped to.

"There's only you. And me. And what I'm going to do to you for touching what's mine."

"Pity." Caelum sighed, genuinely regretful. He gestured.

The army moved.

They came in waves. Dante met them with unleashed power—shadows tearing through dozens at a time. But thousands more waited. The soldiers adapted, found gaps, pressed closer.

More blades got through, more cuts opening. His power flickered as weariness mounted.

She was watching. She needed to know he wouldn't give up on her.

Not ever.

The army pressed harder, surrounding him, forcing him to fight on all sides simultaneously.

He was tiring. Caelum knew it. He could see it in the bastard's smile.

LXVII.
BRYNN

She couldn't look away.

Dante was still fighting, shadows tearing through shells by the dozen, but slowing. Blood marked his skin. A cut across his ribs. Another along his shoulder.

A blade got through his defense, slicing across his forearm. Dark ichor welled from the wound.

But he kept moving forward. One step at a time, carving through the army that stood between them. His shadows flickered with each strike, power draining with every shell he destroyed.

He was going to burn through everything he had left trying to reach her. And she was sitting here useless.

The restraints bit into her wrists, metal burning where it touched. She'd fought them until her skin broke, until blood ran down to her hands, but the restraints held.

Caelum stood a few feet away, that twisted ward-tool still in his hand, watching Dante's approach with interest.

"How much longer, Reaper?" His voice carried across the chaos. "How many more of my soldiers will you destroy before you admit you can't win this?"

Dante didn't answer. Just pushed forward another agonizing step.

Five feet.

The shells pressed harder, trying to overwhelm him before he could reach her. A spear grazed his thigh. He didn't even flinch.

Three feet. She could see his face now—blood on his jaw, dark eyes blazing with determination.

Two feet. The army redoubled its assault, but he pushed through like nothing could stop him.

One foot.

His hand shot out, shadows wrapping around her restraints. The metal that had held her helpless, that had burned and cut and suppressed everything she could do.

Power surged through the connection. The restraints resisted for a moment.

Then shattered.

The metal screamed as it broke. The locks holding her wrists exploded into fragments that bit into her skin.

She gasped as her arms fell free. Blood rushed back into her hands, every nerve ending screaming. The burn on her arm throbbed—blistered flesh, angry and raw, where the tool had touched.

His hand closed around her upper arm.

Real. He was real. He'd come for her.

"Can you stand?" His voice was rough, strained.

She nodded, not trusting her voice. Her legs trembled as she pushed herself up, but she forced them to hold.

Caelum's expression shifted, benevolent concern giving way to something colder.

"You can't escape, Reaper." His voice remained calm. "You've exhausted yourself fighting through my army. You're bleeding. Weakened. And I have thousands more soldiers waiting."

Shells poured into the chamber from every entrance. Hundreds of them, coordinating to surround them.

Dante's shadows exploded outward anyway, creating a barrier between them and the army—buying seconds.

"Stay behind me."

He positioned himself between her and the shells, shoulders set despite exhaustion, shadows flickering as they struggled to maintain the barrier, blood seeping through his clothes.

He was going to die protecting her. Going to burn through what little power he had left, holding them off while she did nothing.

The shells crashed against the barrier. Each impact sent visible shockwaves through Dante's shadows. Through him.

She had to find another way.

Her ward-sense flared suddenly, that instinct she'd always had for reading locks and barriers. But this wasn't directed at any physical restraint.

The entire facility hummed with ward-work. Ancient patterns woven through every surface, every pipe, every extraction chamber. Architecture her ancestors had built, corrupted but still familiar.

She could feel it. All of it.

Power flowed through the refinery like blood through veins. From extraction chambers to collection spheres, from those spheres to a central nexus. And from that nexus, a massive pipeline streamed upward.

To Caelum's paradise.

That was his power source. That was what fueled all of this. If she could reverse the flow, overload the system, give them a chance to escape...

It was what she did. Find the mechanism. Apply pressure. Turn.

"Dante." Her voice came out raw but determined. "I can collapse his power source. Give me thirty seconds."

Caelum's head snapped toward her, surprise flickering across his features before smoothing back to that patient smile. "I wouldn't recommend that, my dear. You don't fully understand—"

"Thirty seconds." She cut him off, eyes locked on Dante's back. "Can you hold them?"

He didn't hesitate. Didn't question.

Just trusted her completely.

"Do it."

His shadows surged outward with renewed force, reinforcing the barrier. The dome around them solidified, buying her the time she needed.

She pressed her burned palm against the floor, ignoring the way charred flesh screamed in protest. Reached deeper with her ward-sense, following the pipeline to its source.

The regulatory valve. Complex ward-work that controlled flow and direction. Patterns she understood instinctively.

Just like picking a lock. Find the mechanism. Apply pressure. Turn.

"No!" Caelum lunged toward her, grace forgotten. "Stop her!"

The shells redoubled their assault. The barrier shuddered, cracks spreading wider. She heard Dante's rough breathing as he poured power into maintaining it.

She grabbed the valve with her magic and twisted.

The ward-work resisted, ages of balance fighting against her, then yielded. Flow reversing. Power that had been streaming upward now rushing downward at double the volume.

The extraction chambers around them flickered. Collection spheres began to glow brighter as they overloaded. The shells attacking the barrier faltered, movements becoming less coordinated.

"Brynn, stop!" Caelum's voice rose, composure cracking. "You don't understand what you're doing!"

She pushed harder, forcing more power backward. Building pressure. Overwhelming the systems.

The barrier around them shattered completely.

Shells flooded in, but they were slower now. Uncoordinated. Dante's shadows kept them away from her while she worked.

She felt the valve giving way, restrictions breaking down, the flow becoming a torrent—

And then she felt what lay beneath.

The valve wasn't blocking flow. It was limiting something. Regulating something that was meant to stay regulated.

The pipeline tore open.

Power exploded through the connection. From everywhere. From all five death courts simultaneously, channeling through ward-work far older than she'd realized.

The collection spheres that had been dimming suddenly blazed with new essence. The extraction chambers roared back to life. The shells that had been faltering surged back to full strength.

And more appeared.

Translucent forms materialized throughout the chamber. Dozens, then hundreds. Souls being pulled from every corner of the death realms, drawn through the gateway she'd accidentally blown wide open.

Horror crashed down as understanding hit.

Warriors who should have gone to the Violent. Artists meant for the Consumed. The unfinished bound for the Lingering. All of them redirected here. Harvested. Refined. Weaponized.

Her ancestors had built bridge points between domains. Had locked them down, limited them to slow trickles.

And her bloodline had just given permission to open completely.

"No," she whispered, yanking her hand back from the floor. "No—"

Dante's shadows wrapped around her waist, pulling her backward as shells flooded the space where she'd been. His barrier reformed—smaller, tighter, barely large enough for both of them.

"What happened?" His voice was rough. Strained. "The power—"

"I opened it." The words came out broken. "I thought I was closing his source but I—"

She couldn't finish. Fresh souls kept appearing. The army doubling. Tripling. All drawing power from the gateway she'd opened.

Caelum had stopped trying to reach her.

His desperation melted away, replaced by something infinitely worse.

Triumph.

"Yes." The word was soft. Tender. "Oh, thank you, my dear. Thank you so very much."

"I could never have opened that gateway myself," he continued, voice taking on that fervent edge. "The ward-architects built in safeguards against external manipulation. But you..." His smile widened. "You commanded it from within. Your bloodline permitted it."

More shells formed. Hundreds. Thousands.

"Every soul that dies now flows through my realm first," Caelum said, spreading his hands like benediction. "Before any of the other

Death Lords can claim them. Your beautiful ward-work channels them here for processing."

Every death. Every soul. For eternity.

"Though why would I send them onward?" He tilted his head. "When I can perfect them here. Make them useful. Give them purpose."

She couldn't move. Couldn't think past the souls multiplying around them.

"I've been building toward this for centuries," Caelum said softly. "Waiting for the right catalyst. You accomplished it in thirty seconds."

"We're leaving." Dante's voice cut through the spiral. "Now."

His shadows wrapped around them both. Darkness so thick it felt like drowning. The refinery disappeared, reality twisting.

They materialized in the Forsaken Court.

His domain. The bone palace rising in the distance. Black roses blooming. Eternal twilight.

Her knees gave out.

She collapsed onto the grass. Her blistered hands caught her, pressing into the soft earth, and the shock of it made her whole body shake.

"Brynn." His hand on her shoulder.

She couldn't look at him.

"I opened it." The words scraped from her throat. "The gateway. Every death flows through his refinery now because I—"

Her voice broke completely.

"We'll fix it."

His grip tightened. Firm enough to anchor her to something beyond the horror spiraling in her mind.

She looked up at him through tears she hadn't realized were falling.

Blood stained his clothes. Dark against fabric, seeping through from too many wounds. His face was pale, jaw tight with exhaustion. But his expression held no accusation. No blame.

Only certainty.

"We'll fix it," he repeated. "Whatever it takes."

"Every soul," she whispered. "Every death in every realm."

The sob that tore from her chest hurt. Everything hurt. Her burned arm, her blistered palms, her throat raw from screaming. But worse than physical pain was the weight crushing down.

She'd tried to be strong. Tried to prove she was more than just something to protect. And she'd handed him victory.

She wrapped her arms around him, burying her face against his chest. Her whole body shook with sobs she couldn't control, couldn't stop, didn't have the strength left to fight.

His arms came around her immediately.

One hand cradling the back of her head. The other wrapped around her back, holding her close while his shadows drew tighter around them both. Creating a cocoon of darkness and safety.

"I destroyed everything," she whispered against bloodstained fabric.

"No." His voice was firm. "Caelum destroyed it. He set the trap. You were trying to save us."

"But I—"

"Enough." He pulled back to see her face, his hand moving to cup her jaw. His thumb brushed away tears. His dark eyes burned with intensity. "You're exhausted. Hurt. We both are."

Before she could protest, he lifted her. One arm beneath her knees, the other supporting her back.

He was injured. He'd fought through an army. He shouldn't be carrying anything.

But she didn't have the strength left to argue. Didn't have anything left at all.

His shadows wrapped around them as he carried her through palace corridors. Past arched bone and flickering blue flame. Toward his chambers.

She tucked herself against his chest, face buried in his shoulder.

He'd come for her. Fought through thousands of soldiers.

"Stop," he said quietly, as if reading her thoughts.

"Stop what?"

"Whatever you're telling yourself. I can feel you spiraling."

"You came for me," she whispered. "And I—"

"You survived." His arms tightened around her. "You stayed alive until I reached you. Everything else we'll handle together."

Together.

She was too exhausted to push him away. Too broken to do anything except let him carry her while catastrophe settled like lead in her chest.

We'll fix it, he'd said.

She wanted to believe him.

She wasn't sure she could.

LXVIII.
DANTE

Dante had known the other Death Lords would demand answers eventually.

He hadn't expected it to be this soon.

One hour since returning from Caelum's refinery. Since carrying her through the palace while she shook with sobs and guilt that wasn't hers to bear. Since getting her to his chambers and spending twenty minutes cleaning blood from her wrists, where those cursed restraints had cut deep.

She'd finally collapsed against his pillows, fatigue dragging her under. But even unconscious, her expression twisted with self-blame.

His shadows had refused to leave her even when he'd stepped away—curled around her wrists over the bandages, threaded through her hair, wrapped around her throat like a possessive collar.

He'd left her to check on his domain.

His realm was failing. The Tower of Screaming Winds had gone silent, no new souls to fuel its purpose. The Weeping Marshes receded, saltwater pools drying without fresh grief. Ward-stones throughout his domain pulsed irregularly.

A day, maybe two, before collapse.

His death-knights were already reporting instability. Souls becoming agitated, confused by the sudden cessation. His servants asking questions he couldn't answer yet. And the other realms were suffering the same, all of them being starved while Caelum harvested everything.

That's when his death-knight had arrived with the summons. A demand from three Death Lords who'd discovered their soul-flow had been completely severed.

A subtle tremor ran through the palace—one of his ward-stones failing somewhere in the outer realms.

The Reaper within him wanted blood. Wanted to return to that facility and tear Caelum apart slowly. But she needed him here. That mattered more than vengeance at the moment.

The shadows brought another warning: multiple powerful presences materializing in his throne room without permission.

His nature snarled at the invasion.

A moment later, his study door opened without a knock.

Aldric stood there, armor scorched from containing the power signatures flooding the throne room.

"My lord. The other Death Lords are here. They transported directly into—"

"I felt it." His jaw clenched. "Who's here?"

"Seraphina, Vex, and Thessa." The knight hesitated. "Lady Seraphina is volatile. They're demanding your presence immediately."

His shadows wound tighter, responding to the anger building in his chest.

"They'll wait." The words came out cold enough to make the knight step back. "I'll deal with them when I'm ready."

But even as he said it, he knew that wasn't an option. If he made them wait, their anger would only build. And they'd take it out on Brynn when they finally faced them.

The floor shuddered beneath his feet. He felt it through his connection to the realm, another ward-stone failing in the Weeping Marshes.

His gaze moved toward his chambers. She needed to face them. Needed to be part of stopping this. Keeping her away would only feed her guilt.

He moved toward his chambers, shadows reaching ahead. They slipped under the door, gentle tendrils wrapping around her to check, to confirm, to reassure himself that she was there and safe.

She was awake when he entered.

Sitting on the edge of his bed, her injured wrists resting in her lap. She looked up at him with weary eyes that held too much guilt.

"The other Death Lords are here." No point in softening it. "Emergency council. They've discovered their soul-flow has stopped."

She stood immediately, like she'd been expecting this. Her balance faltered, and she caught herself against the bedpost with wounded wrists.

His shadows were there before she could fall, settling around her waist. She leaned into them for a moment, and satisfaction pulsed through him at her trust.

Then she forced herself upright.

"They're going to blame me."

"They're going to try." The words came out like a growl before he could control them. "I won't let them."

"Dante, I opened that gateway." Her voice wavered. "I gave Caelum exactly what he needed to—"

"Caelum manipulated you." He moved closer, unable to stay away when she looked like that. His hand cupped her face, thumb brushing across her cheekbone. "Set a trap specifically designed to use your bloodline against you. You were trying to save us. What happened wasn't your fault."

"Then whose fault is it?" Her voice broke completely. "I have the abilities. I commanded the gateway to open. Me. So whose fault is it if not mine?"

His thumb retraced her cheekbone, the dark circles under her eyes more pronounced than before.

"We face this together," he said quietly. "But let me handle the initial politics. They're going to be looking for someone to blame, and I need you to trust me to position this correctly."

She studied his face for a long moment, searching for something.

Finally, she nodded.

He stepped back, giving her space. She went to the washbasin, splashing cold water on her face with careful movements that avoided jarring her injuries. She changed quickly, pulling on the gown his servants had provided. When she straightened, she pushed back some of the fatigue with determination.

There she is. His thief, refusing to break.

His shadows wrapped around her as they left his chambers, and he let them. Let his power reveal that she belonged to him.

They moved with intent, tracing her pulse points—throat, wrists, the hollow behind her ear. Curled around her throat like a visible collar. Slid beneath her clothing to rest against bare skin.

Every shadow-tendril a declaration: touch her and die.

The walk to the throne room was silent except for their footsteps. He could feel the other Death Lords pressing against his wards, adding more strain to systems already weakening.

The throne room's temperature had shifted erratically when they crossed the threshold. Seraphina's wrath mixed with the heat bleeding off Vex's starving power.

The mosaic floor bore fresh cracks from Seraphina's pacing. Vex's hunger had scorched dark patches on the windows. Even Thessa's gentle presence had left frost patterns spreading across surfaces.

He bristled at the invasion.

All three turned when he entered, and their unified focus felt like standing before an execution squad.

His shadows curled around Brynn's ankles, making his position clear before he even spoke.

Seraphina didn't waste time on pleasantries.

"Finally." She kept pacing, hand on her weapon. Each step cracked his floor deeper. "Do you know what's happening, Reaper? My battle-dead aren't reaching my domain. Every soul that should come to me, warriors and murder victims, all of them vanishing at the moment of crossing."

"Mine as well." Vex's voice cracked with desperation. The Lord of Consumption stood rigidly by the windows, hands clenched. Dark circles shadowed his eyes, spreading like bruises across his skin, becoming more transparent by the hour. "The consumed souls that feed my realm are gone. I can feel my power weakening with every death that doesn't reach me."

His form flickered at the edges. He was fading.

"The spirits scream." Thessa drifted near the shadows, her translucent form flickering more violently than usual. Parts of her kept disappearing, an arm vanishing for seconds before reforming, her face losing definition. "They show me souls being pulled away from their destined paths. Harvested before they can even understand what's happening."

Her form solidified just long enough for her eyes to lock on his.

"Something has corrupted the flow of death."

The palace groaned around them. Foundations weakening.

Seraphina's eyes locked on him. Her hand wrapped around her weapon's hilt.

"Your realm seems remarkably intact, Reaper." Her voice dropped. She stepped forward. "Your defenses are perfect, and you're the only one strong enough to pull off something like this."

His shadows drew tighter around Brynn, several threads remaining wound through her bandages even as he stepped forward—putting himself between her and Seraphina's building aggression.

"My realm was attacked too." He moved toward the throne, letting his presence command the space. Drew their focus away from Brynn and onto him. His shadows spread across the floor, reminding them whose domain they were standing in. "My soul-flow stopped an hour ago. The Tower of Screaming Winds has gone silent. The Weeping Marshes are drying up. My ward-stones are failing one by one."

The darkness spread further, pooling around their feet like a tide. The temperature dropped as his power filled the space.

"Convenient timing." Vex's desperation made him reckless. "You discover it first, have time to prepare your story, position yourself as the victim instead of the architect—"

"I discovered it first because I've been investigating the ward sabotage for months." His voice hardened, dropping to that tone that made even other Death Lords reconsider. "This isn't an attack. It's the culmination of a plan that's been building longer than any of us realized."

The floor cracked beneath them.

Thessa drifted closer, her form flickering with agitation.

"The spirits showed me the gateway opening." Her eyes locked on Brynn, fully solidifying with accusation. "Ward-work twisted into something new. Activated by someone with an architect bloodline."

His shadows tightened.

"Someone who's been in all our courts," Thessa continued. "Studying our defenses, learning our vulnerabilities."

Seraphina's pacing stopped. She turned to face Brynn directly.

"The human." Seraphina's voice filled with accusation. "She arrives in your court out of nowhere. You bring her to investigate all of us, learning our vulnerabilities, mapping our wards. Then Caelum makes his move, and suddenly she opens a gateway that gives him control of everything?"

Her jaw clenched.

"She's been playing us from the start. The question is whether you knew, Reaper, or if she played you too."

He felt Brynn tense beside him through the shadow-threads. Felt her guilt rising, her instinct to accept their blame.

"She was captured." His voice dropped to that lethal softness that preceded violence. "Tortured. These—"

He gestured to her wrists, and fresh fury surged through him at the sight of blood seeping through the white fabric.

"Are from suppression cuffs designed specifically to neutralize ward-magic. To prevent her from defending herself or escaping. She watched souls being processed in extraction chambers. Saw the army he's building. Experienced firsthand what he plans for everyone who opposes him."

He stepped closer to Seraphina.

"She knows what they're building, how they're doing it, and what they're planning next." He held her gaze, then looked at the others. "Which is more than any of you can say."

"Or," Vex said, desperation making him reckless enough to challenge the Reaper directly, "she's exactly where the enemy wanted her. Inside your court, your most secure location, with access to your defenses and your trust and your—"

The shadows exploded outward.

Darkness flooded the throne room, rising from floor to ceiling. They pressed against the other Death Lords like hands around their throats, making the threat clear.

The temperature plummeted. Frost crept across the floor, climbing the walls, covering every surface.

The bone walls creaked under the pressure, leaning inward in response to his wrath.

Seraphina's hand tightened on her weapon, but didn't draw. Smart enough to recognize when she was outmatched.

Vex took an involuntary step back. Even Thessa's ethereal presence dimmed.

"Choose your next words carefully." His voice echoed from every shadow in the room. "You're in my realm. Under my protection. And you're questioning my judgment about someone I've claimed."

He pulled the shadows back, muscles tensing as he reined in his power. The darkness settled but didn't disappear.

"You want answers?" He let the question hang. "You want to know who's behind this, how to stop it? Then listen. Because she's the only one who's actually faced the enemy instead of standing in your courts, wondering where your power went."

Seraphina studied him for a long moment. Her eyes moved from him to Brynn, then back, reading the shadows wound possessively through Brynn's bandages, the way his power responded to her presence.

Finally, slowly, she moved her hand away from her weapon.

"Fine." Her voice had lost some of its hostility. "Talk."

Thessa's form solidified slightly. Vex remained by the windows, but his hands unclenched.

Dante turned to Brynn, and pride surged through him at what he saw.

She stood straighter through her exhaustion. Through the pain from her wounds, the burns on her arm, the weight of three Death Lords who'd been ready to blame her. She didn't flinch under their scrutiny.

He gave her a slight nod.

She stepped forward, shoulders back, chin lifted, meeting their gazes.

Her hands shook slightly, but her voice didn't waver.

"I'm not Caelum's accomplice. But I did trigger the gateway that's stealing your souls. And I need to explain how he trapped me into doing it."

She laid out exactly what had happened. Finding what she thought was Caelum's power grid, attempting to collapse his operation, triggering the trap he'd long been building.

He watched their expressions shift as she spoke. Watched suspicion give way to understanding, then to grudging respect as she outlined the scope of what they were facing.

"You opened it?" Seraphina took a step forward, voice rising. "You're confessing to giving Caelum control of the entire soul-flow—"

"I was trying to collapse his operation." Brynn held her gaze without flinching. "I found what I thought was his power grid. A way to shut him down, to save—"

Her eyes flicked toward him for just an instant.

"To save us," she continued. "What I triggered instead was the trap."

"Convenient story," Vex spat, his form wavering. "Caelum sets the perfect trap, you spring it at exactly the right moment—"

"She was trying to stop him and walked into a trap designed specifically for her." His shadows moved, flowing around Brynn's feet. "A trap that required an architect's bloodline to activate. That had been corrupted over the ages. She was manipulated. Used."

The walls shuddered, more violently this time. Dust rained from the ceiling. One of the windows cracked.

"And you?" Seraphina's eyes narrowed. "Were you manipulated too, Reaper? Or did you know exactly what she was doing when you brought her into all our courts?"

"If I were working with Caelum, why would my realm be suffering the same soul-starvation as yours?" His voice came out dangerously quiet. "Why would I let my Tower of Screaming Winds go silent? Why would I watch my Weeping Marshes dry up? Why would I allow my ward-stones to fail one by one while my entire domain crumbles?"

"Why would I risk what I've built?" he continued. "My power, my domain, my people. All of it depends on the same soul-flow he's stealing. What possible reason would I have to destroy my own foundation?"

"Maybe you didn't know he'd betray you too." Thessa's form solidified completely. "The spirits show me that you were meant to be spared. Your realm was supposed to remain intact. Part of whatever deal you'd made."

Her translucent eyes moved between him and Brynn, reading something in the shadows that connected them.

"But something changed. Something he didn't plan for."

A pause.

"He didn't expect you to make her your companion."

The words fell into silence.

He felt Brynn's confusion ripple through the shadow-threads, her spine stiffening as she processed Thessa's words.

She looked up at him, questions in her eyes.

Then she turned back to face the others.

What followed was her explanation of the refinery. The extraction chambers. The assembly lines processing souls like raw materials. The army of weaponized victims.

He watched their expressions shift from suspicion to horror as she laid out the scope of what Caelum had built.

"How do we stop him?" Seraphina asked.

"Not here." He pushed away from the throne. "War room. Follow me."

He led them through palace corridors, Brynn staying close to his side.

The war room had been designed for precisely this purpose. Stone tables dominated the center, their surfaces enchanted to display magical projections. Ward-stone maps covered the walls.

He moved to the central table, shadows pouring across its surface. The enchantments responded, and the three-dimensional map of the ward network materialized above them.

It should have been beautiful. Golden light pulsing, connecting all the realms in perfect harmony.

Instead, most of it bled red. Failing. Corrupted. Dying.

"Show them." He looked at Brynn. "Everything you saw."

She stepped forward, and he watched her confidence grow as she moved into familiar territory. Technical knowledge grounding her, giving her something solid to hold onto.

"The refinery is here." Her hand hovered over the pulsing point in the display. "The extraction chambers process souls and weaponize them before adding them to his army."

She traced the energy flows back through the network. Every channel, every court's pipeline, all of it converging on a single point. Her finger stopped moving.

The Mourned Court. The deep-water harbor. The one place all the roads led.

She'd mapped this exact pattern in the library that night, tracing diagrams by firelight while he watched.

"The refinery isn't the actual target." Her voice quieted. "It's just the surface. He built it directly on top of the ward-core. The gateway is underneath."

"If we can reach it, I can shut it down." Steadier now. "The protocols that created it should respond to my bloodline."

"Will respond or should respond?" Seraphina's challenge was practical now, not hostile.

"Will." Brynn's certainty made pride unfurl in his chest. "I opened it. I can close it."

He studied the map, a lifetime of tactical experience already calculating approaches, weaknesses, opportunities. His shadows traced pathways through the projection.

"A direct assault on the refinery won't work." He began circling the table, mind working through possibilities. "His defenses are too concentrated. He'll expect us to strike there first."

"Then what?" Vex demanded. "We just let him keep harvesting?"

"We divide his attention." His shadows carved four distinct pathways through the projection. "Four simultaneous strikes. Force him to spread his forces thin."

He pointed to the first pathway.

"Seraphina. Your warriors hit his outer defenses here. Draw the bulk of his army away from the refinery. Make him think the assault is coming from your direction."

Her eyes tracked the route, warrior's mind already calculating. She nodded slowly.

"Vex." He indicated the second pathway. "His processing chambers. The souls he's already harvested but not yet weaponized. You consume them before he can use them."

"Consume his stolen power." A smile crossed Vex's gaunt face. "Turn his resources against him."

"Thessa." The third pathway wound through ethereal channels. "The spirits he's holding prisoner. Guide them to their proper destinations. Every soul you free is one less weapon in his army."

Her translucent form solidified with purpose. "The lost will find their way home."

"And us?" Brynn asked quietly.

He met her eyes across the table.

"We anchor the central ward repair." His shadows moved to bracket the gateway's location. "While they handle the military action, we reach the heart of his operation. You close the gateway. I keep you alive long enough to do it."

Understanding settled in her expression.

"The wards will need to be stabilized simultaneously," she added, tracing connections he couldn't see. "Otherwise, closing the gateway might cause a cascade failure. I'll need access to the original wardstones while you—"

"I'll clear your path." The words came out rougher than intended. "Whatever it takes."

Seraphina studied the projection, tactical assessment evident in her gaze. "Dividing our forces. Risky."

"Staying together is riskier." He let his shadows emphasize the four pathways. "He'll expect a unified assault. This way, he has to defend on multiple fronts simultaneously. Can't concentrate his forces if he doesn't know where the real threat is coming from."

The realm lurched around them. The projection flickered. One of the ward-maps on the wall fell, parchment tearing.

"When do we move?" Seraphina asked.

He felt Brynn through the shadows. Carrying everything that had happened and everything still to come—the kind of heaviness that wouldn't lift with sleep.

"We need time to prepare." He made the decision. "Rally our forces. Coordinate timing. Rest and recover our strength." His shadows settled around Brynn's feet. "The assault happens in two days. Tomorrow we gather our armies. The following dawn, we attack."

"Two days." Seraphina nodded. "My warriors will be ready."

"I'll prepare my court." Vex squared his shoulders. "If I'm going to consume his operation, I'll need to gather what power I have left."

"The spirits will guide me." Thessa began to fade. "I'll spend tomorrow opening pathways for the lost souls."

One by one, they departed. Seraphina in violent red energy. Vex in dying amber light. Thessa, fading from sight.

Finally, he and Brynn stood alone in the war room.

The projection still glowed above them, casting their faces in amber and crimson. Red-pulsing failures spread across the ward network like wounds.

Brynn stared up at the display, silent. Her hands shook at her sides.

"You claimed me." Not looking at him. Voice quiet. "In front of them all."

"I did."

Her hands tightened, blood seeping through the bandages again. "I've spent ten years trusting no one. Belonging nowhere. And you just—" Her voice faltered. "You tied yourself to me. In front of everyone."

"You were already mine." He moved closer, unable to stay away. "I just made it official."

"What if I fail?" The words came out barely above a whisper. "What if the gateway won't close, or the wards won't hold, or I can't repair what he's broken? What if I'm not strong enough?"

Her breath hitched.

"You've given me everything. Standing, protection, your name. You. And we might not survive this. I might cost you everything."

His finger slipped beneath her chin, tilting her head up to meet his gaze. Her eyes held weariness, terror, determination. Everything he'd come to recognize as uniquely her.

"Then tonight, I want everything." His thumb traced her lower lip, feeling it quiver under his touch. "No more holding back. You're my companion now. Mine in every way that matters. And I want to make sure you know exactly what that means before we face what's coming."

Her eyes darkened, pupils expanding. Her hands came up to frame his face, palms against his jaw, fingers threading into his hair.

"Then claim me." Her voice dropped to a whisper, rough with want and determination. "Every part of me. Make me yours in the only way we haven't yet. So that if we die tomorrow, at least we'll have had this."

LXIX.
DANTE & BRYNN

Brynn

The words left her mouth before she could stop them. A challenge. An invitation. A plea she couldn't take back.

For a heartbeat, nothing happened.

She watched Dante's eyes darken.

This wasn't like before. Not like the garden, not like the night after the ball when he'd stopped them both at the edge. There was no hesitation in the way he moved toward her now.

His hands found her waist with a grip that brooked no argument. She gasped as strong fingers dug in hard enough to bruise, anchoring her, claiming her. Her legs wrapped around his hips before she could think, heels digging into his lower back, and she ground against him shamelessly. Desperate for friction. Desperate for him.

He pressed her back against the wall. Cold stone bit through her clothes, sharp contrast to the heat rolling off his body. His mouth hovered over hers, close enough she could feel his breath. Warm. Ragged. Laced with everything he'd been holding back.

"I'm going to ruin you." The words vibrated against her pulse.

Her breath stuttered. Her cunt clenched around nothing.

"I'm going to take you apart piece by piece until you forget your own name." His lips brushed the shell of her ear. "Until the only word left in that clever mouth is *mine*."

She was already wet. Could feel the slick heat gathering between her thighs, soaking through her underwear. Her body readying itself for him before her mind could catch up.

He pressed his hips forward, letting her feel every inch of how hard he was. The thick ridge of his cock ground against her core through their clothes, and she whimpered at the pressure. Not enough. Not nearly enough.

"Feel that?" He pressed harder, rocking against her in a slow, torturous rhythm. "That's what you do to me. Every fucking day. Every time you look at me with those defiant eyes, every time you say my name like it belongs to you."

His hand fisted in her hair, yanking her head back hard enough to sting. The pain shot straight to her cunt.

"It does belong to me," she gasped.

He growled against her throat.

"Yes." He bit her earlobe, tugging with his teeth. "And tonight I'm going to make sure you know exactly what that means."

Their mouths crashed together.

His tongue swept against hers, claiming, and she tasted the wildness in him. She kissed him back with equal desperation, her hands fisting in his hair, pulling hard enough to hurt. He groaned into her mouth, a low broken sound that made her grind harder against him.

This time there would be no stopping.

His shadows curled around them both, lifting her away from the wall. Cool tendrils wrapped around her thighs, her waist, sliding against her skin like silk. The sensation made her shiver. Cold where his body burned hot. Smooth where his hands gripped rough. They moved with intent, caressing her through her clothes, dipping beneath her neckline to stroke the tops of her breasts.

The world dissolved into darkness.

Shadow travel. She'd experienced it before, but never like this. Never with his mouth still on hers, his hands gripping her hips, his shadows stroking her skin while the realm blurred around them. It lasted only seconds, but by the time solid ground reformed beneath them, she was dizzy with want.

They tumbled onto the bed together. She landed on her back with him between her thighs, and the weight of him pressed her into the mattress. She could feel his cock straining against his pants, pressing into the soft flesh of her inner thigh. Hard and thick and insistent.

"Too many clothes," she panted against his mouth.

He pulled back. Eyes blazing. "Then do something about it."

She reached for his shirt with fingers that trembled. The fabric tore under her urgency. She heard the stitches give, didn't care. Just needed skin. Her palms found his chest, mapped the hard planes of muscle, the scars that told stories she'd learn later. He was burning hot beneath her hands. When her nails raked down his chest, leaving red trails in their wake, he hissed through his teeth and his hips jerked against her.

"My turn," he growled.

His hands found the laces of her gown, but his patience lasted all of two seconds before shadows joined in. Cool tendrils sliced through fabric like blades, baring her skin inch by inch. The dress fell away in ruined pieces until she lay in nothing but her thin chemise.

He sat back on his heels, looking at her. His eyes traced over her breasts, nipples already hard and visible through the sheer fabric. Down the flat plane of her stomach. To the damp patch between her thighs where she'd soaked through.

"You're wet already," he said. Voice rough with want. "I can see it. Smell it." He inhaled deeply, nostrils flaring, and his cock twitched visibly in his pants. "You smell like honey. Been thinking about me, thief?"

Her face flushed. "Shut up and touch me."

"Answer me first." A shadow slid up her inner thigh, cool and teasing. It pushed between her legs, pressed against her soaked underwear, and she gasped at the sensation. Smooth and cold and firm, rubbing slow circles against her cunt. "Have you touched yourself thinking about me? Slid your fingers into that pretty cunt and pretended they were mine?"

"Yes." The word ripped out of her. The shadow pressed harder, and she whimpered. "Yes, damn you."

His smile showed satisfaction. "Good. So have I. Stroked my cock until I spilled into my own hand, imagining it was your tight little cunt."

The image made her breathless. Dante alone in his chambers, his fist wrapped around his cock, pumping himself while he thought of her. She moaned, hips rolling against the shadow still working her through her underwear.

He yanked the chemise over her head, baring her completely. Then he stripped off his ruined shirt, his pants, until he was naked above her.

Her eyes dropped to his cock.

Thick. Flushed. Straining. A bead of precum glistened at the tip, catching the firelight. It jutted up toward his stomach, the head swollen, veins running along the underside. Her mouth watered at the sight.

"Like what you see?" he asked.

"Come here," she breathed. "I want to taste you."

Dante

HER WORDS NEARLY UNDID HIM.

He let her push him onto his back. Let her climb over him, her bare skin sliding against his, her wet cunt leaving a slick trail on his thigh as she moved down his body. The evidence of her arousal smeared across his skin. Marking him.

She kissed her way down his chest, her tongue tracing the lines of his muscles, teeth nipping at his skin. Lower. Following the trail of dark hair that led to his cock. When her breath ghosted over the head, his hips jerked involuntarily and more precum leaked from the tip.

"Brynn—"

She wrapped her hand around him. Her fingers barely fit around his girth, and the sight of her small hand gripping his shaft made his balls tighten with need. She stroked once, slow, from base to tip, and her thumb swept through the precum beading at the slit.

"You're dripping," she murmured. "All this for me?"

"Every drop."

She lowered her mouth and licked him clean.

The sound that tore from his throat wasn't human. Her tongue swirled around the head, lapping up his precum, and she moaned at the taste. The vibration traveled down his shaft, and his hands fisted in the sheets.

"You taste good," she said, lips brushing his sensitive tip with every word. "Salt and power."

Then she took him into her mouth.

Hot. So fucking hot, and wet, and tight. Her lips stretched around his girth, pink and swollen and obscene. She sank down slowly. Taking as much as she could. He felt himself hit the back of her throat and she gagged, pulled back, then tried again. Determined. Greedy.

"Fuck." His hand tangled in her hair, guiding but not forcing. "Your mouth. So hot. So fucking tight."

She found a rhythm. Bobbing her head, cheeks hollowing with every upstroke, tongue working the sensitive underside of his shaft. Her hand stroked what her mouth couldn't reach, twisting at the base, squeezing just right. The wet sounds filled the chamber—slurping, sucking, every sound proof of how she worked his cock like she was starving for it.

Spit dripped down his shaft, pooling at the base. She was messy. Enthusiastic. Fucking perfect.

"That's it," he groaned. "Take it. Take all of it."

She moaned around him, and the vibration made his hips buck. She gagged but didn't pull away. Just took him deeper, tears pricking the corners of her eyes from the effort, spit and precum smearing across her chin.

He looked down, watching his cock disappear between her swollen lips. Watching her cheeks bulge with his thickness. Her eyes were half-lidded, glazed with lust, and when she looked up at him through her lashes, mouth stuffed full of his cock, tears streaking her face, looking utterly debauched, he nearly came right then.

"You look so pretty with my cock in your mouth," he rasped. "Stuffed full of me. Drooling all over my shaft." He wiped a tear from her cheek with his thumb. "Is this what you imagined when you touched yourself? My cock stretching those pretty lips?"

She pulled off with a wet pop, a string of saliva connecting her mouth to his tip. Her lips were swollen. Red. Slick with spit and precum.

"I imagined a lot of things." She licked the length of him, base to tip, tongue tracing the thick vein. "Your cock in my mouth." Another lick. "Your cock in my cunt." She sucked the head back in, swirling her tongue, then let it pop free. "Your cock in my ass."

His vision went white at the edges.

"Later," he growled, grabbing her. "I'll fuck every hole you have. But right now—"

He flipped them.

Brynn

HER BACK HIT THE MATTRESS, and then he was on top of her—between her thighs. The head of his cock pressed against her entrance, nudging through her soaked folds.

She was drenched. Could feel her arousal coating his shaft as he rubbed against her, slicking them both up. Every drag of his cock through her slit made her whimper. The head caught on her clit and she gasped, hips jerking.

"Please," she begged. "Dante, please—"

"Please what?" He positioned himself at her entrance but didn't push in. Just held there, the thick head stretching her opening, barely breaching her. "Tell me what you want."

"I want you inside me." She tried to roll her hips, to take him in, but his hands pinned her to the mattress. "I want you to fuck me. Please. I need it."

"Need what? Say it."

"Your cock." The words spilled out, shameless and desperate. "I need your cock inside me. Filling me up. I've been empty for so long. Please."

He pushed inside her.

The stretch was intense. She gasped, body arching off the bed, fingers clawing at his shoulders. He was big. So much bigger than her fingers, than anything she'd had before. Her cunt struggled to accommodate him, walls straining around his girth, burning as he forced her open.

"Breathe," he commanded. His jaw was clenched, muscles trembling with the effort of holding still. "Relax. Let me in."

She forced herself to exhale. To relax her muscles. He sank deeper, inch by thick inch, and she felt herself opening for him. Stretching. The burn faded to fullness, and the fullness felt like completion.

"That's it," he murmured. "Good girl. Taking me so well. Your tight little cunt is swallowing me up."

When he was fully seated, his pelvis pressed against her clit and his cock so deep she could feel him in her throat. She was stuffed. Impaled. Completely full of him.

"Look." He grabbed her hand, pressed it to her lower belly. "Feel that? Feel how deep I am?"

She could feel the bulge of him inside her. Could feel his cock pressing against her hand from the inside. Her fingers traced the shape of him through her own skin, and the intimacy of it made her eyes sting.

"You're inside me," she whispered.

"Yes." He pulled back slowly, and she felt every ridge of his cock dragging against her sensitive walls. The friction was exquisite. "And I'm never letting you go."

He thrust back in.

She screamed.

He fucked her with deep, powerful strokes. Each thrust punched a cry from her throat. The sounds of her cunt taking his cock filled the chamber. She was so wet. Drenched. Her arousal coating his shaft, dripping down to pool beneath them. She could hear it. The slick, sloppy sound of her being fucked open.

"Listen to that," he growled, driving harder. His balls slapped against her ass with every thrust. "Listen to how wet you are for me. Soaking my cock. Making a mess of my sheets."

"Dante—" She couldn't form words. Could only moan and writhe and take it.

His shadows joined in.

Cool tendrils wrapped around her wrists, yanking them above her head and pinning them to the headboard. The grip was firm. She tested it, pulled, and the shadows just tightened.

Others slithered around her ankles, pulling her legs wider, spreading her open beneath him until there was nothing left to hide. She was helpless. Exposed. Her cunt stretched around his cock, on display for him to see.

"That's better," he said, looking down at where they were joined. She followed his gaze and saw his thick shaft pistoning in and out of her swollen folds, glistening with her arousal. "Now I can see everything. See your pretty pussy stretched around my cock."

A shadow slid between their bodies, finding her clit.

She jerked at the sensation. Cool and silky, pressing against her swollen nub in tight, precise circles. The shadow worked her with relentless precision.

"Oh hells—" Her back arched off the bed. "Dante, your shadows—"

"They've wanted to touch you for weeks," he said, fucking her harder. "I've had to hold them back. Stop them from crawling under your skirts and making you come in the middle of court."

Another shadow curled around her breast, squeezing the soft flesh. A tendril found her nipple and pinched, rolling the stiff peak between incorporeal fingers. Then it lowered, and something cool and slick wrapped around her nipple and *sucked*.

She cried out, back arching. It felt like a mouth, but cold. Insistent.

She was being touched everywhere. His cock pounding into her cunt. Shadows on her clit, her breasts. Cool sensations sucking her nipples. Tendrils stroking her throat, her thighs, the sensitive crease where her leg met her hip. It was overwhelming. Too much sensation from too many directions.

"I can feel how close you are," he growled. "Your cunt's getting tighter. Squeezing my cock like a fist."

She was. The pressure was building, coiling in her core, fed by every thrust and every shadow-touch. Her whole body trembled on the edge.

"Come for me." He drove deep, grinding against her. "Come all over my cock. Let me feel it."

The shadow on her clit pressed harder. Rubbed faster. The others sucked harder on her nipples.

The orgasm ripped through her. Her cunt clamped down on his cock, pulsing, milking him. Her scream echoed off the walls, his name over and over until her voice cracked. She thrashed against her bonds, body convulsing, and still he fucked her through it.

"That's it," he groaned. "Fuck, you feel good when you come. So tight. Squeezing me so hard. That's it. Give it all to me."

She was still shaking, still spasming around him, when he pulled out.

Dante

HE FLIPPED her onto her stomach.

She went limp as a ragdoll, still trembling from her orgasm, and he arranged her how he wanted her. On her knees. Face pressed into the pillows. Ass up, presented to him like an offering.

He looked down at her cunt—swollen and pink, her folds puffy from use. Glistening with her release, practically dripping with her arousal. Her little hole gaped slightly, stretched from his cock, clenching around nothing. Begging to be filled again.

His cock throbbed at the sight. He was so hard it hurt.

"Look at this pretty pussy," he murmured, running a finger through her folds. She shivered, whimpered. "All wet and used. Already so sloppy for me. And I'm not done with you yet."

He lined himself up and slammed back inside.

She screamed into the pillow.

The angle was different like this. Deeper. He could see his cock disappearing into her body, could see the way she stretched to take him. The rim of her opening clinging to his shaft every time he pulled out, like she was trying to keep him inside.

"Watch," he commanded, and shadows lifted her head, made her turn to look. A mirror materialized from the darkness, angled so she could see everything. "Watch me fuck you."

Her eyes fixed on the reflection. On the image of her own body, ass up, being pounded by the Reaper behind her. On his cock slamming into her cunt, glistening with her wetness. On the way her tits swayed with every thrust, on the way her mouth hung open in constant moans.

"See how good you take me?" He thrust harder, making her cry out. "Made for my cock. Your tight little cunt was made for my cock."

His shadows wrapped around her again. Around her wrists, pulling them behind her back. Others slithered around her thighs, keeping them spread. One slid between her asscheeks, teasing, and she jerked.

"Dante—"

"Shh." The shadow circled her puckered hole. Not pressing in. Just rubbing. Making her aware of it. "Not tonight. But soon, I'm going to fuck you here too. Fill every hole you have. Make you take my cock everywhere."

She moaned, pressing back against the shadow. Against his cock. Taking everything he gave her and begging for more.

He grabbed her hips and fucked her harder. Brutal now. All finesse gone. Just raw need. The slap of his hips against her ass echoed through the chamber. The sound of her pussy taking him over and over. Her moans, muffled by the pillows, growing higher and more desperate.

The shadow on her ass pressed slightly into her hole. Just the tip. Just enough to make her feel it.

She came.

Without warning, without his permission, her cunt clamped

down on him so hard he saw stars. She screamed into the pillow, body shaking, and he felt her release around his cock. Felt it drip down his balls.

"Fuck—" The sensation dragged him to the edge. "I'm close. Where do you want me?"

"Inside," she gasped, still shaking. "Fill me up. I want to feel it. Want to feel you come inside me."

He grabbed her hips hard enough to bruise and fucked her through her orgasm. Chasing his own. Two more thrusts. Three.

He buried himself to the hilt and came.

The orgasm ripped through him with force. His cock pulsed inside her, flooding her cunt with his release. He roared her name, hips jerking, emptying himself completely. Her walls milked him through every pulse, squeezing out every drop.

When it finally stopped, he collapsed over her. Pressed her flat into the mattress with his weight, still buried inside her.

He withdrew slowly. Watched his cum leak from her swollen pussy, white and thick against her pink flesh. It dripped down her thighs. Pooled on the sheets.

"You're dripping," he murmured, running his fingers through the mess, pushing some back inside her. "Full of me."

She made a satisfied sound. "Good."

Brynn

SHE COULDN'T MOVE.

Every muscle in her body had turned to liquid. Her cunt throbbed, tender and well-used, still leaking his release. She could feel it sliding down her thighs, cooling on her skin.

She'd never felt so thoroughly claimed.

"How long before we can do that again?" she asked, voice hoarse from screaming.

His laugh rumbled against her back. "Give me ten minutes."

True to his word, he was hard again before she'd finished catching her breath.

The second time was slower. Sweeter. He laid her out on her back and worshipped her with his mouth. Throat. Breasts. The soft curve of her belly. He licked her clean, his tongue scooping out his own release, groaning at the taste of them together. Then he kissed her so she could taste it too. Salt and musk and the evidence of their claiming.

"I love the taste of us," he murmured against her lips. "Going to eat you out every time I fill you up. Clean you out just so I can fill you again."

He slid back inside her. Easier this time, slick with his cum and her arousal. Made love to her with deep, rolling thrusts. His eyes never left her face, watching every flicker of pleasure.

"Beautiful," he breathed. "So beautiful."

She came twice more before he let himself follow. Spilled inside her again, adding to the mess.

The third time was in the bath.

He carried her on shaking legs, lowered them both into the steaming water. They were supposed to be getting clean. Instead, she ended up in his lap, his cock sliding back inside her well-used cunt. The hot water soothed her tender flesh even as he stretched her open again.

"We're making a mess," she gasped as she rode him, water sloshing over the edge with every roll of her hips.

"Don't care." His hands gripped her ass, spreading her cheeks, helping her move.

She came with his name on her lips. He followed moments later, spilling inside her for the third time that night.

After, they actually managed to wash. His hands gentle on her swollen, sensitive flesh. Cleaning away the sweat and arousal.

They collapsed into bed. His shadows curled around them both.

"Can't walk," she mumbled against him.

A rumble of satisfaction vibrated through his chest. "I should have warned you."

"Smug bastard." But there was no bite to it. She felt too boneless and satisfied to muster any real protest.

"Your smug bastard." He settled beside her and pulled her against his chest. "My thief."

"Your partner," she corrected, eyes already drifting closed.

"That too." His hand stroked through her hair. "Sleep. You need rest."

"So do you." Her fingers traced idle patterns across his chest.

"I will," he replied, his hand continuing its soothing motion. "After I'm sure you're actually sleeping."

She smiled against his skin, exhaustion already pulling her under.

LXX.
DANTE

Dawn light filtered through his study windows. Dante stood alone at his desk, one hand braced on the enchanted surface while the other moved through the glowing projection of the ward network.

Red failure points pulsed across the magical construct. Soul-flow routes corrupted. Junction points compromised, sabotage exposed in detail.

Maps and tactical reports covered every surface. Scout intelligence scrawled in haste, troop positions that kept shifting, power readings from the failing wards that worsened with each update. Casualty projections. Numbers representing souls who would cease to exist if this went wrong.

The sheer scope of what they were attempting should have felt impossible.

Instead, it felt necessary.

His shadows spread across the floor, carrying reports between stacks, reorganizing documents, holding open reference materials at relevant pages, lifting a scout report, sliding it across the desk, then retrieving the next.

Helpful. Obedient. Betraying nothing of the restlessness bleeding through his connection to them.

He'd left Brynn sleeping in his chambers when Lord Aldric arrived before dawn with fresh scout reports. She'd been in a deep sleep, injured wrists curled against the pillow. Face peaceful for the first time in days. Her body surrendered to rest after everything. The torture. The gateway activation. The night that had left marks on both of them he could still feel.

The bite on her shoulder. The bruises on her hips where he'd gripped too hard. The rawness in his own chest where her nails had raked desperate lines.

He'd wanted to stay. Watch over her while she recovered. Keep his power wrapped around her while she healed.

But Caelum was harvesting souls while Dante played lovesick guardian. Every moment spent watching her sleep was another soul being processed. Another victim stripped of everything that made them individual.

So he'd left. Had pressed a kiss to her temple, gentle enough not to wake her, and retreated to coordinate the assault that might save them all.

Four battlefields. Four simultaneous strikes. Precise timing required across multiple realms while the ward network screamed warnings at him.

No room for error. No margin for sentiment.

Lord Aldric had reported moments ago. Their forces were assembling faster than anticipated. Vex's court gathering in the shadowways. Thessa's spirits moving into position. Seraphina's warriors preparing for deployment.

The pieces moving into place.

The timeline had compressed from days to mere hours.

He moved his hand through the projection again, tracing the assault points. Looking for the flaw in his strategy. The weakness he'd missed. The variable that would get them all killed.

Simple in theory. Catastrophic if executed poorly.

If the timing was off by even minutes. If Seraphina's assault stalled. If Vex's hunger overwhelmed his control. If Thessa couldn't reach the victims in time.

If Brynn couldn't close the gateway before Caelum stopped her.

If he lost her.

His jaw clenched. Shadows wound tighter around his feet, responding to the spike of fear that shot through him.

She wasn't allowed to die because he'd been too slow or too weak or too distracted by the way she'd looked in his bed, tangled in his sheets, wearing nothing but his marks. She'd survive this. They'd survive this.

He'd make sure of it even if he had to burn every other realm to ash.

The floor shuddered beneath his feet. Another ward-stone failing somewhere in the outer reaches. He felt it through his connection to the realm like a tooth being pulled. The pain was distant but undeniable.

His domain was dying. Time running out.

Movement in the corridor outside.

His power lifted from the maps instantly, reaching toward the door before he registered the sound. Quick footsteps approaching. That particular rhythm he'd learned to recognize. The cadence of someone who moved like she was still working jobs. Light on her feet. Careful with weight distribution. Ready to shift direction at a moment's notice.

Brynn.

His shoulders dropped. The tension he'd been carrying since leaving her asleep released in a slow exhale.

She was awake. Coming to him instead of staying safely in his bed, where nothing could touch her.

The door opened quietly. She stepped inside, pausing just past the threshold. Taking in her surroundings before committing. A habit he recognized because he did the same thing. Survey, calculate, and decide on the safest path forward.

Her gaze swept the room before landing on him—standing alone at his desk in the pale light, one hand braced on the surface, darkness pooling at his feet.

Her expression softened. That shift from wariness to something gentler surprised him every time, like he was worth approaching instead of avoiding.

Like he was someone to seek out instead of escape.

She crossed to him in silence. There was a noticeable stiffness in her movement, and he caught the wince she tried to hide when her weight shifted.

From him. From what they'd done before dawn.

From being spread across his bed while he'd taken her apart until she'd screamed his name so loud the entire palace must have heard.

His shadows stirred in response to the surge of heat. The Reaper recognizing what was his. The urge to take her against this desk rose immediately. Hear those breathless sounds again. Feel her clench around him while his name fell from her lips.

He clenched his jaw and pulled his attention back to the construct.

The realms were hours from war. This was not the place. Not the time.

Even if everything in him screamed otherwise.

She didn't stop until she was beside him. Her shoulder nearly brushing his arm. Close enough for her scent to reach him, mingled with the faint traces of last night. His shadows reached for her instantly.

Wearing one of his shirts. Soft black fabric that hung loose on her, falling to mid-thigh and leaving her legs bare. Her hair tangled from sleep and his hands. Circles shadowed beneath her lashes. Her wrapped wrists stood out against the dark fabric, white bindings a reminder of what Caelum had done.

And there, just visible above the shirt's collar, the bite mark he'd left on her shoulder. Already purpling.

She looked like she'd been tortured, taken, and had barely slept.

Yet ready for war regardless. Spine straight. Chin up. Gaze sharp through the fatigue.

Her hand reached out, fingertips hovering over the projection where Caelum's fortress glowed. The ward-architecture rippled at her proximity, responding to her bloodline even without direct contact, light pulsing brighter where her fingers passed.

Even half-dead, her power called to the wards.

"You should be sleeping," he said, watching how the wards responded to her. How even projection magic knew what she was.

"So should you." Her voice was rough with sleep. Deeper than usual, scratchy in a way that reminded him exactly how she'd sounded when he'd made her beg. When she'd gasped his name while he'd had her so thoroughly they couldn't tell where one ended and the other began.

"How long have you been working?"

"An hour. Maybe two." He'd lost track after the third report update and the fifth time he'd traced these vectors looking for flaws. "Scout updates came in. The timeline's compressed. We move today instead of tomorrow."

A tremor shuddered through the stone. Noticeable enough that the magical projection flickered briefly before stabilizing. Dust rained from the ceiling. A crack split across the far wall with a sound like breaking bone.

The ward network was protesting the instability. Crying out against the damage Caelum had done to its foundation.

Her attention snapped to him, alarm clear in her expression.

"The wards are deteriorating," he said quietly. "We're running out of time."

She studied the construct in silence, tracking the soul-flow patterns. The way power moved through the network, where it pooled and strengthened, where it bled away through sabotage. The failure points spreading like an infection. The vectors he'd been analyzing.

Looking for patterns. For weaknesses. For the angle he'd missed.

Her mind worked like his did. Seeing systems, understanding how pieces connected, finding the vulnerabilities that others overlooked. It was one of the things that made her valuable.

Then her finger dropped, tapping a specific junction point. The ward-architecture flared bright at the contact.

"Here. This is where we anchor. Right at the convergence of all five major soul-flows. It's the strongest point structurally. If we can stabilize it, the rest of the network will hold even under stress."

He turned his head to look at her. Really look.

Sharp. Focused. Thinking three steps ahead. Recognizing patterns in the ward-architecture that had taken him years to grasp fully. Understanding the system her ancestors built with an instinct he'd never possess.

She wasn't his weapon against Caelum. Wasn't just the companion he'd taken to protect and possess.

She was his match. In strategy. In power. In the way her mind cut through problems to find solutions he'd been circling since dawn.

He reached up. His hand cupped her jaw, thumb brushing across her cheekbone. Felt the softness of her skin, the warmth beneath his touch. The slight flutter that said her heart was racing.

"We need to rally support," he said quietly. "Before we walk into war."

Her brow furrowed. "The other Death Lords are—"

"Not them." His shadows curled around her waist, pulling her closer. "Nightfall. The settlement in my realm where souls who've earned their freedom have chosen to stay. They've survived by staying organized, building something of their own. Warriors. Strategists. Resources we'll need if this is going to work."

Her expression shifted to surprise. "You want to recruit an army from the forsaken."

"I want to give them a choice," he corrected, thumb tracing her cheekbone because he couldn't quite make himself stop touching her. "They deserve to know what's coming. To decide if they'll fight for the freedom they've earned or hope Caelum doesn't find them when he starts harvesting my entire realm."

His hand trailed from her face, down her arm, fingers catching briefly on the bandages at her wrist.

"And if they choose to stand with us, we'll have the numbers to make this work. To hit him from enough angles that something breaks in our favor."

She leaned into him. Slightly, just enough. Her gaze held his with a trust that still surprised him. The way she looked at him like he was capable of protecting her, of winning this, of being more than the Reaper that everyone else feared.

"How do we reach them?"

"Shadow-travel." His thumb traced circles on the inside of her arm, careful of the injuries beneath. "I can have us there in minutes. We rally them, gather what resources they can provide, and return before the convergence point assembly completes. Quick in and out."

"Hours to build an army," she said softly. Then her mouth quirked. "And here I thought planning a heist on short notice was stressful."

The knot in his chest loosened at her humor. At the fact that she could still find lightness when the world was crumbling around them.

"Hours to give them a choice." He let his forehead rest against hers, stealing this moment of quiet before the chaos began. Before they walked into a war that might kill them both.

Her breath was warm against his lips. Her heartbeat even where his hand rested against her throat.

She pulled away first. He watched the shift happen in her expression. From the woman who'd fallen asleep in his arms to the warrior who'd stand beside him in battle.

Both were her. Both were his.

His hand slid from her slowly. The shadows around her waist loosened, reluctant but obedient when he forced them to release her.

"Get dressed," he said. "I had your things moved to my chambers."

The corner of her mouth lifted, mischief glinting in her expression that sent his power surging toward her. "Yes, my lord."

The way she said it. Half-mocking, half-serious. It sent heat through him. Stirred the urge to bend her over this desk and remind her exactly what calling him that did to his control.

She turned toward the door, then paused. Looked over her shoulder, and the dawn light caught in her hair, and his heart turned over in his chest.

"Dante?"

He raised an eyebrow in question, not trusting his voice.

"We're going to win this."

She said it like she believed it. Like she needed him to believe it too.

His shadows reached for her before he could stop them. Unable to resist. Drawn to her like she was magnetic north and they were compasses finding true.

She smiled at them. At him.

Then slipped through the door.

LXXI.
BRYNN

Brynn braced one hand against Dante's dresser and straightened. Her thighs protested. Screamed, actually. Her hips ached in places she hadn't known could ache. Even her core throbbed, a deep reminder of how thoroughly he'd worked her body before dawn. How he'd filled her completely, pushed deeper than she'd thought possible, made her take all of him until she couldn't remember where she ended and he began.

Worth it.

Completely worth it.

But getting to his study ten minutes ago had required more dignity than she'd known she possessed. Every step was a conscious negotiation with muscles that wanted to remind her what she'd done. What he'd done to her. His hands gripping her hips hard enough to bruise. His shadows pinning her while he'd moved inside her. His mouth on her throat, teeth scraping skin, growling her name like a prayer and a curse.

And now she had to gear up for war.

The irony wasn't lost on her.

She moved toward the wardrobe, covering the stiffness as best she could. Silver light filtered through the window, different from the usual purple twilight. Softer somehow, like even the realm recognized that something had shifted overnight. That the Reaper had taken his companion, and the Forsaken Court would never be quite the same.

The formal attire hung on a chair where Naia had probably left it. Black silk and silver threading, designed to complement Dante's court aesthetic while marking her as his equal. Beautiful work. Expensive fabric, tailoring that would have cost more than she'd made in a year.

Quality. The real thing. She'd handled enough to know the difference between craftsmanship and pretty trash—also completely impractical for rallying an army in a settlement of freed souls who'd probably take one look at court finery and decide she was just another noble playing at power.

She ran her fingers over the silk, feeling the weight and drape. Fabric that whispered against skin, that made you feel powerful just wearing it.

Now it was hers. Tailored for her. Waiting for her to step into the role she'd somehow stumbled into.

Warmth rushed through her at the memory of how he'd looked at her in the darkness. Dark eyes blazing with possession. His voice dropping to that rough command that made her pulse race.

She let her hand drop from the silk.

Three sharp knocks at the door.

"Come in."

Naia drifted through, carrying a breakfast tray that smelled like fresh bread and coffee. The servant's form solidified slightly as she set the tray on the table, and Brynn caught the knowing smile before Naia even spoke.

Oh no.

"Good morning, Lady of the Forsaken." Mischief glinted in Naia's expression. "I trust you're finding Lord Reaper's chambers to your liking? Since that's where you live now."

Heat crept up Brynn's face. "Don't."

"The entire palace knows." Naia arranged the breakfast with care, shoulders shaking. "His shadows were practically singing. The death-knights are placing bets on wedding timelines. And the ward-keepers swear the stones glowed at midnight when you—"

"Of course they did." Brynn grabbed for the coffee, needing something to do with her hands before she died of embarrassment. Because apparently her magic had responded to his touch with enough intensity to make the ward-stones light up. Perfect. Nothing said "we had incredible sex" quite like making magical architecture glow.

"Lord Vex looked rather put out when the news reached his court." Naia's tone turned dry. "Apparently, he'd been hoping you might choose differently. The spirits say he spent an hour ranting about 'predictable dramatic declarations' and 'showing off.'"

Good. Let Vex be disappointed. She'd made her choice. Had screamed it loud enough for the entire palace to hear, apparently.

"Vex can—" Brynn stopped herself, sipped the coffee instead. Let the warmth settle her nerves and chase away the embarrassment. "What's the situation? Battle preparations?"

"Straight to business." Naia's amusement softened into something closer to respect. "The palace is mobilizing. Every fighter who can hold a weapon is preparing. The other Death Lords' forces are assembling at their convergence points. Shadow-guards are being deployed to critical positions." She paused, her translucent form flickering slightly. "Word is you're going to Nightfall first."

"We need their support." Brynn studied the formal attire again, her mind already working through the problem. Calculate the variables. Find the angle. Execute perfectly. "But showing up in court finery would be the wrong move. They'd see a noble playing dress-up, not someone who understands what they've survived."

"You're thinking strategically." Approval colored Naia's voice. "They need to see you as one of them. Someone who knows what it means to survive in a realm designed for suffering. But they also need to see you as the Lady Companion. Powerful enough to stand beside the Reaper without being consumed by him."

Consumed. The word sent warmth curling through her. Because he had consumed her. Devoured her completely. Made her burn and break and beg until there was nothing left but sensation and his name on her lips.

Focus. War first. Melting into a puddle of remembered pleasure later.

Brynn moved to the wardrobe, ignoring the way her body protested. Sore muscles could wait. The realms couldn't.

She sorted through the options, looking for something that would work. Practical enough for Nightfall. Authoritative enough to command respect.

She pulled out black leather pants, reinforced at the knees and thighs, designed for someone who expected to fight or run. Then a fitted shirt in silver. The colors of Dante's court without being too formal. A reinforced leather corset to go over it.

The outfit said she belonged to the Forsaken. To the Reaper. But it also said she'd earned her place through more than just sharing his bed.

Even if sharing his bed had been absolutely incredible.

"And this." Naia's voice went quiet. Serious.

Brynn turned.

Naia held a circlet of dark metal, ward symbols etched into its surface, black roses etched alongside them. Their stems intertwined with small carved bones. Designed to rest across the forehead like a crown. Like a declaration.

Her breath caught.

"The Lord Reaper had this commissioned during the night," Naia said softly. "He left it with instructions to give it to you this morning. Said you'd need it for Nightfall."

Tenderness flooded her chest.

During the night. While she'd been sleeping off exhaustion and satisfaction in his bed, he'd been thinking about her. About what she'd need. About how to protect her and mark her as his simultaneously.

She crossed the space between them, thighs protesting, and reached for the metal. Her fingers brushed the surface, and the symbols flared immediately, responding to her bloodline.

But underneath that pulse of recognition, she felt something else.

His darkness.

Woven into the metalwork, reinforcing the structure from within. A blend of their magic. Her ward-architect bloodline, his shadow. Her light and his dark, forged together into something that was neither and both.

Not just jewelry. A statement.

He couldn't say the words easily. Struggled with vulnerability like it was a physical threat. But this spoke volumes. Everyone would know she was his.

She'd be safer this way.

So perfectly him. Protective and infuriating and hers.

"Help me get ready," Brynn said, voice rougher than she intended. "We have work to do."

Naia's form brightened, solidifying more fully. "That's my Lady of Death."

The leather pants fit perfectly. Someone had tailored them to her measurements while she'd been occupied with other things. Probably while she'd been screaming Dante's name into his pillows. The thought sent color flooding her cheeks again.

The silver shirt settled comfortably across her shoulders, the fabric soft but durable. Naia laced the reinforced corset over it, pulling the leather tight enough to provide real protection without restricting movement. Armor that looked decorative but could actually stop a blade if someone got too close.

Naia handed her the circlet last.

Brynn took it, feeling the weight. Heavier than it looked. Black metal, not hollow decorative work. The etchings pulsed against her fingertips, eager and alive. The shadow-work stirred, recognizing her through whatever connection Dante had woven into the metal.

She settled it across her forehead.

The metal was cool at first, then warmed rapidly, responding to her body heat and bloodline. It clicked into place like a lock turning, like it had always belonged there.

His power stirred against her skin. A caress. A reminder.

She turned to the mirror.

The woman looking back wasn't the merchant's daughter who'd lost everything to betrayal. Wasn't the tribute who'd been sent to die in the Forsaken realm as payment for crimes she'd committed.

This woman looked dangerous.

The circlet gleamed against her forehead. Symbols glowing faintly, black roses and carved bones marking her connection to death. The leather and silver made her look like a warrior instead of a noble. And her eyes...

Her eyes looked like someone who'd survived torture, opened a gateway that nearly destroyed everything, and was ready to walk into war anyway.

Lady of the Forsaken. Ward-architect. Strategic commander.

Partner to death incarnate.

The woman who was going to close the gateway she'd opened and make Caelum pay for every soul he'd harvested.

LXXII.
BRYNN

Nightfall was dying like the rest of the realm.

Brynn saw it the moment they materialized at the settlement's edge. Cracks branching across buildings that had stood for ages, ward-stones flickering, gardens withering to grey.

Caelum's sabotage had been killing this place slowly. Her gateway had ripped the wound wide open.

But even failing, she could see what Nightfall had been. What these souls had built with their freedom.

The same black stone and bone that made Dante's palace cold and imposing had been shaped into something else here. Buildings pressed shoulder to shoulder, sharing walls, the architecture of people who'd died alone and refused to live that way again. Shadow-lanterns hung between rooftops on braided wire, their pale light guttering now but clearly strung with care. Someone had decided this corner of the Forsaken realm deserved to be lit. Most of the doorways had no doors at all, just open arches, because people who'd been abandoned had chosen to never shut each other out.

Now the lanterns were dimming. Cracks climbed the shared walls. The open doorways gaped like wounds.

Dante's arm was still around her waist from shadow-travel, his chest solid against her back, and she needed to step away. Needed to stop leaning into him like he was the only solid thing in a collapsing world.

She didn't move.

His shadows trailed across her hips as they retreated, slow and reluctant. "They're already gathering." His breath stirred her hair, low and too intimate for what was coming.

She stepped out of his embrace and immediately missed it. Souls emerged from doorways across the settlement, watching. Warriors checked weapons. Parents pulled children close.

Their eyes watched Dante with wary distance—the look of people who'd served their time and earned their freedom, now watching the system that had tormented them walk back into their home.

"They won't want to hear from you," she said quietly.

"No." He didn't sound offended. "They earned their freedom from Death Lords. Asking them to follow one into battle would feel like being dragged back into chains."

"So what, I give the speech?" She laughed, but there was no humor in it. "The outsider who made everything worse?"

"The mortal who stands beside me without flinching." His gaze was unwavering. "The woman who came here to fix what she damaged instead of hiding behind my power. They've spent decades learning that Death Lords take. You're offering to give."

The ground shuddered. A crack split the cobblestones at her feet. The tremor rolled through Nightfall like a death rattle, and a wardstone at the nearest intersection flickered twice and went dark.

"Besides." His mouth curved, just slightly. "You're better at making people believe in impossible things."

"That's not—"

"It is." He caught her hand, squeezed once, then released her. "I'll be there. They'll know my power backs whatever you say. But the words should be yours."

She stared at him. The Reaper. Stepping back so a mortal could lead.

"You're sure about this?"

"I'm sure about you."

Her throat tightened. No time to process that. No time for any of it.

She started toward the central square.

The path wound between close-built houses, and even now she could see traces of the life here. A communal table set beneath a bone-arch canopy, long enough for dozens, its surface scarred from shared meals. Window boxes where someone had coaxed pale silver moss into growing, the only living thing she'd seen in the Forsaken realm that wasn't one of Dante's black roses. A children's corner where smooth stones had been stacked into small towers, a game abandoned mid-build.

These people had taken the materials of despair and made a home from them. And it was falling apart.

The square was packed when they arrived. Hundreds of souls pressing close, translucent forms shimmering in the dying light. Warriors ringed the perimeter. Families huddled in tight clusters.

Dante stopped at the platform's edge. Didn't follow her up.

The crowd noticed. Murmurs rippled outward. The Reaper hanging back. The mortal woman stepping forward alone.

Brynn felt every eye on her as she climbed onto the raised stone. The cold circlet pressed against her forehead. The bandages on her wrists stood out stark white.

A broad-shouldered blacksmith pushed to the front, arms folded. "We know what's happening to the realm. What we want to know is why we should listen to you."

Fair. Brutally fair.

She hadn't prepared for this. Hadn't expected to be the one standing here with a crowd waiting for answers. Her hands wanted to shake. She didn't let them.

"Because I owe you the truth about what's killing your home."

She held the blacksmith's gaze.

"Caelum of the Mourned has been sabotaging the wards for months. Weakening the barriers. Destabilizing the realm piece by piece. Everything you've been feeling—the tremors, the failing wardstones, the corruption in the air—that's him. That's been him all along."

The murmurs that rippled through the crowd carried shock. They'd expected anyone but him.

"But I made it worse." She didn't let herself look away. "The gateway I opened tore through defenses that were already barely holding. I didn't know. That doesn't matter. I accelerated the collapse, and I'm not here to pretend otherwise."

Someone in the crowd made a sound of disgust. A woman pulled her children back another step.

"So you're here to apologize?" The blacksmith's voice was flat. "While our home crumbles?"

"No. I'm here because I'm the only one who can close what I opened. And I can't do it alone."

The ground heaved. Stone cracked near the fountain with a sound like snapping bones, and a child cried out. When the tremor passed, no one had fled.

They were listening.

"Caelum's been harvesting souls. Stripping away everything that makes you you—memories, choices, your entire self extracted and discarded. He's building an army of empty shells, and when he's done with the tormented courts, he'll come for the free settlements. For everything you've built."

She stepped to the platform's edge. Close enough to see the fear in their faces, the anger, the desperate hope they were trying not to feel.

"He calls it mercy. Calls it peace." Her voice hardened. "It's annihilation. And I will burn in every hell that exists before I let him do to you what he's done to thousands of others."

The circlet flared hot against her skin. Responding to her fury, to the ward-magic threaded through every soul here.

"You don't owe me anything. I'm the outsider who made your situation worse. You have every right to tell me to go to hell and handle this myself."

Her chest ached. Her wrists throbbed beneath the bandages.

"But I'm asking anyway. Fight with me. Not for the Reaper—" she gestured toward Dante without looking at him, "—not for any Death

Lord. For what you built here. For the freedom you bled for. For every soul who'll face the same choice after you."

Silence stretched. The crowd barely breathed.

The blacksmith studied her for a long moment. "You admit you made it worse."

"Yes."

"And you think you can fix it."

"I can close the gateway. Stop the hemorrhaging. Whether we win the war against the one who started all this—" She shook her head. "I won't promise what I can't guarantee. But I'll die trying."

He looked past her, at Dante standing motionless at the platform's edge. "And him? Why isn't the Reaper the one asking?"

"Because he had the sense to know you'd rather hear it from me." She finally glanced back at Dante, then returned her attention to the blacksmith. "You earned your freedom from Death Lords. He's not here to command you. He's here to fight beside you, if you'll have him."

The blacksmith's eyebrows rose. He looked at the Reaper, standing silent at the edge of his own rally. Letting a mortal speak for them both.

Something shifted in the crowd.

"My steel doesn't fail." The blacksmith's voice had changed. Rough with something that might have been respect. "Neither do I."

An older woman stepped forward, translucent at the edges. "My wards are yours, my lady."

Then more. A tactical officer pledging his warriors. Craftsmen. Scouts. Voices overlapping until she lost count.

Some souls vanished into side streets without a word.

Parents slipped away with their children.

But enough stayed.

Enough looked at her and chose to believe.

The square dissolved into organized chaos. Another tremor hit, harder than before, and the urgency turned desperate.

An elderly soul caught Brynn's hand as she moved through the crowd. Her grip was iron, even as her form faded. "Stubborn. Too brave for your own good." The old woman's smile was sad and knowing. "Go save our world, child."

Dante materialized at her side the moment she stepped away from the last cluster of volunteers.

"Ninety minutes," he announced, voice carrying over the chaos. "Fighters by specialty. Non-combatants evacuated. Move."

Then his hand closed around her elbow, pulling her into the shadow of a doorway where the crowd couldn't see. His body caged hers against the wall, close enough that she felt heat radiating off him without quite touching.

"You told them I'm here to fight beside them." His voice was low. Rough. "Not to command."

Her pulse jumped. "It's what they needed to hear."

"It's also true." His thumb traced the inside of her wrist, right above the bandage. "You understand something I never learned. How to make people want to follow."

"Dante—"

"I've commanded armies through fear for centuries." His shadows wound around her waist, pulling her closer. "Watching you do it through faith is the most terrifying thing I've ever seen."

His mouth hovered an inch from hers. She could feel his breath, warm against her lips.

"Terrifying," she managed. "That's romantic."

"It is." His eyes held hers. "You have no idea what you've become."

Then he stepped back.

His shadows released her slowly, trailing across her hips like a promise.

"Ninety minutes." His voice had dropped low enough to make her knees unreliable. "Then after we win this war..."

He didn't finish. Didn't need to.

She pushed off the wall on legs that weren't entirely steady. "Try to keep up, Reaper."

His smile was the most dangerous thing she'd seen all night.

She walked back into the chaos, skin still burning where his shadows had touched her.

LXXIII.
DANTE

A thousand freed souls stood in his courtyard.

Dante let that number sink in. A thousand who'd looked at a mortal woman and decided to follow her into war. Who'd watched the Reaper stand silent at the edge of his own rally and chosen to believe anyway.

Brynn had done that. Given them something he never could.

She stood beside him now, the circlet gleaming against her dark hair as the transport circle's light faded behind them. Ward-symbols etched into the black metal hummed with residual power. He could feel it where his shadows brushed her skin. Her magic and his, tangling together like they couldn't help themselves.

The mobilization was already underway.

His death-knights had moved. Weapons were distributed in orderly lines, armor checked and reinforced. Shadow-guards coordinated with ward-keepers, movements precise as clockwork—twenty-five hundred of his own warriors who'd served him since before mortal memory, who knew his commands before he gave them.

Combined with Nightfall's thousand, that made thirty-five hundred souls under his direct command.

Thirty-five hundred souls he was about to lead into a battle—some of them wouldn't survive.

Aldric approached, armor scarred from years of service. "Palace forces ready. Nightfall integration underway. They'll be battle-ready within the hour."

"Casualty projections?"

Aldric's form flickered. The only sign of emotion in a warrior who'd died facing impossible odds and chose to keep fighting anyway. "Forty percent if we're fortunate. Sixty if Caelum commits his full force."

Forty percent.

Fourteen hundred souls. Ceasing to exist. Because he'd asked them to fight.

The number lodged somewhere behind his ribs and refused to move.

"Coordinate with the other Death Lords," he said. The words came out even. They had to. "Communication signals active two hours before we move."

Aldric saluted and moved off.

Dante's gaze found Brynn across the courtyard. She stood with the ward-keepers, hands moving through magical constructs, circlet glowing as she synchronized the communication network.

He knew that look. Had seen it on warriors before battle, when acknowledging terror meant breaking.

His shadows reached for her without permission. Crossing the courtyard, needing to touch her even from a distance.

She wouldn't last two hours like that. And he needed her sharp when they hit Caelum's fortress—needed her whole, not hollowed out by fear she refused to face.

But she had to finish the synchronization first. And he had coordination to handle.

He'd find her after.

Dante moved through the preparations on instinct. Confirming positions. Checking supply lines. Answering questions from captains who needed orders. The whole time, part of him watched her across the courtyard. Watched her shoulders creep higher with tension she wouldn't release. Watched her hands move faster, more desperate, like she could outrun her own fear if she just worked hard enough.

When she finally slipped away from the ward-keepers and disappeared into the palace, he gave himself five minutes. Let her have a moment alone before he followed.

He found her on the eastern balcony.

She stood with her back to him, hands gripping the stone railing hard enough that her knuckles had gone white. Below her, thirty-five hundred souls checked weapons. Reinforced armor. Said goodbye to people they might never see again.

Her whole body was rigid. Braced against something that was coming, whether she was ready or not.

He crossed the balcony without a sound, shadows reaching her first—tendrils curling around her ankles, announcing his presence.

She didn't turn.

"Forty to sixty percent casualties." Her voice barely carried. "That's what Aldric said."

Shadows wound around her waist. He pulled her back against his chest—an anchor in the dark.

"Yes."

"Fourteen hundred to two thousand souls. Who trusted us. Who believed what we said." A tremor ran through her. "They're going to die because we asked them to fight."

"They're going to die because they chose to." He covered her hand on the stone, feeling how cold her fingers were. "Everyone down there knows the cost. They came anyway."

Her laugh was bitter. "Is that supposed to make it better?"

"No." He pressed his mouth to her hair. "Nothing makes it better. You just carry it."

She went quiet. Below them, the blacksmith directed younger fighters toward the armory. Ward-magic flared bright as the network linked across realms. Somewhere, someone was crying. Somewhere else, someone was laughing too loud, the way people did when they were terrified.

"I should check the ward calculations." She pulled away from the railing, from him. "Make sure the synchronization is perfect. If there's any weakness—"

He caught her wrist.

"Brynn."

She wouldn't look at him. Kept her eyes on the courtyard, the preparations, anywhere but his face.

His shadows wound around her other wrist. "Look at me."

"I can't." Her voice cracked. "If I look at you right now, I'll fall apart. And I can't afford to fall apart. I need to stay focused. I need to keep working. If I stop—"

He pulled her into the shadowed alcove beside the balcony doors. Away from the courtyard. Away from watching eyes. Into darkness where nothing existed but his power and her heartbeat.

"Dante—"

He backed her against the wall. Framed her face with his hands, gentle in a way that contradicted everything he was.

"I need you focused when we hit that fortress." Rough. Almost breaking. "Not drowning. Not paralyzed. And you won't get there by running from this."

"Too late." Her hands fisted in his shirt. "I'm already drowning. I can't stop thinking about all the ways this goes wrong. Losing you. You losing me. Both of us dying and Caelum winning anyway." Her breath hitched. "All those souls are going to die because I opened that gateway. Because I walked into his trap like an idiot. They're cleaning up my mess with their lives, Dante."

His shadows wound tight around them both.

"Caelum built this. Not you." His thumbs brushed her cheekbones. "He corrupted the wards. He spent ages planning. You were just the catalyst he manipulated."

"That makes it worse." Her eyes were bright with tears she refused to let fall. "I should have seen it. I should have known. And instead I handed him everything he wanted."

Something cracked open behind his ribs. The same place where fourteen hundred casualties had lodged and wouldn't let go.

He kissed her.

Hard and desperate, edged with the terror of tomorrow. She gasped against his mouth and then kissed him back just as fiercely. Her hands slid into his hair, fisting, pulling him closer like she could crawl inside him and hide.

Shadows wrapped them in darkness until the alcove disappeared. Until the war disappeared. Until nothing existed but her body against his, her hands in his hair, her mouth moving like she was trying to memorize him.

When they broke apart, both breathing hard, he kept her close. Forehead pressed to hers. Shadows holding them in their own private world.

"Promise me something." Barely a whisper.

His hands tightened on her face. Thumbs brushing away tears she probably didn't know were falling. "Anything."

"If it comes down to closing the gateway or saving me..." Her green eyes burned into his. "Close the gateway. Don't let Caelum win because you chose me."

Everything in him rebelled.

"No."

"Dante—"

"No." His grip turned frantic. Shadows lashed out hard enough to crack the stone behind her. "Don't ask me to watch you die and do nothing. Don't ask me to finish the mission like you meant nothing."

"I'm asking you to save the realms." Her hands covered his, holding them against her face. "Even if it costs—"

"Everything." Darkness solidified around them. Frost crawled across the stone. "It would cost everything. You don't understand what you're asking."

"I do." She held his gaze, unflinching, tears streaming down her face. "That's why you have to promise. If I'm worried you'll sacrifice the world for me, I'll hesitate. I'll look for another way. And Caelum wins."

His shadows writhed.

She was right.

If he fell protecting her and Caelum won, she'd die anyway. Everything would die. The realms would collapse. Reality would fracture.

But choosing the mission over her—

He closed his eyes.

"The same applies to you." The words scraped out of him like broken glass. "If I fall, you finish it. Close the gateway. Survive. No heroic sacrifices. You live, Brynn."

"Dante—"

"That's the deal." His thumb traced her cheekbone. "We both come back. Or we finish the mission, and whoever survives carries that weight forever. Knowing they chose duty over the person who mattered most."

His forehead pressed harder against hers. Shadows wrapped them deeper into darkness.

"But know this." His voice dropped to something that barely qualified as human. "If death tries to take you from me, I will tear through every realm to bring you back. I will unmake reality itself before I let you go." His hand slid to the back of her neck. "You're mine. And I keep what's mine. Even if I have to rebuild existence to do it."

Her breath shuddered.

Then she was kissing him again.

He slowed it this time. Made it aching. Tender. Memorizing the taste of her mouth. The way she fit against him. The sound she made when his shadows traced her spine.

In case this was the last time.

She matched him. Fierce and fragile at once. Her hands sliding around his neck, holding on like he was the only solid thing left.

When they finally pulled apart, neither moved far. Shadows wrapped around them both like armor against everything waiting outside.

Crimson light flared across the courtyard. Seraphina's signal, burning violently against the twilight.

Time was up.

Brynn glanced toward it. Something shifted in her face. Fear and grief folding themselves away, buried under focus. "That's Seraphina. The armies are ready."

"I know." His hands lingered on her waist. "Two hours."

"Two hours." She straightened. He watched her rebuild her walls, brick by brick. "Every signal synchronized. Every contingency planned. We can do this."

"Brynn."

"I'm fine." She touched his face. "We'll do what needs doing. Both of us."

They'd both come back.

Or they'd finish the mission and carry that weight forever.

He took her hand. Threaded his fingers through hers. Led her out of the shadows and back toward the courtyard.

Back into the twilight and thirty-five hundred souls preparing for war.

LXXIV.
BRYNN

Her boots hit ground that rippled with each step—solid stone becoming soft, then solid again, like walking on something that couldn't make up its mind. Above her, the sky had cracked where the realms collided—purple and red and silver bleeding through the fractures like light through a broken window. And seeping through all of it, Caelum's golden glow. The color of warm honey. The feeling of something rotting underneath.

Thirty-five hundred souls materialized around her. Death-knights. Shadow-guards. A thousand freed souls from Nightfall who'd believed her when she said this was worth dying for.

What if she was wrong?

The thought came to her before she could stop it. What if she couldn't close the gateway? What if she froze at the critical moment and everyone who'd followed her here paid for her failure with their existence?

"Brynn." Dante's voice cut through. His shadows brushed her wrist. "Stay with me."

She nodded. Shoved the doubt down where it couldn't paralyze her. Straightened her spine.

Other transport circles flared across the convergence point.

Seraphina's army hit the ground to the east like a storm making landfall—four thousand warriors in red-stone armor, war machines towering behind them. Frames of fused bone built from the dead of wars they'd already won.

Vex's forces materialized to the west—two thousand beautiful nightmares that prowled instead of standing, vibrating with hunger that made the air shimmer.

Thessa's spirits drifted in from the north. Fifteen hundred ghostly presences haunting forward through the fractured light.

Eleven thousand against thirty thousand.

The math kept running in her head.

The Death Lords converged at the center. Brynn stayed with Dante, the circlet blazing against her forehead, and tried to look like she belonged among immortals.

Seraphina reached them first, six feet of scarred warrior queen. Her eyes swept Brynn with the casual appraisal of someone who'd watched empires burn.

"The human lives." Approval underneath. "Still breathing after everything—"

"Tell me," Vex interrupted, prowling closer, form flickering at the edges, "did the Reaper consume you? Make you beg for—"

Shadows erupted between them. Dante's darkness formed a wall, temperature plummeting until frost cracked across the ground.

"Mine." The word came out barely human.

Vex laughed, backing off. Seraphina's mouth curved with something like amusement. And Thessa simply materialized at Brynn's shoulder without warning, close enough that the chill of her ghostly form sent goosebumps prickling down Brynn's neck.

"You're standing at a crossroads, child."

Brynn flinched. Thessa's eyes held that distant look.

"The gateway closes. That much is certain." Her translucent form flickered, revealing glimpses layered over one another. Brynn bloody but standing. Brynn on her knees, screaming. Brynn alone in darkness, reaching for someone who wasn't there anymore. "What you sacrifice in the closing... that choice is still being made."

The images burned into Brynn's mind. Alone. Reaching for someone who wasn't there.

Dante.

She couldn't breathe.

"Enough prophecy." Seraphina's voice cracked like a whip. "We have a war to fight. Save the riddles for after we've won."

Thessa smiled sadly and began expanding outward, ghostly threads reaching toward each army. The death-link taking shape.

The first connection hit Brynn like a fist to the chest.

Four thousand warriors breathing as one, their battle-hunger vibrating through her bones. Then Vex's forces crashed into her awareness, restless and burning and consuming until she wanted to tear something apart with her bare hands—

Cold cut through. Thessa's spirits joining, steadying the chaos like ice water over fire.

And beneath it all, anchoring her: Dante. Solid. Immovable. His shadows tightened around her waist as eleven thousand souls pressed against her awareness.

"Breathe." His presence bled through the link. "I've got you."

She let the flood settle into patterns instead of drowning.

His voice carried across the death-link: "Final positions. Seraphina draws their main force east. Vex hits harvesting chambers from below. Thessa extracts victims through the spirit-paths. I take the central approach with the Architect. She closes the gateway." A pause that felt weighted. "We end this today."

Acknowledgments pulsed back. Seraphina's determination, sharp as shattered glass. Vex's hungry anticipation. Thessa's gentle certainty.

Brynn made herself look toward their destination.

The horizon pulsed with sickly gold. And in that light, movement. Shapes beyond counting. Soul-soldiers emptied of everything that made them human, waiting in perfect, silent rows.

Thirty thousand.

The number she couldn't stop counting.

Through the death-link, she felt their forces register the same thing. The collective flinch. The moment of raw terror before training and purpose clamped down over survival instinct.

They knew. Every soul here knew most of them wouldn't survive.

They were standing anyway. Because she'd asked them to.

"They chose this." Dante's voice, quiet beneath the link's noise. "You gave them something worth choosing."

"And if I can't close it?" The words slipped out before she could stop them. "If I freeze and they all die for nothing?"

His hand found hers, squeezed once, hard enough to bruise.

"Then I'll burn through every soul between here and that gateway to give you another chance." His dark eyes held hers. "And another after that. However many it takes. You won't fail alone, Brynn. You won't fail at all."

Her throat closed.

She didn't have words. So she squeezed back, just as hard, and let that be enough.

The sky lightened, dawn bleeding across the fractured horizon.

The death-link pulsed: all positions ready.

Dante's hand released hers. But his shadows tightened around her waist one last time. A private claim beneath the weight of eleven thousand watching souls.

"Together," she said.

"Together." He made it sound like a vow. Like something that could survive even this.

Dawn broke.

Seraphina's battle-cry split the morning, four thousand warriors surging forward in a tide of violence. Vex's infiltrators vanished underground. Thessa's spirits drifted toward the paths like fog with terrible purpose.

And their thirty-five hundred advanced. Toward the corrupted paradise. Toward the gateway she'd opened and had to close. Toward thirty thousand empty shells waiting to tear them apart.

The circlet burned against her forehead. Ward-symbols flaring bright enough to taste.

Eleven thousand souls at her back. One impossible task ahead.

Brynn stopped counting and started walking.

LXXV.
DANTE

The smell hit him before his feet touched stone: blood and ash and that sickly-sweet corruption that meant Caelum's magic was close.

His shadows had already mapped the chamber during descent. Twenty soldiers at choke points. Another thirty flooding from side passages. Moving with coordination that shouldn't be possible for empty shells.

They'd walked into a trap.

"Death-knights, advance! Shadow-guards, flanks!" His shadows struck in every direction, buying seconds. "Ward-keepers, hold position!"

The chamber erupted.

Death-knights met the first wave with shields and steel. The impact shook the ground hard enough to crack stone beneath their feet. Metal screaming against metal. The copper smell of blood hitting air. Shadow-guards swept wide, cutting into exposed flanks while the center held.

But these shells had tactics. Strategy. Three surrounded each death-knight simultaneously, coordinated strikes forcing his warriors back step by step. Another group punched through the line, heading straight for the ward-keepers.

For her.

Dante's shadows intercepted them. Wrapping around empty forms, crushing the corrupted bindings that held them together. Shells crumbled to ash. But more kept coming, pouring from passages like water through broken stone.

"Contact rear!" Aldric's voice, sharp. "Through the walls—"

Stone exploded behind their formation.

Soldiers burst through solid rock. Not breaking through. Emerging. Like they'd been waiting inside the walls themselves.

The Nightfall blacksmith's apprentice went down first. She'd stood in the square twelve hours ago, voice clear, promising her steel wouldn't fail. Two shells tore her apart before anyone could reach her. Dante felt her die through the link. Brief terror. A cry for help that wouldn't come. Then nothing.

A death-knight fell seconds later. Then two shadow-guards, fighting back to back until shells simply crushed them under numbers. Then, three Nightfall volunteers. Then more.

"Defensive circle!" His shadows spread in a black wave. "Death-knights anchor! Ward-keepers—"

"The exits!" Brynn's voice cut through. Her circlet blazed as she thrust her hands toward the breached walls. "I can seal them!"

Ward-magic pulsed from her bloodline. Ancient mechanisms responded like they'd been waiting for precisely this. Stone doors ground shut on the passages, shells caught between grinding to nothing.

"Now!" Dante's shadows struck with renewed force.

The tide turned. Death-knights held, shields locked, driving forward.

Then the elite soldier crashed through their line.

Twice the size of the others. Blazing with concentrated golden light. It moved too fast for its mass, physics bending around it. A death-knight raised his shield. The elite backhanded him into the wall. The crack of breaking bone echoed through the chamber.

Then it turned toward the ward-keepers.

Dante's shadows wrapped around it mid-charge. Crushing force. Everything he had.

The elite didn't slow. Tore through his bindings like cobwebs.

Cold shot through his chest. His power. Being resisted.

He shadow-stepped into its path. Locked his hands around its throat. Poured death magic into restraining it, his nature against whatever animated this thing.

Four seconds of locked combat. Neither giving ground. His arms shook with effort. His vision blurred at the edges.

For the first time in centuries, he thought: I might not win this.

The ground gave way.

Brynn had triggered something in the floor. Architecture responding to her command. The stone opened. The elite plunged through. Its roar cut off as the mechanism snapped shut with grinding finality.

Dante stared at the sealed floor. Chest heaving.

Brynn was pale. Shaking. Blood across her face that wasn't hers.

He reached through his shadows. Brushed her wrist once. Still here.

The last shell fell. Then silence.

"Casualty report."

Forty-three dead. Eight death-knights. Twelve shadow-guards. Twenty-three Nightfall volunteers.

He let it settle into his bones. The weight of forty-three souls who'd trusted him.

"Secure this level. Wounded fall back. Everyone else, with me."

The door ground open. Stairs descended into darkness that seemed to swallow light.

From below, the sound of hundreds of feet in perfect coordination.

"HOLD THE STAIRS!"

Death-knights formed a wall across the entrance. Shields locked. The narrow space was their only advantage against numbers that should have overwhelmed them in seconds.

Shells poured upward. Wave after wave. Throwing themselves against the defense with no regard for self-preservation.

Because there was no self left to preserve.

The first wave broke against the shield wall. Death-knights cut them down. For thirty seconds, it almost felt manageable.

Then the second wave hit before they could reset.

A death-knight stumbled. Shells dragged him down before he could recover. The man had served Dante for four hundred years. Had survived wars that toppled empires. Died in a stairwell, drowning under empty bodies.

"Close the gap!"

Shadow-guards surged forward. Filled the hole. Held.

The third wave came. And the fourth. And the fifth.

It stopped being a battle. Became something more like drowning. Like being buried alive under bodies that kept coming, no matter how many they killed. Dante's shadows lashed out constantly, destroying shells by the dozen, but for every one that fell, three more pushed forward.

His arms burned. His chest ached with every breath. Sweat ran down his spine. He'd fought for his whole existence without tiring like this. Now his body screamed for rest it wouldn't get.

Aldric went down.

Not dead. A shell's blade caught his shoulder, spinning him into the wall. Two shadow-guards pulled him back before the tide could swallow him. But the captain who'd served Dante longer than civilizations had existed was bleeding badly, face grey with pain.

"Keep fighting," Aldric snarled at the guards trying to tend him. "I'll bleed later."

Another death-knight fell. Then three volunteers in quick succession, pulled from the line and torn apart before anyone could reach them. A ward-keeper named Sera, who'd been teaching the younger ones during the march, took a blade meant for someone else. She crumpled without a sound.

Each death pulse carved absence into Dante's awareness. Each one made the weight heavier.

The shells kept coming. Endless. Relentless. Like the stairs went down forever, and every level was full of them.

"They're not stopping!"

"We don't need to kill them all." Dante's voice came out steady. Had to. "Brynn, how far to the ward-core?"

"Four more levels." She was at the wall, tracing symbols with bloody fingers. "But there's a service passage. Emergency route. Bypasses everything."

Four more levels would break them. Would leave bodies stacked on every stair.

"Can you access it?"

"One minute."

Sixty seconds.

Another wave surged up the stairs. The shield wall buckled. A shell broke through, heading for the ward-keepers. A Nightfall volunteer intercepted it. They went down together, her knife in its throat, its hands around hers. Neither got back up.

Forty seconds.

"The line's failing!" Someone's voice, high with panic.

Dante threw more power into the defense. His shadows spread thin, trying to plug gaps that kept opening. His nose started bleeding. He ignored it.

Thirty seconds.

Shells pushed through the gap where the volunteer had fallen. Shadow-guards threw themselves into the breach, buying seconds with their lives. One. Then another. Then a third. Each one a death pulse. Each one an absence.

Twenty seconds.

Blood slicked the stairs. The air tasted like copper and death. His people were dying faster than they could hold. The weight was crushing. Suffocating. Every instinct screamed to retreat, to run, to survive.

They held anyway.

"When I say move, you move. Brynn first. Ward-keepers protect her. Everyone else follows."

Trust pulsed through the link.

"Ready!" Stone ground open beside the stairwell.

"NOW!"

His power exploded down the stairs.

Pure force with nowhere for enemies to run. Death magic so

concentrated it turned the air black. Shells disintegrated by the dozen. Fifty. A hundred.

The cost was immense. His vision went dark. His knees buckled.

Not yet.

"MOVE!"

His forces surged into the passage. Dante was last. Shadows forming one final barrier as shells closed from all sides.

"Seal it!"

The door boomed shut.

Dante collapsed against the wall. Hands shaking against the stone.

Brynn was beside him instantly. Her hand on his arm.

"How bad?"

"I'll make it." He wasn't sure. Had to be sure.

Her fingers tightened. "You'd better. I'm not doing this alone."

He looked at her. Blood-spattered. Exhausted. Eyes fierce with something that looked like fear, wearing the mask of determination.

This might be the last time we speak, he thought. If the next chamber is worse. If he's waiting for us. If—

"Whatever happens in there," he said roughly, "I need you to know—"

"Don't." Her voice cracked. "Don't say it like goodbye. Say it after. When we've won."

He held her gaze. Nodded once.

"After."

She helped him stand. His body screamed protest. He ignored it.

"Casualties?"

"Hundred and twelve." Aldric's voice was raw. "Sixty-four from the stairwell."

Hundred and twelve souls. His to carry.

Updates pulsed from the other fronts:

Seraphina: "Six hundred dead. Whatever you're doing, do it faster."

Vex: "He's rebuilding. Move, brother."

Thessa: "So many we can't save. Hurry."

Everyone buying time with blood.

"Move out. Double-time."

They ran. Ward-stones flickered to life as Brynn passed, emergency lighting greeting her bloodline. Down through levels, they would have had to fight through, past chambers full of shells they'd never face.

The passage opened into a massive space.

The ward-core chamber.

Dante stopped breathing.

It should have been beautiful. Patterns carved by masters. Ward-stones positioned with perfection. Channels guiding power with elegant efficiency.

His partner's birthright. The legacy her ancestors had built to last forever.

Caelum had butchered it.

Ward-stones pulsed sickly gold instead of blue-white. The channels meant to distribute power across five courts had been reshaped. Violated. All flowing toward the center now.

Toward the gateway.

It hung above the chamber's heart, pouring golden light that hurt to look at. Soul-energy from every realm. Every death across five courts. Being harvested. Processed. Erased.

Brynn stepped forward. Her grief struck him like a blade between the ribs.

"He destroyed it." Barely a whisper. "Everything they built."

He wanted to pull her close. To shield her from seeing her heritage desecrated. But there wasn't time. There was never enough time.

"Death-knights, perimeter. Shadow-guards, entrances. Ward-keepers, on Brynn."

His people moved. What remained of them.

He sent one final message: "Ward-core reached. Beginning closure. Hold."

Seraphina: "Until we can't. Then longer."

Vex: "About damn time."

Thessa: "The spirits are with you."

Brynn approached the gateway. Every ward-stone pulsed in

response. Recognition. Authority. A daughter of architects come home to sacred ground that had been violated in her absence.

She placed her hands on the corrupted ward-stone at the gateway's base.

Her circlet blazed.

The war held its breath.

LXXVI.
BRYNN

The moment Brynn's hands touched the corrupted ward-stone, something tore open behind her eyes.

Something worse than pain. Her mind was forced to contain years of corruption all at once. Caelum's modifications clawing at her awareness, fighting her attempt to undo them—like the work was alive, refusing to die.

Her circlet blazed white.

Ward-sight flooded in. She saw the original architecture her ancestors had built, with clean lines and every angle precise, now buried under rot, golden corruption threading through the patterns like veins of infection. Spreading. Growing. But underneath, still intact, still waiting: the original protocols, sleeping for ages, hoping someone with the right bloodline would come.

Her ward magic poured through the patterns, ripping at the corruption like peeling back dead tissue to find what was still alive beneath. The gateway convulsed, golden light pulsing erratically, fighting her.

The stone burned beneath her palms—skin blistering, flesh cooking against ward-work that didn't want to be fixed. The bandages on her wrists, already soaked from Caelum's torture, went hot and wet, blood running down her arms and dripping onto the stone.

Her blood mixing with her ancestors' work.

"Channel! Now!"

Power slammed into her from behind.

The ward-keepers responded. The entire network opened. Every stone they'd synchronized, every point in Dante's realm—all of it flowing through her mortal body at once.

Her spine arched. Every nerve lit up. Magic that should have killed her poured through in torrents.

This is what it feels like to burn alive from the inside.

The gateway howled, reality screaming as she forced it to change.

Soul-flow channels flickered. For one moment, they stopped flowing inward. The corruption wavered.

Then it surged back twice as hard.

Copper flooded her mouth. She'd bitten through her tongue. Every muscle locked as centuries of Caelum's work pushed back at once.

Opening had been turning a key.

This was holding a wound closed while something on the other side tried to tear it open.

Her hands were melting.

She could smell her own flesh. Sharp. Nauseating. But if she let go now, she'd lose everything. Every soul who'd died to get her here.

Updates crashed through the death-link:

Seraphina: "Taking heavy losses. Can't hold much longer. Finish it NOW."

Vex: "He knows. His army is converging. MOVE FASTER."

Thessa: "Spirit-paths collapsing. So many trapped in processing..."

She pushed harder—blood running from her nose. Vision fracturing. Her magic tore through corrupted patterns with desperate violence.

One modification burned away. Then another. Ward-stones began grinding back toward their original positions. A channel was redirected. Light shifted from sickly gold to clean blue-white.

The chamber shook from the gateway itself, from corruption that had grown into the stone like roots.

Dante's voice across the link: "INCOMING! Hundreds! All entrances!"

She couldn't look away. A second of broken concentration would undo everything.

But she heard it.

Steel on shells. Temperature dropping as Dante unleashed the Reaper. Death-knights shouting. Shadow-guards fighting. Dying.

Someone screamed, cut off mid-sound.

The death pulse hit like a blade. Terror, pain, nothing.

A hundred and thirteen. They'd lost a hundred and twelve getting here, and now—

Another pulse.

A hundred and fourteen.

A third: Jill, the ward-keeper who'd stood beside her during the synchronization, whose last thought was confusion because she'd been in the back, she'd been safe, how had they reached her—

A hundred and fifteen.

Tears and blood ran down her face. Her body was breaking—blood vessels bursting in her eyes, muscles tearing.

She was dying, the magic burning her hollow.

But the gateway was closing.

Another stone ground into place. Another channel snapped back, light shifting gold to white and holding. Her ancestors' work remembering itself.

Behind her, the battle raged—Dante's voice calm, certain, coordinating the defense.

He was out there. Could be dying right now. Could already be gone and she wouldn't know because she couldn't turn around, couldn't check, couldn't do anything but stand here with her hands fused to stone while he—

Don't. Don't think it. Don't let it in.

But she couldn't stop her mind from showing her: Dante falling. Dante's shadows going still. Dante's voice cutting off mid-command the way Jill's scream had cut off, there and then not, alive and then just—nothing.

She poured everything into the closure. Every drop. Every spark.

The ward-stones blazed like stars.

Perfect patterns. What her ancestors had built to last.

The soul-flow channels redirected with a sound like bones setting, like the world remembering how to breathe.

The gateway sealed.

Her hands tore free from the stone—skin peeling away, bloody handprints left behind.

Her legs buckled.

"It's done." The words came out barely a whisper. "It's closed."

She turned, needing to see him, needing to know—

Chaos. Shells flooding through every entrance. Death-knights falling back. Shadow-guards desperate. Dante's shadows everywhere, coordinating retreat.

His voice through the link: "Fighting retreat! Wounded first—"

Still alive.

Golden light erupted across the chamber.

Caelum materialized at the center.

Light blazed around him like a dying sun. His mouth twisted. His hands shook at his sides. Every trace of the compassionate mask had cracked away, leaving something raw underneath—something that had been hiding.

"You closed it." The words came out broken, incredulous. "You actually—"

He looked at the sealed gateway. The restored ward-stones glowing blue-white. Centuries of his work undone.

His masterpiece. Burned to nothing.

When his eyes found her, they were empty of everything except one thing.

She'd seen rage before, had survived his torture, endured his attempts to break her.

This wasn't rage.

This was a god denied his heaven. And she was the one who'd taken it from him.

Some things couldn't be forgiven. Some things demanded blood.

She had just enough time to think: *He's going to kill me himself.*

Then Caelum moved.

LXXVII.
DANTE

The gateway sealed with a pulse of magic that Dante felt through every shadow in the chamber.

Brynn had done it.

Through the death-link, he felt her exhaustion. Bone-deep. Her triumph was fierce even as pain wracked her body.

She was alive. She'd succeeded.

But the battle was still raging.

Shells poured through all three entrances. Hundreds of them, maybe thousands, momentum carrying them forward even though their purpose was gone. His death-knights were breaking under the pressure. A hundred and eighteen casualties now, death-pulses hitting the network in rapid succession.

"Fighting retreat!" His command cracked through the death-link. "Death-knights, fall back by sections! Shadow-guards, cover the ward-keepers! Everyone through the service passage. NOW!"

His forces responded instantly. Death-knights fell back in coordinated groups, shields locked. Shadow-guards formed a rear guard, weapons flashing.

Updates pulsed from other fronts:

Seraphina, fury bleeding into exhaustion: "Gateway's sealed. Withdrawing. Lost over six hundred, but we held them."

Six hundred. Six hundred souls who'd followed her and wouldn't come home.

Vex, manic energy settling: "Harvesting stopped. Pulling out."

Thessa voice came through, sorrow, and satisfaction mixed: "Extraction complete. So many saved. So many we couldn't reach."

Dante's shadows spread wider, covering the retreat. Forming walls of darkness that shells crashed against uselessly. Death-knights moving through the service passage in organized groups. Ward-keepers following. Almost clear. Almost safe.

A shell broke through on the left flank.

One of his death-knights went down under four of them before anyone could reach her. The death-pulse hit the network. Shock, pain, the desperate thought that this couldn't be how it ended.

A hundred and nineteen.

Dante's shadows lashed out, destroying the shells, sealing the gap.

"Keep moving! Don't stop for the dead—"

Golden light erupted across the chamber.

From everywhere at once.

The ward-stones cracked under the surge. Every instinct he possessed screamed warning.

He spun toward the center.

Caelum stood there.

Light blazed around him. Power radiated in waves that made the stone crack beneath his feet. His perfect features twisted with rage.

A man watching everything crumble to ash.

His gaze swept the chamber. The sealed gateway. The restored ward-stones. The evidence of his failure.

Then landed on Brynn.

She was swaying near the sealed gateway. Exhausted beyond anything a mortal should survive. Blood running from her nose and mouth. Hands charred from touching corrupted ward-work.

But alive. Triumphant.

The mortal who'd destroyed his perfect plan.

Dante saw the exact moment Caelum's rage fixed on her.

"You." Caelum took a step toward her. His voice shook. "A thief. A mortal criminal. You ruined everything."

Dante shadow-stepped between them before thought could form. His shadows spread wide, creating a wall of darkness between Caelum and everything that mattered.

"It's over, Caelum." His voice was dead calm. The quiet that preceded annihilation. "Your harvest is done. Your gateway is sealed. Stand down."

"Over?" Caelum's laugh cracked. "OVER? Centuries of work. Perfection within my grasp. And you think one mortal thief can just—"

"She closed your gateway. She undid your corruption in minutes. She won."

Caelum's smile turned vicious. "A thief. The great Reaper, reduced to protecting street trash. She'll be dust in decades while you remain for eternity. Was she really worth—"

Behind Dante, another shell broke through.

A death-knight's scream cut off mid-sound.

A hundred and twenty.

His attention split for one second. One critical heartbeat as he coordinated the response.

And Caelum moved.

Light gathered in his hands. Concentrated. Building. Every soul he'd ever harvested. Every bit of stolen essence. All of it poured into one attack.

"If I can't have my paradise—" His voice dropped to something cold and final. "—neither shall you have your architect."

Dante's head snapped back. Saw the attack forming. Saw where it was aimed.

"NO!"

He shadow-stepped, trying to intercept—

Too slow. One second too slow.

The light exploded across the chamber.

Time seemed to slow. Every detail clear. The way the light moved through the air was like liquid fire. The way Brynn's eyes widened in that final moment. The way her lips formed his name.

The blast hit her directly in the chest.

She made a sound—half gasp, half scream, his name torn from her throat. A sound that would echo in his nightmares for eternity.

"Dante—"

Her body arced backward. The circlet blazed one final time, ward-symbols flaring bright enough to sear the eyes. Her ancestors' work trying desperately to protect her.

Then went dark.

Blood erupted from her nose. Her mouth. Her eyes. The impact lifted her off her feet like she weighed nothing.

She hit the ground hard, stone cracking beneath her.

Didn't move.

Didn't breathe.

The world stopped.

Everything. The battle raging around them. The retreat. The shells still pouring through entrances. The death-link carrying thousands of souls. All of it ceased to exist in that moment.

There was only Brynn.

Lying on blood-stained stone.

Still. So impossibly still.

His heart forgot how to beat. His lungs forgot how to breathe. His legs forgot how to hold him upright.

He reached for her presence through the shadows wrapped around her waist. That connection he'd felt since his power had first touched her. The awareness of her had become as natural as breathing.

It was there.

But fading. Fragmenting. Scattering like smoke in the wind.

"Brynn." Her name came out raw. "Brynn, no. Please—"

He took one step toward her.

Caelum moved between them, light still blazing, features twisted into something vicious and triumphant.

"Look at her. Dying. Your precious mortal couldn't survive what I can create. She was always too weak. Too fragile—"

Something inside Dante shattered.

He felt it break. Every wall he'd ever built collapsing simultaneously. Every thread holding his restraint together snapping at once.

Because she was dying.

The only person who'd looked at what he truly was and seen him beneath it. Who'd chosen him, knowing exactly what he was. Who'd said "you don't scare me" and meant it with her whole heart.

Who'd made him want to be something more than what he was born to be.

And she was broken because he'd looked away for one second.

The temperature plummeted instantly. Frost spread across every surface in seconds. The ward-stones. The walls. The ceiling. Even the blood pooling beneath Brynn's body.

His shadows erupted.

They swallowed Caelum's golden light whole. Consumed it. Devoured it like starving things finally allowed to feed. His form became less solid, less defined. The shape he wore out of convenience beginning to dissolve.

Death incarnate.

The Reaper.

Finally unleashed.

The chamber walls cracked. Stone screaming under pressure. Reality fracturing at the edges where his shadows touched.

Caelum's expression cracked like porcelain. His smug smile faltered as he felt the weight of what he'd done, what he'd unleashed.

"Reaper—" He backed up. His voice lost its arrogance. "I didn't mean—she was just a mortal, we can find another—"

"Don't." The word made the walls shake. Made reality shudder. "Don't speak. Don't breathe. Don't dare continue existing in my presence."

"She was nothing—"

Wrong answer.

"She survived losing everything and learned to steal hope from the darkness." Dante's voice was cold. "She is every forsaken soul who refused to break, distilled into one impossible woman."

His form shifted further, less human with every word. More concept. More of what he'd always been beneath the restraint.

"And she is mine."

The possessive snarl echoed through the chamber. Through the death-link. Through every realm simultaneously.

Caelum threw up barriers. Light flaring in layers. Every defense he'd learned over millennia.

Dante's shadows touched them.

They exploded like glass.

His power didn't break through. It erased them. Made them cease to be because death didn't negotiate with those who'd forfeited their right to exist.

Caelum's face went white. "Brother, please—we can bring her back, there are ways, rituals—"

"I was never cursed, Caelum." Barely recognizable as language now. "I was born this way. Death given form and will."

His shadows surrounded Caelum. Cutting off every escape.

"I choose to be gentle. I choose to show mercy. I choose to protect instead of destroy."

Caelum's breathing came in gasps. "Brother—"

"But she falls because of you." Dante stopped an arm's length away. Close enough to smell his fear. "And I choose nothing for you. No mercy. No restraint. No gentleness."

His hand moved to his right glove.

"I am the Reaper." His fingers found the edge. "I am the monster every soul fears. I am what walks in your nightmares and whispers in your final moments."

He pulled the glove off.

Slowly. Deliberately.

Let Caelum see his bare hand. Let him understand exactly what was coming. Let terror have time to sink in.

The skin was pale—almost normal—Except for the way reality bent away from it. The way the air avoided contact. The way the stone cracked where his fingers passed.

This was the hand that had harvested countless souls over millennia. That could drain life with a touch. That had earned him the name every soul whispered with terror.

"You took her from me."

His bare hand reached out.

Caelum tried to scream.

Dante's fingers closed around his throat.

"Now let me show you what happens when you steal from the Reaper."

He let his true nature rise fully. Let himself be exactly what he was born to be.

Caelum's light started to dim. Slowly. Because Dante wasn't just killing him.

He was erasing him.

Every soul's essence Caelum had harvested. Every piece of magic, memory, consciousness. All of it flowing into Dante's hand, being drawn out like poison from a wound.

Caelum's scream lasted three seconds before his voice gave out.

Dante didn't stop.

He felt Caelum's stolen power flooding through his palm. Felt the souls Caelum had consumed crying out as they were torn free—thousands of them, finally released from their prison of peaceful oblivion. Finally allowed to feel again, even if what they felt was the agony of their captor's destruction.

Let them feel it. Let them know their torturer burns.

Caelum's features cracked. Skin splitting, form fragmenting as the magic holding it together was torn away.

His eyes went dull. Awareness fading like candles snuffed out one by one.

But still conscious enough to feel it happening. Still aware enough to understand that this was worse than death. That this was erasure.

Dante squeezed harder.

Caelum's mouth moved. Forming soundless words. Maybe begging. Maybe apologizing.

Dante didn't care.

The harvesting intensified. Every second stripping away more until there was nothing left.

Just a shell. Empty. Everything that had made him a Death Lord —gone.

Caelum's body crumbled. Disintegrating from the extremities inward. Fingers to ash. Arms following. Chest collapsing.

His eyes went dark. No awareness. No spark.

Dante's hand tightened one final time.

And Caelum ceased.

The ash was scattered. The light faded into darkness so complete it was like it had never existed. Reality sealed over the space where he'd been.

The death realm itself wouldn't remember him.

Dante's hand dropped.

His shadows contracted. Pulled back into him like a tide retreating. His form solidified, became physical again because he needed hands now. Needed to hold her. Needed to be human-shaped for what came next.

The temperature rose. The frost stopped spreading.

Because destroying Caelum meant nothing if she was gone.

He turned toward where she lay.

His legs barely worked. The world tilting. Shadows sluggish from the expenditure.

He dropped to his knees beside her. Hands shaking as he reached for her, afraid to touch her, afraid he'd hurt her more.

Her eyes were closed. Blood running from her nose, her mouth, her ears. The circlet sat dark against her forehead. Her chest barely moving. Each breath shallow and labored.

"Brynn." His voice broke completely. "Please. Please don't leave me."

He reached for their connection through his shadows.

It was there.

But so faint. Fading with every heartbeat.

LXXVIII.
DANTE

The rage drained out of him. Left nothing but emptiness. His bare hands were already on her face, cupping her cheeks. So cold. Her skin was so cold.

"Stay with me." The words came out broken. "Brynn, stay with me."

Her chest barely moved. Shallow breaths that stuttered and caught. Each one was wet, labored, like something vital had been damaged and was filling with blood.

He could hear her heartbeat with his enhanced hearing. Growing weaker. Skipping beats. Struggling to continue when everything in her body was failing.

Her face was pale, lips going blue. The bandages around her wrists were soaked through. She'd pushed herself too hard maintaining the wards while under attack. The circlet on her forehead had gone dark, ward-symbols that had blazed so brightly now dim as dying embers.

Dying.

She was dying in his arms.

"Don't." His voice cracked. "Not after everything. Not now."

She didn't respond. Didn't open her eyes. Didn't make a sound.

Just kept taking those shallow, stuttering breaths that were getting further and further apart.

His hands moved to her shoulders. Shook her gently. "Brynn. You're stronger than this. You survived the Forsaken realm. You faced down Caelum. You can survive this."

Nothing.

Her chest rose. Fell.

Didn't rise again.

Three seconds. Four. Five.

His own breathing stopped. Waiting. Willing her lungs to work.

Six seconds. Seven.

Then a gasping breath that sounded like drowning.

He pulled her against his chest, cradling her. Her body was limp in his arms. The woman who'd never stopped fighting had finally gone still.

Because he could see it now.

Her soul.

It was separating.

Translucent, shimmering, like heat-haze rising from summer stone. The essence of everything that made Brynn who she was. Her fierce defiance, her sharp wit, her refusal to back down even when facing monsters.

All of it pulling away from her body.

The connection between soul and body was visible to him. Threads of silver light anchoring her essence to her physical form.

They were fraying.

Snapping one by one.

Even as he watched, one thread broke. The sound was silent, but he felt it in his own body. A tearing sensation behind his ribs, like something was being ripped out of him too. His stomach dropped. His vision swam.

Her soul lifted. An inch above her body now.

"No." His hands tightened on her. Fingers digging into her shoulders. "No, no, no."

Another thread snapped.

Her soul rose higher. Still connected, but the pull was getting stronger.

He could feel it starting. Multiple directions. Different courts reaching for her.

The Violent court wanted her warrior's death. She'd fallen in battle, fighting to the last. The Consumed reached for her obsessive determination. The way she'd poured everything into closing that gateway. The Lingering pulled at her unfinished business. All the things left unsaid between them.

And the Forsaken.

His realm.

Reaching for her because she'd died while he was consumed by rage. Unable to protect her. The exact moment of abandonment that defined those who came to his court.

He saw it with horrible clarity. Her consciousness fragmenting. Pieces of who she was torn apart and scattered across realms. Each piece aware. Each piece suffering. Each piece calling for the others that would never come.

Part of her trapped in the Tower of Screaming Winds, replaying Caelum's attack forever. Golden light hitting her chest. The impact. The pain. Over and over and over. Screaming his name while he never came.

And he would hear it.

Every scream. Every sob. Every time she called for him and he couldn't answer.

Her voice echoing through his realm for eternity while he stood on the other side of barriers he couldn't cross. Unable to free her. Unable to grant her peace. Unable to do anything but listen while the woman he loved suffered in his own domain.

Forever.

The image gutted him. His hands spasmed against her shoulders. For a moment, he couldn't see anything except that vision. Brynn screaming, Brynn suffering, Brynn calling his name into darkness.

His hands started shaking.

"Please." The word came out strangled. His throat closing. "Take anything else. Everything else. But not her."

No answer came.

Another thread snapped.

Her soul lifted higher. Connected by only the thinnest strands now.

He could see the courts fighting for her. Golden light from the edges of where the Mourned had been. Red from the Violent. Hungry darkness from the Consumed. Mist from the Lingering. And his own shadows, reaching without his permission.

All of them wanting pieces of her.

She didn't move. Didn't react.

Three threads left.

Through the death-link, he felt his commanders' confusion and concern. They couldn't see what he saw, her soul departing, but they felt his anguish bleeding through the network.

My lord? Aldric's voice came through the link. *Are you—*

Dante couldn't answer. His throat had closed completely.

Could only watch as she died.

Two threads left.

He'd held her with these same hands just hours ago—her body warm and alive, her heart beating strong against his palm, her skin flushed with heat and life and want.

She'd looked up at him with those fierce eyes and said she wasn't doing this alone, that they'd finish it together. That whatever happened, they'd face it side by side.

And now she was slipping away while he knelt here uselessly.

He was death incarnate. The Reaper. One of the most powerful beings in any realm.

He could destroy armies. Could harvest souls with a touch. Could unmake a Death Lord so completely that reality forgot he'd existed.

He had just erased Caelum from existence. Had consumed ages of stolen power like it was nothing. Had made the walls of reality tremble under the weight of his rage.

And none of it mattered.

Because he couldn't save her.

All that power. All that destruction. All that time of being the thing every soul feared.

And he was kneeling here watching her die like the most helpless creature in any realm. His hands were useless on her body. His power useless in his veins. Everything he was. Useless.

One thread left.

The final anchor between soul and body stretched so thin it was nearly invisible.

About to break.

Time seemed to slow.

He could see every individual fiber of the connection coming apart. Her soul pulling upward. Her body going completely still beneath his hands. That struggling breathing had stopped entirely now.

The last thread began to fray.

His whole body was shaking now. His jaw ached from clenching. His fingernails had cut crescents into his palms without him noticing.

His mind screamed. Do something. Anything. There has to be—

He stared at his bare hands on her chest. Right where Caelum had struck. Where her soul was trying to depart.

These hands had only ever taken. Had only ever harvested. Had only ever ended.

But she was the one person they'd never hurt.

The thought cut through his panic like lightning.

What if he could do more than touch her safely?

He could channel. He always channeled. It was his nature. But what if he channeled differently?

Not harvest. Not take.

Give.

Force his power to work in reverse. Pour his essence into her instead of draining hers away. Anchor her soul with threads of his own power. Share enough of what he was to tether her to existence.

The idea was reckless. Desperate. The kind of thing that only occurred to someone watching everything they loved slip away.

His nature didn't work that way. He took life. That was what he was built for, what he'd always been.

It might not work.

Might kill her faster.

Might destroy them both.

Three fibers left in that final thread.

But doing nothing meant watching her die.

Two fibers.

And he'd rather risk everything, including himself, than lose her without trying.

One fiber.

That heart had beaten so strongly against his palm just hours ago. Had raced when he kissed her. Had belonged to him as surely as his belonged to her.

It was barely beating now.

But it was still beating.

Which meant there was still a chance.

"Stay with me." His voice came out rough. Desperate. "Don't you dare leave me."

The last fiber began to tear.

Dante stopped thinking.

Stopped questioning.

Just acted.

He reached deep inside himself. Past the control. Past the restraint. Past a lifetime of discipline.

Reached for the core of what he was.

And he let his power flow.

Not to take away.

But to give.

LXXIX.
BRYNN

She couldn't find her edges.

That was the first thing that was off. She'd always known where she ended and the world began. You had to, as a thief. Knowing the exact space your body occupied. Every finger. Every breath.

Now there was nothing to find. She was edgeless. Formless. Aware without being anything at all.

Just consciousness floating in nothing.

Was this death?

The memories came slowly. Disconnected. Fragmented.

Caelum's attack. Golden light blazing toward her chest. His face twisted with rage. His voice: *neither shall you have your architect.*

The impact. Pain exploding through her chest, so much pain it erased everything except the knowledge that she was ending.

Then nothing.

Then this.

She tried to feel her body. Couldn't. Couldn't even remember what "feeling" meant when you had nothing to feel with.

Tried to open her eyes. Had no eyes.

Tried to move her hands. Had no hands. No form. Nothing to move.

Dead, then. Or dying. Or caught somewhere between.

Forces were pulling at her.

Multiple directions at once.

Reaching for her from different places. Trying to claim her. Trying to tear pieces away like she was something to be divided.

Her awareness was fragmenting. She could feel it happening. The sense of *I* becoming *we* becoming *pieces*, her thoughts starting to run in different directions at once, memories already beginning to sort themselves into piles for different destinations. Here, the violence. There, the obsession. Somewhere else, the unfinished business. Parts of her being catalogued for distribution.

Like an estate sale. Like inventory being divided among creditors.

She was being liquidated.

No.

The thought came from somewhere the fragmenting hadn't reached yet. Some stubborn core that had kept her alive when her parents died. That had kept her stealing when she should have starved. That had kept her mouth running when smarter people would have stayed silent.

Absolutely fucking not.

She'd survived worse than this. She'd survived betrayal and starvation and ten years of running. She'd survived the Forsaken realm. She'd survived Caelum's torture with her mind intact.

She was not going to let herself be parceled out like disputed property.

And Dante—

He was there. Somewhere. She could feel him, faintly. A presence at the edges of her awareness. Familiar. Safe. Hers in ways she didn't have words for.

He'd come for her. She knew it with certainty.

The pulling intensified. The courts fighting harder.

She could sense them now.

The Violent court wanting her warrior's death. The Consumed reaching for her obsessive determination. The Lingering court pulling at her unfinished business.

And the Forsaken.

His realm.

Reaching for her because she'd died while he was consumed by rage. Unable to protect her. The exact moment of abandonment that defined those who came to his domain.

The Tower of Screaming Winds was calling. She could feel it. The place where she'd relive Caelum's attack until the concept of time lost meaning. Where she'd scream for help that would never come. Where she'd become nothing but suffering echoing through stone.

And Dante would hear. Every scream. Unable to reach her. Unable to stop it. Listening to her break while he stood helpless on the other side of barriers he couldn't cross.

She would rather cease entirely.

She refused to scatter. Refused to break. She was going back.

To him.

To her body.

To life.

She reached for the familiar presence. The sense of him at the edges of her awareness.

Reached and pulled with everything she had.

The pulling from the courts suddenly changed.

Something else was reaching for her now.

Darkness. Familiar shadows that had always been safe.

His power.

Threads of death magic reaching through the void. Anchoring instead of harvesting. Holding instead of claiming.

Multiple threads, white and black intertwined, wrapping around her like hands catching her before she fell. Tethering her. Holding her together when she should have been fragmenting.

And shadows. His shadows. Weaving through the threads. Dark and protective and possessive.

Claiming her.

Marking her as his.

Refusing to let the courts have even a single piece of what belonged to him.

Stay with me. His voice came from somewhere. Distant. Rough.

Desperate in ways she'd never heard from him. *Don't you dare leave me.*

The threads strengthened. More appeared, branching out like roots or veins. A whole network forming around her. Catching every piece. Holding her together.

Pulling her toward her body.

She could sense it now. Distant but approaching. The physical form she'd left behind. There. Intact. Breathing somehow. Heart beating when it should have stopped.

Because he was keeping it alive.

Thief. Steal this. Steal my power. Steal my immortality. Steal whatever you need to come back to me.

His voice again. Broken. Raw.

And through the connection forming between them, she felt what he wasn't saying. What it was costing him.

His body was failing. She could sense his hands shaking against her physical form, his breath coming ragged, his heartbeat growing erratic. Power flowing out of him in torrents. Not a stream. A flood. Everything he was pouring into her with no thought for what it would leave behind.

He was emptying himself. Draining his own existence to fill the void in hers.

He was dying. Giving her his life because he couldn't bear to watch her lose hers.

He wasn't just saving her. He was trading himself for her.

No. No, you stubborn, impossible—

She pulled harder along the threads. Moving faster toward her form. Toward him. If she could get back, maybe she could stop him. Make him stop giving. Make him keep enough to survive.

The shadows helped. Guiding her. Supporting her. Like hands pulling her home.

Her awareness touched her form.

The reconnection snapped into place like a bone setting.

Cold.

That was the first thing. The stone beneath her back, the air against her skin, her own flesh somehow freezing from the inside. Cold like she'd never be warm again.

Then everything else crashed in. Weight. Lungs burning for air. Her heart stuttering, forgetting its rhythm, finding it again. Pain radiating from her chest where Caelum had struck.

Her back arched against stone. Air rushed into her lungs in a gasping breath.

Alive.

But changed.

She could feel him. Inside her. Part of her now.

Not beside her. *Inside.*

Like a second heartbeat under her own. Like a voice in the back of her skull that she'd never be rid of. His presence taking up space in her consciousness, rearranging things to make room for himself. Settling in like he'd always belonged there.

Their consciousnesses connected. His thoughts brushing against hers. His emotions bleeding into her awareness. The edges of where she ended and he began had blurred.

And through that connection, she felt him clearly now.

Felt how much he'd given. Felt the hollowness where his power had been. Felt his body trembling with exhaustion, his lungs barely working, his heart struggling to beat. He'd poured so much of himself into saving her that there was almost nothing left.

He was a fire burning down to embers. Slipping away while she lay here in the body he'd saved.

She tried to move. To open her eyes. To reach for him.

Her body wouldn't respond.

Too exhausted. Too damaged. Her awareness was back, but her body needed rest.

No. He needs you. He's dying because he saved you and you need to MOVE.

Her fingers twitched. That was all she could manage. Her hand, she could feel his hand in hers, firm but weakening, trembling, his grip loosening as his strength failed.

I'm here, she tried to tell him through the bond. *I came back. You saved me. Now stop. Stop giving. Keep something for yourself.*

She didn't know if he could hear her.

Through the bond, his presence flickered. The steady flame becoming erratic. Fading.

He'd given too much and was slipping away while she lay here unable to help. Dying because he'd chosen her life over his own.

Dante!

She screamed it through the bond. Tried to push strength to him the way he'd anchored her. Tried to give instead of take. Tried to shove her own life force through the connection, anything to keep him from fading.

But she didn't know how. Didn't understand this new magic or how to save him when he was the one who'd always saved her.

So she gave him the only thing she could.

She squeezed his hand.

One weak squeeze. Everything she had. Her fingers closing around his with all the strength left in her broken body.

I'm here. I'm alive. Don't you dare leave me now. Don't you dare make this a trade.

His presence flickered again.

Weaker.

Darkness pulled at her. Exhaustion dragged her under even as she fought it.

Her last thought before awareness left was fierce and desperate and absolutely certain:

You brought me back. I'm bringing you back too. Whatever it takes. Even if I have to steal your death right out from under you.

Then nothing.

Just darkness.

And his hand still in hers.

LXXX.
DANTE

Dante counted her breaths.

He'd lost track of the total since the battle. Thousands. Maybe tens of thousands. Each one tallied like a miser hoarding coins.

In. Out. In. Out.

His hand gripped the armrest, splinters biting into his palm. He didn't move it—the pain was real, grounding, proof he was still here, still watching.

Two days since Caelum's death, since he'd poured more of himself into her than he should have.

Two days since he'd collapsed beside her, his body giving out the moment hers started breathing again. He'd woken hours later with Nathaniel standing over him, demanding he rest. He'd refused. Dragged himself to this chair instead.

Two days of watching her lie motionless while he slowly came apart.

The door opened. He didn't look up.

"My Lord." Nathaniel's voice came from the doorway.

Dante said nothing. His gaze stayed fixed on her face. On the rise and fall of her chest. Still breathing. That was all that mattered.

"You need to rest." Nathaniel didn't step into the room. "You've been here for forty-eight hours straight. Haven't eaten. Haven't slept. You're still recovering—"

"Leave."

The word came out flat. Empty. His shadows clung to him in wisps, depleted. His hands hadn't stopped trembling in two days. And her chest kept rising, falling. That fragile rhythm was the only thing keeping him from shattering completely.

A pause. Then footsteps retreating. The door closed with a soft click.

Silence again. Just her breathing. That precious, necessary sound.

He leaned forward, elbows on his knees, head bowing under a weight that had nothing to do with exhaustion. He'd given so much of himself that his power was recovering more slowly than it should. Depleted. Raw. There was a hollowness behind his ribs where part of him used to live, like a room with half the furniture missing. His muscles ached from sitting in this chair. His eyes burned from not sleeping. His stomach had stopped complaining about food sometime yesterday.

But he didn't care about any of that. All that mattered was her.

And she still hadn't woken.

Her vitals were strong. He could feel her steady pulse through the bond, sense her body recovering from wounds that should have killed her. That had killed her, before he'd dragged her back.

But what if he'd saved her body and lost her soul anyway? What if she opened her eyes and the person looking back wasn't really her anymore?

Stop. He forced the thoughts away, focused on the bond instead. On the thread connecting them that pulsed with life and warmth. She was in there. She had to be.

Her fingers twitched.

Dante's head snapped up. Every muscle went rigid.

Her hand. Resting on the blanket. Her fingers had moved. Just slightly—barely a tremor—but they'd moved.

He stopped breathing. Afraid any sound would shatter this moment.

Her eyelids fluttered. She made a sound, her head turning slightly on the pillow. Unconscious movement, instinctive, but it was *movement*.

He wanted to reach for her. Touch her. Make sure this was real. But his body had locked in place and his heart was pounding so hard he could hear it in his ears.

Her eyes opened.

Slowly. Unfocused at first, blinking against the dim light. She stared at the ceiling, brow furrowing.

Then her gaze slid sideways and found him.

His heart stopped. One beat, two, three, before it remembered how to work again. His vision blurred at the edges. His hands clenched the armrests so hard the bone groaned.

The confusion in her expression cleared. Her eyes widened, focused on his face with that intelligence he'd come to crave more than his next breath.

"Dante?"

The word came out hoarse, barely a whisper.

But it was his name. His name in her voice, the voice he'd been terrified he would never hear again. The sound broke something open in him. Two days of held breath, held hope, held terror, cracking apart at the sound of two syllables.

She knew him. Recognized him. *Remembered*.

The breath he'd been holding tore out of him. His whole body released forty-eight hours of held tension in a single exhale—shoulders dropping, spine curving, hands finally unclenching. His shadows exploded outward, darkening the room, writhing along the walls.

"You're awake." His voice came out wrecked. "You're really awake."

She blinked at him, processing, then tried to sit up. Her arms trembled. She got maybe an inch off the pillow before her strength gave out.

He moved without thinking.

One hand behind her back, the other supporting her arm, lifting her carefully. Her muscles were weak from disuse, her body still recovering.

But she was moving. Breathing. Here.

He got her settled against the pillows, adjusting them with more care than he'd shown anything in ages. His hands lingered on her shoulders, not quite able to let go yet.

She looked up at him. Her eyes swept over his face, taking in the exhaustion written in every line, the way his shadows clung weakly to him. Cataloguing his state.

"How long?" she asked.

"Two days." He pulled his hands back. Forced himself to give her space even though everything in him wanted to hold on. "You've been unconscious."

Her eyes widened. "Two—" She stopped, then her gaze sharpened on him. "You look terrible."

A rough sound escaped him that was almost a laugh. "I'm fine."

"You're not." Her hand lifted, reached for his face. "You've been here the whole time, haven't you?"

Her fingers touched his jaw. The contact sent warmth flooding through the bond. His hand came up instinctively, covering hers and holding it against his cheek.

"Yes," he admitted quietly.

"Dante—"

"You died." The words scraped his throat raw. "You died in my arms and I couldn't—" His voice broke. "I wasn't leaving."

Her expression softened. Her thumb brushed his cheekbone.

"But I came back," she said simply. "We both did."

His eyes closed just for a moment. Letting himself feel her touch, her presence. When he opened them again, she was watching him with understanding.

"What happened?" she asked quietly. "After Caelum's attack. I remember the pain. Then..." Her brow furrowed. "Then nothing. Just darkness. And then I felt you. Pulling me back."

Dante pulled the chair closer with shadows, positioned it so they were at eye level. Her hand slipped from his face but he caught it, held it in both of his.

"Caelum's strike tore your soul from your body." His voice came out even. Like he could control this if he just explained it properly.

"The courts were pulling at you. Fighting over you. You were fragmenting. Coming apart."

His grip tightened.

She went very still. Her pulse jumped beneath his fingers.

"I remember," she whispered. "The pulling. Different directions. Coming apart."

She'd felt it. Known what was happening to her. The knowledge sat in his chest like broken glass.

"I couldn't let that happen. So I anchored you. Poured my death magic into you. Enough to tether your soul. To hold you together."

Her gaze searched his face.

"You gave me part of yourself to save me."

"Yes."

"And now we're..." She trailed off. He felt her reaching through the bond, testing it.

"Bound." His jaw clenched. "Our souls are connected. I can feel you now. Constantly. Your presence. Your emotions once you're strong enough to project them clearly." He forced himself to keep going. "You're carrying my shadows. My mark. I'm woven through everything you are."

He watched her, bracing for the fear. The anger. The regret.

Instead she smiled.

"Good," she whispered.

He blinked. "Good?"

"I felt you," she said, meeting his gaze. "When I was dying. When the courts were pulling. I felt you reaching for me. And I reached back." She said it like it was simple. "So yes. Good."

Something in his chest loosened. Let go.

"I changed you," he said quietly. "Made you into something you weren't. You didn't have a choice."

"I chose." Her free hand came up, covered both of his. "When I was dying, I chose. I could have let go. Let the courts take me. But I didn't. I fought to come back. To you. So don't you dare feel guilty for saving me."

His throat closed. She'd chosen him. Even while dying, she'd chosen him.

She shifted, wincing slightly, then looked down at her hands. Her brow furrowed in concentration. He felt what she was doing—reaching for his gift, testing it.

Shadows stirred beneath her skin.

Dante stopped breathing.

Tendrils emerged from her fingertips, white-edged in silver. Not his black shadows. Something new. Something uniquely hers, born from his darkness and her own essence.

They moved with her will, responding to her thoughts. Dancing between her fingers, curious, testing, exploring their range before curling back beneath her skin like they'd always belonged there.

His chest ached. His eyes burned with something that might have been tears if he'd had the strength left for them. She was beautiful. Beautiful with his power transformed through her, made into something neither of them had been alone. Something better.

She looked up at him, eyes bright with wonder.

"They're part of me now," she whispered. "I can feel them. Like another limb. Like they've always been there."

"Yes. You're connected to me now. In ways that go beyond any bond I've known."

"Show me."

He blinked. "What?"

"The bond. I can feel something." She pressed a hand to her chest. "Like there's a thread between us. But I don't understand it yet. Show me."

Dante hesitated. Opening the bond fully would expose everything. His exhaustion, his lingering fear, what her death had done to him.

But she was asking. And he'd already laid himself bare in every other way.

He slowly opened his side of the connection.

Her vitals, strong and steady—the exhaustion in her muscles that would fade with rest, the confusion still lingering. And beneath it all, the core of who she was. Her soul wrapped in his shadows, anchored by his power.

Her eyes widened. Her hand pressed harder against her chest.

"I can feel you," she breathed. "Your presence. Like you're inside me."

"Yes."

"And you can feel me the same way?"

"Yes." Always. Forever. He would feel her like his own heartbeat. Would know if she was hurt, scared, or safe.

She stared at him, her chin lifting slightly as understanding settled over her features.

"We can't be separated," she said. "Can we? Not really. Not anymore."

"No." He held her gaze. "Even if we're in different realms. Different courts. I'll always know where you are. How you are. And you'll know the same about me."

"Forever?"

"Forever."

She should look scared. Trapped. Instead, her smile widened, and the frozen thing that had lived in his chest for two days finally cracked apart.

"Good," she said again. Then grimaced. "Though right now I feel disgusting. Two days unconscious probably means I smell terrible."

The shift caught him off guard. From profound connection to practical concerns in a heartbeat. But that was Brynn. Facing down death and eternity with the same attitude she'd use for a sticky lock.

"You want to clean up?" he asked.

"Desperately. But..." She tested her legs, managed to move them, but the weakness was obvious. "I don't think I can walk yet."

"I'll help."

"Dante, you barely look like you can stand—"

"Let me take care of you." He met her gaze, let her see how much he needed this. The desperate urge to do something, anything, to prove she was really here. "Please."

Her expression softened. The protest died on her lips.

"Alright," she said quietly.

He stood. His legs protested after two days in that chair. He pulled back the blankets, then bent and lifted her.

The weight of her in his arms. The warmth of her body against his chest. The way her head fit perfectly against his shoulder. He'd carried her before, but never like this. Never after two days of watching her breathe and being unable to touch her, help her, do anything but count breaths and pray to gods he didn't believe in. She was lighter than she should be, and he filed that away. Something to fix. Food, water, rest. He would take care of all of it.

Her arms came around his neck. He could feel her heartbeat against his chest.

"You know," she murmured, "I could probably walk with help."

"Indulge me."

"Fine." He felt her smile against his skin. "But only because I really do feel gross."

He carried her toward the bathing chamber, each step grounding him further. Reminding him she was solid in his arms.

LXXXI.
DANTE

The bathing chamber was exactly as he'd left it hours ago.

The sunken tub is already filled with steaming water. Servants had prepared it this morning on his orders, just like every morning for the past two days—hoping she'd wake, hoping he'd need it.

The hope had felt like madness at the time—like counting her breaths, like refusing to leave her side.

Now she was here in his arms, solid and real, and the madness had paid off.

He crossed to the tub and set her down on the tiled edge. She steadied herself with one hand on his shoulder, the other gripping his forearm. Even that contact sent warmth through him—proof she was here, alive, touching him.

"You had this ready."

"I hoped." He tested the temperature, giving his hands something to do. "Every morning. Just in case."

Her expression softened. "Dante."

His name in her voice. Tender. Aching. His throat tightened and he looked away. Two days of holding it together and now that she was awake, his control was fracturing. "Can you undress yourself or do you need help?"

She tested her arms. Lifted them slightly. The trembling was obvious. "I think I need help."

He nodded. Knelt in front of her, bringing them eye to eye. "Tell me if anything hurts."

His hands found the hem of the sleeping gown—cotton, the one he'd dressed her in two days ago—when her own clothes had been ruined with blood. His fingers brushed her thighs as he gathered the fabric.

She sucked in a breath.

He froze. His gaze flicked up to hers.

Her pupils were dilated. Her pulse visible at her throat, beating faster than it should for someone just sitting still.

She felt it too. This awareness. This hunger to touch and be touched after coming so close to never touching again.

He forced himself to focus. Lifted the fabric slowly, watching her face for any sign of pain. The gown slid up her legs, her hips, her stomach. Her skin was warm beneath his fingers where they accidentally brushed. She raised her arms as much as she could. He pulled the fabric over her head and set it aside.

She sat naked in front of him.

His jaw clenched. His shadows stirred restlessly around his shoulders.

Her skin was pale in the lamplight. Marked with fading bruises around her ribs where Caelum's magic had struck, purple and yellow evidence of how close he'd come to losing her. The bruises were healing but still visible.

Still there. Still proof she'd died in his arms.

His hands curled into fists at his sides.

"I'm alright. It looks worse than it feels."

He didn't trust himself to speak, just offered his hand to help her into the water.

She took it. Used his stability to slide into the tub.

The sound she made when the heat surrounded her, a low moan of pure relief, hit him somewhere below his ribs. His stomach tightened. His breath caught. Her eyes closed, head tilting back as she sank down until water reached her shoulders.

"This feels amazing."

He started to stand. Started to give her privacy.

Her hand shot out and caught his wrist. "Where are you going?"

"To give you space—"

"Don't." She opened her eyes and looked up at him, something raw in her expression. "Stay. Please."

The *please* broke something in him.

He nodded, started unfastening his shirt because he'd been wearing the same clothes for two days and they deserved to be burned. His fingers fumbled with the buttons, exhaustion and lingering weakness making simple tasks harder than they should be.

She watched him struggle. "You're shaking."

"I'm fine." The lie tasted bitter.

"You're not. You gave too much. Pushed too far. You're barely standing."

He took off his shirt, let it fall. The cool air hit his bare chest, raising goosebumps. Or maybe that was her gaze tracking over him. "I'll recover."

"How long?"

"A few more days. Maybe a week." He stripped completely, too tired to care about modesty. Too aware that modesty between them had died somewhere around the time he'd poured part of his soul into hers. "My power is returning—just slowly."

He stepped into the tub on the opposite side. The hot water felt incredible against muscles that had been locked in one position for forty-eight hours. He sank down with a sound he couldn't suppress.

When he opened his eyes, she was watching him.

Even weakened, his shadows curled.

"You look exhausted."

"I am." No point denying what she could feel through the bond anyway.

She shifted slightly. Winced.

"Sore?"

"Everywhere." She tried to smile. Failed. "Apparently, almost dying means every muscle hurts."

"Let me help." He moved through the water toward her. "I can wash your hair. The rest." He paused. "If you want."

"Please."

He positioned himself behind her. Close enough to reach but not quite touching. The water rippled between them.

"Lean back."

She did. Trusted him completely as she let her head fall back, let him support her weight with one hand while the other wet her hair. His fingers moved through the strands, dark silk beneath the water, heavy against his palms, spreading around her.

Beautiful. She was so fucking beautiful it made his chest ache.

He reached for the soap. The scent filled the space between them —jasmine and night-blooming flowers, something he'd had made specifically for her weeks ago—before the battle, before everything changed.

Back when he'd pretended this was just a political alliance.

The lies he'd told himself seemed laughable now.

He lathered his hands and brought them to her scalp. Began working the soap through her hair with gentle pressure. Starting at the crown, massaging slowly, his fingertips tracing circles against the delicate skin, working down to where her hair met her neck, the soft give of her scalp beneath his touch.

She made a sound. Soft. Almost a moan.

Her shoulders dropped, relaxing under his touch. Her head tilted slightly, giving him better access.

His hands stilled for half a second.

The heat of her body so close. The way she melted under his touch. The smell of her skin mixing with jasmine. The want rising in him when exhaustion should have made it impossible.

Control. He forced his hands to continue their work—fingers moving through her hair, making sure every strand was clean.

He rinsed her hair, cupping water in his hands and pouring it over her head. Making sure no soap got in her eyes. Taking longer than necessary because stopping meant acknowledging what came next.

Then he reached for the washing cloth.

Paused with it in his hand.

His gaze traveled down. The curve of her neck. Her shoulders. The line of her spine disappearing beneath the water. Lower to where the bruises marked her ribs. Evidence of her death. Her resurrection. His claim on her that went soul-deep.

He let out a breath and lathered the cloth.

"Arms first." His voice came out rougher than intended.

She lifted one arm without hesitation.

He started at her shoulder, the cloth moving slowly down. Over the curve of her elbow, along her forearm, where he could see her pulse beating. Her wrist, where her skin was so soft.

She leaned into his touch. Just slightly. Just enough that he knew she felt it too.

Down her back, the cloth trailed along her spine. Her skin was fever-warm beneath the water. His shadows stirred, wanting to wrap around the fading bruises.

Mine, they whispered. *Ours. Almost lost her.*

Across her sides, avoiding the bruises.

His grip on the cloth tightened. His other hand had somehow landed on her hip, steadying her. Or steadying himself. Skin to skin beneath the water.

Stop. He pulled back. Handed her the cloth. "You can do the rest."

She took it. Her fingers brushed his, lingering just a moment too long to be an accident. The tension thickened as she finished washing the places he'd avoided, places he wanted to touch. Not yet. Not when they were both barely holding together.

When she was done, she set the cloth aside and settled back against the tub with an exhale. Her eyes closed. Water lapping at her collarbones.

He moved back to his side of the tub and began washing himself quickly.

When he looked up, her eyes were dark. Lips parted slightly. Heat in her expression.

"What?"

"Come here."

"Brynn—"

"Please."

He moved through the water toward her. She met him halfway, and suddenly they were inches apart, close enough that he could see silver threading through her irises—his mark, his essence, proof of what he'd done. What they'd become.

Her hands found his chest, fingers splayed against his skin, right over his heart, where she could probably feel it racing.

"I felt you fading."

His lungs seized. Every muscle locked.

"At the end. Through the bond. When you were saving me, you were pouring everything into me, and I felt you slipping away. Your presence getting weaker and weaker." Her fingers pressed harder against his chest. "And I couldn't do anything. Couldn't help you. Couldn't stop it. I just had to feel you dying while I lay there unable to move—"

Her voice broke.

His hands came to her face, cupped her cheeks, tilted her head up so she had to look at him. "I'm sorry. I'm so sorry you felt that—"

"Don't apologize." Her eyes were bright with tears. "You saved me. I just... I needed you to know. That it wasn't just you watching me die. That I felt you dying too, and it was—" She stopped. Swallowed hard. "It was the worst thing I've ever felt."

His throat closed. He pulled her against his chest, held her tight enough that she had to feel his heartbeat. "I'm here. I'm alright."

"Promise me something." Her arms wrapped around him, clinging.

"Anything."

"Promise me you won't sacrifice yourself for me again. That if it comes down to a choice, you'll choose yourself."

His jaw clenched. The words she was asking for stuck in his throat. "I can't promise that."

She pulled back enough to look at him. "Dante—"

"Would you make that promise to me?" He held her gaze, let her see the truth he couldn't hide. "If our positions were reversed? If I was dying? Would you choose yourself over me?"

She opened her mouth. Closed it. Because they both knew the

answer. Had known it since the moment she'd reached back for him while scattering. Since the moment he'd poured his soul into her dying body.

"Exactly." His voice came out quiet. "So don't ask me to promise something you couldn't promise either."

"I hate that you're right." She pressed her forehead against his chest, right over his heart. "I don't want to lose you."

"You won't." His arms tightened around her. One hand sliding up her back, the other cupping the back of her head. Holding her like she was precious. Like she was everything. "We're bound now. Where you go, I go. Even death can't separate us anymore."

They stayed like that, just holding each other in the warm water while steam rose around them. His chin rested on top of her head. Her heartbeat steady against his chest. Their breathing falling into sync.

This. This was what he'd been terrified of losing. Not just her life. But these moments. This connection. The way she fit against him like she'd been made for his arms.

Finally, she tilted her head back. Looked up at him with eyes that had gone dark.

"Kiss me."

His hands tightened on her reflexively. "You should rest—"

"I want you." Her hands slid up his chest, over his shoulders, fingers curling into his hair. "I want to feel you. Want to prove you're really here and I'm really here and we're both alive." Her voice dropped lower. "Please."

His hand came up to cup her face, thumb brushing across her cheekbone, feeling the warmth of her skin. Her pulse fluttered beneath his palm, where it curved around her jaw.

Alive. She was alive.

He closed the distance and kissed her.

LXXXII.
BRYNN

The moment his mouth met hers, everything else fell away.

The fear. The exhaustion. The lingering terror of almost losing him.

All of it disappeared under the heat of his kiss.

He started gently, like she might shatter if he wasn't cautious enough.

She didn't want gentle. She wanted proof that they were both alive.

She deepened the kiss, parting her lips, tasting him—water and something darker, something uniquely him that made her head spin. Her hands tangled in his wet hair, pulling him closer, demanding more.

His control slipped.

She felt it in the way his hands tightened on her waist, fingers digging into her hips hard enough to leave marks she'd welcome. The way his mouth claimed hers, harder, hungrier, all that restraint burning away like paper.

The bond between them flared.

Heat and want flooded through the connection until she couldn't tell where her desire ended and his began. Every sensation doubled, amplified, feeding back through their link until she was drowning in it. Her need. His need. Theirs. One overwhelming force that made her dizzy.

She pressed against him, seeking more contact—skin to skin in the cooling water, nothing between them except want and desperation and relief so fierce it felt like pain.

His groan vibrated against her mouth. The sound went straight through her, made her body clench with need, made her ache for things they were both too weak for, but she wanted anyway.

Her hands moved down his chest. Hard muscle and smooth skin under her palms. Over the ridges of his stomach that flexed under her touch. Lower, following the line of dark hair that disappeared beneath the water.

He caught her wrists.

Broke the kiss.

Pulled back just enough that she could see his face. His pupils were dilated, eyes black with hunger that he was clearly fighting. His chest heaved, matching her own ragged breathing.

"Not tonight."

She blinked at him, dazed, her body still thrumming with unfulfilled want. "What?"

"Not tonight." His hold on her wrists was firm, grounding them both. His breathing still ragged, his whole body tense with the effort of pulling back.

"Why not?" The words came out sharper than she intended.

He didn't answer immediately. Just stared at her with want obvious in every line of his body, in the way his shadows writhed around them. But something else too. Something more vulnerable.

"Dante—"

"I just need—" He stopped. His jaw clenched. Started again. "Tonight I just need to hold you. That's all."

The rawness in his voice stopped her protests cold.

She looked at him. Really looked. The weariness carved into every line of his face. The way his hands trembled where they held her wrists. The shadows clinging to him weakly instead of with their usual strength. Two days of hell written in his eyes.

He wasn't saying no because he didn't want her. He was saying no because he needed something else more. Needed to hold her, feel her breathe, know she was alive without the complications of everything else.

She understood that. Had felt the same fatigue pulling at her, the way her body demanded rest even as it ached for him.

"Alright," she said softly.

His eyes widened slightly, like he'd expected a fight.

She cupped his face with one hand, feeling the scrape of stubble against her palm. "Today we rest."

The tension in his shoulders eased.

"Tomorrow—"

"Tomorrow," she interrupted, holding his gaze with promise, "you give me everything."

Heat flared in his eyes. Dark and wanting and full of promises that made her thighs clench.

He pulled her hands to his mouth. Kissed her knuckles one by one. Then her wrists, his lips lingering against her pulse point. The touch sent shivers through her even in the warm water.

More intimate than the kiss.

"Come on. Let's go to bed."

He stood, lifting her with him. Water cascaded off both of them, and she shivered as cool air hit her heated skin. He stepped out of the tub and reached for a thick towel, wrapping it around her with more care than necessary.

His hands lingered as he dried her. Starting with her arms, running the soft fabric over her shoulders, squeezing water from her hair. Every touch grounding.

She watched his face as he worked. The concentration. The tenderness. The Reaper who'd ruled for so long, treating her like something irreplaceable.

Then he grabbed another towel for himself, wrapping it low around his waist before sweeping her up into his arms.

She settled against his chest without protest. Her head found his shoulder naturally, like her body knew exactly where it belonged. His pulse beneath her cheek.

He carried her back to the bedroom. To the bed where he'd kept watch. The reminder sent a pang through her. Forty-eight hours of him sitting there, refusing to leave, slowly coming apart.

He set her down on the edge of the mattress. "Stay here. I'll get you something to wear."

Weariness was creeping back in now, making her thoughts slow and her limbs heavy. The adrenaline from the kiss was fading, leaving only tiredness behind.

He found one of his shirts, a silk that would be far too large on her, and brought it back.

By then, she'd already lain down, unable to fight gravity any longer, the towel discarded beside her. She was on her side, eyes half-closed, fighting to stay awake just a little longer.

"Arms up."

She lifted them with effort, muscles protesting. He slid the shirt over her head and helped her get her arms through the sleeves. The fabric pooled around her, drowning her in silk and his scent.

He pulled on sleep pants. Nothing else. The fabric hung low on his hips, showing every line of his torso.

When she looked up, he was watching her. Eyes dark. Jaw clenched. Fighting the same battle.

Her cheeks warmed.

Then he climbed into bed beside her, and she didn't hesitate.

She wrapped herself around him immediately. Her head on his chest, right over his heart. Her arm across his waist. Her leg hooking over his, tangling them together.

He went still for half a second, like her touch surprised him, like he hadn't expected her to cling. Then his arms came around her, pulling her closer. Holding her tight enough that she could barely breathe, but she didn't care.

"I'm right here. I'm not going anywhere."

His embrace tightened. "You almost did."

The words were quiet. Broken. Full of terror he'd been carrying alone.

"But I didn't." Her hand found his face, made him look down at her. "I came back. And I'm stronger now because of what you did."

He stared at her. Searching. His eyes were raw and exposed in a way she'd never seen before.

"I know," he said finally.

He pulled her closer again. One hand sliding up her back, the other cradling her head against his chest. Holding her like she was everything.

She settled against him, letting his steady rhythm calm her. Strong and sure beneath her ear.

His breathing changed almost immediately, slowed, deepened, evened out. The adrenaline that had been keeping him upright finally giving out now that she was safe in his arms. Now that he could finally stop fighting.

His hold loosened slightly, but he didn't let go, even as sleep took him.

She stayed still, feeling his chest rise and fall. He'd barely slept for two days. Of course his body was demanding payment now.

She should close her own eyes.

But she couldn't stop looking at him. The way his face relaxed in sleep, the harsh lines softening. The way his shadows finally went quiet, no longer writhing with anxiety. The way he looked younger somehow, less like an ancient Death Lord and more like just a man. Exhausted and vulnerable and hers.

Mine, she thought, and felt the bond pulse in agreement. *My Reaper. Mine.*

Her own tiredness pulled at her, dragging her eyelids down.

Even as sleep took her, wrapped in his arms with his heart beating beneath her ear, one thought remained crystal clear:

Tomorrow. Tomorrow she'd show him exactly what she meant.

Tomorrow, there would be no stopping. No holding back.

Tomorrow she'd claim him as thoroughly as he'd claimed her.

LXXXIII.
DANTE

The brush of a foreign presence against his wards woke him instantly.

Multiple presences. All powerful. All in his throne room.

Again.

Dante's eyes opened to pre-dawn twilight filtering through the windows. To the weight of Brynn draped across his chest, her arm wrapped around his waist like she was afraid he'd disappear if she let go.

Her breathing was slow and even against his skin. Deep sleep. The kind that came from feeling safe.

He didn't want to move. Wanted to stay here with her warmth pressed against him, her pulse beneath his palm where his hand rested on her back. Wanted to ignore the three presences currently in his throne room like they had any right.

But they wouldn't have come if it wasn't important.

He groaned softly against her hair, breathing in jasmine and citrus. His arms tightened around her sleeping form for one more moment before reality intruded.

Then he slowly extracted himself from the tangle of limbs and sheets.

She made a sound of protest, her hand reaching for him even in sleep. The bond between them flickered with confusion, her subconscious registering his absence.

He paused, watching her settle back into the pillows. Her face relaxed again, features softened by sleep. Beautiful. She was so fucking beautiful it made his chest ache.

She needed the rest. They both did, though apparently he wasn't going to get it.

He found a shirt and shrugged it on, leaving most of the buttons undone. Whoever had decided to invade his domain at this hour could deal with his irritation and informal attire. His body still felt hollowed out from what he'd done. Power returning but slowly, muscles protesting as he moved.

The palace corridors were empty this early. His bare feet made no sound on stone as he stalked toward the throne room. Shadows curled around his shoulders, still half-feral from sleep.

The doors stood open like an invitation he hadn't extended.

All three of them had made themselves comfortable in his throne room like they owned it.

Seraphina leaned against one of the bone-carved pillars, examining the edge of a blade she'd apparently brought with her. Vex lounged in a chair that hadn't been there yesterday, legs crossed, looking far too pleased with himself. Thessa stood near the windows, her form catching the light and making her look even more ghostly than usual.

"Why." Dante's voice came out flat as he crossed the threshold, darkness coiling irritably around him. "Are you here?"

Seraphina didn't look up from her blade. "We tried sending messengers."

"I sent them away." Three times. He'd been busy watching Brynn breathe, counting the beats of her heart, making sure she was real.

"We noticed." Vex raised an eyebrow, his gaze taking in Dante's disheveled state with obvious amusement.

"I was occupied."

"How is she?" Thessa turned from the window, concern softening her features.

Dante's shoulders eased slightly. "Recovering."

"We felt the transformation." Seraphina finally sheathed her blade and straightened. "The whole death realm felt it. Your power signature changed. Merged with something new."

Dante's shoulders tensed. The bond with Brynn thrummed beneath his ribs, a second presence that was somehow also his own. He could feel her even from here, sleeping peacefully, her dreams quiet, her warmth something he'd never known he needed until it was almost taken from him.

"Show us what happened." Vex leaned forward.

For a moment, Dante considered refusing. The memory was too raw.

But they needed to understand what she was now. What she'd become. What he'd made her.

He let his shadows flow outward.

The memory took shape in the air between them.

Brynn collapsing. Her soul tearing free, fragmenting, pieces of her essence scattering toward different realms like she was being pulled apart.

His stomach dropped. His hands started shaking before he could stop them.

His memory-self's hands closing around translucent soul-stuff that tried to slip through his fingers. The decision made in a heartbeat. Pour his own death magic into her, rebuild her from the inside out, give her enough of himself that death couldn't claim her.

Living through it again was almost as bad as the first time. His throat closed. His chest constricted. His shadows writhed with the remembered terror, the desperate need, the fear that everything he gave still wouldn't be enough.

Her body convulsing as immortality burned through mortal flesh. Shadows erupting from her skin, white edged in silver.

Silence held the throne room for a long moment while Dante fought to control his breathing.

"Great." Seraphina's lips curved. "Now there are two of you."

"She's considerably more dangerous than I am." The words came out with a pride he didn't bother to hide. His thief, his companion, his equal. Now immortal and powerful and capable of things that would make other courts think twice about challenging them.

"That," Vex said, his smile turning sharp, "is what concerns us."

Seraphina snorted. "You look pleased about it."

Vex winked at her, utterly shameless.

"The death realm recognizes her." Thessa's voice echoed strangely in the chamber, layered with something otherworldly. "The wards stabilized the moment she transformed. The barriers between realms strengthened. She is what we needed without knowing we needed it."

She belonged here. The realm had claimed her as one of its own.

"Which brings us to why we're actually here." Seraphina sobered, all trace of amusement vanishing. "Caelum's shells. They're gone."

Every shadow in the room went completely still.

Dante's voice came out forcibly even. "All of them?"

"Every single empty husk he created." Thessa's tone was soft but grim. "We've spent the past two days returning fragmented souls to their proper domains. Piecing together what was left of them after his... harvesting." She said the word like it tasted foul.

"The Mourned realm is stable," Vex added, his usual levity completely absent. "The souls who survived, those he hadn't fully drained yet, are still there. Living in that paradise he built for them."

"But they need a leader." Seraphina crossed her arms. "Someone to guide them. To restore what natural death should actually mean, not Caelum's twisted version of it."

Dante's shadows drew in, defensive. "I'm not taking another domain." He could barely manage his own court right now, and Brynn needed him.

"We know." Vex stood, his usual laziness dropping away to reveal the power beneath. "Which is why we brought someone else."

A figure stepped forward from the shadowed alcove near the far wall where Dante's wards should have alerted him to their presence but apparently hadn't.

Dante went completely still.

He was tall, with blonde curls falling to his neck and light blue eyes that held none of Caelum's false warmth. There was a calmness to him. Peace, not the artificial serenity Caelum had manufactured. The kind that came from guiding souls gently, not consuming them.

"Gabriel," Dante said slowly, searching his memory for the last time he'd seen this Death Lord. Centuries ago. Before Caelum claimed he'd faded into nothing.

"Lord Reaper." Gabriel inclined his head with respect that felt earned, not performed. "It's been a long time."

"Caelum said you diminished." Dante studied him, shadows reaching out to test his presence. "Long ago. That you faded from existence."

"He lied." The words came out bitter, edged with rage that Gabriel was clearly fighting to control. "I discovered what he was planning. The soul harvesting. The paradise prison. I tried to stop him, tried to make him see it was wrong."

Gabriel's hands clenched at his sides, knuckles white.

"He locked me in the deepest chamber of the Mourned palace. Bound me with wards I couldn't break, wards keyed to my own power so that fighting them only made them stronger." His voice dropped lower, thick with anger and helplessness. "Forced me to watch as he collected souls, drained them, turned them into empty shells. Made me see his plan manifest piece by piece while I could do nothing to stop it."

Dante's gut twisted. His jaw clenched so hard his teeth ached.

Trapped. Helpless. Watching atrocity unfold and being unable to prevent it. He knew that particular hell. Had lived it while Brynn lay dying and he could do nothing but count her breaths.

"I'm sorry," Gabriel said, meeting each of their eyes in turn. The guilt in his face was genuine, carved deep. "I should have found a way. Should have broken free sooner. Should have warned you before it came to this."

"That wasn't on you." Seraphina cut through Gabriel's self-recrimination. "Caelum was powerful. If he wanted you contained, you stayed contained. We all know what that's like."

"We all missed the signs," Vex added. "His deception ran deep. He fooled us all this time."

"The betrayal is his alone," Thessa said gently. "Not yours."

Gabriel's shoulders eased slightly, but guilt still shadowed his features.

"There's something I still don't understand." Dante moved closer, his power reaching toward Gabriel as if testing his sincerity. "How did Caelum sabotage the wards in our realms without us noticing? Each court would have felt his presence the moment he crossed our boundaries."

Gabriel's face darkened, lips pressing into a thin line. "The power he gained from harvesting souls, it wasn't just about quantity. He learned how to use it to mask his signature. Make himself undetectable to even the most sensitive wards."

"Impossible," Seraphina said flatly. "We would have felt the void where he should have been."

"Not if he replaced his signature with borrowed souls." Gabriel's voice was hollow, haunted by what he'd witnessed. "He would drain a soul nearly completely, then wrap himself in what remained of their life force like wearing someone else's skin. To your wards, he appeared as nothing more than a wandering spirit, something beneath notice. Too weak to be a threat."

Vex cursed under his breath.

Dante's hands clenched into fists. His shadows surged outward before he wrestled them back under control.

"He used to brag about it." Gabriel's expression hardened with disgust. "After he'd return from one of his sabotage missions, he'd come to my cell and laugh about how easy it was. How you were all too ignorant to notice him walking through your courts. Breaking your wards. Planting the seeds of collapse right under your noses while you looked right through him."

The violation of it hit Dante. His vision tunneled. His skin crawled.

Caelum had been here. In his domain. Walking his corridors. Touching his wards. Studying his defenses. Multiple times. While wearing the hollowed-out remnants of souls he'd murdered.

And Dante had never known.

His darkness erupted outward in a wave of black rage, filling the room, darkening every corner. Frost formed on the windows.

"All of ours," Seraphina said, her tone deadly quiet in a way that promised violence if there was anyone left to inflict it on. "That's how he knew exactly which wards to target. He studied our defenses from the inside."

"While wearing the stolen souls he'd drained." Thessa's form flickered with anger rare for her gentle nature.

Dante forced his breathing to even out through sheer force of will. The fury wanted to consume him, wanted to rage and destroy and hurt something for the violation. But Caelum was already destroyed. Already erased from existence, consumed soul and all until nothing remained.

There was nowhere left for the rage to go except inward.

He wrestled his power back under control. "The Mourned realm needs a leader," he said slowly, pulling the conversation back to the present.

"Yes." Gabriel held his gaze. "Someone who can restore genuine peace. Help souls find real rest, not false paradise. Undo the damage Caelum did to the very concept of natural death."

"You want the position."

"I want to make this right." Gabriel's voice was determined, certain. "I want to give those souls what they deserved from the beginning. Honest guidance toward natural rest. No harvesting. No draining. No paradise prisons. Just peace for those who are ready for it."

Dante looked at the other three Death Lords. Seraphina nodded once, sharp and approving. Vex's look was thoughtful but clearly in agreement. Thessa smiled gently, her form brightening slightly.

"The five courts need to be balanced," Seraphina said. "Gabriel knows the Mourned realm better than any of us. He opposed Caelum's plan from the beginning."

"The realm calls for him," Thessa said softly. "I can hear it through the boundaries. It wants someone who understands peace without domination."

Dante studied Gabriel for a long moment. Shadows still testing, searching for deception. But all he saw was remorse. Determination. A core of compassion that Caelum had never possessed.

"The Mourned realm accepts you?" Dante asked.

"It does." Gabriel's voice was quiet but certain. "I've already begun the work of restoration. The souls there recognize me from before Caelum's corruption."

Dante's shadows settled. "Then you have my support."

"Mine as well," Seraphina said.

"And mine," Vex added.

"The death realm approves," Thessa said softly, and something in the air seemed to resonate with truth.

Gabriel straightened, standing taller. "I won't fail you. Any of you."

Through the bond, Dante felt Brynn.

Felt her reaching for him across the distance, awareness flooding through their connection. Felt the moment she remembered yesterday, the kiss, the promise, the tomorrow you give me everything.

Desire pulsed through their connection like heat. His body responded instantly, pulse quickening, skin warming, breath catching.

Mine, his shadows whispered. *Waiting. Wanting. Ours.*

"If that's everything—" he started, already turning toward the door.

"Go." Seraphina waved him away, amusement clear in her voice. "You don't want to keep her waiting too long."

"Try not to break anything," Vex added, his smile turning knowing.

Dante ignored them. "Get out of my court."

They left still chuckling, Gabriel following with a confused look. The throne room doors closed behind them with a soft boom.

He stood alone for a moment, letting the silence settle. Letting anticipation build in his chest like pressure.

Yesterday, he'd needed to hold her. He'd needed to reassure himself she was real, whole, his. To feel her pulse and know she was alive.

Today, he'd promised, she could have everything.

He turned and walked back toward their chambers. His pace started controlled. But with each step, the bond pulled tighter. Her desire was bleeding through, mixing with his own until he couldn't tell where one ended and the other began.

His pace quickened. Then quickened again. His heart was pounding now. His skin felt too tight. Every step brought another wave of her want crashing through the bond, stoking the heat building in his chest until he was nearly running.

He reached their chambers. His hand closed around the door handle, cool against his palm.

Pushed it open.

And stopped dead in the doorway.

LXXXIV.
DANTE & BRYNN

Dante

Brynn stood naked in the center of the room, her back to him, and she was glowing.

Her shadows moved across her skin. But where his were black as void, hers were white. They traced the curve of her hip, wound around her thigh, cupped her breast, and squeezed before spiraling away. She gasped softly at her own touch, head falling back, and the sound went straight to his cock.

She'd been practicing while he was gone.

He gripped the doorframe, knuckles going white. Heat surged through him so fast it made him dizzy. She was magnificent. Transformed. No longer the fragile mortal he'd been so careful with. She was equal in every way.

And she was touching herself with her shadows while he watched.

"Brynn." Her name came out thick, warning and want tangled together.

She turned, meeting his gaze head-on. Fearless as ever. Her eyes had changed when she'd transformed, silver threading through the green, and right now they blazed with power and mischief.

"Where were you?" Her voice was light, casual, but her shadows tightened, framing her body. Drawing his eyes to her breasts, her waist, the dark curls between her thighs.

He stepped inside and shut the door. It took every ounce of control he had not to cross the room and take her against the wall.

"The other Death Lords." He forced the words out. "Caelum's shells are destroyed. The souls are home."

Her shadows writhed, one tendril sliding down her stomach, dipping between her legs. She let out a soft moan, and his cock throbbed.

"Gabriel's leading the Mourned realm now," he managed, watching her shadow stroke through her folds. "He was Caelum's second. Disappeared long ago. Locked away for trying to stop the harvesting."

She walked toward him. Her shadows reached out ahead of her, brushing across his chest through his shirt. The warmth surprised him. He'd expected cold, like his own, but hers burned with gentle heat.

"The courts are balanced again." His voice was strained now, barely functional, as her shadows slipped beneath his collar to stroke his throat. "Gabriel explained how Caelum hid. Using drained souls as camouflage."

She stopped inches from him. Close enough that he could smell her arousal, rich and intoxicating. Close enough to see the wetness glistening on her inner thighs.

"Is that all?" She looked up at him through her lashes.

"Yes."

Her shadows slid down his chest, his stomach, and cupped him through his pants. He hissed, hips jerking into the touch. His own shadows surged instinctively, black tendrils reaching for her, but she batted them away with a flick of white.

"Not yet," she purred.

His jaw clenched. "Brynn—"

"Take off your clothes."

Arousal surged through him. The thief giving orders to the Reaper. She'd come back as something new, and now she wanted him on his knees.

He should resist. Should remind her who ruled this realm. Who'd made her scream his name so many times she'd lost count.

Instead, he reached for his shirt.

Her smile was wicked and triumphant. She stepped back to watch as he pulled the fabric off and dropped it to the floor.

"Slower," she commanded.

He hooked his thumbs in his waistband and paused. Held her gaze as he pushed down, inch by torturous inch. The fabric dragged over his hips, his thighs, and his cock sprang free. Hard. Aching. Already leaking at the tip.

Her eyes dropped to his length, and her tongue swept across her lower lip.

"On the bed."

He moved toward the mattress, but her shadows got there first. White tendrils pressed against his chest. They didn't just push. They guided. Owned. Demanded.

They drove him back until his legs hit the bed, and he let himself fall onto the sheets.

Her shadows followed. They slithered up his arms, slow and possessive, and wound around his wrists. Pulled them above his head. Bound him to the headboard with tendrils of pure white light.

He flexed, testing the restraint.

They held.

His shadows surged, ready to tear through the bindings, but he forced them back. Forced himself to submit. To give her this.

The look on her face was worth it. Pure power. Pure satisfaction.

"I knew you could behave," she murmured, climbing onto the bed between his spread thighs.

Brynn

He was beautiful like this.

The most powerful being in the death realm, bound and helpless beneath her. His muscles strained against her shadows, his chest heaving, his cock jutting up thick and flushed and dripping.

She traced her palms up his thighs, nails dragging, leaving red trails on his pale skin. He shivered at the sting, hips lifting slightly.

"Brynn—"

She leaned down and pressed her lips to his inner thigh. Felt the muscle jump beneath her mouth. Trailed higher, tongue flicking out to taste the salt of his skin, until her breath ghosted over his cock.

He groaned. "Please—"

She pulled back.

"Not yet." Her hand closed around his length, grip firm and sure. She dragged upward, agonizingly slow, watching his face contort. "I'm going to take my time with you."

Her palm smeared through the slick gathering at his tip, spreading it down his shaft until he glistened. He was so hard he throbbed against her fingers. So desperate, his hips tried to thrust into her grip.

She lowered her head and traced the slit with her tongue, gathering every drop.

The taste of him flooded her mouth. She circled the crown with the flat of her tongue, pressing into the sensitive spot just beneath the head, and his whole body shuddered.

"Fuck." His voice was wrecked. "Your mouth. Please. I need—"

She swallowed him down in one smooth slide, taking all of it. Her lips stretched wide around his girth as she sank until her nose pressed against his pelvis, his cock lodged in her throat, and she held there. Swallowing around him. Letting him feel the tight squeeze of her throat working his length.

His curse was guttural. Animal.

She pulled back with aching slowness, suction so hard her cheeks caved, tongue dragging the sensitive underside. Then plunged down again.

She found a punishing rhythm. Deep and relentless. Her mouth fucking him while her hand twisted around the base, squeezing in counterpoint. Saliva welled up, ran down his shaft in rivulets, and made everything slippery.

But she wasn't alone anymore.

Her shadows responded to her desire. White tendrils slid up his thighs, warm and tingling. One wrapped around the root of his cock, pulsing in rhythm with her mouth. Another cupped his balls, rolling them with steady pressure. A third traced up his stomach, his chest, found his nipple, and pinched hard enough to make him cry out.

He bucked beneath her. Overwhelmed from every direction.

"Brynn—fuck—too much—"

She moaned around him, letting him feel the vibration travel down his length, and pulled off just as his balls drew up tight.

"Not yet," she breathed against his twitching cock.

His groan was desperate. His shaft jerked against her lips, angry and denied, precum dripping off the tip.

She licked it away. Sucked just the head back into her mouth, tongue swirling, then released him again.

Edged him. Again. And again. Bringing him to the cliff with her mouth and her shadows, then yanking him back. Until sweat sheened his chest. Until his muscles trembled with the effort of not coming. Until words stopped working and he could only make sounds—broken, pleading, inhuman sounds.

"Please—Brynn—I can't—I need to come—please—"

The Reaper. The most feared death lord in existence. Begging for her mouth.

She released him with one final slow lick from root to tip and climbed up his body.

Dante

She straddled his hips, her soaked cunt pressing against his stomach.

He could feel how wet she was. Her arousal smeared across his skin as she settled her weight on him. The heat of her core hovered just above his aching cock.

She reached between them and gripped his shaft. Angled him to slide through her folds.

The sensation nearly broke him.

She rocked her hips, dragging her slick slit along his length, coating him with her arousal. The head of his cock caught on her clit with every pass, making her gasp. Making him throb.

"Look at you," she breathed, grinding down. "The Reaper. Bound and desperate." She leaned forward, her tits swaying inches from his face. "Begging for my pussy."

"Brynn—" He couldn't form words. Could barely think. All he knew was the wet heat sliding against him, the need burning through his veins.

She positioned him at her entrance. The swollen head pressed against her opening, so hot, so wet.

Then she rocked away.

He groaned, hips surging up, but her weight and her shadows held him down.

"Say please." Her voice was smooth and commanding.

"I'm not—" His pride fought his need. The Reaper didn't beg. He was the apex predator. He was—

She sank down an inch. Just enough that his head breached her entrance. Her cunt gripped him like a fist, tight and scorching, and his vision went white.

Then she lifted off.

"Say it."

Something inside him snapped.

"Please." The word tore out of him. "Please, Brynn. I need you. Need your cunt. Need to feel you around my cock. Please let me inside you. I'll do anything. Please."

Her smile was pure triumph.

She sank down in one smooth motion, taking him to the hilt.

Brynn

THE STRETCH WAS EXQUISITE.

He filled her completely. Thick and hard, splitting her open, hitting so deep she felt him in her chest. For a moment, she just sat there, fully seated, savoring the fullness. The way her cunt clenched around him. The way he pulsed inside her.

"Move," he begged. "Please. Fucking move."

She planted her hands on his chest and lifted her hips slowly. Let him feel every inch of his cock dragging against her walls.

Then she sank back down.

His groan was broken.

She found her rhythm. Rising and falling on his cock, taking her pleasure from him. Her shadows kept his wrists bound, but now they did more. White tendrils slid across his chest, his stomach, teasing his nipples. One wrapped around the base of his cock, squeezing every time she lifted up. Another traced down, finding the sensitive skin behind his balls, pressing.

He was surrounded. Overwhelmed. Her body and her shadows were working him from every angle.

"Brynn—" He couldn't even form her name properly. Just sounds. Groans and curses and desperate pleas.

She rode him harder. Faster. Her tits bouncing with each movement. The sounds of her cunt taking his cock filled the chamber. Her arousal dripped down his shaft, soaked his balls, made everything slick and messy.

"You feel so good," she moaned, grinding down. "So thick. Stretching me open." She clenched around him deliberately. "Your cock was made for me."

His hips bucked up, meeting her rhythm. Even bound, even helpless, he was powerful. Every thrust punched deep, hit that spot that made her see stars.

She reached down to rub her clit. Her own fingers circling while she bounced on his cock. The pressure built fast, coiling tight in her core.

"Yes," she gasped. "Right there. Fuck. I'm close—"

His shadows surged.

Her white tendrils shattered like glass.

Dante

His control snapped.

He grabbed her hips and rolled them, flipping her beneath him in one savage motion. Her back hit the mattress and he was on her, between her thighs, his cock still buried deep.

She gasped. Eyes wide.

He smiled down at her. All teeth. All predator.

"My turn."

He pulled back and slammed into her.

She screamed.

He fucked her hard. His hands gripped her hips hard enough to bruise, holding her in place while he drove into her.

The slap of his hips against her echoed through the chamber. The obscene sounds of her cunt taking his cock. Her moans climbing higher with every thrust.

"You think your shadows can hold me?" he growled against her throat. "You think you can control the Reaper?"

She clenched around him, squeezing his cock with her inner muscles, and he choked on a curse. His rhythm faltered.

"Whatever you say," she gasped, breathless but smiling. "My lord."

Even pinned beneath him, she could still wreck him.

He grabbed her thighs and pushed them up, folding her nearly in half. The angle let him sink impossibly deep.

He thrust hard, grinding against her cervix.

"Yes—" She could barely speak. "Don't stop."

He pulled out until just the tip remained. Looked down at where they joined. Her cunt gaped slightly, pink and swollen, trying to pull him back in. Their combined arousal dripped from her opening.

"Look at this greedy pussy," he murmured. "Doesn't want to let me go."

He slammed back in. Watched her eyes roll back.

He pulled out and flipped her onto her stomach. Drove back inside from behind.

The new angle made her scream into the sheets.

"That's it." He gripped her hips, watching his cock disappear into her body. "Take it. All of it."

He pounded into her. Her ass rippled with every thrust. Her arousal dripped down her thighs.

White tendrils rose from her skin and wrapped around him. Around his back, his ass, pulling him deeper with every thrust. One curled around his balls, tugging in rhythm with his strokes. Another found his nipple and pinched, twisted, made him hiss against her neck.

"Fuck—" His rhythm stuttered. "Your shadows—"

"Feel good?" She clenched around him, squeezing his cock, and felt his whole body shudder.

"Now you know what it's like."

His laugh was dark and breathless. "Two can play."

His shadows surged.

Black tendrils wrapped around her thighs, spreading her wider. One found her clit and pressed, rubbing in tight circles while he fucked her. Another coiled around her breast, squeezing, the tip flicking her nipple. And one slid lower. Between her cheeks. Found that tight, untouched hole and circled.

She moaned, pushing back against him. "Dante—"

"You want it?" He pressed gently. "Want my shadow in your ass while I fuck your cunt?"

"Yes. Please. Yes."

A thick tendril of cool darkness slid into her ass, stretching her open, filling her alongside his cock. She cried out at the overwhelming fullness. Stuffed in both holes, working her in tandem.

"There it is," he groaned, feeling her clench around him. "So tight. So fucking full of me."

He needed to see her.

He pulled her up, her back against his chest, his cock still buried inside. One arm wrapped around her waist. The other hand fisted in her hair, yanking her head back to expose her throat.

"Look," he commanded.

Her eyes found the mirror across the room.

The image stole her breath. His dark form behind her, muscles straining, face savage with need. Her body impaled on his cock, bouncing with every thrust. And their shadows tangling around them both. Black and white intertwining. Weaving together. Light and dark becoming one.

"Your shadows and mine," he breathed against her neck, teeth scraping. "Do you see what we are? What you are?"

His hand slid from her waist to her cunt. Found her swollen, slippery clit. Rubbed in fast, tight circles while he fucked up into her.

She couldn't think. Couldn't speak. Could only moan and shake as he fucked her cunt while his shadow fucked her ass, his hand on her clit, her shadows squeezing and pulling at every inch of him.

"Mine," he growled.

"Yours." She was shaking, trembling, right on the edge.

His shadows and hers responded to their words. The tendrils wove tighter together, black and white spiraling, creating patterns that seemed to pulse with power.

"Death couldn't keep you from me." He thrust deep. "Nothing will."

Her orgasm ripped through her. Her pussy clamped down on him, pulsing, milking his cock. She screamed his name, body convulsing, and her white shadows exploded outward in brilliant tendrils.

He followed her over the edge.

His release crashed through him, his cock jerking as he spilled inside her. His cum flooded her cunt, filling her until it leaked around his shaft, dripped down her thighs. His black shadows surged to meet hers, and for one blinding moment, their power merged completely.

Light and dark. Death and life. Two halves of the same whole.

The shockwave of their combined release flooded the chamber, rattling the walls, making the candles flare.

When it finally faded, they collapsed together onto ruined sheets.

Brynn

THE ROOM WAS DESTROYED.

Candles blown out. Mirror cracked. Headboard splintered. Scorch marks on the ceiling where their power had surged.

She'd laugh about that later. Right now, she could barely breathe.

Their shadows settled around them slowly.

Her own shadow lifted lazily, tracing along his jaw. She hadn't told it to do that. It just wanted to touch him.

He caught the tendril, pressed a kiss to it, and she felt the sensation ghost across her skin.

"I felt that," she breathed.

"I know." His smile was exhausted but smug. "You'll learn. The shadows are part of you now. Everything they touch, you feel."

She filed that information away for later. Much later.

For now, she just melted into him. Felt the solid weight of his body, the steady thrum of their bond, the reality that she was here.

"I can't feel my legs...again," she murmured against his chest.

"Good." The satisfaction in his voice was insufferable. "Then you won't be going anywhere."

He pulled her closer, pressing a kiss to her temple. When he spoke again, his voice was softer.

"I have forever with you now." His arms tightened around her. "I don't intend to waste a single moment."

She turned in his arms, meeting his dark eyes. Saw the emotion there. The wonder. The disbelief that she'd come back to him. That she'd chosen him.

"Forever," she agreed, and kissed him.

When they broke apart, he was smiling. That rare, real smile that transformed his face.

"There are so many more surfaces in this room," he murmured against her lips. "And I intend to use every one of them."

She grinned, want already stirring again. "Then we'd better get started."

LXXXV.
BRYNN

One Month Later

"Hold still, my lady." Naia's fingers worked through another section of Brynn's hair, weaving it into a pattern that pulled at her scalp with each twist. Sharp enough to remind her she was still real.

"I don't understand why we need this." Brynn shifted on the stool, earning a sharper tug in response.

"The people need ceremony." Naia secured another pin. "They need to see their rulers in all their glory. Makes them feel the realm is stable."

"The realm *is* stable." Brynn caught her eye in the mirror, saw silver threading through her irises that hadn't been there a month ago. "We fixed the wards. Caelum's gone. Gabriel's handling the Mourned Court. This feels—"

She stopped. Elaborate display. Performance. All the hallmarks of the cons she used to run, except this time she wasn't working the angle.

"Unnecessary?" Naia supplied.

"Like showing off."

"When has necessity ever stopped the Death Lords from being dramatic?" Naia's voice held amusement. "Besides, Lord Reaper specifically requested you look..." She paused. "*Devastating*."

Warmth crept up Brynn's neck. Of course he had.

"One month of relative peace and now he wants to parade me around like—"

"Like his equal?" Naia interrupted, meeting her gaze in the mirror. "Like the Lady of Boundaries who saved all the realms?"

Brynn's mouth opened. Closed.

"There." Naia stepped back, admiring her work. "Now let's get you into that dress."

Her hair was swept up into a tight braided crown that wrapped around her head before knotting at her nape. Pieces framed her face, softening the severity just enough.

Behind the dressing screen, the gown waited, black fabric with silver thread that shifted like constellations. At certain angles, ward-symbols appeared in the threading before dissolving back into shadow.

She let her white shadows rise, working the fastenings with more dexterity than her hands could manage. The fabric settled against her skin, heavier than it looked. The silver threads pulsed faintly in response to her.

"That dress isn't just about looking beautiful," Naia said from the other side of the screen. "It's armor. Political armor. Every Death Lord who sees you tonight will understand exactly what you are."

Brynn smoothed her hands down the fabric, feeling ward-magic woven through every thread. "And what's that?"

"Untouchable. Permanent. *His*."

The possessiveness in that last word sent warmth pooling low in her stomach. One month of being claimed by the Reaper, and her body had learned to respond to that edge.

She emerged from behind the screen.

Naia whistled low. "Forget what I said earlier. You won't even make it to the throne room looking like that."

"We have to make it to the throne room."

"Here." Naia retrieved the familiar crown from its velvet-lined box. Black metal worked into patterns that looked like frozen shadows, set with stones that absorbed light instead of reflecting it. "He insisted you wear this one tonight. The one he gave you right after he claimed you."

Before the battle. Before her transformation. When being his equal had felt like a dream she didn't dare believe in.

The circlet settled onto her braided hair. The weight of it familiar and right.

"The whole court's taking bets on how long before he drags you back here," Naia added, amusement dancing in her voice.

"Naia!"

"What? I'm just saying what everyone's thinking." Her smile turned knowing. "The palace has learned to avoid the west wing between midnight and dawn."

Brynn's cheeks flushed. "We're not that—"

"You are. And good for you. A Death Lord who looks at his companion like she's the only thing in existence? That's rarer than you'd think."

Brynn turned back to the mirror before Naia could see how much those words affected her.

His presence moved through the palace corridors like a storm approaching. Her pulse jumped before she even felt his attention focus on her.

Here, she felt through the bond.

The door opened.

Dante stood in the doorway, dressed in his Death Lord attire. All black and silver with bone details. His dark eyes traveled slowly down her body.

His shoulders tensed. His shadows surged. His fingers curled at his sides.

Want flooded through the bond.

"Naia." He didn't look away from Brynn. "Out."

The servant curtsied quickly, shooting Brynn a knowing look. "I hope you at least make the presentation."

The door clicked shut.

The air changed. Charged.

Dante crossed the room in three strides, backing Brynn against the vanity. His hands braced on either side of her, caging her in without touching. Close enough that she could feel his body heat, that his scent surrounded her.

Close enough that her body arched toward him without permission.

"We have to go," she managed, but her voice came out breathier than intended.

"We do." His eyes hadn't left hers, pupils dilated. "In a moment."

"The other Death Lords—"

"Can wait." His voice dropped to that dangerous tone that made her core clench. "But first, let me make something very clear."

His shadows curled possessively around her waist, not quite touching but close enough that she could feel their presence. Her own shadows rose to meet them. Light meeting dark, intertwining.

"You will only be dancing with me tonight."

Brynn's eyebrow arched. Challenge sparked in her chest. "Is that so?"

"If another man so much as thinks about asking you to dance—" His voice went darker, edged with possession. "If you even consider accepting—"

He pulled back just enough to meet her gaze. His eyes were pure black now. "I will drag you back to these chambers and ensure you can't walk for a week."

Her breath caught. She knew he could see it in the flush spreading across her chest, in the way her pupils dilated, in the pulse jumping at her throat.

His satisfaction bled through the bond.

"Is that supposed to be a threat?" She kept her voice level.

"It's a promise."

She leaned forward slightly. Testing. "Because it only makes me want to test your limits."

His teeth ground together. His shadows tightened around her waist, still not touching, but the pressure was there. The vanity beneath his palms creaked.

She could feel him fighting. Fighting the urge to make good on his threat right now. Fighting the need to pin her against this vanity and show her exactly what happened when she pushed him.

"Later," he growled, the single word holding enough promise to make her shiver.

"I look forward to it," she whispered, and watched something dangerous flash in his eyes.

For a moment, she thought he might forget the ball entirely. His shadows pulled her closer, finally making contact, wrapping around her waist like bands of darkness. Her own shadows surged to meet them.

His control hung by a thread. The war between duty and desire was playing out across his face.

Then footsteps echoed in the corridor. Voices. Other Death Lords were arriving.

Dante stepped back with visible effort, every muscle tense. His shadows retreated reluctantly, trailing across her skin before pulling away completely.

He offered his arm, hunger still burning in his eyes. "Shall we, Lady of the Boundaries?"

She placed her hand on his arm and felt him tense. A simple touch made devastating by everything left unsaid. "Lead the way, Lord Reaper."

His shadows writhed around his shoulders, betraying what his face tried to hide.

She thought about trailing her mouth—

His grip on her arm tightened in response. "You're testing my control."

"I know."

"It won't end well for you."

She smiled. "I'm counting on that."

LXXXVI.
BRYNN

The throne room doors opened to chaos.

Hundreds of voices argued, debated, laughed. The press of bodies creating a wall of sound. Then they stepped inside and everything died.

Silence. Complete silence that made her ears ring.

Death Lords in their attire stood at positions like pieces on a game board. Courtiers from all five domains filled the vast space, some beautiful enough to make mortals weep, others terrifying enough to stop hearts. Servants lined the walls. Shadow-guards stood at attention, more formal than she'd ever seen them.

Every face turned toward them.

Her instincts screamed *run. Find an exit. Disappear.*

But she wasn't running anymore.

Dante's hand covered hers on his arm.

I'm here, she felt through the bond. *You're not alone.*

I know. Still terrifying.

You've faced worse.

Have I?

His thumb brushed her knuckles where no one could see. *You faced me.*

They began the long walk toward the center. Her dress whispered against the floor. Their footsteps echoed. Her shadows and his twisted together behind them like a train. White and silver threading through black, creating patterns that made several courtiers step back.

She kept her chin high, meeting the eyes of anyone brave enough to hold her gaze, noting who looked respectful, versus resentful, versus terrified.

Most looked away immediately.

Seraphina looked magnificent in fitted leather and metal scales that flowed like fabric, crimson and black, both armor and gown. She gave Brynn a nod that felt like a salute between warriors.

Vex had chosen robes of silk that shifted color with each movement, deep purple melting into gold, then amber. Jewels glinted at his throat. His smile held warmth, and he winked at her.

Thessa floated more than stood, wrapped in flowing fabric that faded from solid grey silk to pure mist at the hem. Her pale eyes held approval that felt ancient.

Gabriel stood with quiet dignity in robes of soft gold, the Mourned Court's colors gentler under his stewardship than they'd ever been under Caelum's. He inclined his head to her, warmth in his expression.

They reached the center. Dante stopped, turning to face the assembly.

Then every being in the chamber knelt.

The movement rippled outward, hundreds of bodies lowering in acknowledgment, fabric and armor rustling like wind through dead leaves.

Death Lords. Courtiers. Servants. Guards. Every soul in the Forsaken realm bowed to them both.

Brynn's breath caught. Her grip on Dante's arm tightened.

They were bowing to *her*. Not just to him with her as an accessory. To *her*.

Movement in the Mourned section made her heart stop.

Two figures stood apart from the kneeling masses.

Her parents.

Her knees almost buckled. Something cracked open inside her.

Ten years of grief and guilt and longing rising up her throat like a scream she'd been holding since the night they died.

They weren't the twisted memory she'd carried for a decade. They were her parents as they truly were. Her father's sharp eyes had softened with pride. Her mother smiled even as tears tracked down ghostly cheeks.

Papa. Mama.

The words stuck in her throat. Her vision blurred. Her hands were shaking.

Her mother opened her arms.

The tears came without permission.

Dante leaned close. "Gabriel showed them the truth. They know you never betrayed them. They're at peace now, and you can visit whenever you wish."

"Go to them," Dante said, letting her go.

Dignity be damned.

Brynn ran.

She picked up her skirts and sprinted across the hall, not caring how it looked, not caring about anything except reaching them.

The assembly parted. Her parents met her halfway, solid enough to catch her as all three collided in a tangle of arms and tears.

"My little haggler," her father whispered against her hair, using the nickname from when she'd argue prices at his stalls. "My brave, brilliant girl."

"I'm so sorry." The words tore from her throat. "I tried to clear your names. Tried to prove your innocence. I tried—"

"Shh." Her mother's hands framed her face, ethereal but warm, thumbs wiping tears. "You survived, baby. You survived and became something extraordinary." Her voice cracked. "That's all we ever wanted."

Her father touched the crown on her head with gentle fingers. "The Lady of Boundaries. Our daughter, ruling beside a Death Lord."

"We couldn't be prouder," her mother whispered.

Brynn held them tighter, years of grief cracking apart. They knew. They finally knew the truth.

"I love you both so much."

"We love you too." Her mother pulled back slightly. "But this is your moment. Your night." She glanced toward the front of the room. "And your Death Lord is waiting."

Brynn turned, still holding her mother's hand.

Dante stood exactly where she'd left him, one arm extended toward her across the distance. The entire assembly remained on their knees around him, frozen.

"Go," her parents said together. "We'll be here. We have eternity now."

She squeezed their hands once more, then straightened her spine. Wiped her face. Drew in a breath that hurt.

She walked back through the parted gathering with her head high. Not running this time. Walking like the Death Lady she'd become.

She placed her hand in Dante's outstretched palm.

His fingers closed around hers immediately. Anchoring her.

"Thank you," she whispered.

His thumb brushed over her knuckles. *For you. Always for you.*

He turned to address the assembly. "Rise."

The gathering stood as one.

"Tonight, we recognize formally what has already been established through blood and bond." His darkness spread outward, filling the chamber. "The Lady of Boundaries. Master of the ward-systems. Architect of the barriers between realms."

Her shadows joined his on their own accord, white threading through black in a display that made several courtiers gasp. The intertwining patterns created something new. Something theirs.

"She who saved the realms from collapse." His voice dropped lower. "She who holds power equal to any Death Lord. She who stands beside me not as a companion, but as a partner. As co-ruler of the Forsaken throne."

Those words landed inside her and stayed there.

"Any who questions her authority," his eyes swept the assembly, "questions mine."

Several courtiers who'd been cruel to her in the past, Lady Morwyn prominent among them, visibly paled.

"Lord Reaper." Gabriel stepped forward. "May I speak?"

Dante inclined his head.

"The Mourned realm owes the Lady of Boundaries a debt that can never be repaid." Gabriel's eyes found hers. "She exposed Caelum's corruption. Freed the souls he'd enslaved. Restored natural death to its proper place." He bowed deeply, not formal court protocol, but something more personal. "The Mourned realm recognizes her authority and offers its eternal gratitude."

Seraphina moved forward next, shoulders squared, chin lifted. "The Violent realm recognizes the Lady of Boundaries. My warriors will defend her as they would defend me." Her lips curved slightly. "And they're very good at their job."

A ripple of laughter went through the hall.

"The Consumed realm celebrates our new sister in power," Vex added with theatrical flair. He swept into an elaborate bow that made his robes billow. "May her reign be as eternal as her beauty, and may she always remember that I am the most charming of her fellow Death Lords."

More laughter. Seraphina rolled her eyes but smiled.

Thessa drifted forward last, brightening until she almost glowed. "The Lingering realm has always known she would come." Her voice echoed with layers of power. "The spirits whispered of her before she was born. The Lady of Boundaries was written in the very fabric of death itself." Her pale eyes fixed on Brynn with intensity that felt like being seen to her soul. "You were always meant to be here."

Brynn's skin prickled.

"The five courts stand united," Dante said. "The ward-systems are restored. The realms are balanced." He looked down at her, pride evident. "And the Forsaken court has its lady at last."

The hall erupted. Cheers and applause filled the space. Crystal rang against crystal as toasts were raised.

But Dante only had eyes for her. "Come. Your throne awaits."

They ascended the steps together.

Two thrones. Identical in scale and majesty.

Hers matched his perfectly, carved bone inlaid with silver ward-patterns where his held shadows. The same height. The same grandeur.

"Your throne," Dante said. "Lady of Boundaries."

She sat slowly. The bone was cool beneath her palms at first, then warmed as if recognizing her. Her white shadows spread from the base, intertwining with the darkness already woven through the Forsaken court.

The throne fit.

Dante sat beside her, and suddenly the picture was complete. Two halves of a terrifying whole.

Servants approached with wine in crystal goblets. The liquid inside was dark as blood, swirling with silver threads that matched her shadows.

"To the Lady of Boundaries," someone called.

"To the balance of the realms!"

"To the union that saved us all!"

Toast after toast rang out. Brynn accepted her goblet, raised it to those gathered, and drank wine that tasted rich and smooth, with an aftertaste that lingered like smoke.

Through it all, she noticed one figure pushing through the onlookers. Lady Morwyn, the courtier who'd been so vicious at that first dinner, who'd made it clear she thought Brynn beneath notice.

Morwyn stopped at the foot of the dais and dropped into a curtsey deeper than protocol required.

"Lady of Boundaries," Morwyn said. "I offer my service and my sincere apology for my earlier... shortsightedness."

Brynn studied her over the rim of her goblet, searching for mockery or hidden resentment. Found none.

Morwyn's face held respect. Perhaps even fear.

But mercy had more power than vengeance.

"Your acknowledgment honors me, Lady Morwyn," Brynn said, letting her voice carry authority. "Your service to the Forsaken court is valued."

Relief flickered across Morwyn's features. She bowed again and retreated.

Brynn caught several other courtiers exchanging glances.

Through the bond, she felt Dante's approval. *Well played.*

I learned from the best.

Flattery will get you whatever you want.

Warmth pooled low in her stomach. *Impatient?*

You have no idea.

Music began to flow through the chamber. The melody was slower than typical court fare, richer, with a rhythm that pulled at something low in her belly.

Dante stood, extending his hand. The look in his eyes made her pulse skip.

"Dance with me."

She placed her hand in his. "Always."

His smile was pure satisfaction and promise as he led her down from the dais.

The assembly parted, forming a perfect circle. Other couples waited at the edges, but no one would move until the Lord and Lady of the Forsaken took the floor first.

Dante drew her against him, one hand at her waist, the other holding hers. His grip was possessive, holding her close enough that she could feel every line of his body through their clothes.

They began to move, and their shadows erupted around them.

White and black twisted together, silver threads catching the light.

"Everyone's watching," she murmured as he spun her.

"Let them." His hand at her waist tightened, eliminating the space between them. "Let them all see who you belong to."

"And who do you belong to?" she challenged.

"You." The word came out rough, edged with possession. "Always you. Forever you."

He dipped her low, their darkness creating a canopy above them. For a moment, suspended in his arms with his eyes burning into hers, the rest of the world ceased to exist.

He brought her back up, spinning her so her back pressed against his chest. His arm wrapped around her waist, holding her against him. His breath was hot against her ear.

"How much longer do we have to stay?"

"The whole night," she said, breathless. "Naia said—"

"I don't care what Naia said." His arm tightened, his palm splaying across her stomach. "You wore this dress knowing what it would do to me." His voice dropped lower. "Wore it in front of everyone. Let every male in this room see you looking like sin and starlight." His lips brushed her ear. "You're not playing fair, *my thief*."

The nickname, spoken in public, sent fire through her veins.

"Am I not, *my reaper*?"

"No," he growled, spinning her back to face him with enough force that she braced herself against his chest. His eyes were pure black. "But I've been patient. And my patience is running out."

The song ended, but he didn't let her go.

Through the bond, she felt his control hanging by a thread.

"One hour," she negotiated.

"Half an hour."

"Forty-five minutes."

"Done." He leaned down until his lips nearly brushed hers, a promise without delivery. "But when those forty-five minutes are up, we leave. I don't care if the realm is collapsing again."

"Agreed."

Another song began. He drew her back into motion, and other couples finally ventured onto the floor. The ball continued around them in swirls of color and shadow.

Her parents danced together in the Mourned section, ghostly and beautiful. Gabriel stood with them, watching with approval. The other Death Lords had accepted her. The courts were balanced. The ward-systems hummed with strength she could feel in her bones.

As Dante spun her through another turn, she thought about that first day. When they'd dragged her before the Reaper, expecting her to cower.

Instead, she'd looked him in the eye and said, "You don't scare me."

She'd been lying. Terrified and desperate not to show it.

But she'd learned that fear and courage weren't opposites. Courage was doing the terrifying thing anyway.

"I love you," she said quietly, just for him.

His steps faltered. Just for a moment.

"I love you too," he said against her hair. "My thief. My architect. My everything."

They danced together under the eternal twilight of the Forsaken realm, surrounded by court and power and ceremony.

But all Brynn felt was this: *home*.

ACKNOWLEDGMENTS

To my partner: Thank you for tolerating the months of me muttering about shadow magic, for not judging me when I said things like "I need to make this death scene sexier," and for bringing me coffee without being asked. You're my real-life slow burn, and I love you.

To that one friend (you know who you are): You received unhinged drafts, every "does this make sense??" text, every crisis at odd hours. You cheered me on when I doubted everything and celebrated every small victory like it was yours. This book wouldn't exist without you in my corner. Thank you for never getting tired of me.

To the people who listened to me ramble about fictional Death Lords like they were real people, who cheered me on when I wanted to quit, and who never once suggested I "try something more normal"—thank you. Your support means more than you know.

And to everyone who picks up this book: Thank you for taking a chance on a thief and her Reaper. I wrote the story I needed to read, and I hope it becomes something you needed too.

See you in the next one.

Nora Nightingale

www.ingramcontent.com/pod-product-compliance
Lightning Source LLC
LaVergne TN
LVHW091651070526
838199LV00050B/2145